PHOEBE CONN

ZEBRA BOOKS
KENSINGTON PUBLISHING CORP.

ZEBRA BOOKS

are published by

Kensington Publishing Corp.
475 Park Avenue South
New York, NY 10016

First printing: April, 1988

Printed in the United States of America

This book is dedicated to my many friends who have been so generous with their encouragement of my writing career. Your good wishes mean more to me than you will ever know. I'd especially like to thank Margo Farrin, who has been my friend since first grade, Jeanne Cain, whom I met when we attended the University of Arizona, and Betty Morín and Sandra Simon, who shared my days as a teacher and coordinator at Hammel Street School in East Los Angeles. God bless you all for helping to make my dreams come true.

Acknowledgment

I would like to thank Lori Davisson at the Arizona Heritage Center in Tucson, not only for sharing her expertise, but for providing a wealth of historical data on the city in the 1870's. When such a generous amount of valuable research is so readily available, writing is pure pleasure.

Prologue

Mexico . . . Autumn, 1870

Lance Garrett leaned back on his elbows and crossed his ankles to get more comfortable. He had grown so fond of the warm nights in Sonora he felt as though he did not truly come alive until the moment the last of the desert sun's scorching rays disappeared below the horizon. He was stretched out on the grass in front of the bunkhouse, his six-foot-two-inch frame clothed in dusty Levis and a faded cotton shirt. His boots were scuffed and his Stetson hat far from new, but he had not felt so blissfully content in years. There was a *fiesta* underway at the house of the *patrón* and he was enjoying the lively sound of the *mariachi's* blaring trumpets far more than he had the elegant stringed quartets to which he had been forced to listen as a child. One of the other *vaqueros* passed him a bottle of *tequila* and he took a long drink, not fond of the Mexican liquor but in far too sociable a mood to refuse such a generous gesture of friendship. When he saw a flurry of white ruffles coming their way, he groaned loudly and took another fortifying gulp before returning the half-empty bottle to its owner.

"Viene aquí la señorita!" Ernesto used his elbow to give Lance a sharp poke in the ribs as he whispered his warning.

The clear blue of Lance's eyes darkened menacingly as

he rose to his feet. It was too late to pretend he had not seen her and walk away, so he attempted to make the best of what he knew would be another extremely uncomfortable conversation. *"Buenos tardes,* Rosalba."

Ignoring his polite greeting, the brunette immediately began to complain in a petulant whine, "I am very angry with you, Lance Garrett. Why have you not come to my party? You know how much I wanted to dance with you." Rosalba stamped her tiny foot for emphasis, sending the ruffled tiers of her skirt into a fluttering dance of their own. She knew she was a very pretty girl. Her brown eyes were large and exceptionally bright. Her long, ebony curls were gleaming with the shine it took many hours of brushing to produce, and she did not understand why Lance had not come to the party she had personally invited him to attend. "Why are you not dressed in your best clothes?" she asked accusingly.

Lance lowered his voice so only Rosalba would hear, but his tone was hostile rather than seductive. "Your father employs many *vaqueros*. Why was I the only one to be invited to tonight's party? The other men also enjoy music and dancing."

"Why must you always be so difficult?" Rosalba reached out to take his hands as she began to flirt coquettishly. "I care nothing for the others. You know you are the only one I love."

His flesh crawling at her possessive touch, Lance quickly brushed her hands aside. "Your father has invited many fine gentlemen to your home. When they are all eager to amuse you, it is very rude of you to ignore them."

"It is more rude of you to ignore me!" Rosalba cried out unhappily. "When I love you so, why do you pretend to care nothing for me?"

Ignoring her question since his total lack of interest in the willful girl was most definitely not a pretense, Lance continued his efforts to send her on her way. "I will walk you back to the house. Perhaps no one has missed you yet."

"When I say that I love you, why have you nothing as

sweet to say to me?" Rosalba demanded with a haughty toss of her long curls. "Are you a man with no heart to give?"

Exasperated with her incessant declarations of love, Lance could not abide another minute of her cloying company. He put his arm around her waist and with a long, sure stride propelled her toward the brightly illuminated house. When they reached the rear of the rambling adobe home he stepped back into the shadows. "Now stay where you belong, *niña,* and I will do the same."

As she pranced through the wrought-iron gate to return to the patio where the festivities were taking place, Rosalba's sweet features were contorted into a fierce pout. Although she did not look back, she vowed never to forgive Lance Garrett for spurning her affection when she had planned that the evening would be the perfect one for them to spend together. She would make him pay, and dearly, for again treating her like a spoiled child rather than a woman in love.

Lance walked back to the group of *vaqueros* sprawled upon the grass and resumed his comfortable pose. "I'll thank you all to keep quiet about that little scene. Rosalba's daddy has spoiled her terribly. She's much too young to know what love is, let alone to love me as she continually insists she does."

"I do not think she shares that opinion, *amigo,*" a slurred voice from the darkness declared. The *vaqueros* then fell into a good-natured argument over the ability of any woman to truly love a man. While they all enjoyed the company of pretty women, none trusted them.

"I tell you a rattlesnake is a better companion than a young woman like Rosalba Lujan who has both wealth and beauty. It is a fatal combination," Ernesto insisted emphatically, as though his experience with such pampered females was extensive.

Lance protested the harshness of that philosophy in his usual lazy drawl. "No, you are wrong. It is neither beauty nor wealth that makes a woman dangerous, but the lust to control a man, to dominate his every thought. I'll never be any woman's pet."

"Ya lo creo!" several of the others said in unison. Recognizing the truth when they heard it, the *vaqueros* nonetheless continued to tease Lance about Rosalba's passion for him, but he turned their jokes aside with good humor and reached for the bottle of *tequila,* the taste of which seemed to improve with each additional swallow.

Before Lance could ride out the next morning, he was summoned to the main house by the *patrón* himself. Don Ricardo Lujan was seated at his massive desk and looked up only long enough to toss Lance a small leather pouch. "Take your wages and go, Garrett. I want you off the *hacienda* by noon."

Lance took a deep breath in a vain attempt to hold his temper in check. He thought it likely that Rosalba was behind this unwarranted dismissal and did not hesitate to confirm his suspicion. "Your daughter is very young, sir. Infatuations are natural at her age, but not at mine. You have no cause to worry that I'll take advantage of her."

Don Ricardo raised his dark brows in surprise. "I believe my daughter, Garrett. She says you are the one who is infatuated with her and she is tired of avoiding your unwanted attentions."

"That's a damn lie!" Lance thought the man a fool for not knowing his own daughter better than that. "She follows me around like a homeless puppy despite the fact that I do absolutely nothing to encourage her affection."

Rising to his feet, Don Ricardo pointed toward the door. "I have not raised my daughter to flirt with *vaqueros,* not even handsome *norteamericanos. Vaya con Dios."*

Lance tossed the heavy pouch into the air, then caught it in a tight clasp. He debated with himself for no more than an instant, then decided it was not worth his trouble to correct the man's mistaken notion of just how great a flirt Rosalba truly was. The little bitch had gotten even with him, but somehow he suspected she had actually done him a favor. He shoved his hat down upon his thick black curls and, touching the brim in a jaunty salute, bid his former employer farewell. "*Adios,* Don Ricardo, but I think you are the one who is going to need God's help. Kiss Rosalba good-bye for me." He laughed as he strode out the door, for he could not recall ever having heard of anyone being run out of Mexico, but he meant to head straight for the border. It was time to move on anyway and the Arizona Territory was as good a place to go as any.

Chapter I

Lance ate sparingly of the rations he had gathered before his hasty departure from Don Ricardo's *hacienda* and shot small game to supplement his diet as he followed the trail blazed across the desert by the Spanish explorer, Francisco de Coronado, in 1540. Using as landmarks first the Huachuca Mountains to the west and then the Santa Rita, he traveled at a steady pace through a landscape dotted with tall saguaro cactus, the spindly arms of which were raised in a silent salute as he rode by. They reminded him all too vividly of the long lines of troops it had once been his duty to inspect. Five years after the end of the Civil War that had wrenched the heart of America in two, he could still not forget the bright faces of those soldiers or how many of those fine young men he had seen die. To distract himself from such painful memories he whistled the dance tunes he could remember and acted out in his imagination the most exciting adventures from the many books he had read. While he did not mind having no more than his own company and that of his glossy black stallion, Amigo, Lance could not help but look forward to his arrival in Tucson, where he hoped to find another job herding cattle and, if he was really lucky, make a few good friends. He had been on the move so long it no longer bothered him that he had no real home, and he reminded himself now, as he often did, that a ranch hand needed nothing more than a well-trained horse, a comfortable saddle, and a strong constitution to find steady employment. He chuckled to himself as he thought how fortunate he was to have been blessed with all three, for his vagabond existence suited his tastes perfectly.

There was no noticeable change in the parched terrain as Lance left Sonora, Mexico and crossed into the Arizona Territory. The United States had gained the barren land in 1848, at the end of the Mexican War, and men from the East eager for ranch land had flooded the territory hoping to carve prosperous cattle ranches from the wilderness of the desert. Some had become so discouraged by the enormity of that task they had returned home to resume a far easier life. Others had followed their dreams on to California, but a sufficient number had possessed the determination to remain and had given Arizona a decidedly American flavor.

Riding at night to avoid annoying the hostile bands of Apaches who roamed that desolate stretch of land, it took Lance more than a week to reach the thriving town that had sprung from the sleepy *pueblo* of Tucson. Founded in 1776 as a Spanish *presidio,* the settlement located upon the east bank of the Rio Santa Cruz had now grown to nine hundred one-story adobe buildings. While Tucson could not match the towns in the East for elegance of overall design or variety of architectural styles, the dusty city did have the distinction of being the capital of territorial Arizona. Nearly two hundred years after its birth, it had little in the way of beauty, but Tucson's existence had long proven vital to the hearty residents of the Southwest. Home of an Army post, the troops of which were charged with the responsibility of subduing the warlike Apaches, it also functioned as a military supply depot. Provisions arrived from the East in long lines of heavy freight wagons pulled by teams of mules or oxen. That nearly endless stream of traffic made the city a center of commerce for ranches, farms, and the flourishing silver mining industry in the Santa Cruz Valley to the south.

As he entered the crowded streets of the bustling town, Lance followed his usual routine and went shopping for new clothes. He stopped at the general store run by A. and L. Zeckendorf, one of the many prosperous freighter-merchant concerns, to buy a new pair of Levis and two shirts. Deciding to treat himself to some new boots, he spent the better part of an hour searching for a pair as comfortable as the ones he had just worn out. His new wardrobe then complete, he found a barber shop and took a leisurely bath before having a shave and haircut. Clean shaven for the first time in more than a week and dressed in new clothes, he was satisfied he looked presentable, and after asking the directions to the nearest saloon, he strolled into the newly built Congress Hall. While he leaned against the long, highly polished bar and sipped a beer, he listened to the talk buzzing around him, hoping to get a lead on a job, but all too quickly he found himself embroiled in the kind of argument he had always done his best to avoid.

Rex Hatcher enjoyed nothing more than throwing his considerable weight around and whenever he saw a stranger he did his damnedest to intimidate him. He could usually tell which men were easy marks, but he mistook Lance's new clothes for a signal that he was a recent arrival in the territory and unfamiliar with the harsh realities of life in the West. He bumped into him deliberately, then tried to make it appear that the accident had been Lance's fault. "Hey, watch yourself!" he barked crossly.

Rather than respond, Lance simply turned his back on the heavyset man. He had had his fill of men who would pick a fight for no reason and asked the barkeep for another beer. He knew if the obnoxious man were smart he would go away, but unfortunately Rex Hatcher was not known for having even average intelligence.

"Hey, ain't you got no manners? I'm talking to you!" Rex jabbed his stubby fingers into Lance's shoulder to spin him around, but what he got in return was the muzzle of a Colt .45 pointed straight at his straining belt buckle. He tried to back away, but the men standing behind him at the crowded bar did not budge and he was forced to stand his ground.

Lance held the pistol steady as he replied, "I came in for a beer, not conversation. Now get lost."

Rex had seen gunslingers before, plenty of them, but he had not recognized this well-dressed stranger as one of that dangerous breed until too late. This man had the very same cold gleam in his bright blue eyes the others always had. It was a terrifying sight to behold, for it meant he had absolutely no fear of anything or anyone. His pride would not let him back down, but since it would be suicidal to face such a man alone, Rex tipped his sweat-stained hat politely and left the saloon at a brisk walk that was as close to a run as a man of his cumbersome bulk could manage.

The man behind the long bar had swiftly reached for his shotgun but put it back on the wall when Lance replaced his revolver in its holster. "Let me give you a valuable piece of advice, mister. Rex Hatcher is a stupid fool, but he has five brothers who make him look smart. I'd look both ways when I left here if I were you."

"Thanks," Lance replied with a cocky grin, greatly appreciating that helpful tip since it might well save his life. He sipped his beer and wondered why bullies always traveled in packs when the bravest men he had ever known had all been loners. Perhaps cowardice was contagious, he mused with a sardonic chuckle. He had nearly finished his second beer when he recalled the primary reason he had come into the Congress Hall. "You wouldn't happen to know which spreads are shorthanded, would you?"

"Damn near all of them," the barkeep replied with a broad smile, but before he could make any specific suggestions, Rex Hatcher came back through the swinging doors with three of his brothers. "The back door's to your right," he whispered in warning.

Lance had already seen the Hatcher brothers in the mirror above the bar and turned slowly to face them. "You boys just enjoy makin' trouble for some reason?" he asked with the slow drawl that instantly revealed his Southern origins.

"Come outside!" Rex shouted. "We'll settle this in the street."

"There's nothing to settle," Lance replied calmly.

Rex looked toward his brothers with an anxious glance, undecided what to do now that his demand had been turned aside so coolly. Finally summoning all his courage, he yelled again, "Well, I say there is!"

"Are you calling me a liar?" Lance appeared to be relaxed, leaning against the bar with a careless nonchalance, but his fingertips were already brushing the ivory handle of his Colt.

The question confused Rex completely, for he had not expected that the challenge he had issued would be thrown back at him. "Are you coming outside or not?"

Lance shook his head. "The beer's cold and the women pretty. Why, it might be hours before I decide to leave," he responded in his deceptively lazy drawl. He could readily imagine what Mr. and Mrs. Hatcher must look like since four of their sons looked exactly alike. They were tall but so overweight their bellies hung down over their belts. The fronts of their faded plaid shirts were stained with grease, making it obvious they were unacquainted with the merits of using napkins when they ate. Their thinning brown hair was unkempt, their small, squinty eyes watery gray, their large noses bulbous, and to add to that remarkably unattractive assortment of features, each had several days' growth of beard. He could not recall ever having seen a sorrier group of brothers but was far too polite to make such a comment out loud.

Bored by the stalemate, Randy, the youngest of the Hatchers, offered what he considered a fine solution. "Come on, let's just drag him outside." Ready to lead the others, he lunged forward, but he took no more than one swaggering stride before a shot rang out. He sat down with a tremendous thud, a bullet having passed clear through his massive thigh just inches from his groin. "He shot me! The bastard shot me!" the injured man screamed, then pathetically burst into tears.

Lance shook his head apologetically. "Some folks just

won't learn. I hope you boys aren't like that, but I'll be happy to shoot each one of you in turn if that's what it takes to teach you I don't like to be bothered when I'm enjoyin' a relaxin' afternoon."

The patrons of the Congress Hall saloon scattered for cover as Randy continued to holler in tear-choked gasps, "He shot me, I tell you! Go get him!"

Not about to risk getting himself shot too, Rex motioned for his two uninjured brothers, Rad and Donald, to help him, and the three struggled to pick up Randy and carry him outside before any of the rest of them got hurt.

Lance cast an inquisitive glance at the other men in the bar, but none seemed in the least bit upset by what he had done; in fact, most were laughing as though he had just succeeded in ridding the place of vermin they were all relieved to see gone. The brightly painted and gaudily dressed women, however, were eyeing him with open admiration that bordered on lust. Confident he would not be shot in the back, he turned around to the bar and finished his beer, but before he could order another, a man wearing a gold star pinned to a worn leather vest entered the Congress Hall. Tall and lean, he had a face so deeply creased by years of exposure to the blistering desert sun that his skin looked as tough as the soles of Lance's new boots. Seldom had he had reason to smile, and this was most definitely not one of those times.

Walking up to Lance, he announced gruffly, "All right, we'll have no more gunplay in here. I don't care who you are, you're coming to jail with me."

"Damn it, Brad, that don't make a bit of sense," the barkeep argued persuasively, "Randy had it coming to him. You know the Hatchers don't ever come into town unless they're looking for a fight."

Much to Lance's amazement, the men standing nearby were all quick to agree with the bartender's version of the incident and swore he had done no more than shoot in self-defense. With a roomful of eyewitnesses, the lawman had no choice but to back down.

"Well, there hasn't been enough time for you all to agree to tell the same story, so I guess it must be the truth," he announced with obvious reluctance. "I don't want anymore of it, though. If you were just passing through, I suggest you git a move on right now, because if you stay I'm gonna watch every move you make. We don't like strangers riding in here and stirrin' up trouble."

"I came lookin' for work, sir, not trouble," Lance assured him politely.

Thomas MacDowell had noticed the soft-spoken young man when he had first come through the swinging doors. Having been favorably impressed by what he had seen, he rose from his table in the far corner and walked over to join in the discussion. "You can find him at my place then, Brad. I'll be proud to give him a job. MacDowell's my name, Thomas MacDowell."

Lance reached out to shake the hand he had been offered, "Thank you, sir. Lance Garrett is mine." He judged MacDowell to be about twenty years his senior. The man had a stocky build, reddish blond hair, lively green eyes, and a smile so genuinely warm it instantly inspired trust.

Frustrated to find his services were not required to keep the peace, the lawman muttered a few uncomplimentary words about the Hatcher brothers and walked out. Taking that as a sign the incident was over, several of the more boisterous patrons of the crowded bar offered to buy Lance a drink.

Thinking the young man would probably want to spend the night in town, Thomas MacDowell made a gracious offer. "I'm on my way out to the ranch now, but I can send someone back to get you tomorrow if you like."

Since what had begun as a pleasant afternoon had taken such a disappointing turn, Lance had no interest in staying in Tucson. It was unlikely that the Hatchers would be the only ones to wish him harm. When the story got around that he was handy with a gun, some other fool would surely try to push him into a fight. He had gotten away with one shooting, but the second might prove far more difficult to explain and he had absolutely no desire to feel a hangman's noose around his neck. "That's very kind of you, but I'll come with you now, sir." He tipped the barkeep generously for his help, then followed his new employer out to the street. There were no sidewalks, and those wishing to patronize the shops had to constantly dodge out of the way of passing wagons and their sweat-drenched teams. Deciding it was imperative to always be alert in such a confusing place, Lance waited impatiently for Thomas MacDowell to drive his buckboard up to the front of the Congress Hall. He then tied Amigo's reins to the back of the wagon and climbed up into the seat. While the day certainly had not gone as he had hoped it would, things had not turned out too badly and he was cautiously optimistic about the future. When MacDowell made no attempt to begin a conversation as they rode out of town, he was content to share the comfortable silence. The lush grass that blanketed the Santa Cruz Valley provided a refreshing change in scenery and he welcomed the chance to ride in the wagon after being in the saddle all week.

Thomas pulled the team to a halt when they reached the ramshackle gate marking the northern boundary of his land. There had once been a sign proclaiming the entrance to the MacDowell Ranch, but it had disappeared long ago, the victim of a windstorm, and had never been replaced. "This is where my spread begins, Garrett, but before we reach the house, I have a few questions I'd like to ask."

Instantly suspicious, Lance asked skeptically, "Just what sorts of questions might they be, sir?"

"You have a cool head. I admire that in a man. I can tell by your speech you're a Southerner, and from the looks of you and the way you handle yourself, I'd say you served the Confederacy as an officer. Am I right?"

Lance took a deep breath, for he was not nearly as coolheaded as this man mistakenly believed. "The war ended five years ago, Mr. MacDowell. There's no need for us to fight it all over again." This Lance had no intention of doing, no matter how helpful MacDowell had been in town. He had gone to Mexico to avoid the men who had

had some personal score to settle and unfortunately had chosen him as a target for their revenge.

Always in high spirits, Thomas slapped the young man on the thigh. "Lord no, that's not what I meant at all, son. I supplied horses to the Confederacy, so you needn't look at me as though I were the enemy. What I mean is you look like a gentleman to me, or at least you were one and quite recently too."

Insulted by his observation, Lance narrowed his keen gaze slightly. "I'd say I'm a gentleman still, sir." He was uncertain what Thomas MacDowell wanted of him and that made him very uneasy. Unconsciously his hand slid down to the revolver strapped to his right thigh. On guard, he waited for the man to make his point clear before he drew on him.

Unaware of the tensions he had created within the handsome young man, Thomas continued in an offhand manner. "Of course, gentlemen are born, aren't they? What was your rank at the end of the war?"

Seeing no point to the question, Lance replied reluctantly, "I was a major, but there were damn few of us left, so you mustn't think I was all that important." Despite his words, the pride in his deep voice was unmistakable.

"Well now, I think you might be wrong there." Glancing back at Amigo, MacDowell offered a sincere compliment for the stallion who was tossing his well-shaped head, impatient to continue their journey. "I don't ever recall seeing a ranch hand with such a fine mount. Did you have him during the war?"

"No, sir, I won him in a poker game last year," Lance admitted with a sly grin, "but he's as fine a horse as any I've ever owned."

"Owned quite a few, have you?" Thomas asked casually.

"Yes, sir," Lance replied, and although he could see that the man expected him to elaborate on his response, he did not.

When Thomas MacDowell realized that the maddeningly taciturn young man would never willingly volunteer any information about himself, he knew he would have to rely upon what his eyes told him. Lance Garrett was not only remarkably handsome but displayed such obvious good breeding that the older man suspected he would now be a vital member of the South's landed gentry if the Civil War had not interrupted his youth. The war had drastically changed a great many lives, however, and he was certain Lance's had been one of them. The elegant ways of the old Southern plantations were gone forever, but he considered himself extremely fortunate to have found himself a real Southern gentleman, since that was precisely who he needed most. "You're mighty fast on the draw and I'll bet you hit Randy right where you wanted to. Ever earned your living as a hired gun?"

"Only durin' the war," Lance replied with bitter irony.

Thomas agreed with a thoughtful chuckle, certain his high opinion of this courteous stranger was well justified. "When I first laid eyes on you I knew you were precisely the man I needed. I have a proposition for you."

Lance took a deep breath and held it a moment too long. "What sort of proposition?" he finally asked suspiciously. "If it's a killin' you want, you've got the wrong man."

"Killing? Good heavens, no! It's nothing at all like that." Thomas found his mistaken impression highly amusing and again slapped Lance on the thigh as though they were close friends. "My problem is that I have a nineteen-year-old daughter and—"

That was all Lance needed to hear. He stood up and jumped down from the buckboard, "Thank you for tellin' the sheriff I had a job, but that's not the sort of work I'll take."

"Come back here, damn it!" The stocky man gestured emphatically, but Lance stood rooted in place. "I don't want you to marry MaLou. That's not my proposition at all!" Thomas was frustrated at not making more sense than he was and began again. "Just hear me out. MaLou's mother and I were divorced when she was small. Lily was a good woman, but she just couldn't abide living in the desert. She missed her home and family so much that nothing I did seemed to please her. Rather than continue to make the only woman I'd ever loved miserable, I sent her back home to Boston and I was supposed to send MaLou to her for an education when she was old enough to go. Well, the war made travel back East too dangerous to send her alone, and with the Army troops gone it was all we could do to stay ahead of the Apaches, so I couldn't leave to take her." He shuddered at that gruesome memory, then continued. "MaLou didn't get to go back to Boston until the war was over. She was fourteen by then and after only two weeks with her mother she turned around and came home. That she and Lily didn't get along was all my fault though. You see, I'd raised her as best I could, but with no women around—"

Understanding the situation well, Lance scuffed the toe of his new boot in the dust of the rutted road as he interjected, "What you mean is you raised her like a son. Isn't that it?"

Thomas nodded. "I sure did. It didn't seem to matter that she liked to wear Levis and ride with the hands when she was small, but now—"

Lance started to laugh, for the situation was too humorous to ignore any longer. "Mr. MacDowell, I lost my last job because my boss thought I'd been flirtin' with his daughter. What exactly is it you want me to do with yours?"

"Come on back up here and sit down. I promise it's nothing so terrifying that you'll want to run away." Thomas waited for Lance to climb back up into the seat beside him before he continued. "MaLou is a pretty little thing, so this won't be difficult. I just want you to treat her like a woman instead of like one of the hands as the other men do. You needn't flirt with her, just be respectful. You Southerners all seem to be naturally polite, so I know you can do this for me."

Lance thought over the outlandish proposition for a long minute and then nodded. "Just say, 'Yes, ma'am,' like I noticed she was female? That's all there is to it?"

"That should do for a start. I just want her to see there

are some advantages to being a woman. I want her to get married and have a family of her own, but you don't need to do more than put the idea in her head that she might like to try being a woman for a change. Once she sees how nice it is, I think she'll do all right on her own."

After the way he had been kicked off Don Ricardo Lujan's *hacienda,* Lance had his doubts. "I know you must love your daughter, sir, but are you certain this plan of yours is a wise one? What if MaLou wants me to do more than be respectful? I don't mean to sound boastful, but women often find me attractive and your daughter just might take a likin' to me too."

Thomas frowned as he considered the question. While he knew he could do far worse, he could not see himself having a handsome drifter for a son-in-law, even though Lance claimed to have been a major in the Confederate Army. "Now MaLou would be furious with me for telling you this, but she's always liked our neighbor, Alex Spencer's son, Josh. He's fond of her, too, but not about to propose marriage to her when she'd probably be mistaken for his kid brother rather than his wife. I can't ask him to help me when he'll be the one she'll want to impress."

Lance gave the request a good deal of thought before he agreed. "Well, as I see it, I owe you one favor at least, Mr. MacDowell. If helpin' you teach your daughter how a lady behaves is what you want, I'll give it a try, but I don't want to hear any complaints if this scheme of yours backfires."

"How can it?" Thomas wanted to know. "You're coming in new. She'll never suspect I've put you up to this."

Lance gave him a skeptical glance. "Let's just hope not."

The ranch was a large one and by the time they pulled up in front of Thomas MacDowell's one-story adobe house, Lance had had more than enough time to regret his decision. He had given his word, however, and he never went back on it, no matter how difficult things became. He followed Thomas over to the corral where a dozen men appeared to be attempting unsuccessfully to break a lively brown and white pinto mare.

"She's a mean one, Mr. MacDowell. If Nathan can't stay on her back, then nobody can," one of the men called out by way of greeting.

"Nathan's my foreman. I'd better introduce you to him. He'll see you have a place in the bunkhouse." Thomas waited until the foreman had picked himself up, dusted himself off, and climbed upon the top rail of the corral to catch his breath before he led Lance over to meet him.

Nathan looked Lance's powerful build up and down slowly, his expression suspicious rather than friendly. "Didn't realize we needed another hand, Mr. MacDowell. Guess he'll do. Ever break a horse, Garrett?"

"A few." When all eyes focused on him, Lance knew there would be no way to avoid giving the mare a try. He was tired and would have much preferred having an early supper and turning in, but he knew the new man always had to prove himself and wanted to get that ordeal over with quickly. Two of the spectators exchanged knowing grins as they held the pinto still while he climbed over the gate and got into the saddle. The stirrups were too short for his legs and he had to wait while they were adjusted for a man of his height. Then all that was required was that he had more guts than the horse had and he was sure he would beat the mare handily since other men had already ridden her and had undoubtedly sapped some of her strength.

When the stirrups were ready, he jammed the toes of his boots into them and shouted, "Turn her loose!" For an instant the mare froze, then she exploded in a wild burst of flying leaps that carried him around the corral in a choking cloud of dust. If she was not the worst bucking horse he had ever had the misfortune to ride, she was damn close, but just when he thought he had finally subdued the last of the wild streak raging within her, she slammed into the side of the corral with a force that threatened to crush his knee. Recoiling from the pain of that brutal jolt, he lost his balance and went flying off into the dirt. As he struggled to avoid the mare's dancing hooves and scramble to his feet, a soft, feminine voice whispered in his ear.

"You were marvelous! You managed to break the mare without making Nathan look like a fool. Good work!"

Astonished by the totally unexpected praise since he had not noticed a girl among the men, Lance looked up into a pair of long-lashed green eyes vibrantly sparkling with mischief. Their owner was a slender blonde dressed in buckskins who darted off without giving him a chance to reply. She caught the pinto's trailing reins and leapt into the saddle. Shouting for the men to open the gate, she rode the mare out upon the open plain. Fascinated by the young woman's spirited grace, Lance brushed off his new clothes, leaned against the top rail of the corral, and watched until he could see no more than a spot of dust on the horizon. The mare had incredible speed, but the girl had clearly been in complete control and he did not worry about her being thrown.

Thomas MacDowell sauntered up to the young man's side and apologized. "I should have mentioned that MaLou's a trifle headstrong too."

Lance nodded but did not reply, for he had found MaLou MacDowell's lively charm so unexpectedly appealing that he had not the slightest desire to help her father change her ways. Besides, from the ease with which she had taken charge of the pinto, he doubted such a feat would even be possible.

Chapter II

Lance limped into the cookhouse the next morning, his right knee so stiff and sore he could barely bend it. It was not the first time he had suffered such an injury and he was confident that in a few days' time he would be as good as new. He took a plate and joined the line, hoping the breakfast would taste half as good as the tantalizing aroma that had lured him from his bunk. When he reached the serving table, he was startled to find MaLou MacDowell standing beside the cook, chatting with the men as she dished up generous portions of scrambled eggs. She was dressed in jeans but also in a delightfully feminine red silk blouse and she had caught her blond curls atop her head with a red ribbon. After he had had the opportunity to observe her for several minutes, Lance was certain her father had greatly underestimated her appeal, for she was far more than merely pretty. She was a fair beauty with the enchanting sparkle of a bright spring morning. She gave him a pleasant smile, but it was no warmer than the one she gave the other hands and he limped over to a table wondering if he should not start planning to move on right away. She looked content with her life, so why couldn't her father just leave well enough alone? he asked himself. From what he had seen, she would make a fine wife for a rancher, and if this Josh Spencer was too stupid to see that, then he was a damn fool.

When most of the men had finished eating and had gone

outdoors, MaLou slid onto the bench opposite Lance. After wiping her hand on her apron, she held it out to him. "I didn't have a chance to meet you properly yesterday. My name's Marie Louise, but everyone's always called me MaLou. Dad said you made fools of the Hatchers, and that's enough to make me your friend for life."

Lance rose as quickly as his battered knee would allow and shook her hand politely. "I'm pleased to meet you, ma'am. My name's Lance Garrett and from what I saw, makin' fools of the Hatchers isn't overly difficult to do."

MaLou's sparkling green eyes widened in dismay as she looked up at him, for she had absolutely no idea why he had leapt to his feet so suddenly. "Please sit down. I didn't mean to interrupt your breakfast," she apologized with a deep blush. She was embarrassed that she had disturbed him and tried to make up for it with a sincerely worded compliment. "I like the way you talk. Your accent is very charming. Where's your home?"

Lance recoiled inwardly at that oft-repeated question, but he gave her an easy grin as he resumed his seat. "Since yesterday, it's right here."

While his manner was still pleasant, MaLou was astonished by the bolt of fury that had flashed across the glorious sapphire blue of his eyes. The look had come and gone in an instant, but she was positive she had not misread the anger in his glance. Her question had been such an innocent one that she was sorely disappointed in his response. Why didn't he want to talk with her when she had done her best to be friendly? If he could not trust her with the truth about such a simple matter as his home, she was certain any further attempts at conversation would be pointless. Thoroughly disgusted to find that Lance Garrett was not nearly as nice a man as his fine appearance had led her to believe, she took her leave. "Forgive me for disturbing you. Finish your breakfast." She rose to her feet in a nimble leap. Her chores completed for the morning, she tossed her apron to the cook, then strode out the door without a backward glance.

Lance had seen that same proud walk too recently to

mistake its meaning. Though he had obviously gotten off to a very poor start with MaLou MacDowell, he did not think his accent was "charming." It tied him to a past best left forgotten and he vowed to make an effort to talk with the same careless haste MaLou used herself. He finished the rest of his breakfast, then stopped to pay the cook a heartfelt compliment, for he had found that a ranch cook who could actually prepare tasty meals was a rarity and he wanted the man to know that his talents were greatly appreciated.

MaLou ripped the ribbon from her hair as she slammed her bedroom door shut. She unbuttoned the bright red blouse with trembling fingers, tossed it atop her bed, and replaced it with one of the faded cotton shirts she usually favored. She had hoped that since the new hand was so handsome he would be different, but he sure as hell wasn't. There wasn't a man on the ranch who had noticed she wasn't built like one of them and she felt like a jackass for having tried so hard to impress Lance Garrett when his personality wasn't nearly as appealing as his looks. She had liked him the minute she had seen him the previous afternoon, but for some reason he certainly did not like her.

Wondering what sort of women he did like, MaLou studied her reflection in the mirror above her dresser while she wound her flowing blond curls atop her head and covered them with a straw hat. What she saw was a remarkably pretty girl with a healthy tan that gave the subtle peach tones of her fair skin a warm, golden glow. A thick fringe of long, dark lashes framed emerald eyes made far too bright by unshed tears. Her nose had a slight upturn and her lips a charming fullness, which invited the kisses she had yet to receive. She had never given her appearance much thought but decided now that while her father had said she was pretty, it could not possibly be true. Tucson had more bachelors than family men, but not one had ever noticed her. She had been a stupid fool to think

Lance Garrett would be any different. With his black curls and deep tan she had mistaken him for a Mexican until she had gazed into the startling bright blue of his eyes. Perhaps since he was dark, he only liked brunettes. Although she had heard that most men liked blondes best, she certainly had no experience to prove it. She knew her father would tell her to try wearing a dress if she wanted to impress a man, but there was too much work to be done to waste time swishing around in a cumbersome skirt. No, a dress would have made no difference anyway.

Maybe Garrett was like so many of the drifters her father had brought home, she mused, men with little on their minds other than how they would spend their next month's pay. He would probably only stay on the ranch for a few months and then be gone, so there was no point in wanting him to like her, no point at all. With a wistful sigh of regret, she shoved all thought of Lance Garrett from her mind, turned away from her mirror, and went to saddle the pinto for her morning ride.

After a week on the MacDowell ranch, Lance's fine horsemanship had earned him the respect of the other hands. He had found several who spoke Spanish so he could stay in practice, but he had had no second chance to speak with MaLou, and Thomas MacDowell had chided him about that repeatedly. While Lance knew that the man had no real idea what he was asking, he also knew he would have to do something soon since he liked his job and wanted to keep it. As he went about his business, he made it a point to keep his eye out for MaLou and found her routine as predictable as his own.

She usually helped the cook at breakfast, and occasionally at noon. She rode the pinto each morning and sometimes was not back until afternoon, but no one paid the slightest attention to her comings and goings, not even her father. She tended the kitchen garden in back of the house she and her father shared, but she worked there only briefly, as if she had no real talent or interest in gardening.

There was a long porch built across the front of the adobe house with bright pink geraniums planted in hanging baskets and an exotic magenta bougainvillea growing up and over the west end of the porch, providing an abundance of color as well as refreshing shade. He had noticed that each afternoon she spent several minutes watering the flowers and occasionally she stayed on the porch to read, but most days she disappeared into the house and he would not see her again until morning. While he enjoyed watching her, it saddened him to see that she spent so much of her time alone. Not once had she left the ranch, nor had anyone come to visit her. Having grown up surrounded by a large family, many friends, and numerous servants, he thought her solitary existence had to be impossibly lonely, though that was not the problem her father had asked him to correct. His difficulty was that he did not blame her in the least for dressing so casually, and while he had expected to see her in a dress on Sunday, no young man had come to call and he understood clearly why she had failed to dress any differently on that day.

When Lance happened to see MaLou currying her mare's glossy brown and white coat outside the barn one morning, he walked over to her as though he had business in the barn.

"Mornin', Miss MacDowell. What have you named the mare?" He pushed his hat to the back of his head, tucked his hands in his back pockets, and tried to look as though he were more interested in the horse than in her.

MaLou shrugged. "I haven't bothered to give her a name yet. Do you have any suggestions?" She glanced at him only briefly but was not surprised that her first impression of his looks had not changed any. His deep tan enhanced his finely chiseled features and the vivid blue of his eyes easily made him the most attractive man she had ever seen, but she reminded herself how little he thought of her and concentrated instead on the mare.

MaLou was again dressed in soft tan buckskins and as she reached up to curry the horse's mane, Lance found the saucy curve of her fanny impossibly distracting. He felt like a fool for being unable to keep his thoughts more proper but tried not to sound like one. "No, but I'll give it some thought."

"You do that." MaLou's pretty mouth was set in a firm line, her mood an openly hostile one.

Lance looked around quickly and seeing no one about moved a step closer. "I never meant to insult you, ma'am. I was born in Georgia if it matters so much to you."

"It doesn't matter in the slightest to me, but I admire honesty in a man. It's a pity you didn't realize that last week," MaLou replied flippantly.

Knowing he would need some plausible excuse for a remark she had clearly interpreted as rudeness, Lance gave the mare an affectionate pat on the rump and moved closer still. "Your horse damn near broke my leg. I was doing good to get out of bed that mornin', let alone carry on an honest conversation."

Appalled she had not known he had been hurt, MaLou dropped her hands to her sides as she turned toward him. "Well, why didn't you say so? I thought you'd just taken an instant dislike to me and I couldn't understand why."

Lance chuckled as he shook his head. "You're far too pretty for a man to ever dislike, ma'am." When her fair complexion brightened with a deep blush, he offered his hand. "Friends?"

MaLou hesitated a moment, then her tiny hand nearly disappeared inside his grip. "On one condition. You've got to stop calling me 'ma'am.' It sounds like you're talking to my mother." At that request Lance flashed a ready grin, showing off teeth that were not only even but a sparkling white. She then watched in rapt fascination as a slow, sweet smile played across his lips. When he leaned down slightly, she thought he meant to kiss her hand, but instead he drew her close. His lips brushed hers ever so lightly, a mere whisper of a caress, but it was a kiss all the same. As swiftly as it had begun it was over. He gave her hand a loving squeeze before releasing her and walked away without uttering a single word of farewell.

Trying to catch her breath, MaLou simply stared in

frustrated silence, unable to tell Lance what she thought of his manners as she watched him enter the barn. She was tempted to hurl the currycomb at his back but forced herself to resist the impulse. Josh had kissed her once, long ago, before he had ridden off to join the Union Army. His kiss had been every bit as brief but not nearly as pleasant. But shouldn't a kiss be returned? Apparently Lance Garrett had not thought the wait worth his while. The man had confused her completely again, and what sort of friend was that? "A poor one," she murmured to herself, and after saddling the mare she rode out across the prairie toward the Santa Rita Mountains, where the silence would calm the yearnings for affection Lance's kiss had aroused but not satisfied. "Damn him!" She wiped away the single tear that had escaped her lashes to trickle down her cheek and vowed not to be taken in by the charming Southerner ever again.

Before he had taken ten paces, Lance realized he had just made the worst mistake of his entire life. Rosalba had followed him around when he had never given her any hint he found her company enjoyable. His task was not to make the same sort of pet of MaLou but to inspire her to accept the veneer of femininity. How could he have been so stupid as to have kissed her? He had not given his action a second's thought. When she had placed her hand in his, it had seemed only natural to draw her near for a kiss. Her mouth was almost irresistibly appealing and he had had to restrain himself from savoring the sweetness of her taste more fully. That was what he had really wanted to do, though he had somehow managed to stop himself with the briefest of kisses instead. But now MaLou would expect something more and before long he would find himself in the same kind of mess that had cost him his job with Don Ricardo. "Damn her!" he swore to himself, sorry he had ever agreed to work for Thomas MacDowell in the first place.

Rather than skip breakfast the next morning since he

was desperately hungry, Lance waited until most of the men had eaten before he entered the cookhouse, hoping that if MaLou had been helping the cook that day she would already have left to go riding. Unfortunately for him, she was still serving stacks of flapjacks. Bracing himself for a confrontation of some sort, he did his best to give her a friendly smile. "Good mornin', Miss MacDowell."

"Good morning, Mr. Garrett." MaLou slid three buckwheat pancakes onto his plate and topped them with a thick slab of butter. "Syrup's on the table," she remarked absently without bothering to look up at him a second time.

Lance stood there, simply staring at her until the next man, impatient to eat, gave him a firm nudge. He realized with surprise bordering on shame that his kiss had not made the slightest impression upon MaLou MacDowell. As he choked down his breakfast, he watched her serve the last of the men with far more charm than she had shown him, and he ate hurriedly, disgusted that the kiss he had given her had caused him such a sleepless night when clearly it had not mattered at all to her.

Manuel Ortiz was one of the several Mexican *vaqueros* employed by Thomas MacDowell. While slight of build, he was as tough as a whip and greatly amused by Lance's discomfort, since its cause was so readily apparent. "If you want a woman, there are many pretty ones on Maiden Lane. Do not waste your time courting MaLou, *amigo*. She is no more than a beautiful child."

Startled by the unexpected advice, Lance looked up quickly. Manuel had been one of the first to welcome him to the ranch and he did not want to ruin the friendship they had just begun to build. "And if I happen to think differently?"

Manuel chuckled. "I will bet you ten dollars you cannot get so much as a kiss from her."

"Then pay up now because I already have," Lance replied with a cocky grin.

"Madre de Dios!" Manuel exclaimed excitedly. "Mac-

Dowell will kill you if he learns of it!"

"Care to risk another ten on that?" Lance dared with what Manuel mistook for reckless bravado.

MaLou glanced over at Lance at intervals spaced so that she was certain they would not cause comment and wondered just what he and Manuel had found so very amusing. Probably some filthy joke they would not share with her. She loved jokes, for her father had raised her to appreciate the type of humor most young girls never knew existed. Well, at least Lance seemed to be enjoying himself, so maybe he would stay around longer than the usual drifter did. Not that it mattered to her, she reminded herself coolly.

Lance found Manuel's good-natured teasing far easier to tolerate than MaLou's polite aloofness, which did not grow any warmer as the week progressed. He was doing such a poor job of repaying the favor to Thomas MacDowell that he strolled over to his house on Sunday afternoon, hoping the man would have a few minutes to talk with him. He had not expected MaLou to be seated on the porch reading, but she looked up and smiled as she saw him approaching. As he drew closer, he watched her cheeks fill with a pretty blush and realized she thought he had come to see her. His heart fell as he recalled the lack of visitors upon the road to her door. He made his choice quickly, sat down upon the edge of the porch in front of her, and leaned back against a post to get comfortable. "I've been thinkin' about your pinto, about givin' her a good name." In truth he had thought of no suitable names for the horse since he had been so preoccupied with thoughts of her maddeningly indifferent mistress.

"That's very nice of you, Mr. Garrett." MaLou had been sprawled across the chair, her left knee slung over the arm, and she tried hurriedly to move into a more graceful pose without calling undue attention to herself. She then closed her book and laid it aside. "Although I doubt she's suffered any for having none. I'm sorry you were injured breaking her. I would have ridden her myself that day, but Nathan wouldn't have it since my father wasn't here."

"He permits you to break wild horses?" Lance sat up so suddenly he nearly slipped off the porch but managed to prevent such a dreadful show of clumsiness by slamming the heel of his right boot into the dirt with an awkward jerk that jarred his whole spine.

MaLou laughed at his stricken expression. "Oh, I won't pretend I haven't been thrown, and plenty of times, but I'm as good at it as most of the men."

Lance leaned back again, uncertain how to respond to her boast—if it was a boast. Perhaps she was merely stating a proven fact. "You should keep such prowess a secret, Miss MacDowell. Most men don't like to be beaten in anythin' by a woman."

MaLou looked away for a moment, her glance following a red-tailed hawk that circled lazily overhead. "I've done it again, haven't I?" she asked softly, addressing that question more to herself than to him.

"Done what?" Lance asked curiously.

MaLou shrugged, unwilling to put her faults into words if they were not obvious to him. "Never mind. What names did you want to suggest for my mare?" she asked instead.

Lance was sorry he had criticized her, for the teasing sparkle had instantly vanished from her eyes and the sadness he saw reflected in their emerald depths filled him with an inexplicable sorrow. He had not meant to hurt her feelings again, but clearly he had, and that knowledge pained him greatly. Who was this young woman who behaved so differently from all the others he had ever met? He could not seem to do something as simple as pass the time of day with her, and yet he could not deny the attraction that existed between them for it was a most compelling one. He had always had an easy confidence where women were concerned, but MaLou MacDowell proved to be more of a challenge with each passing minute. He finally realized she was watching him with rapt interest, waiting for a list of names, so he hastily supplied some. "'Freckles' is too cute, but 'Pecosa' has a nice sound to it. That's the same thing in Spanish.

'Mancha' means 'spot'—that's appropriate too—but I like 'Querida' best."

MaLou gave him a skeptical glance. "'My Darling'?"

"I didn't realize you spoke Spanish or I'd not have translated for you," Lance apologized quickly, afraid he had insulted her again.

"I had a Mexican nanny when I was small, but doesn't every woman in the Arizona Territory recognize that word?"

"Well, they certainly should," Lance agreed with a rakish grin. "I've only just come here from Sonora though, so I've no idea whether all the women here do or not."

"From the looks of you I'd say you soon will," MaLou replied matter-of-factly.

"Miss MacDowell!" Lance tried to hide his shock and failed completely. "That's not the sort of thing a lady says to a man."

"Why not? You're very handsome. If I think so, surely other women will too."

"Well now, I certainly hope so, but it's still not a proper thing for a young lady to say." Lance shook his head, amazed that she had not known that.

MaLou sighed wearily. "If a lady isn't allowed to say what she thinks or tell the truth, then what's the point of being one?" She got up, skipped down the porch steps, and started off toward the hills, her stride a long, sure one despite her diminutive size.

Lance realized that the problems Thomas MacDowell had with his lively daughter were a lot more complex than the man had at first revealed. Putting a dress on MaLou would not change her free-spirited opinions, nor her penchant for expressing them. He rose slowly, knowing he had just been dismissed, but as far as he was concerned they still had plenty more to say. After a moment's hesitation, he started after her and with a few quick strides reached her side. "As I said, I'm new to the Territory and perhaps what I consider to be good manners strikes you as being old-fashioned."

MaLou stopped abruptly, surprised to find him by her

side. "Old-fashioned? I doubt such fine manners as you have can be called that. You don't really consider your ideas old-fashioned, do you? You're a very young man to have such thoughts." At least she thought he was quite young. His face was deeply tanned, giving the blue of his eyes an added sparkle, a very handsome and intriguing gleam, she realized, but she doubted he was much older than she. "You're not thirty . . . I'd say closer to twenty-five," she mused out loud.

"I'm twenty-seven, which is another question you shouldn't have just come right out and asked me." Lance could not suppress a deep chuckle, for the young woman was clearly incorrigible and yet he found her lack of guile very appealing. She had a child's innocence despite having the face and figure of a lovely young woman. It was a remarkable combination, and a most unnerving one too.

"I'd say twenty-seven is far too young to begin worrying about whether or not your ideas are old-fashioned, Mr. Garrett. Come and talk with me any time you wish. You needn't invent an excuse like wanting to name my mare, either."

Her smile was so delightfully sweet that Lance was not in the least bit tempted to reveal he had not come to see her in the first place. "That was not an excuse," he argued instead. "The horse does need a name." He watched her smile fade and knew she could sense a lie better than anyone he had ever known. He scuffed the toe of his boot in the sandy soil and tried to think of some way to salvage their conversation before it became an out-and-out fight.

"Well, stay away from me then, if that's what you want!" MaLou put her hands on her hips as her defiant glance raked over him. The man exasperated her completely, for while she loved to hear him talk, he said little worth hearing. "Think of some more names if it will save your pride, and I'll be happy to consider them." She walked back to her house, then slammed the front door shut soundly behind her. She knew she had embarrassed Lance, but she was furious that he had tried to lecture her exactly like her father did. That was useless, since she simply was not cut out to be a lady, and no amount of advice from anyone was going to change the way she felt inside.

Lance was the first man in line for breakfast the next morning. He ate hurriedly and left without speaking more than a terse "Good morning" to MaLou, but when she went to the barn to saddle her horse for her morning ride, she found him waiting for her.

Lance led the pinto out into the sunshine as he explained his purpose. "Take a look at the brown patch on her hip. What does that look like to you?"

The well-built young man was in such a hostile mood MaLou did not ask his reason for posing such an unusual question. She lifted her hand and slowly traced the outline of the patch as though she actually understood what it was he was asking. "It's almost a perfect oval, only the top has two pieces missing."

"Precisely," Lance agreed promptly. "It looks exactly like a tulip. That should be her name."

MaLou frowned. "Tulips don't grow here in the desert, Garrett. They can't survive the heat. This mare was born here and this is where she'll live. Tulip would be a ridiculously inappropriate name for such a horse."

While Lance could not argue with MaLou's logic, he could not recall ever having met a female who gave so little effort to impressing him favorably. He drew himself up to his full height as he handed her the reins. "Miss MacDowell, I believe pleasin' you to be an impossibility and I'll no longer waste my time tryin' to do it!"

Before MaLou could reply, her father waved to her from the back door. He strode across the yard calling as he came close enough to be understood, "I have to send MaLou into town, Garrett. Hitch a team to the buckboard and go with her."

"Yes, sir." Grabbing back the pinto's reins, Lance led her away as he stormed off to attend to the errand, but MaLou immediately began to argue.

"Why do I need to go into Tucson?"

"Because I asked you to, sweetheart. Just get these

things for me. Here's the list."

MaLou scanned the brief list quickly. "These are all the cook's supplies. Why doesn't he go for them?"

"Jake's not feeling well and I told him to get some sleep."

"Then who will cook for the men at noon?" MaLou asked with an exasperated sigh. "Send Garrett and one of the other men and I'll stay here and help Jake."

"He's not feeling that poorly, MaLou, but it won't hurt you to go into town for him. It is a small favor."

MaLou did not want to argue with her father, but the last thing she had expected to do that morning was spend her time with Lance Garrett and she tried frantically to think of some way to get out of such an ordeal. Hearing the rattle of the buckboard as Lance drove it around to the front of the barn, she gave her father one last pleading glance and whispered, "Can you send one of the other men with me then?"

"Garrett's a good man. Now you're wasting time. Get going." He gave her a light kiss upon the cheek, then winked slyly at Lance when she turned to climb up into the seat beside him.

MaLou was too upset to think clearly and made one final gesture of rebellion. "Shall I stop by Candelaria's to give her your love?" she inquired with unmistakable sarcasm.

"Lord, no!" Thomas turned away, having no time to waste on one of their perpetual arguments.

Lance waited until he had swung the buckboard out onto the road before he dared ask, "Who is Candelaria?"

"My father's mistress." MaLou's expression grew bitter as she explained, "He won't marry her because he's still in love with my mother. He just uses her."

Lance could not allow her remark to pass unchallenged. "Do you never think before you open that pretty mouth of yours? Whether or not a man has a mistress is his own business, certainly not that of his daughter!"

MaLou gave him a withering glance. "Then why did you bother to ask me about Candelaria if you didn't really want to know who she is?"

"I suppose I thought you'd have the sense to say she was a friend of your father's without tellin' me she was such a close one," he admitted reluctantly, not understanding how he could have expected such a show of discretion from her.

"Alex Spencer is a friend of my father's. Candelaria is his mistress. There's a great deal of difference between the two," MaLou insisted emphatically.

"I won't argue that, but still—"

"Oh, let's just forget you ever asked me the question."

After a moment's thought, Lance began to see the humor in their situation and couldn't help but laugh. "I think you're just plain jealous."

"Jealous? Of whom?" MaLou asked indignantly.

"Candelaria, of course," Lance explained. "Most girls don't want to share their daddy with another woman. I'll bet you're no different."

"That's disgusting, Mr. Garrett, and if we were going anywhere but into town to run an important errand for Jake I'd get out and walk home!"

"Yeah, I just bet you would." Lance continued to chuckle though, then offered a more revealing opinion. "I think you've been your daddy's little girl far too long, Miss MacDowell. It's time you had a man of your own."

MaLou pretended not to listen, but her cheeks burned with a bright blush. She wasn't opposed to falling in love—it just hadn't happened to her and Josh as she'd thought it would, that's all. She wouldn't apologize for the lack of men in her life, for surely it wasn't her fault.

When MaLou made no response, Lance clucked to the team to hurry them along. "It's a shame there wasn't time for you to change your clothes."

"What's the matter with my clothes?" MaLou looked down at the faded cotton blouse and jeans. "They're clean. I'm certainly not ashamed of the way I look."

"Oh no, I didn't mean that you should be," Lance agreed. "You look very pretty, but I know you must prefer to wear a dress into town so I'm sorry your daddy sent us off without givin' you the time to put one on."

"Mr. Garrett, did my father put you up to this?"

Alarmed she would consider that a possibility, Lance attempted to shrug nonchalantly. "I'd like to see you in a dress sometime, that's all. If your daddy feels the same way, I'm not surprised. Most men like to see their women in pretty clothes."

"Their women?" MaLou asked in disbelief. "Just who do you think you are?"

"Lance Garrett, ma'am, but you already knew that."

"That's not what I meant and you know it!" MaLou found his satisfied smirk impossible to bear. She was tempted to go into town by herself and make him walk back to the ranch, but she knew her father would be furious if she did that. There were dangers in the desert for a woman alone too numerous to contemplate. Renegade Indians and fools like the Hatchers were two of them, but she feared the good-looking rake by her side was twice as dangerous as those two perils combined.

Chapter III

This time Lance was prepared for the chaos that filled the dusty streets of Tucson, but MaLou's helpful suggestions on how to traverse them easily proved invaluable. She not only knew dozens of shortcuts that took them swiftly from one store to the next, but she also took the time to point out landmarks so he could find the same route when he came on his own. "You certainly know your way around town. It would have taken me half the day just to find the mill without you."

That she would know the town well scarcely seemed remarkable to MaLou. "I've lived here all my life, Garrett. Why wouldn't I know my way around?" she asked incredulously.

Lance dared to take his eyes from the crowded roadway for a brief second to flash her a teasing grin. "I know Tucson's grown rapidly. It must be difficult to keep up with all the buildin' goin' on."

"Well, that's certainly true enough," MaLou agreed. "In the mid-sixties there were only about fifteen hundred living here, mostly Mexican families who'd called Tucson their home for several generations. Last year's census showed there were more than eight thousand residents, and most of us American. So the town's not only grown but also changed a whole lot."

"For the better?" Lance asked curiously.

"Some say so and others don't," MaLou replied

noncommittally. She paused a moment to push a stray curl back up under her hat, then pointed to the cross street as they approached the corner. "I'll bet you've heard about Maiden Lane."

Lance frowned slightly as he recalled that Manuel had mentioned something about it and pretty girls. Afraid she was about to give him the directions to the most popular whorehouse, he raised his hand. "Now, MaLou, I don't think that part of town ought to be on your guided tour."

The pretty blonde gave Lance a disgusted glance. "Honestly, Garrett, do you think I have no sense at all? I was sure you'd heard about what goes on there. I just wondered if you'd heard where the street got its name since it's an interesting story."

"Are you sure it's a story that's fit to tell?" Lance asked with well-warranted apprehension.

"Just listen, and then you be the judge," MaLou responded icily, thinking he was only baiting her. "In the days when Tucson was a *presidio*, there was an Indian maiden who went to live with one of the Mexican officers. When he died, neither his people nor hers would take her in. The street was named for her: Calle de la India Triste."

"Street of the Sad Indian Girl? No wonder she was sad. I'll bet she was downright miserable," Lance remarked with a melancholy frown, obviously touched by the unfairness of the poor woman's fate.

Surprised he was so genuinely moved by her tale, MaLou gave Lance's arm a comforting squeeze. When he flinched at her touch, she instantly regretted the display of sympathy and clasped her hands tightly in her lap as she replied flippantly, "It's just an old story, Garrett. It probably never really happened at all."

"Oh, I'm sure it happened," Lance argued perversely, "and probably not just once but dozens of times."

"Well, maybe it happened and maybe it didn't, but the street's called Maiden Lane still." Afraid they were on the verge of a bitter argument over whether or not the mistreated Indian had actually existed, MaLou grabbed the first excuse that came to mind and changed the subject.

"Just pull over anywhere you can. I want to run into the *Citizen* Building and get a copy of the paper for Dad."

Lance was so grateful the perky blonde had shown an uncharacteristic restraint and had described only the origin of the name rather than the pleasures available on the brothel-lined street, he swiftly dismissed the homeless Indian maiden from his thoughts. Finding an open space in front of the newspaper office, he pulled the team to a halt. MaLou disappeared inside and while she was gone a notice in the window caught his eye. He wrapped the reins securely around the brake handle, then leapt down to study it more closely. The poster advertised a dance on the coming Saturday at the hall of the Pioneer Brewery. A few minutes later when MaLou came out the door, he reached for her hand to draw her to his side and pointed out the advertisement. "What do you know about this place?" he asked with an encouraging smile, thinking that if the young men of Tucson would be there, then that was exactly where MaLou ought to be too.

MaLou used the latest issue of the *Citizen* to fan her flushed cheeks lightly as she read the annoucement silently to herself before responding to his question. "Alexander Levin came to town a couple of years ago and opened the brewery. He built a big hall and has parties and dances there all the time. I suppose it's good advertising for his business."

"Who goes to these dances?"

Not seeing his point, the petite blonde shrugged. "I have no idea. I guess any man who wants to go is welcome."

Lance reached out to draw her close as a heavyset man lumbered by. For a moment he had thought it might be one of the Hatchers, but the fellow was far too pleasant to be part of that surly brood. After wishing them a friendly "Good morning," the man passed on by. His curiosity far from satisfied, Lance continued to probe. "You've never gone to any of the dances?"

Exasperated, MaLou tried to turn away, but Lance held her shoulders fast and she saw she would not be able to escape him before she had answered his question fully. "Single men can go alone, but not women. That's totally unfair, but I don't care about going to dances anyway so I haven't bothered to complain to Mr. Levin about his rules."

Before Lance could offer the opinion that no respectable young woman should attend such a gathering without an escort, their conversation was interrupted by a young man who had halted at the doorway of the *Citizen*. Amused to find MaLou and her companion studying the announcement for the dance, he greeted her with a teasing sarcasm. "It's high time you finally decided to take up dancing, MaLou."

Instantly recognizing his voice, MaLou wheeled around ready to whip Josh Spencer up one side and down the other with the folded newspaper in her hand. Had Lance not grabbed the back of her belt to reel her in a foot she would have done it too. "So what if I have, Josh? That's no business of yours," she responded petulantly.

Ignoring the fiery sparks that gave MaLou's eyes the hypnotic gleam of a demon's, Josh looked over her head to introduce himself. "I'm Joshua Spencer. Are you Garrett?"

Startled to find the young man knew his name, Lance nodded cautiously. "Have we met somewhere?" Until that very minute he had given Josh Spencer no thought, but he could readily understand why MaLou had always been fond of this fair-haired young man. Josh was almost as tall as he, although not nearly as well built. His hazel eyes reflected the warmth of his teasing laughter while his sparkling smile was framed by a neatly trimmed blond mustache. Undoubtedly his boyish charm impressed most women favorably, but Lance could not help but notice that MaLou's reaction to his teasing greeting had been anything but cordial.

Josh leaned around the still-seething girl to extend his hand. "We've met now," he explained with an admiring glance. "Everyone's heard how you drilled a hole clean through Randy Hatcher's leg. In case you didn't know it, that makes you one of the most popular men in town."

"I can do without that kind of popularity, thank you." Lance observed MaLou's expression from the corner of his eye. She still appeared miffed, but she had yet to take her eyes off Josh, and the glow in their emerald depths held a curious mixture of fury and awe. Hoping to lighten the mood, he attempted to draw Josh into their conversation. "We were just talkin' about this dance," he remarked with a casual gesture toward the poster. "Do you and your friends ever go to them?"

"Sure. They're lots of fun and nearly everyone goes. Once in awhile things get somewhat out of hand late in the evening, but since everyone knows you know how to handle yourself, you'll have no trouble with drunks just wanting to be obnoxious."

"Nor with anyone else, I'll wager," Lance offered slyly.

Amused by his confident boast, Josh reached out to give Lance a hearty slap on the shoulder. "Hey, you're all right for a reb." Then, as though she were not standing right by his side, Josh lowered his voice and began talking about MaLou. "When we were little kids, MaLou and I used to dance together at parties. She was such a tiny little thing I could just pick her up and carry her around in my arms so she never learned how to do the steps." As an afterthought, he finally glanced down at the brightly blushing blonde. "I bet you don't even remember that, do you?"

While she treasured those memories as some of the dearest of her childhood, it had been a good many years since MaLou had thought of herself as a child. It was painfully obvious, however, that Josh still considered her one. "I think I probably remember more than you do," she revealed proudly.

Lance watched the amusement fill Josh's eyes, but when the young man did not make any sort of favorable reply, he encouraged one himself. "I imagine MaLou is a very fine dancer now."

Josh shrugged slightly. "You couldn't prove it by me. Say, is your father still providing the beef for General Stoneman's feeding stations?"

Startled that he had changed the subject so completely, MaLou needed a moment to reply. "I know you and your father are opposed to showing the Apaches any sort of kindness in the hopes it will lead to peace, but my dad agrees with the government's policies. He's happy to sell the Army beef for the Indians."

Josh tapped the paper she held as he offered some advice. "Tell him to read the editorial this week because he'll see that's a mighty unpopular view. The Army ought to be chasing those thieving bandits over the border rather than providing them with free rations."

Since Lance knew Apache raids were no more welcome in Sonora than they were anywhere else, he opened his mouth to disagree, but before he could interject a single word, Josh turned away and with a jaunty wave entered the *Citizen* Building. Lance was as perplexed as MaLou that they had been dismissed so abruptly. He thought he had provided Josh with ample opportunity to invite MaLou to the dance. That the young man had shown so little interest in taking her had been appalling. The more he thought about it, the more disgusted Lance became, for Josh had behaved like a jackass. He had either ignored MaLou during their conversation or treated her in a rudely condescending manner. If that was the best Tucson had to offer, then he was afraid the pretty blonde would die a spinster. "Would you like to go to the dance, MaLou?" he asked in a tone so charming he hoped she would have no idea how furious he truly was.

"Hm?" MaLou asked absently, still numbed by Josh's total disregard for her as a person. She knew even when he had looked straight at her he still hadn't really seen her.

Lance placed his hands upon her shoulders to again turn her around to face him. "I said, 'Would you like to go to the dance'?"

Her eyes filling with hot tears of anger, MaLou shook her head so violently her hat was in grave danger of flying off into the street. She reached up quickly to make a grab for it but was too late to prevent her bright curls from spilling down upon her shoulders in charming disarray.

Clutching the well-worn straw hat tightly to her breast, she tried one last time to make Lance understand her plight. "I told you women can't go alone and I certainly didn't hear Josh invite me, did you?"

Stung that she had not realized he was extending an invitation, Lance was sorely tempted to drop the matter right there, but he reminded himself that she was completely inexperienced when it came to pleasing men and tried again. "MaLou, I am trying to invite you to go with me. Would you do me that honor?"

MaLou gasped in surprise, then hastily tried to dry her eyes on the back of her hand. She was horribly embarrassed, simply mortified, that she had not understood his question the first time he had asked it. "Oh, I am so sorry," she apologized with a bright blush, "but I really can't go. Josh is right. I don't know how to dance and I have no pretty clothes and—"

Lance ignored the fact that they were standing at the edge of a busy street and pulled her into his arms for a reassuring hug. Cradling her head softly against his shoulder, he explained his plan. "If you want to impress Josh, then you'll have to go to the dance. This is only Monday. We can buy you a new dress, slippers, whatever else you need today, and I'll teach you how to dance. I'm positive you'll be the prettiest girl there and Josh will kick himself all the way home that you weren't there with him."

Surrounded by the comforting warmth of his embrace, MaLou found it surprisingly difficult even to remember who Josh was. That realization confused her all the more. "I don't know. Do you really think he'd notice me?" she asked hesitantly, the hope in her voice tinged with doubt.

"You heard him. I have suddenly become one of Tucson's most popular citizens and everyone will notice my date."

That teasing promise made MaLou laugh. She stepped out of Lance's arms and raised her hands quickly to cover a smile she feared had grown much too wide. "Could we really do it, Lance? Could we?"

That she wanted to impress Josh so badly made Lance's heart ache, and he nodded enthusiastically. "Of course we can do it. Now if you needed a satin ball gown you'd have to hire a seamstress, but I think we ought to be able to find a nice ready-made dress somewhere here in town that would be suitable for this dance. You told me your father wants you to wear dresses so why not buy several, since you're sure to have plenty of callers after Saturday night?"

Ordinarily MaLou would have laughed at such a comment, but Lance's enthusiasm was contagious and she agreed to go shopping without putting up any argument at all. When they found only two dresses to her liking at Zeckendorf's, one pink and one blue, she took him to a store operated by another of the freighter-merchant companies: Tully, Ochoa, and DeLong. The clerk there began by showing her a dress of peppermint-striped polished cotton with its own bright red petticoat and she fell in love with it instantly. It was more expensive than the others, but with Lance's encouragement she quickly decided it was well worth the cost. After she had put it on her father's account, she added three bars of gardenia-scented soap and a tiny bottle of French perfume. When Lance gathered up her purchases to carry them out to the buckboard, she suddenly realized they had given no attention to the fact he might need something new to wear.

"Wait a minute," she called as she caught up with him. "Won't you need new clothes too?"

Lance was not concerned about the meager state of his own wardrobe. He still had most of the pay Don Ricardo had given him, but he did not have it with him. "I can't expect your father to pay for my clothes too. I'll come into town on Saturday and get what I need."

"No, I don't think that's fair," MaLou insisted anxiously. Drawing him aside where their conversation could not be overheard, she explained the reason for her decision. "Look, this isn't a real date, now is it? You're only acting as my escort to help me impress Josh. Isn't that the truth?"

Since it was plain in the innocent delight of her

expression that she regarded his invitation as part of a deception rather than a sincere request to enjoy her company, Lance thought better of putting up an argument. Thomas MacDowell wanted his daughter to dress like a lady and show a healthy interest in men. It now seemed to Lance that task had been accomplished with astonishing ease. He had done nothing at all, however, to honor his promise to his employer, his conscience chided him painfully. MaLou had taken one look at Josh Spencer and had made all the right choices herself. Still, he would not allow her to purchase his clothes too. "I will buy what I need myself," he declared firmly. "Now, we've been gone so long Nathan probably has a search party out lookin' for us. We better get goin'."

Alarmed by that thought since it could so easily be true, MaLou quickly hustled him out the door. "I'm sorry. I'd completely lost track of the time." She took the bundles from his arms and placed them in the buckboard along with their other purchases. "My father would like nothing better than for me to marry Josh. Not a day goes by that he doesn't mention his name. He won't be mad at us for taking so long when I explain it was for such a good cause."

Lance knew that was certainly true enough, but he dared not admit it. "I sure hope not, ma'am."

Exasperated, MaLou climbed up into the seat with an agile leap. "I asked you not to call me 'ma'am'!" she implored again.

"How about 'honey' then?" Lance replied with a cocky grin.

"Honey?" MaLou was aghast at his suggestion. "Now you just wait a minute—"

"If we are going to make Joshua Spencer jealous, you'll have to pretend to like me, MaLou. Do you think you can do that?"

As MaLou stared into the dreamy blue of his eyes, she dimly recalled that just a few hours earlier she hadn't wanted him to escort her into town, but for some reason she couldn't remember why. His grin was so charming that she thought for a minute he might be teasing her, but then she decided his question was sincere. "I do like you," she declared with a saucy smile, but, frightened their conversation was becoming too personal, she promptly turned it in another direction. "What do you call that black stallion of yours?"

Lance clucked to the team as they turned out into the street to begin the long ride back home. "He's a Mexican horse so his name is Spanish, which should please your passion for logic. I call him Amigo, since a cowboy's best friend is most definitely his horse."

MaLou glanced away at the mention of the word "passion," for it embarrassed her to think he believed her to have strong feelings only for logic. "That's a nice name." After paying that compliment she sat dreamily thinking about Saturday night and praying she would not look like a fool in the pretty red and white dress. "Are you any good at dancing, Mr. Garrett?" she asked suddenly.

"Superb," Lance replied with a reassuring wink. He chuckled to himself as he remembered how disappointed Rosalba had been when he had refused to dance with her. "You mustn't worry, MaLou. All a lady need do is follow the man's lead. By Saturday night you'll be able to dance with whomever you choose without worryin' you'll trip over his feet."

MaLou was not nearly as confident in her ability to master the art of dance, but she smiled shyly as she continued to pray the sweet talking Southerner was speaking the truth.

Lance cast Thomas a warning glance, silently beseeching him not to argue as MaLou described their plans. The man was clearly astonished and perhaps a trifle annoyed, but he managed to wait until MaLou completed her rambling explanation and stopped to take a breath before he made his first comment.

"Now let me get this straight. There's a dance at the Pioneer Brewery on Saturday night and it's likely Josh will be there with some of his buddies. Just whose idea was it that Lance be your escort, baby, yours or his?"

MaLou's golden tan again took on a rose tint as she turned to look up at the handsome ranch hand. "It was his idea, but it's a damn good one all the same."

The offhand compliment brought a deep burst of laughter from Lance. "She's right, sir. Joshua Spencer seems like a nice young man, but he can't be too bright if he didn't think of invitin' MaLou to the dance himself. I figure all he needs is a chance to see her in one of her pretty new dresses and he'll realize what an awful mistake he made." He smiled happily then, as though he were positive the sight of MaLou decked out in a dress would turn Josh's blood to flame.

Thomas turned away to hide his smile, for he had almost given up on Lance Garrett when the man had not had any immediate effect upon his willful daughter's boyish habits. He tried to appear reluctant to permit her to attend the dance as he turned back to face her. "I'd like for you to be able to go to nice dances, MaLou. I just wonder if this one at the brewery is the proper place to begin."

Accurately guessing the man was merely playing his part in their ruse, Lance assured him there was no cause for alarm. "I can readily understand your concern, sir, but I promise to bring MaLou straight home at the first sign of trouble. She'll come to no harm as long as she's with me."

"Well, now, I don't know." Thomas rubbed his chin thoughtfully, appearing to be carefully weighing his options. Finally he held out his arms and began to smile. "Come give me a hug, darlin'. If you want to go to the dance with Garrett I guess it will be all right."

Lance's smile was genuine as he watched MaLou leap into her father's outstretched arms. He was confident that in a dress, with her hair worn up in a softly feminine style, she would attract everyone's eye, and he knew that while Josh might be a tad stupid, he wasn't blind.

Unfortunately Lance had not considered MaLou's lack

of dancing skills much of a problem until after he had begun trying to teach her. He had come back to the house after supper, but he soon found that giving instruction while she was dressed in buckskins provided an obstacle he had not foreseen. He tried to keep his hand at her waist, but all too often when she turned or bent forward slightly his fingertips would slide up to the spot where her breast began to swell and then he would be so distracted he would forget what it was he was trying to teach.

Despite his momentary lapses in attention, MaLou was frowning with deep concentration. She was trying so hard to please him, but Lance was afraid she lacked even the smallest amount of talent. He was beginning to think Josh had had the right idea and the best way to dance with her would be to lift her clean off her feet and carry her around the dance floor. But suddenly he had a better idea. She would surely be more graceful dressed as a lady, and when she donned a corset he would not be so easily distracted either. Hoping to solve two problems at once, he dropped his arms to his sides and phrased his request as tactfully as he possibly could.

"This is a mite difficult without music, but I think it can be done. So it will feel more natural to you on Saturday night, why don't you put on one of your new dresses, and then we'll begin again."

MaLou could not imagine what her attire had to do with it, but since she was afraid it was her fault the lesson was progressing so slowly, she readily excused herself and went to her bedroom to change.

Thomas chose the few minutes they would have alone to confide in Lance in a low whisper. "You're gonna need a world of patience, son. The poor child can't even walk like a lady. It's no wonder she can't dance like one."

Lance kept his eye on the doorway to make certain his remarks would not be overheard. "She's bound to appear more graceful in a dress, sir. Just give her a chance and she won't disappoint you." He downed the whiskey Thomas offered in a single gulp but refused another, thinking he would need all his wits about him that night. "Josh

Spencer said somethin' about your supplyin' beef for feedin' stations for the Apaches. Can you tell me how they work?" Lance was intrigued by the idea since this was the first he had heard of such stations.

"Sure. It's a simple concept. General George Stoneman is the department commander of Arizona. He's merely carrying out orders from President Grant to provide temporary locations where Indians who've surrendered can receive rations until a permanent reservation can be established. I send cattle up to Camp Grant every couple of weeks to provide beef both for the Army and for the Apaches who've settled near there. I think it's a good idea myself, but plenty of people in Tucson don't agree. They want Stoneman to use his troops to slaughter every Indian he can find until there's not one Apache left. That's not my idea of being civilized. Is it yours?"

"No, sir, it isn't, but I can understand why most settlers don't trust Indians to adopt a peaceful way of life."

"Would you if you and your family were being run off the land you'd roamed for centuries?" Thomas asked pointedly, his sympathy clearly with the Apaches.

Lance straightened up proudly as he pointed out a relationship the elder man clearly had not seen. "As a matter of fact, no, sir, but when General Lee surrendered I had no choice but to follow orders and lay down my arms too."

Afraid he had unintentionally insulted Lance, Thomas apologized hurriedly. "I didn't mean anything by that remark, Garrett. Try to remember I was on your side. A lot of us here were."

Since Lance believed the less said about the war the better, he was angry with himself for bringing it up and quickly turned the conversation back to its original topic. "If you don't mind, I'd sort of like to read that editorial in the *Citizen* to see what it says."

"Sure, sit down and make yourself comfortable. Looks like MaLou needs longer to dress than I thought." Thomas picked up the newspaper from a nearby table and handed it to Lance. He then looked down at his watch and decided it was definitely time for another drink.

After a lengthy mental debate, MaLou decided to wear the pink dress and save her favorite for the party. Not that the pink dress wasn't very pretty too. The fullness of the skirt was gathered at the back of her waist in a softly padded bustle. She turned this way and that in front of her mirror, attempting to ascertain whether or not the fashionable style was actually as flattering as the clerk had sworn it to be. She thought padding a gown on the fanny was silly, but she knew she paid so little attention to women's fashions that she could not truly act as judge. She was so slender she had no need for a corset to nip in her waist and hadn't even bothered to buy one. The square neckline of the gown was trimmed with a lace ruffle so it could not be called immodest, but she could not help thinking that it did show off just a bit too much of the fullness of her breasts. That worried her, for she did not want her apparel to suggest that she was a flirt.

Reminding herself she had no plans to appear anywhere except her own parlor for the moment, she used several combs to catch her hair atop her head. When the result was not all that neat, she simply ignored the stray curls that had escaped her efforts at taming and had fallen in wispy ringlets upon her shoulders. Her new kid slippers were comfortable but felt nothing like her boots, and she tied them snugly around her ankles to make certain they would not come loose. Thinking herself as ready as she would ever be, she hurried back out to the parlor, hoping she had not kept Lance waiting too long.

A breathless smile on her lips, MaLou was not simply attractive but so hauntingly lovely that her father and Lance were flabbergasted by the remarkable change in her appearance and could do little more than stare in amazement. Lance leapt to his feet, but a long moment passed before he had the presence of mind to pay her the compliment she so richly deserved. "Your new dress is lovely and so are you." When MaLou looked more skeptical than pleased, he could only wonder at the fact that she had absolutely no idea what a treasure she was. With her father standing no more than three feet away, however, he dared not do more than pay her that one compliment. Since she had spent so much time getting dressed, he hastened to resume their lesson. "Now, why don't we just stroll around the room a few times so you'll have a chance to practice walking in a long skirt."

"I have worn a dress before, Garrett," MaLou assured him with a self-conscious laugh. "I don't think we have any time to waste on just prancing around." Eager to get on with the dancing lesson, she stepped into his arms and looked up at him with an expectant smile.

She had suddenly become so incredibly beautiful it was all Lance could do to stifle the impulse to crush her in his embrace and shower her face with fevered kisses. He showed remarkable restraint, however, and did no more than step back and take her hand. "I am serious, MaLou. It is far more difficult to walk in a long gown than in pants. Now humor me and let's just pretend we are walkin' up to the dance, passin' through the doorway, and movin' across the floor to talk with your friends. Whatever you'd like to imagine is fine." She still seemed reluctant to grant his request, so he slipped his arm around her waist to start her along. It did not take him but a second to realize she still was not wearing a corset, but he knew there was no way he could send her back to her room to don one. He felt only the warmth of her fair skin beneath his fingertips, for the fabric of her gown was soft and sheer, but by summoning a great deal of willpower he kept his hand away from the enticing curve of her breast.

After repeatedly tripping upon her hem, MaLou understood the vital importance of mastering a basic walk first. "I never realized I'm so dreadfully clumsy," she apologized nervously, her sweet expression filled with dismay.

"You are not in the least bit clumsy, MaLou." Lance wished they had more room in which to practice. The entrance hall in his family home had been larger than Thomas MacDowell's modest parlor. He had not thought of that gracious house in years, but suddenly he yearned to see MaLou in her pretty pink dress come gliding gracefully down the curving staircase, a sweet smile lighting her delicate features as she rushed to meet him. While such fantasy was delightful, he was forced to confront the fact that the lively girl could not seem to manage a graceful walk on a flat surface, let alone while descending a flight of stairs. "Pick up just a bit of your skirt to raise the hem slightly. Yes, that's it. Just look up and smile at your partner, and if you should happen to trip, he'll be certain it was his fault and he'll apologize profusely. I guarantee it."

"Not all men have your fine manners, Mr. Garrett." Nor your splendid looks, MaLou thought impishly, but she kept that opinion to herself. They spent the better part of two hours practicing only a few simple moves, yet he never once got angry with her for not immediately mastering the steps. She was certain they would have been easy for anyone else, but she just could not seem to manage the full skirt of her gown and produce the required steps simultaneously. Discouraged, she dropped his hand and sank down upon the settee in a careless heap. "It's no use, Garrett. I'm never going to learn how to dance by Saturday night."

Lance groaned inwardly, for she obviously had no idea how to sit down gracefully either. She looked more like a cowboy perched on the top rail of a corral than a young lady seated demurely in her parlor. "No," he contradicted convincingly, "you are doing beautifully. It's been a long day and it's no wonder you're tired. Let's stop now and continue tomorrow night."

"I hate to waste so much of your time," MaLou replied

with a wistful sigh. "You're a wonderful teacher, but I'm afraid this is hopeless."

"No, if you can break a horse, then you can learn to dance," Lance assured her with a teasing wink, but as he strolled across the yard to the bunkhouse, he reflected that it was an awful shame he wasn't taking her to a rodeo instead of a dance.

Chapter IV

Lance had found his bunk surprisingly comfortable on other nights, but now sleep had eluded him for so many hours he felt as though he were lying upon a bed of nails. He was tired, but apparently not nearly tired enough to escape his memories and fall asleep. He lay with his hands behind his head, gazing up into the darkness, attempting unsuccessfully to ignore the gnawing emptiness that filled him with an all-too-familiar ache. It was persistent, not unlike pangs of hunger, but he knew that no meal, no matter how delicious, would still this recurring pain. He had allowed himself to become involved in the MacDowells' lives when he had first agreed to Thomas's request to provide the encouragement MaLou needed to become the woman she had been born to be. They were nice people—he couldn't help but like them—but the petite blonde had begun to stir feelings inside him he didn't want to give in to ever again. He had taken far too personal an interest in her, and he would bring that to an immediate end. He would not allow her prettiness to affect him again. Giving dancing lessons was merely part of his job, a ridiculous part perhaps, but he would regard it as no more than that. To do otherwise would simply deepen the involvement he had done his best to avoid since the end of the war. He had lost far too much during those hellish years ever to risk opening his heart again.

He had not been teasing MaLou about Josh Spencer. He

was certain that once the young man saw her dressed as a lady he would swiftly cease regarding her as a willful child and come calling. Unless, of course, he was a bigger fool than he had appeared from their brief meeting that day and Lance did not think that was possible. He forced himself to concentrate upon that aspect of Thomas's scheme. He was tutoring MaLou so she would receive the attention she deserved from the young men of Tucson. That was it. It was a job like any other and he would do it well and then move on. With any luck, Josh would be so smitten with the delightful blonde that he would propose to her Saturday night. When that thought brought absolutely no consolation, Lance grew even more stern and told himself that protecting his own emotions would also protect MaLou's. If he didn't keep his own feelings in check, she might begin to care for him, and what an awful mess that would create. It would be unspeakably cruel to encourage her affection when he had no intention of returning it. He had suffered far too much from the pain of loss himself to inflict that same grief upon a young woman as sweet as she. No, when it came to women, where he belonged was on Maiden Street with the other cowhands who cared only about sharing the charms of a pretty woman's body without any wish to touch her heart. Strangely, the prospect of paying for easy affection left him feeling all the more alone. As always, he was overwhelmed with bitterness when he thought about spending the rest of his life without the love of the wife and family he had once assumed he would have, but it was his choice, and the only one he would ever make.

Far from rested, Lance entered the cookhouse the following morning feeling every one of his twenty-seven years. Then he saw MaLou. She gave him no more than the usual pretty smile she gave everyone, but then she winked at him. It was a saucy wink, reminding him instantly that she had no idea his motives were more than merely helpful where she was concerned. He tried to return her smile but was only partially successful. He ate hurriedly and then left to begin the endless chores running a cattle ranch entailed.

MaLou wore her new blue dress that night. She had spent more than an hour practicing with her hairbrush and combs to achieve a more sophisticated upsweep of curls. She did not understand how women could sit still while a maid attended to their grooming, but she hoped the fact that she had done it herself would not be too obvious to Lance. He was right on time, as pleasant as before in his compliments and as patient in his manner. His mood was so much more restrained, however, that MaLou soon began to worry if her lack of grace was the cause. "It's hopeless, isn't it?" she asked apprehensively. "You're a wonderful teacher, but even when I remember the steps, I don't do them well."

In truth, Lance had been so lost in his own thoughts that he had not noticed whether or not she was having difficulty. He could scarcely admit that to her, though. "This is only Tuesday so we still have three more nights to practice. Please don't worry so. Try to relax. Dancing is supposed to be fun, not the ordeal you're makin' it," he teased softly.

MaLou reached up to poke a stray curl back into place. Her hairstyle had been attractive when they had begun to dance, but now, an hour later, it felt uncomfortably loose and she was afraid if she wasn't careful her curls might soon spill down her back in a tangled mess. Lance had been as sympathetic as always, but then, she reminded herself, he was such a fine gentleman he seldom told the truth. "Whatever am I going to do if I don't get any better?"

Lance found her worried frown so troubling he made the best suggestion he could. "We'll simply plan to arrive late then. That will give Josh time to have several beers. He'll see only how pretty you are but never notice if your dancin' is less than perfect."

MaLou was not certain that Lance was serious, but since his plan was so sensible she agreed. "The way I dance, we might have to arrive very late," she suggested with a lilting giggle but then suddenly had second thoughts. "Oh no, we don't dare do that. It would cause far too much gossip. We'll have to be on time and I'll have to be able to dance at least passably well or everyone will laugh at me. But I'm afraid there just isn't enough time for me to learn everything I should have learned years ago."

Inspired by desperation, Lance tried a new tack to dispel her fears. "You are not goin' to be presented to a bunch of snobs at a society ball on Saturday night, MaLou. You're goin' to a dance at a brewery where everyone will be far more interested in havin' a good time than anythin' else. Now just think about what fun it will be and stop worryin'."

Intrigued, MaLou laid her hand in his to again try the series of steps she had been attempting to master. "You've been to society balls, haven't you, Lance? My mother was hoping to present me as a debutante, but without someone in Boston as patient as you to teach me, I'm certain I'd never have made her proud of me."

She was not complaining, or feeling sorry for herself, but merely stating what she considered to be a fact. Lance had no idea what her mother was like, but he took an instant dislike to the woman, for he was certain a mother's pride should not be based solely upon a child's accomplishments. "There are plenty of things more important than being a debutante, MaLou. Don't give the fact you weren't presented to society at a lavish ball another thought," he commanded somewhat stiffly. "That's the best thing about the West. We can make our own traditions here without any ties to the past."

Thomas MacDowell was seated in a chair he had pulled into the far corner to be out of their way. He had a book in his hands, but he had been eavesdropping on their conversation rather than concentrating on the story. Finally he had to speak up. "MaLou, I thought you really wanted to go to the dance. If you're going to worry so about it, though, why don't you just forget the idea?"

"No!" Lance responded instantly, then realized too late the question had not been addressed to him. Both MaLou and her father were staring at him in wide-eyed dismay and he quickly apologized. "What I mean is, MaLou already has a stunnin' new dress. I'll be sure to dance the first few dances with her so she gains some confidence and I'm certain the dance will be well worth our efforts to attend. If Josh Spencer needs to have a fire lit under him to notice MaLou, then Saturday night we'll start a blaze."

Thomas pursed his lips thoughtfully, thinking that perhaps Lance was putting too much enthusiasm into getting MaLou off his hands. He spoke directly to his daughter this time. "Josh should be so thrilled to see you in a dress he'll never notice you can't dance like a ballerina. I just don't want you so worried you won't have a good time, baby, that's all."

MaLou was still looking up at Lance, wondering why her desire to make a good impression upon Josh had become so important to him. Deciding he was a man who welcomed challenges, she knew she had surely given him a fine one. "I think that's the problem. Having a good time is not nearly as important to me as not looking like a fool."

"All right then, you needn't dance with anyone but me," Lance assured her. "I know we'll look good together after all the time we'll have spent practicin', and it will make the other men all the more eager to dance with you themselves. Then when you're ready, go ahead and accept one of their invitations to dance. Do you like that plan? Will it make you more confident if you don't have to dance with anyone but me unless you really want to?"

"Yes, it would, but none of the young men I know have such nice manners as yours, Lance," MaLou warned him shyly. "I wouldn't want you to wind up in a fight when you're just trying to do me a favor."

"I can take care of myself," Lance reminded her impatiently, yet he knew damn well that the fact he was taking such a pretty girl to a dance in hopes of impressing another man was clear proof the situation was totally beyond his control. "Now let's just concentrate on the steps and let Saturday night take care of itself."

His tone of voice was far too emphatic to inspire further argument and MaLou looked down at their hands. He had been holding hers through most of the conversation in a very warm and pleasant clasp and she could not help but wonder about the fine ladies he had escorted to elegant balls in Georgia before the war. Surely none of them had had as many doubts as she. "You're being very kind to help me, Mr. Garrett. I'm sorry if I seemed ungrateful."

She moved to his side to begin again, yet Lance felt little relief that they had returned to the task at hand. He knew the best advice he could give her was simply to be herself, and he still thought it a great pity that Joshua Spencer did not see that too.

Taking care not to make her lesson so long she would be tired as well as frustrated, he left a short while later, and as he approached the bunkhouse he found several of the hands lounging on the steps. "You're wasting your time there, Garrett," a man named Charlie advised with a deep chuckle. "MaLou's probably not even noticed you're a man."

But Lance was most definitely a man in the truest sense of the word and he would not allow such teasing remarks to go unchallenged when ignoring them would only encourage more. He reached down, grabbed the noisy fellow by the front of his shirt, and yanked him to his feet. "It seems you overlooked that fact too. That was your first mistake. Now if I ever hear you speak another insultin' word about Miss MacDowell, I'll make certain you're even more sorry than you are now. Do you understand me?"

Lance had such a firm hold on him, only the toes of Charlie's boots scraped the old wood of the steps, and dangling in mid-air, he nodded frantically. "I was only teasing! I didn't mean nothing!"

"Well, I mean exactly what I say!" Lance snarled and with that he released the sniveling man who then went bouncing down the steps on the seat of his pants, accompanied by his friends' hearty laughter. Satisfied he had taught enough lessons for one night, Lance moved on into the bunkhouse.

Wednesday night he thought he actually detected some small signs of improvement in MaLou's performance and Lance was so tickled to think his time was not being wasted after all he offered a steady stream of encouraging compliments. He made certain his manner was that of a friendly older brother or uncle, however, so she would not mistake his praise for flirting. He kept his distance both in his tone and actions and was quite pleased with himself when he left the house.

That night it was Nathan who was waiting for him. "I don't know what you're up to, Garrett, but you're real stupid if you're trying to impress MacDowell by courting MaLou. If you think you can get him to fire me and hire you as foreman, you got another think coming."

Nathan had never been friendly, but Lance was surprised to find him so openly hostile, especially since it was totally without cause. The man was not quite six feet tall, lanky, with sharp features that more often than not bore a menacing scowl. His hair was neither blond nor brown but a nondescript shade in between, while his eyes were a dull gray, though they glowed that night with a surprising amount of hatred. Since he could scarcely reveal the truth, and he had no wish to share it with Nathan anyway, Lance made no effort to put the aggressive foreman's doubts about him to rest. "I happen to enjoy Miss MacDowell's company, but that's my business and no concern of yours," he countered with a taunting smile.

The foreman disagreed. "We all know MaLou a lot better than you ever will. No man would call on her every night without something to gain, and I'm warning you it's not going to be my job."

Lance looked away, stealing the time to get a firm hold on his temper before he lashed out at Nathan in a low, threatening whisper. "You wouldn't know a lady if you met Mrs. Grant on the street in Tucson! Now I intend to call on MaLou whenever I damn well please and as long as she's happy to see me I'll expect you to keep your ridiculous opinions to yourself. She's MacDowell's daughter, not yours, and it's up to him to say who can call on her and who can't. You think I can't do the job I'm being paid to do, then you've got a right to complain to the boss; otherwise, keep your damn mouth shut!"

He stared coldly at the foreman, thinking him an obnoxious fool. When Nathan did no more than return his icy stare before ambling off, Lance spit into the dirt and turned away too. MaLou might be worried about fights on Saturday night, but it sure looked to him like he'd be in one long before then.

Since he was still the foreman, Nathan wasted no time in using that power to get even with Lance. Thursday morning he sent him out with Manuel Ortiz and three others to search the outer boundaries of the MacDowell ranch for strays. He had not expected the men to return before nightfall, but they rode in about four in the afternoon with two dozen head they had found roaming wild. While he was impressed they had rounded up so many strays, Nathan did not show it. "I said to cover the whole spread, Garrett, not just to go out, sleep under a saguaro all afternoon, and then come back."

Lance glanced at the men who had accompanied him and was pleased to see by their disgusted expressions that they were as insulted as he, for they had spent the whole day chasing cattle out of rocky *barrancas* and deserved some praise for their efforts. He swung down out of Amigo's saddle and walked up to the foreman. "Don't call the others lazy when I'm the only one you're tryin' to insult." He knew exactly what the man had done. He had wanted him to be gone so long he would not have time to visit MaLou that night. Naturally Nathan was furious that his plan had not succeeded. Lance knew that if everything went well on Saturday night, he might just move on right then, so he had no reason to back down. "Let's just settle this score now since it's just between you and me."

Lance was taller than Nathan, and more muscular, but the feisty foreman had won plenty of fistfights against bigger man and did not consider himself at a disadvantage. "All right," he agreed confidently, "but take off your gun belt and leave your knife with it. The fight has to be strictly hand to hand."

"That's fine with me," Lance replied with a deceptively agreeable grin. He tossed his own weapons aside, and the instant Nathan had dropped his he hit him with a solid right that broke the foreman's nose and catapulted him backward six feet. He landed on his seat in the dirt, blood flowing from his battered nose. His expression was one of utter disbelief, for he had expected Lance to begin this fight as all his other opponents had, with tentative jabs, not such a devastatingly brutal punch. The men who had been with Lance were out of their saddles now, cheering so wildly every man within earshot came running to see what had happened. Many had old scores to settle with the foreman themselves and they were eager to cheer for Lance, who waited patiently for Nathan to rise and come forward before he hit him again. The foreman refused to go down this time, however, and clung to the Southerner, attempting to knock him off balance and wrestle him down into the dirt.

Thomas MacDowell had been working on his accounts, adding up columns of figures in a vain attempt to make them balance, when he heard the shouting. "What's going on out there?" he called to MaLou.

MaLou stepped out onto the porch and knew from the dust flying into the air and the number of men crowded around that it had to be a fight. "Some sort of fight, Dad, but I can't see who it is."

Not overly distressed to have to lay his ledger aside, Thomas strode out the door. Though his intention was to allow the fight to run its course, when he saw that with methodical precision Lance appeared to be beating Nathan to death Thomas had no choice but to draw his Colt and fire into the air. "Get back, Garrett. I don't tolerate fighting here."

Manuel Ortiz was one of the many who quickly spoke up to explain that Nathan's insults had started the fight and that he was getting exactly what he deserved. Confronted by more than a dozen men who held the same opinion, Thomas had no idea what to do. If he had found any other man scuffling with his foreman, he would have fired him on the spot and taken Nathan aside to warn him privately not to provoke anyone else, but there was no way he could fire Lance Garrett when his job as a cowhand was not really the one he had been hired to do. Stalling for time in hopes he would think of something, he turned first to Nathan. "Well, what do you have to say for yourself?"

Nathan did not look at him but at Lance, eyeing him with a savage stare. "Not a thing, sir."

"And you, Garrett?"

Lance shook his head. "No, sir, it was a private matter."

"Well, I want you two to settle any other 'private matters' in a more private fashion!" Seeing the cook on the edge of the crowd, he motioned for him to come forward. "Jake, take Nathan into the cookhouse and do what you can to clean him up. You look like you can take care of yourself, Garrett." After issuing those orders, he turned around and walked back to his house, but MaLou did not follow. She waited as the cowhands shuffled off in twos and threes until Lance was left standing by himself trying with some difficulty to fasten the buckle on his gun belt.

"You've cut up your hands pretty badly," she commented sympathetically. "Better come with me."

"I'll be all right," Lance protested as he continued to fumble with the buckle.

Thinking him too stubborn for his own good, MaLou tried again. "I don't understand why Dad didn't fire you for fighting with Nathan, but if you don't follow me this instant I'll insist that he does. Is that clear?" MaLou put her hands on her hips, ready for a long argument if necessary, but she was certain his injuries needed looking after and she was determined to do it herself.

Lance finally succeeded in getting the buckle secured, then leaned down to pick up his hat. He dusted it off, then looked up with a defiant stare. "Is that an order, Miss MacDowell?"

"You're damn right it is. Now follow me." She started off toward the house but walked around to the back rather than leading him in through the front door. She did not look back, but when she stopped at the back door and turned around she was pleased to see that Lance was no more than two paces behind her. "Just sit down here on the steps and I'll get some water."

"You needn't help me, MaLou. This is nothin'," Lance insisted as he turned his hands over to examine the scrapes that had torn most of the skin from his knuckles.

"Just sit down, Garrett," MaLou ordered even more firmly.

"Yes, ma'am," Lance replied sarcastically, obviously not eager for her attentions.

MaLou gave him an equally cool glance as she slipped through the back door. In a few minutes she returned with a pail of water, an empty bowl, and a small jar of medicinal salve. She poured some of the water into the large bowl, then stood back. "First take off your shirt," she ordered again in a no-nonsense tone.

"What?" Lance asked, startled by her request.

MaLou sighed impatiently. "I've seen plenty of men without their shirts, Garrett, and it doesn't drive me wild. I think that's Nathan's blood you've got splattered all over you, but if we soak the shirt in cold water now the bloodstains will come out when you wash it. We'll just leave it in the bucket while you soak your hands in the bowl."

Lance felt rather foolish to find she was more interested in his laundry than in any injuries he might have suffered. He yanked off his hat, set it down on the step beside him, and unbuttoned his shirt. This was no small task, for his hands ached badly.

MaLou stood by the bucket, silently observing Lance and thinking he certainly looked a lot better without his shirt than most of the hands did. His tan did not end at his collar and cuffs but covered the muscular planes of his chest and back with an even bronze glow. Clearly he went without a shirt often, but she did not think it would be wise to inquire about his clothing habits. His broad chest was covered with a thick mat of dark curls that tapered to a thin line as they grew over his flat belly, providing a handsome accent to his powerful build rather than obscuring it. She was certain he would offer a still more attractive sight nude but knew without having to be reminded that ladies did not speak those kind of thoughts aloud. When he handed her the shirt, she dropped it into the pail. "That's a nice plaid. I hope it isn't ruined."

Lance leaned back against the back door, tired after working all day on a dirty job for which he had gotten no credit. He lowered his right hand into the bowl she had placed by his side and watched the cool water gradually take on a pink tinge. It soon became obvious that his hand had only a few scrapes and that most of the blood discoloring the water was Nathan's.

As she so frequently did, MaLou was wearing her buckskins that day. She sat down beside him and, bending one knee, hugged it tightly to strike a comfortable if totally unladylike pose. "You can tell me and I promise not to tell Dad. What were you and Nathan fighting about? I know he's rather cold, but most of the hands seem to get along with him. Why couldn't you?"

Lance found it difficult to believe that the inquisitive tomboy seated next to him was the same lovely young woman he had been trying to teach how to dance. He did not scold her for the way she was sitting but tried in a roundabout way to answer her question. Since he knew she had a high regard for the truth, he decided to tell her at least part of it. "Some men are uncomfortable with giving me orders, MaLou. They think I'd rather give them myself, although that's the last thing I want anymore. I give a full day's work for my pay and that's all I need to be happy. I have no other ambitions despite what men like Nathan mistakenly fear."

"You don't actually believe that, do you?" the perceptive blonde inquired curiously.

"Of course!" Lance replied gruffly, sorry now that he had made the mistake of confiding in her, even in an oblique manner.

"The hell you do," MaLou replied as she lazily shooed away a fly. "You're not the first Confederate drifter we've had working here, even if you are the brightest. You've got more than half your life ahead of you and if you throw it away by being no more than a ranch hand just because you were on the losing side of the war, then the Union will have whipped you twice. Are you going to let them get away with that?"

Had he been struck by lightning, Lance could not have been more shaken, for she had just succeeded in summing up the futility of his aimless existence in one sentence. He pulled his right hand out of the water and replaced it with his left as he tried to think of a convincing way to deny she had hit upon the truth. It was not just the war he had lost though, but so much more.

As he wrestled with his conscience, MaLou watched in rapt fascination as a full range of emotions from despair to anger played across Lance's finely chiseled features, but when he finally looked up, the coldness of his sky blue gaze sent a shiver of dread down her spine. She had been far too blunt, she realized instantly and feared she had succeeded only in reopening old wounds rather than in jarring him out of his obstinate complacency. Before he could open his mouth for what she was certain would be the worst of insults, she spoke. "So Nathan's afraid you want to be foreman, is that it?" she asked rather than give any more advice about how he had chosen to lead—or, in her opinion, waste—his life.

"Yes," Lance readily admitted, glad she did not suspect that his nightly visits to her house had had anything to do with their fight.

"He's been here six or seven years and I guess the job means a lot to him, even if it wouldn't be much of a challenge for a man like you."

"I thought I just explained that I didn't want any challenges," Lance replied with the first hint of a smile he had shown.

MaLou rose to her feet and stepped over to the pail of water to check on his shirt. "Any man who'd volunteer to give me dancing lessons has got to love challenges," she teased playfully, relieved he had not given in to the anger she had seen so clearly in his eyes. "The blood's soaking out. Your shirt isn't ruined after all. I'll just leave it in the bucket overnight and toss it over the line in the morning."

"You don't have to do my laundry, MaLou." Lance pulled his left hand from the water and flexed it cautiously. Both his hands would be stiff in the morning, but he had suffered far worse.

"I didn't say I'd wash and iron your shirt, Garrett. All I offered to do was toss it over the line to dry." MaLou watched as he rose and straightened up to his full height. She knew now that she shouldn't have offered him advice when he hadn't asked for it, but she sensed that apologizing would only make things all the more strained between them. "Put some of the salve on your knuckles. Dad gets it from Candelaria. She brews up all sorts of concoctions from desert plants and he brings them home for us."

Lance was skeptical the herb cream would have any beneficial effect but tried it anyway rather than start another argument with MaLou. Surprisingly, it felt cool and immediately numbed the pain of his scrapes. "Thanks, this feels good."

"You're welcome." MaLou hesitated a moment, then offered generously, "Take the night off. I know you don't feel like dancing."

Lance shook his head, not wanting to give Nathan the mistaken impression their fight had influenced him to stop seeing MaLou. "No, you're wrong. That's exactly what I feel like doin'. I'll be over after supper."

MaLou knew she would never understand the man. He looked dead tired to her, but if he wanted to dance, she would put on a dress and try her best not to step on his feet.

Lance stared at MaLou as he came through her front door. She was again wearing her pink dress, but there was something different about her appearance although he could not quite decide what it was. She was remarkably pretty and as they moved through the basic steps he had had such a difficult time teaching her, he was positive her motions were at long last taking on a more fluid grace. As he looked down at her, he flashed a charming smile. "All you need do is dance as well as you did just now and I'm certain you'll enchant all the men Saturday night. Josh Spencer will probably ask if he can bring you home."

"Oh, do you think so? I never even thought of that possibility." MaLou looked quite worried by this unexpected prospect and called over to her father, who was again seated in the far corner pretending to read. "Daddy, what shall I do if Josh asks to bring me home?"

"You'll have our buggy, MaLou. Come home with whomever you like," Thomas suggested with a hearty laugh, obviously thinking it unlikely she would receive any such invitation.

MaLou looked up at Lance and was disappointed he appeared to be amused by her father's response. "You won't think it so funny, Mr. Garrett, if I leave you with no way to get home that night."

It was her hair, he realized then. She had combed it so expertly there were no wispy tendrils escaping the mass of curls at her crown. He had rather liked the soft curls that had brushed her nape and was sorry she had not left one or two loose. "You mustn't give my comfort any thought that night. In fact, if it wouldn't look suspicious, I'd tie Amigo to the back of the buggy so I'd have him if there were a need."

MaLou thought such a precaution unnecessary. "No, you needn't do that. If Josh were to bring me home you could ride his horse here and that way he'd have his own mount to ride back to his ranch."

Lance nodded, thinking her idea the best. "Of course. That settles that question. If you want to ride home with Josh, or anyone else, I'll just ride his horse." He could see MaLou still was not happy, however. "Is something else botherin' you?"

MaLou was embarrassed to admit that after all their efforts she was still afraid Josh wouldn't even notice her, but that was far too humiliating a fear to share. "No, let's just try the turns a couple more times and call it a night."

She had done so well he did not argue, but when she went to her room and he left the house, Thomas MacDowell followed him. The usually jovial man did not speak until they had walked a good distance, for he did not want MaLou to overhear their conversation. "You've done right well with my little girl, Garrett, but I can't let you get away with many fights like the one today without her and everyone else catching on as to why you're here."

"I doubt I'll have any more trouble with Nathan, Mr. MacDowell," Lance replied optimistically. He was tempted to say that if he did he would just move on, but for the first time in five years the prospect of facing a problem rather than turning his back on it was suddenly appealing. The Nathans of the world were so numerous he knew he would just encounter the same man with a different name on his next job anyway. "I like it here," he said more to himself than to the older man.

"Well, if you want to stay, try to keep on Nathan's good side, will you?" Thomas asked, hoping to secure such a promise.

"I don't think that's possible, sir, since from what I've seen he hasn't got one."

Thomas was still laughing at the joke when he returned to the house, but he stopped smiling when he found MaLou standing at the window where clearly she had been watching him. "I thought you'd gone to bed, baby," he remarked as he closed the door.

"Were you two talking about me just now?" MaLou

asked suspiciously.

Thomas chuckled as he shook his head. "No, I was just warning Lance again not to get into any more fights. He's a good man and I'd hate to have to fire him for something as stupid as that."

MaLou was still somewhat surprised the man had not quit that afternoon when she had been so bold about offering him advice. His glance had been so murderous she had been certain he had been about to do it. He had not even argued with her opinion of him, although she knew he had been angry, and she still found that puzzling. "He'll not stay long, Dad. His type never does."

"No, I think Lance Garrett is one of a kind," Thomas assured her. "But it's Joshua Spencer you're hoping to impress come Saturday night and I think you'll do just fine."

MaLou kissed her father good night and this time stayed in her room to undress and prepare for bed. As she brushed out her long curls, she could not shake the feeling that if Josh were as fine a man as she had always thought he was, he would have shown her the same courteous respect Lance had. She stared into her mirror for a long while, wondering if perhaps she wasn't baiting a trap for the wrong man.

Chapter V

Lance rode into Tucson on Saturday hoping to find a suit that would fit him without more alterations than could be completed in a single afternoon. Since he had taken MaLou shopping, he at least had an idea where to go, but he found the men's clothing available in the boisterous city a far cry from the finely tailored suits he had once worn. The friendly clerk at Tully, Ochoa and DeLong instantly recognized him as a gentleman and a discerning one at that from the requests he made, and brought out their finest merchandise.

"It is a pleasure to wait on a man who knows quality goods," he complimented sincerely. "I think this suit will please you."

Lance tried on the black frock coat and when he stepped in front of the mirror he was quite pleasantly surprised by how well it fit through the shoulders and yet tapered sufficiently to compliment his trim waist. The last suit he had worn had been Mexican in design. It had been black too, but the short jacket and flared pants had been liberally decorated with braid and silver so it had not seemed nearly as austere as this one. Deciding that the coat had the best fit he would be likely to find, he tried on the pants and had the clerk pin them up to the proper length. "This reminds me too much of President Lincoln for my taste," he joked with a sly chuckle, "but at least the dark color is practical."

"Oh, that it is. If you'd like more color, I have a splendid selection of brocade waistcoats. Would you like to see them?" The clerk was a slightly built man in his forties who had made a career of working for fine haberdashers on the East Coast. He had been lured west by the promise of easy riches but had soon discovered he much preferred waiting on customers to the backbreaking work of mining for silver and so had quite willingly returned to his former profession.

"Why not?" Lance agreed, thinking he might as well buy one, but he chose a soft silver satin rather than bright red or blue. He added a fine linen shirt and a tie, then gave the helpful clerk one final request. "I'll be back in an hour to pick up everythin', so please have the pants hemmed so I'll not be kept waitin'." He spoke with a confidence that sent the man scurrying off to fetch the tailor. Lance chuckled to himself as he stepped back into the sunshine, knowing the fellow would earn the generous tip he planned to give him.

Lance's next stop was a small shop he had noticed when he had been with MaLou, although they had not visited it. The display window was discreetly curtained in lace, while the neat gold-lettered sign advertised Ladies' Intimate Apparel. He had never shopped for women's lingerie, but since MaLou had not once worn a corset under her new gowns, he was fairly certain she did not own one. He wanted her to be popular that night, but not because she was the only young woman present without a corset. Deciding his request would sound more reasonable if he explained he was shopping for his wife, Lance described MaLou's petite stature and slender build to the proprietress, hoping she would be able to recommend a garment of the proper size.

While she was greatly amused by her handsome customer's request, Claire Duchamp was too clever a businesswoman to let it show in her expression. She clothed her ample figure in elegant fabrics of subdued colors, displaying the excellent taste she knew everyone believed a well-bred lady should have. Her background, however, was not one that would bear close scrutiny.

When she had arrived in Tucson she had introduced herself to the business community as a widow with sufficient funds to open a small specialty shop. She provided a measure of the style and culture the fast-growing town had sorely lacked, had immediately been successful, and no one had ever wondered if her story was true. Her hair, which was piled atop her head in elaborate curls, was now more white than blond, but she was still an attractive woman and especially so when she had a handsome man at whom to smile. "May I assume your wife usually wears more casual garments every day and wants something new for a special occasion?" she asked in her most charming manner. She doubted he was married and thought it far more likely he simply wanted to buy a gift for one of his favorites on Maiden Lane, but, no stranger to deceit herself, she did not question his motives aloud.

"Yes, ma'am, that's exactly the case. Her figure is quite lovely on its own and needs little in the way of enhancement, but under a fine gown a woman needs somethin' in the way of lingerie."

Claire nodded, her opinion of her customer improving each time he spoke, and she realized she had let his casual attire influence her too greatly. He might be dressed as a cowhand, but she was certain he was a most unusual one. Still, most of Tucson's male citizens were single and she doubted that he really had a wife. "Of course, but a young woman with a pretty figure doesn't require a cumbersome corset but merely one with a hint of whalebone to nip in the waist. Let me show you some of our latest designs. They are from France and the lace is exquisite."

Lance was more concerned about MaLou's appearance than anything else and he was not embarrassed to be shopping for her. When Mrs. Duchamp showed him three garments she felt would be the proper size, he chose the prettiest: a pale pink silk, attractively adorned with satin ribbons and rows of delicate lace. "This one will be fine," he told her confidently. Even after paying for his own new clothes, he had plenty of money left and thought such a necessary item well worth the expense. "Wrap it up for me and I'll pick it up later this afternoon."

Claire was pleased he had not shown the slightest concern about the price and hoped he would come back often, regardless of who the woman he had in mind might be. "If for any reason the fit is not superb, have your wife come in next week and I will alter the corset or exchange it for another."

Since the silk garment laced up the back while the front merely provided a slight uplift without covering the bust, Lance thought MaLou would be able to loosen or tighten the laces to adjust the fit herself. "I'm certain it will be fine, thank you."

Claire waited until after he had left the shop to wrap up his purchase. "I should have had sense enough to sell him a complete set of lingerie," she scolded herself crossly, thinking when next he came shopping she would see he left with an armload of packages.

There were plenty of bars in town, but Lance strolled down to the Congress Hall, hoping that if the Hatcher brothers were in town they would be elsewhere. He paused a moment at the swinging doors to glance around the crowded room to make certain they were not inside, then entered. He went up to the bar and ordered a beer.

The barkeep remembered him and chuckled as he recalled how they had met. "Haven't seen the Hatchers from that day to this, which is fine with me. I don't miss 'em one bit."

"Well, it's a shame you lost their business," Lance replied with a broad grin, "but it looks like you're still doing pretty well."

"That we are," the man agreed, and then summoned by a patron at the far end of the long bar, he left Lance to finish his beer alone.

Lance used the mirror behind the bar to study the faces of the men standing nearby. Most looked like ranch hands, but he thought others were most likely miners hoping to make a fortune in silver. From the unkempt looks of them, none had struck it rich as yet. Then he noticed Joshua

Spencer seated at a table near the center of the room. He was playing poker with three other men who also appeared to be in their mid-twenties. As Lance watched, one man threw down his cards and pushed back his chair, obviously out of both money and luck. Josh seemed to be the big winner and when he glanced over at the bar looking for a fourth man for their game, the first person he saw was Lance.

"Hey, Garrett!" he called out as he waved. "Want to get in our game?"

Lance picked up his beer mug and walked over to the table. For a reason he could not explain even to himself, he knew he would get a perverse thrill out of beating Josh at poker and he sat down in the newly vacated chair opposite him. "It's been quite a while since I played," he apologized with a slight frown.

"Hell, that don't matter," Josh assured him. "This is just a friendly game. This is Seth Gardener on my left, and Carl Perry on my right. This, boys, is Lance Garrett, the man who drilled such a neat hole through Randy Hatcher." He waited while Lance shook hands with each of his friends, then continued. "We've all been playing together since we were kids, but none of us is much good. Ain't that right?"

"I'm afraid so," Seth agreed. He was a heavy-set young man with bright red hair, pale blue eyes, and fair skin liberally sprinkled with large freckles. He had arranged his chips in front of him in neat stacks and was now leaning back in his chair sipping a beer as he waited for the next hand to be dealt.

Carl Perry was blond like Josh but clean shaven and brown eyed. He was so tall and lean his clothes hung on him like a scarecrow's, but his smile reflected a genuine warmth. "I count myself lucky to break even, Garrett, so you needn't worry you'll lose all your money to me."

"I'll try not to lose it to anyone else either," Lance replied in a lazy drawl that brought hearty laughter from his companions. Carl was acting as banker and Lance asked how much he would need to buy in, then handed him the required ten dollars to get his chips. He then tossed a white chip on the table for the ante and set back to watch Josh deal. While he appeared to be giving his full attention to the cards, he was actually observing Josh and his two friends. They were no different from a thousand other men he had met over a poker table. He hated to take Seth's and Carl's money, but they were in the game and there was no way he could avoid cleaning them out too unless they dropped out early on each hand. Four was really too small a number for a good poker game, but from what he could see of the bar's other patrons, they were either already playing at other tables or leaning against the bar wistfully wishing they could afford to wile away their time gambling.

Lance finished his beer and, preparing for a more lengthy stay at the Congress Hall than he had anticipated, ordered another. He had started playing poker with his daddy as soon as he had gotten old enough to learn the names of the cards. The first thing his father had taught him was that poker was a game of strategy rather than chance and a man who appreciated that fact could do real well for himself. While he preferred stud to draw, as the newcomer he knew it would be considered poor manners to suggest they change their game. He hesitated when the betting passed to him, then merely called rather than raise the bet, deliberately giving the impression he had little confidence in his hand until only he and Josh were left in the game. When Josh laid down three kings, Lance tried to look surprised.

"Imagine that. I thought I'd need somethin' better than a straight to win that pot, but it sure looks like I've won." He laid down his hand to show he held five cards in sequence, scooped up his winnings, and still shaking his head in disbelief, finished the last of his beer. "I'm usually not so lucky," he revealed with a sheepish grin. "But at least now I've got the cash to stay in the game a while longer."

Josh frowned slightly as he glanced at his two friends. They played often with none of them ever winning more than a couple of hands in succession, so each usually left the table close to breaking even. Since he had invited Lance to join them, he could not very well tell him to leave after he had played his first hand. Besides, he wanted a chance to win back his money.

Lance shuffled the cards rather clumsily when it came his turn to deal. It was not out of a desire to mislead the others at the table, but simply due to the remaining stiffness in his hands from his fight with Nathan. He played the first few hands conservatively until he had gotten a good idea of each man's style. Josh's eyes would narrow when he held a good hand and he would bet with a reckless bravado that swiftly forced the others to toss in their cards, so he kept himself from winning the largest pots. When Seth drew a good hand he would sweat so profusely Lance soon got wise to him, though his friends did not seem to notice how often he pulled out his handkerchief to wipe his brow. Carl shifted in his chair almost constantly, but when he sat still Lance knew he was holding a hand he considered a winner. When the behavior of all three indicated that each thought he had a chance at winning, Lance would drive the bidding up until one by one they would lose confidence in their cards and fold. He won more than one hand that way, by bluffing until the others dropped out, and then he could claim the pot without having to show his hand. He would fold occasionally himself just to let the others win enough to keep them interested in the game, but they were no match for his skill, and his stacks of chips continued to grow taller while theirs dwindled rapidly. They had to pull money out of their pockets more than once to buy more chips, while he had no more than his original ten dollars invested in the game.

Seth was the first to decide he had had enough. "I got to get going," he remarked as he tossed his few remaining chips to Carl to exchange for cash. "I don't want to be late for the dance tonight and it's a long way home and back."

"See you later," Josh replied without looking up. "You still in the game, Carl?"

"Yeah, I can't afford to go home until I win back some of my money," the lanky man explained with one of his frequent smiles. "What about you, Garrett?"

"I've got time to play only one more hand before I've got to be goin' home too. What do you say we double the stakes?" Lance offered in a challenging tone he was certain Josh would not be able to resist.

Seeing a chance to recover his losses, Josh quickly agreed. "That's fine with me. It's your deal, Carl."

At one time Lance had been intensely competitive in all aspects of his life. Since the war, however, he had found that the only form of competition he still enjoyed was playing cards. He had had to be careful that afternoon not to let the other men at the table see how greatly he relished winning. His opponents blamed bad luck each time they lost a hand and he did not voice his opinion that it was skill rather than luck that determined how each man played a hand and whether or not he turned it into a winner. For the final hand he was dealt a pair of jacks, a pair of sevens, and a ten, so his opening bet was a deliberately modest one. He then exchanged the ten for another card and was dealt a third jack. Knowing it was unlikely either Carl or Josh would have anything better than the full house he now held, when it was his turn to bet he not only called Josh's bet, but raised it ten dollars.

Carl shifted nervously in his chair, then folded. "That's it for me. I should have left with Seth," he grumbled as he tossed in his cards, more angry with himself for losing so much money than with Lance for winning most of it.

Josh thought he held the winning hand, too, and cursed the fact he had not brought more money into town with him, but he had enough left to call Lance's bet.

A slow smile crossed Lance's lips as he then called Josh's bet and raised it another ten dollars. Josh did not have enough chips left to meet that amount but still refused to give in.

"I'll sign a note to cover my bet. The whole town knows I'm good for it," he boasted proudly.

"Well, that might be true, but I'm new here and I don't

want the bother of collectin' on anyone's notes. Not even yours." Lance laid his cards face down on the table and started to reach for the pot.

"What do you mean you won't take my note?" Josh cried out so loud everyone in the noisy bar heard him. "I thought you were a gentleman!"

"It's not the value of my notes that are in question here," Lance reminded him with a wicked grin, hoping he was embarrassing Josh as much as the arrogant young man had embarrassed MaLou by not asking her to the dance.

Josh yanked the gold ring off his left hand and tossed it into the pot. "There, that ring is worth more than enough to call your bet." He looked up to grin at the men who had drawn near to see how their game would end since it appeared to be an exciting one.

Lance still had a sizable stack of chips left and glanced down at them, apparently about to call Josh's bet until he saw the color drain from the young man's face. He laughed then as he turned over his cards. "I am a gentleman or I'd take you for whatever else you'd be foolish enough to wager."

Josh looked at Lance's cards and swore under his breath. "A full house," he announced to no one in particular as he turned over a straight. "The pot's yours."

"Damn right it is," Lance agreed. "That's what I tried to tell you before you wagered this ring." He picked it up, judging its weight in his grasp. It was a heavy signet ring engraved with the letter *S*. "This is of no use to me, but I'll keep it until you can raise the cash to buy it back."

Josh looked ready to explode as he rose from his chair. "Are you coming with me, Carl?" he asked gruffly, infuriated he'd been the one to invite Lance to play poker in the first place since the man had proven not only to be good at the game but too damn lucky as well.

"Yeah, I'm comin' as soon as I give Garrett the money for his chips. I was the banker today, remember?"

Josh was too angry to wait around and left without Carl. The men who had crowded around their table returned to the bar and when he had a neat stack of bills instead of chips, Lance stood up, slipped them into his pocket, and reached out his hand. "I'm glad we met, Carl. You goin' to the dance tonight too?"

"Yeah, sure am. What about you?" the blond asked as they started for the saloon's swinging doors.

"I'm takin' MaLou MacDowell," Lance revealed quite willingly, hoping the information would swiftly reach Joshua Spencer's ears. "See you later." He strode off before Carl could reply, but he had seen his astonished expression and could barely suppress his laughter as he started up the street to pick up his purchases. When he heard someone call his name, he wheeled around, ready to draw on anyone who might be foolish enough to think he could help himself to his winnings. The man who had followed him from the saloon had no such intentions, however.

Lance saw before him a well-dressed Mexican and, except for the dark brown of his eyes, the man resembled Lance so closely he was astounded.

"Yes, I noticed it too," the man remarked with a friendly smile. "Do you have Spanish blood? Perhaps we are distant cousins."

"Well, cousin or not, I'm sorry but I'm in a hurry to get back home." Lance turned away, but the man moved swiftly to his side.

"I will walk with you to your horse. Permit me to introduce myself. I am Jesse Cordova. My family has been in Tucson for several generations and there are many of us. Since 1848 we've found ourselves on the wrong side of the Mexican border, but that has not inspired us to move."

They had reached Mrs. Duchamp's shop and Lance hesitated at the door, not wanting the man to follow him inside. Jesse was dressed in a short, close-fitting suede jacket and flaring brown pants, the hems of which did not hide the wicked pointed wheels on his silver spurs. Lance recognized him instantly for what he was: a wealthy and intelligent man. It was never wise to insult a man to whom honor was important, and he was certain it would be to Cordova. "I'm afraid this afternoon I don't have the time to trace our families searchin' for common roots, Señor Cordova. Perhaps another time."

Jesse flashed an engaging grin. "No, you misunderstood me. I noticed you first because we look so much alike, but that is probably no more than coincidence. What you did to Joshua Spencer was far more entertaining for us looking on than for him. You play poker very well, Mr. Garrett, far too well to be working as a cowhand for Thomas MacDowell. I'd like to offer you a job working in my saloon."

"If you own a saloon of your own, what were you doin' in the Congress Hall?" Lance inquired suspiciously.

Jesse shrugged. "My establishment is not yet open, but it will be soon and I'd like you to come work for me there. You took Spencer's money so easily he did not even suspect you were leading him into a trap. With talent like that, you might soon become my partner."

"You're the second person to tell me lately I'm too damn clever to be a cowhand, but I don't think I'd be happy dealin' cards in a saloon."

Jesse had a charming grin he used often on men as well as women and he tried it again. "I would not insult you by offering you work as a dealer. What I wish to offer you is the job of manager first and if it proves agreeable to us both, a partnership when you can afford to purchase one."

"Do you go around offerin' partnerships to every man you see winnin' a few hands of poker?" Lance asked skeptically, wondering if perhaps the handsome Mexican was a bit daft.

"No, of course not, but from what I hear you can handle men like the Hatchers as well as you handle cards, and that is an invaluable combination."

Lance rested his hand lightly on the brass doorknob, thinking that if Joshua actually did propose to MaLou that night he might be wise to leave the MacDowell ranch in the morning so he would not have to see the fool when he came calling. Then again, managing a saloon was not all that appealing an alternative.

"Let me think about it," he finally replied, knowing

Thomas MacDowell would surely have heard of Cordova and know something about the man.

Jesse held out his hand and seemed pleased when Lance took it. "A man can avoid his destiny only so long, Mr. Garrett. Do not delay in making your decision."

Lance watched as the Mexican moved back up the street, not understanding what destiny had to do with his job offer. The Mexican people were all romantic creatures from what he had seen though, and he dismissed the encounter from his mind as he entered the lingerie shop.

"Ah, Mr. Garrett." Claire Duchamp positively beamed when she saw him. "It was very thoughtless of me not to suggest additional garments for your wife. Perhaps she requires new camisoles, pantaloons, slips, stockings, or a nightgown?"

Lance had removed his hat as he came through the door and fingered the brim while he considered making the additional purchases. Since the money that now filled his pockets had recently belonged to Josh and his friends, he thought it only fitting to buy something for MaLou with it. "Yes, of course, she should have a complete set of lingerie, and stockings too. Do you have silk stockings?"

"Of course," Claire replied sweetly, pleased her ploy had worked so well. Again Lance chose the most expensive items in her stock and she wished him an enthusiastic farewell as he left her establishment and made his way to the haberdasher's.

Lance tipped the clerk who had sold him the suit even more generously than he had at first intended and left town at a gallop in order to make it back to the ranch in time to prepare for the evening. He had won more than five hundred dollars from Josh and his friends and while that seemed like a small sum to him, he knew there were plenty of men who would kill for far less and he kept a sharp lookout for strangers on the way home.

MaLou was huddled in the chair on the front porch, her chin trembling as she fought back her tears. She knew

Lance Garrett had been gone for hours and she was desperately afraid he wasn't coming back. Surely he had gone into town and forgotten all about her. He had probably gotten drunk like the other hands liked to do and was sleeping it off in some whore's bed on Maiden Lane. That thought absolutely mortified her. "If that scoundrel ever shows his face around here again I'll see he's fired so fast it'll make his head swim!" she vowed to herself. When a thin puff of dust appeared on the trail leading to the ranch, she dared not hope it would be he, but when she saw the light of the setting sun gleaming upon Amigo's jet black hide, she knew Garrett had come home after all. Scrambling to her feet, she brushed away her tears and grabbed the watering can so he would think she had been tending her flowers rather than watching the road for some sign of him.

Lance rode up to the house, leapt down, and untied the parcel from Mrs. Duchamp's, which he had lashed behind his saddle. "I've brought you a present!" he called as he approached MaLou. "I'm glad you're not already dressed. I've got somethin' else for you to wear."

"You're very late, you know," MaLou scolded crossly. She gripped the watering can's handle tightly so she would not be tempted to slap the insolent grin from his face, but her expression showed her anger clearly.

Lance's smile disappeared as he realized the pretty girl was truly angry with him. "I didn't mean to worry you," he apologized.

"Why should I be worried?" MaLou replied flippantly. "Just because you went into town and didn't come back until the day was over shouldn't have worried me, should it?"

Lance was sorry she had been upset, but he was also disgusted she did not know him any better than that. "I'm a man of my word, MaLou. I invited you to the dance tonight and I meant to be here to take you. Now, here, these things are for you. Don't argue that I shouldn't have bought them because I already have. Just keep them and wear them when you wear your pretty new dresses."

Hesitantly, MaLou set the watering can aside and reached out to take the package from Lance. That he had spent at least some of his time shopping for her embarrassed her terribly. "You didn't need to buy me presents, Lance," she replied self-consciously.

Lance brushed her comment aside. "They're not exactly presents, just a few things we forgot to buy the day we went shoppin'. I won some money playin' poker, so don't worry about the expense."

"That's where you've been all afternoon, playing poker?"

Lance couldn't help but laugh at the wide-eyed blonde's puzzled expression. "Yes, ma'am, and there are plenty of witnesses too. What did you think I was doin'?" As her cheeks filled with a bright blush, he raised his hand. "No, don't say it. I know what you thought, but you were wrong."

Noticing Josh's ring on his hand, MaLou was quick to ask about it. "Where'd you get that gold ring?"

Lance had slid it on the third finger of his right hand just to bring it home. "Your friend Josh bet it on a poker hand and lost. I won't keep it though. I expect him to buy it back real soon."

"You were playing poker with Josh?" MaLou licked her lips nervously, for she knew Josh gambled in his every spare moment, but she had always thought he won more frequently than he lost.

"He invited me to play with his friends, Seth and Carl. Unfortunately they aren't any better at the game than he is. Do you know them?"

"Oh dear." MaLou was not pleased at all. "They won't be happy to see you there tonight if you won all their money."

"That, my dear, was the whole idea," Lance confided with a sly wink. "Now I've got to go and get dressed. You'd better hurry up too because I don't like to be kept waitin'."

MaLou was sorely tempted to hurl the package he had given her right back at him, but she was far too curious about what it contained to be that impulsive. She settled for giving him a withering glance and carried the mysterious bundle into the house. She ran to her bedroom, then closed and locked the door to be certain her father would not glance in while she was unwrapping it. When she found a billowing lace-trimmed slip with matching pantaloons, a camisole so sheer it was transparent, the pink silk corset, and three pairs of silk stockings, she sank down on the side of her bed and simply stared at the lovely lingerie for she had never, ever, owned anything even remotely like it. Her undergarments were woven of a fine muslin, which was comfortable if not stylish, but Lance had bought her the fancy lingerie a real lady wore, and while she was pleased, it made the tears well up in her eyes all over again. She ran her fingertips over the ribbons on the corset and knew she should wrap up the package and tell him to return everything to the store where he had purchased it, for surely she should not accept such shockingly intimate gifts from any man.

"He said they weren't really gifts though," she reminded herself, frantically searching for some way to keep the pretty lingerie for her own. When she had bought the three new dresses, she had remembered only to get slippers, but she had forgotten everything that went underneath and truly she did need nice lingerie to wear with her new gowns. Her mental debate was extremely one-sided. It was definitely improper for her to accept a gift of lingerie from a man, but since Lance had insisted it was not really a gift and she desperately needed the pretty lace-trimmed garments, she decided the only practical solution was to keep them. She then leapt to her feet and went to warm water for her bath, thinking that if Lance Garrett wanted to share his poker winnings with her, then it was all right with her, but she looked forward to playing the game with him herself sometime soon.

Chapter VI

When Thomas MacDowell went to the door, he was so startled it took him a moment to recognize Lance, for the man who stood before him was no longer merely a good-looking drifter with a remarkably cool manner. The Southerner's well-tailored black suit not only enhanced his vivid coloring but complimented his proud posture handsomely. It suddenly struck Thomas that Lance was indeed the gentleman he had assumed him to be and therefore far too fine a man to be involved in their present scheme. He was horribly embarrassed he had revealed his hopes that MaLou would someday marry Joshua Spencer and had asked Lance's help to accomplish that seemingly impossible feat. Feeling very foolish, he stepped aside to let Lance enter, then nodded toward the hall leading to the bedrooms. "I want to thank you again for taking MaLou to the dance tonight. She's spent a couple of hours getting dressed, but I think she's almost ready. Can I get you a drink?"

"No, thank you, sir," Lance responded with a smile, wondering why his employer seemed so nervous. "There is somethin' you could do for me, though. Do you have a safe of some kind here?"

"Sure, a small one I keep the payroll in sometimes. Why?"

Lance withdrew a sealed envelope from his coat pocket. It bore his signature across the front and the date. "I won some money playin' poker this afternoon and I'd rather not leave it in the bunkhouse or carry it with me tonight. I'd be grateful if you'd keep it in your safe and I'll try and get into town next week to open an account at the bank."

Thomas took the envelope and decided by its thickness that Lance must have done quite well. "I'll keep it for you as long as you like. In fact, your money is probably a lot safer here than in any of Tucson's banks."

Lance thought that was probably true, but before he could agree, he caught sight of MaLou out of the corner of his eye. She was standing hesitantly at the doorway and he turned to give her an encouraging smile. She looked very self-conscious, as though she longed to remain a child who could wear comfortable buckskins forever. At the same time the elegant lines of the red-and-white-striped dress displayed her figure to every advantage, proclaiming seductively that she was an incredibly beautiful young woman. He might have given her the confidence to attend the dance, but her anxiety was so plain he could see he still had a great deal of work cut out for him. It was then he finally noticed she was staring at him quite openly. That proved somewhat disconcerting, since for some reason her father's initial reaction to him had also been one of surprise. He was certain he looked quite proper and could not understand why they both seemed dismayed. He walked over to MaLou and took her hand to draw her into the middle of the parlor. "You look especially pretty tonight, Miss MacDowell. I thought both the pink and blue dresses were flatterin' with your fair colorin', but I'd forgotten how attractive that one is. You should wear red all the time."

MaLou had always thought Lance handsome, but that night he looked so splendid she now felt even more like an imposter. When she had looked in her mirror she had seen a stranger's reflection rather than her own, a pretty blonde who resembled her but who was not really her at all. "Thank you, Mr. Garrett," she responded in a breathless rush. "I think you look absolutely magnificent."

Lance could not help but laugh at so lavish a

compliment. "Well, thank you. I don't recall ever being described as lookin' 'magnificent' before, but I'll do my best to live up to it."

Puzzled to find her compliment had amused him when that had not been her intention, MaLou was tempted to take it back. "Just what do all the other women say?"

The sparks of anger that flared brightly in MaLou's eyes saddened Lance, for he had not meant to insult her. As always she had said exactly what was on her mind. He knew she had been sincere and he should have known better than to laugh and hurt her feelings. "To tell you the truth, it's been so long since a woman paid me a compliment I can't even recall. If you're ready to go, I'll bring the buggy around to the front of the house."

"Let me put this away and I'll get it for you," Thomas quickly volunteered, since he had promised to put Lance's money in the safe. "Just wait for me out on the porch." When he went out the back door he saw that one of his favorite horses, a big buckskin gelding he had named Buck for lack of a more original name, had already been hitched to the buggy. As he began to untie Buck's reins from the corral post, he heard a peculiar clatter coming from inside the barn and curious as to its source, he decided to investigate. He pulled open one of the heavy double doors but had taken no more than one step inside when he was drenched with nearly a full bucket of whitewash. The interior of the barn was too dark for him to recognize the culprit who had hurled it at him and before his eyes could adjust to the shadows he heard the door at the opposite end of the long building slam shut. He swore as he looked down at his pants, for they were now more white than navy blue and he doubted they would ever come clean. His plaid shirt had been sprayed with the white paint too. "Damn fool!" he yelled into the now empty barn. Wanting only to see MaLou on her way so he could change out of his ruined clothes and fire whoever had thought such a stupid prank amusing, he slammed the barn door shut, circled back around the buggy, grabbed Buck's reins, and started for the front porch with a ponderous gait and murderous expression.

"Oh, Daddy!" MaLou cried out as he rounded the corner of the house. "What happened to you?"

Thomas looked up at Lance, thinking he now had a better idea about what had caused his fight with Nathan. "Well, one of the boys must have been playing a stupid prank, but I don't think he meant to cover me with paint. Do you, Garrett?"

"No, sir," Lance agreed, even more disgusted with what had happened than Thomas was. "Someone must have seen me hitching Buck to the buggy and expected me to be the one who would come back for him."

"But who would have done something as mean as that?" MaLou asked. "Your new clothes would have been ruined and—" She hesitated then, not wanting him to think she was more concerned about getting to the dance than with what someone had tried to do to him. "Oh, damn it all, who could have been so spiteful?"

"Don't you bother your pretty little head about it another minute, baby. You just go on into town and have a good time. I'm going to change my clothes and then fire the bastard I find with the slightest trace of whitewash on his boots or cuffs. Since the stuff splattered all over me, it's bound to have gotten on him too."

Lance thought it doubtful that Nathan had had the strength to do it himself after the beating he had given him, but he was certain the hostile foreman had been behind it. He kept those thoughts to himself, though. It was an awkward way for the evening to begin and he hoped that it did not mean it would all go poorly. Again taking MaLou's hand, he helped her up into the buggy, then walked around to take Buck's reins from her father and climbed in himself. "I'll see she's home early, sir," he promised with a sly wink the pretty girl could not see.

"I know you will, son." Thomas stood in front of his house as he watched the buggy roll across his front yard and angle toward the road. He had forgotten that the small black carriage would need washing, but Lance apparently had not overlooked that chore, for it was so sparkling clean it looked brand new. Buck had been brushed until his coat shone too. "Damn it if Lance and MaLou don't make a handsome couple," he mused softly to himself as they rode away, but he had his fingers crossed she would come home with Josh Spencer by her side instead.

Lance really did think MaLou's appearance was absolute perfection. Her hair was attractively curled atop her head, but several of the wispy tendrils he found so charming had escaped her combs to tickle her neck. He could catch a whiff of the scent of gardenias from her perfumed soap and thought it remarkable she could be so astonishingly pretty without even a touch of makeup. Her lashes were thick and dark, providing her bright green eyes with a frame that was both innocent and alluring. He liked the slight upturn to her nose and the way she carried herself so the elegant line of her throat led his eye to her creamy smooth shoulders. She looked like a lady, truly she did, but she was fidgeting so nervously he could not help but worry about her mood. Seeking to distract her, he asked the first question that popped into his mind. "Have you ever met a man named Jesse Cordova?"

"Good-looking fellow with lots of teeth?" MaLou asked with a slightly raised brow.

"Well, I don't know if he has more teeth than anyone else, but yes, he does grin a lot. What can you tell me about him?"

MaLou found it difficult to look at Lance and think clearly enough to speak at the same time. It was not only that he was so handsome, but that he looked like such a polished gentleman. She simply could not understand his desire to do nothing with his life but chase cattle. Surely a man who could look so damn good ought to have more in the way of ambition, but she did not want to start a fight with him on the way into town and so answered his question rather than ask some of her own. "He's Candelaria's nephew," she began rather flippantly. "The

Cordovas are one of Tucson's original Mexican families. They had enormous land grants and the way the city's grown, they've been able to make a lot of money selling property and they still own plenty more. They own several businesses too. Most of them are respectable citizens, but I guess you could call Jesse the black sheep of the family. He owns one of the biggest whorehouses on Maiden Lane."

Lance made a valiant attempt to hold his temper as he made his usual request to the lively blonde to consider her remarks more fully before she made them. "'Brothel' is a less offensive term, MaLou," he offered a little too sternly.

"You mean ladies call whorehouses 'brothels'?" she replied sarcastically.

"No, ladies don't refer to such establishments at all," Lance insisted even more emphatically.

"Why did you ask me about Jesse if you didn't want me to tell you the truth?" MaLou asked with an exasperated sigh. "The man owns a whorehouse. Oh hell, a brothel, if you like. I can't very well tell you he owns the mill, can I?"

MaLou looked so lovely, and yet she was the same irrepressible young woman she had always been. At least she no longer seemed so anxious about the evening and he considered that a welcome improvement. "I'm just tryin' to give you all the help I can, MaLou, and I didn't mean to sound critical. It's just that I know you want Josh to see you as a lady and I'm tryin' to help you act that way."

MaLou clamped her jaws shut, unwilling to respond until she could speak in a far more pleasant tone than she had been about to use. "That's all this is, Garrett. I'm trying to act like a lady just as though I were an actress playing a part in a play. What if it works though? What if Josh likes seeing me all dressed up and talking only in excruciatingly polite words but saying nothing? What am I supposed to do then, play a part for the rest of my life?"

Lance was tempted to tell her they were all forced to play parts at one time or another, but he knew that was not what she needed to hear. "We're just tryin' to make Josh notice you're a woman, MaLou. Once he does, well, then you two can get to know each other all over again and you won't have to pretend to be somethin' you're not."

"Suppose I find out it's only the pretense that he likes?" MaLou asked apprehensively. "That could happen, you know."

"Sure it could," Lance agreed, feeling like he had just painted himself into a very tight corner. "Most men like women who make them feel more like men though. It's as simple as that. They like to hear a woman tell them they're smart and strong or good-lookin', whatever. That doesn't mean it isn't true, that she's lyin' to him just because she's tellin' him what he likes to hear."

After a moment's reflection, MaLou thought she finally had the idea. "Oh, I see," she agreed suddenly. "If I tell all the handsome men they're good-looking but don't say they're smart if they're not, they'll be happy?"

Lance chuckled to himself, thinking he was definitely the wrong person to be teaching her how to flirt. He remembered Mrs. Duchamp then and thought it a great shame Thomas had not hired her to tutor MaLou, since she certainly had an abundance of feminine wiles. "Yes, ma'am, that's it. Compliment a man for an asset he knows he has and he'll think you're not only pretty but clever too."

"Well, Josh is handsome and he's reasonably bright. He's lots of fun too, but he can behave like an awful ass at times." When Lance gave her another disapproving glance, MaLou grew even more emphatic. "He does! He definitely wastes far too much time playing poker and I'm sure he's no stranger to the . . . the brothels on Maiden Lane."

Since he was not overly impressed with Joshua Spencer himself, Lance had a difficult time defending him, but he tried. "He's just young, MaLou, that's all. He'll settle down and maybe a lot sooner than you think."

MaLou doubted he would, even though she hoped it was true. She twisted her hands nervously in her lap, then fearing she would wrinkle her dress, she quickly smoothed out the folds in the crisp red and white fabric. "Thank you for the lingerie. It is the prettiest I've ever owned. I should have thanked you for it before we left the house."

"Did you tell your daddy about it?"

"No, I didn't think I should, so I hope you won't either, but I do want to thank you all the same."

"You're welcome," Lance responded politely, wondering why he was getting more depressed the closer they came to town. MaLou was more than lovely. She was absolutely gorgeous. Josh would fall madly in love with her for certain and then he would be off the hook. But rather than eagerly anticipating the happy outcome of their ruse, he just wanted it over. "Look, if Josh asks to bring you home, don't worry about me. I'll find a way to get home myself without borrowin' his horse."

MaLou was puzzled by her companion's dark scowl until she realized they had spent all their time worrying about her making a good impression and had not once thought about how he would spend the evening. "Oh, Lance, I'm so sorry," she apologized with a deep blush. "I should have given more thought to you. Maybe you'll meet someone you'd like to escort home and you'll be stuck with me. You can't explain we're just friends either or it might get back to Josh and he'd know I'm just trying to fool him. Oh, what an awful mess. I'm sorry and I won't ever ask you to take me anywhere ever again."

The pretty blonde now looked miserable and Lance could not bear to have her worrying about him. "MaLou, I invited you to the dance," he reminded her. "You didn't ask me to take you."

"Well, yes, I suppose that's true, but it wasn't really an invitation. You were just trying to help me and—"

"Forget it!" Lance shouted much too loud. "Let's just try to have a good time tonight and not spend another minute worrying about it!"

Not wishing to cause her handsome companion another second's grief, MaLou tried to sit back and relax as they rode the rest of the way into town in an uneasy silence. She could not help but feel that nothing she was doing that night was honest. Lance was not really her escort and she was not really the lovely young woman she had seen in her mirror. Yet as they neared the Pioneer Brewery, she could hear the music and see the bright lights and prayed that for just a few hours she could actually be the fine lady Lance had tried so hard to teach her how to be.

Just as Lance had known he would, Carl Perry had wasted no time before running to tell Josh that MaLou would be at the dance that night and with whom. At first Josh had been amused that the Southerner would want to take the headstrong tomboy anywhere, let alone to a dance. Then he got mad. He and MaLou had been close when they were children because she had not been like the other little girls who had always been worrying about keeping their dresses spotlessly clean. Hell, MaLou MacDowell had been as cute as a button, but she had not even owned a dress as far as he could recall. When he had come home at the end of the war he had expected to find her all grown up, but the little blonde had been the same reckless sprite he had left behind four years earlier. He had been more disappointed in that than he had let on, but while he had certainly not staked any claim on her himself, he still did not want her going out with any sweet-talking Southerners.

Josh had taken care to dress up that night and thought he looked mighty fine. He had scrubbed himself clean, shaved real close, and trimmed his mustache to precisely the right length to show off his smile. While he had not bothered to wear a suit to other dances, he had put one on that night. He enjoyed good beer, and being from Germany, Alex Levin certainly knew how to brew it. Levin also knew how to throw parties, so he expected to have a good time. Knowing Lance Garrett would be there with MaLou merely annoyed him because he was certain the lucky bastard would be wearing his gold ring and he hadn't had nearly enough time to get together the cash to buy it back.

At seven he stood in the courtyard of the Pioneer Brewery with Carl and Seth, smiling and calling to all the pretty girls as they arrived so they would be sure to know he would dance with them later. He was not really looking for MaLou, but he was curious about what she would wear and how she would look. He thought it was silly to remember how much fun they had had together as children until he saw her drive up with Lance Garrett. Had she not been with the man who had beaten him so handily that afternoon at poker, he would not even have recognized her. In fact, he was not all that certain the stunning blonde with Garrett was MaLou until she returned his smile with a slight wave. Nothing about her seemed in the least bit boyish that night. Her hair was arranged in pretty curls and the waves at her temples provided a flattering accent to her delicate features. Her green eyes shone as always with mischief, but tonight their sparkle hinted at the passion he had never suspected she possessed. Her cheeks held a faint blush, her lips an inviting trace of rose, and her stylish gown showed off a figure that was clearly a grown woman's. He felt like a bigger fool than he had that afternoon when he had seen Garrett slip on his ring. MaLou had grown up. She had become the beautiful young woman he had always hoped she would be and he had been too stupid to notice while it was clear Lance Garrett certainly had. "Evenin', MaLou, Mr. Garrett." Josh greeted Lance coolly, wondering if the money he had lost to him had paid for the man's clothes.

"Gentlemen," Lance responded with a ready grin, taking a great deal of pride in the astonishment he had seen in all their eyes. It was clear Seth and Carl were just as shocked as Josh by the transformation of MaLou, and he hoped they all felt like the stupid fools they were for ignoring her for so long. Everywhere he looked he saw admiring glances directed his way too, yet when he had still been in his teens he had gotten thoroughly bored with people who were attracted to him solely because he was handsome. He seldom gave his appearance a moment's thought now and that night had wanted to look his best simply to provide MaLou with a presentable escort. He was thrilled her newly displayed beauty appeared to be dazzling everyone and had no intention of competing with her for attention. He meant to dance the first few dances with her, then step back into the shadows until it was time for them to leave for home, but he did not get even one dance before she was surrounded by young men clamoring to be her partner. Whether or not she had decided to merely act the part of a lady he did not know, but as she gave him a sweet smile and moved out onto the dance floor with the first of her partners, she seemed perfectly at ease. The dance was one he had taught her and she managed to complete the figures with a lively step that made it appear she had been to a hundred dances instead of just this one. She danced very well and as the music ended Josh reached her side before any of the other young men could leave their partners to claim her. He had noticed her all right, and his adoring expression was all MaLou had hoped to inspire. They had done exactly what they had set out to do: drive Joshua Spencer so mad with desire he might actually propose that very night. So why did Lance feel like he had just been kicked in the stomach?

Jesse Cordova was a man who always got what he wanted and what he wanted that night was to cement his friendship with Lance Garrett. He walked up to him and offered a comment as though he had every right to make such an observation. "You are even more clever than I thought, Mr. Garrett. A pretty young woman naturally enjoys the attentions of many men, but I'm sure she will soon realize that none compares with you."

"I don't expect MaLou to compare anyone to me. I just want her to have a good time tonight, that's all." Lance knew that sounded ridiculous even as he said it. She was easily the prettiest girl there and would have dozens of men vying to dance with her regardless of what his feelings were in the matter. That several of those men wore blue Army uniforms was something he was trying hard to ignore.

"That cannot possibly be MaLou MacDowell!" Jesse

scoffed. "She is also blonde and petite, but surely that is not Miss MacDowell."

"Oh yes it is," Lance boasted proudly, his satisfaction genuine on that score.

Jesse contemplated this astonishing fact for a moment, then shook his head. "I am ashamed I did not think of his daughter when I asked you why you'd rather work for MacDowell than me. He is in good health, but no one lives forever, and were you to marry his daughter—"

Lance turned toward him so quickly his shoulder slammed right into Jesse's chest, knocking the breath out of him in mid-sentence. "Offering me work in a saloon was demeaning enough. Don't make the mistake of callin' me a fortune hunter too."

Alarmed by the fierceness of Lance's expression as well as his threatening words, Jesse stepped back quickly. "Forgive me. I did not mean to insult you. Had I known she was so pretty, I'd have been courting her myself. I have no interest in marrying for money either, but beauty holds a fascination all its own."

The worst thing about Jesse Cordova was that he resembled him so closely. Lance felt as though he were arguing with his conscience and that already pained him badly enough as it was. "I doubt your brand of superficial charm would work on her, but why don't you go ahead and try it just to see for yourself?"

Rather than take offense at his blatant insult, Jesse laughed and clapped Lance on the shoulder. "We are even, Mr. Garrett. Since Miss MacDowell arrived with you, I would not dream of flirting with her. I treat my friends well and I would like to number you among them."

For once Jesse had failed to flash his engaging grin and Lance thought he might actually be sincere. That was so welcome a change he decided not to argue the point. Instead he offered his hand. "No one ever has too many friends, *amigo,*" he stated simply.

Jesse grasped Lance's hand firmly, uncertain just how he had managed to impress the man but glad he had finally succeeded in doing so. He turned back to watch the dancers, but MaLou was no longer in sight.

MaLou tried to smile as Josh again stepped on her toes and again apologized profusely. She had never known the young man to be either so nervous or so clumsy as he was that night, but she did not realize she was causing his anxiety herself. She had been delighted to find all of Lance's predictions were true. It was easy to follow a man's lead and her partner seemed to regard it as his fault when he stepped on her feet rather than hers for getting in his way. She still did not think she danced that well, but the hall was crowded with couples who all seemed to be having too good a time to notice if she missed a beat or two. She was concentrating so hard upon not getting her feet stepped on again she did not hear what Josh was saying and had to ask him to repeat it. "I beg your pardon?"

"I asked if you could forgive me for not realizing you'd grown up long before this."

He looked so mortified by his oversight that MaLou was tempted to forgive him immediately, but then she saw no point in denying she had been hurt by her formerly dear friend's neglect and so kept still.

"Well, will you forgive me or not?"

His hand tightened upon hers and MaLou knew she would have to say something. Finally she decided to speak the truth as she always had. "I think you're the one who's taking much too long to grow up, Josh, not me." The music ended then and just as Josh had, another man reached for her hand before she could be escorted off the dance floor. It was not until three dances later that Josh again became her partner and she realized that while she had spent all week worrying about impressing him, the fact that she obviously had was not in the least bit satisfying. Whatever was wrong with her? Josh was practically drooling as he looked down at her, but she did not feel any excitement at being in his arms. He was very handsome, his deep tan making his hazel eyes glow like quicksilver, and she had always liked the way his mustache framed his smile, but all she felt for him was the warmth of the friendship they had shared as children. Maybe she was not grown up after all, for surely a woman should feel more than that sweet affection.

Josh smiled often as he tried to please MaLou with the compliments all the other girls liked to hear, but she paid so little attention to his words he soon fell silent and tried to impress her solely with his dancing. Since Tucson had so many more men than women, he knew he would not be able to dance with her often, but the fact that she did not seem to care whether he did or not drove him to distraction. He was considered a fine catch by everyone, so why wasn't she making an attempt to impress him as all the other girls were? Redoubling his efforts at charm, he pulled her close and whispered in her ear, "Let's go outside so we can talk a while."

MaLou could not think of a single thing to say to him, not even one, so she quickly refused. "I'd rather dance," she responded with a slight smile, and when he glared down at her as though she had just insulted him, she could not understand why.

She danced next with Seth, who began like all the others by saying he had never realized she was so pretty. "You've known me all my life, Seth. Surely I don't look that different tonight."

"Oh, but you do!" the husky young man insisted. "You look like a girl for a change."

"Thank you, Seth," MaLou responded coolly, not bothering to ask how she had looked before, since obviously he must have thought it was awful.

"I didn't mean that the way it sounded, MaLou."

"Oh yes you did." Ignoring his bright blush, which made his freckles all the more apparent, MaLou concentrated on dancing gracefully and did not bother to acknowledge his continuing apologies. She had heard the same thing, with only a few original variations, from each of her partners. For nineteen years she had scarcely been noticed and now tonight everyone noticed her, but she wanted to scream at them all that it was too late. She held her tongue, but as the evening progressed she began to feel her sudden popularity was more insulting than flattering and grew increasingly depressed. When next she danced with Josh, she thought he might again ask her to step outside and talk, but when he did not, she suggested it herself. "I would like to rest for a few minutes if you'd still like to talk."

Thinking his charm had finally begun to work on her, Josh agreed readily. He lowered his arm to encircle her waist and escorted her through the door. "The courtyard's kinda crowded, MaLou. Let's take a little walk."

"Oh Josh, must we? Isn't there some place we could sit down and rest?"

"What about your buggy?" Josh suggested slyly. "Come on, it's just over here a little ways."

MaLou did not question her friend's motives until he had taken his place beside her in the dark carriage and had tried to draw her into his arms. "Josh," she laughed, thinking he was teasing her again, but when she realized he wasn't, she did not know what to do. "Joshua Spencer, you stop that this minute!" she whispered hoarsely, not wanting to embarrass either of them by calling out loudly for help. Thinking her merely coy, Josh ignored her attempts to escape his embrace and pushed her back against the seat as he tried again to kiss her.

"Josh!" MaLou pleaded softly before the young man's mouth covered hers in a bruising kiss that left her gasping for breath when he at last drew away.

"Hold still, MaLou!" Josh scolded. "I've waited too long for this to stop with no more than one kiss."

Thinking his mood anything but romantic, MaLou placed her hands on his chest and tried to shove him away. When that proved totally ineffective, she ceased to struggle, hoping her indifference to his affection would cool his ardor, but she hated both his confining embrace and his sloppy kisses. When he tried to shove his tongue down her throat as he clutched her breasts, she could take no more of his mauling. She tore her mouth from his, grabbed his hair to turn his head, then bit his left earlobe so savagely he was the one to scream for help. When she tasted blood she released him, scrambled out of the carriage, and dashed back into the brightly lit hall. She had seen Lance from time to time either dancing or talking with the other men, but as she searched the crowd frantically for him now, she could not seem to find him. Shaking with both rage and humiliation, she was near tears when finally she saw him coming toward her.

Lance had seen MaLou leaving the hall with Josh and had been hoping the fool would have the sense to treat her sweetly, but obviously he had not or she would not have come running back through the door alone. Before she could begin what he was certain would be a vivid description of a most unfortunate encounter, he swept her out onto the dance floor. "Hush," he cautioned. "Dance with me and then I'll take you home. Is that what you want?"

Not trusting herself to speak, MaLou nodded. Being in his arms was like coming home and she felt safe again. The musicians were doing their best to play a waltz, and while it was clearly not their best number, Lance danced beautifully all the same. Had she danced the first dance with him, she knew she never would have accepted any other invitations, and more confused than ever, she closed her eyes and pretended they were all alone in her parlor. She obviously had no talent as an actress, and while she knew the dance would last until midnight, she could not pretend to be a lady any longer and just wanted to go home.

When the music ended, Lance gave MaLou an encouraging smile and led her toward the door, ignoring the chorus of eager bachelors who wanted another chance to dance with her. As they stepped out into the courtyard, he saw Josh talking excitedly with Carl. He was holding a bloody handkerchief to his ear. Amazed to think MaLou had actually drawn blood, Lance shot her a quizzical glance.

"The little bitch bit me!" Josh screamed accusingly as

they walked by him.

"Excuse me a minute," Lance told MaLou, then dropping her hand, he approached the injured man. "I couldn't possibly have understood you. What did you say?"

Josh waved the bloody handkerchief this time. "She damn near bit my ear off!" he yelled.

"Really?" Lance asked incredulously, then while Josh's attention was still focused on MaLou, he drew back his hand and punched him so hard in the chin he landed flat on his back in the dirt. He waited a moment for him to get up, but Josh was out cold.

Carl knelt down beside his friend, then tried to find the pulse in his throat without success. "I think you've killed him!"

"Oh hell, just pour a beer on him and he'll come around. When he does, tell him if he doesn't learn some manners real fast, I'll be around to teach him some."

Since he had seen a sample of how Lance taught his lessons, Carl quickly agreed. "I'll be sure to tell him just that."

"Good." Lance found MaLou still standing right where he had left her. He escorted her the rest of the way to their buggy, helped her up into the seat, then swiftly took his place at her side and turned Buck out onto the road. As he yanked off his tie, he began to swear under his breath. "From beginnin' to end this has been one terrific evenin'. Yes, ma'am, it sure has. I can hardly wait to see what happens to us on the way home!"

Chapter VII

With the need to impress Josh over, MaLou yanked the combs from her hair, then raked her fingers through her curls as they spilled about her shoulders. Relieved she no longer had to worry about her appearance, she leaned back and drew the first deep breath she had taken all day. There was a full moon to light their way home, and bathed in its soft glow, her sweet features were scarcely marred by her savage frown. She had managed to look like a lady for a few hours at least, but she knew by morning the news would be all over town that she still did not know how to act like one. Strangely though, she did not even care.

While MaLou's mood was understandably dark, Lance was merely perplexed. He truly did not know whether to laugh or cry, but because he knew MaLou would react badly to either alternative, he tried to strike a balance between the two emotional extremes. Since he felt at least partly responsible for the way the evening had turned out, he said so. "I'm the one who made the mistake, MaLou. I taught you how to dance, but I didn't think far enough ahead and teach you how to handle overly amorous suitors."

"I did all right on my own, Garrett," MaLou contradicted sharply. "Joshua Spencer will think more than twice before he tries to kiss me again."

Her hostile response both surprised and exasperated Lance. "You'll have to forgive me for being confused, but I thought the whole point of goin' to the dance tonight was to make Josh want to kiss you. Are you sayin' now you don't care for him after all?" Lance could not believe his ears and knew if he lived to be a hundred he would never understand the feminine mind.

"I know you must think me impossibly fickle . . ." MaLou began rather hesitantly, for she had been far more surprised than he to discover she had so little interest in the man she had always hoped to marry.

"Why no, not at all," Lance assured her, taking care to hide his smile, though he thought "fickle" far too genteel a term to describe her actions.

"I'd hoped Josh would notice me—of course I did—but I didn't expect him to fall all over himself to impress me the way he did. He was just like all the other boys I've known all my life. It was as though they'd never seen me before tonight when they've seen me thousands of times. Just putting on a dress couldn't possibly have made me look all that different."

"Well now, I'll have to disagree with you there, MaLou. You're real cute in your buckskins, but you are one beautiful woman in that dress."

MaLou stared at Lance, trying to figure out why both his words and voice sounded somewhat peculiar. His accent was as appealing as ever, even if it was slightly slurred. "How many glasses of beer did you drink tonight?" she was finally perceptive enough to ask.

"Lost count," Lance admitted with a devilish chuckle.

"It sounds like it." Deciding conversing with him was pointless, MaLou again fell into a sullen silence.

When he realized MaLou thought he had had too much to drink to make his remarks worth hearing, Lance started to argue. "I'm a long way from drunk, MaLou. Now just let me finish what I was tryin' to say. In the first place, you know Josh a whole lot better than I do, but it's never a good idea for a woman to leave a party alone with a man, even if he only invites her to step outside for a breath of air. I don't care what Josh said to lure you outside, it's plain once you got there you didn't like what he had in mind."

"Are you saying it's my fault Josh made such an ass of himself just because I went outside with him?" MaLou shrieked in dismay.

"No, of course not," Lance replied calmly, distressed he had upset her. "Just don't leave a dance or party to go outside alone with a man for any reason. That way you'll avoid creatin' the problem in the first place."

"I did not *create* this problem!" MaLou insisted defiantly. "Why you're going out of your way to insult me I don't know, but I don't appreciate your line of thinking one bit."

"No, I don't mean your behavior prompted Josh to act like an ass—he does that well enough on his own—but you sure gave him the opportunity to do it. Don't make that same mistake again. That's all I'm sayin'."

"Do you want to get out and walk home?" MaLou asked in a vicious whisper. "That's what you'll deserve if you don't shut up! I ought to blame the whole wretched incident on you anyway since you were supposed to be taking care of me and didn't!"

"And how was I supposed to do that when you were surrounded by so many men each time the music ended I couldn't even see you? Tell me that, why don't you?" Lance shot right back at her.

Astonished that he had noticed how popular she had been, MaLou could not imagine why he cared. "If you'd wanted to dance with me, all you had to do was ask me, Lance. This is no time to complain about that oversight now."

"Frankly, I didn't want to have to stand in line," Lance confided sarcastically.

"The others all thought I was worth it," MaLou countered defensively.

"Well I know better!" Lance heard her gasp and reached out to catch her wrist when she drew back her hand to slap him. "I'm sorry. I shouldn't have said that," he apologized immediately, shocked he had made such an ill-mannered remark. Maybe he had had too much to drink after all, but he would not use overindulgence as an excuse.

When he released her hand, MaLou moved as far away from Lance as she could get in the confines of the small buggy and turned her back to him. First Josh and now Lance. She felt as though she had been betrayed twice that night and was thoroughly depressed for ever having trusted either of them.

"MaLou? I said I was sorry." Lance did not really expect her to reply, and when she did not, he concentrated on driving the buggy until they reached the gate at the entrance to her ranch. He then pulled Buck to a halt and wrapped the reins around the brake handle, thinking he would be smart to have both of his hands free if her mood had not improved any. "Look, we ought to get our stories straight before your father asks how the evenin' went. Don't you think that's a good idea?"

MaLou cast a suspicious glance over her shoulder. "It's obvious what happened. You don't need to make excuses for me, because I don't intend to make them for myself. I'm just no damn good at playing a lady and that's all there is to it."

Still certain he was partly to blame for what had happened, Lance could not allow her to think she was at fault and began to argue again. "That's not true at all, MaLou. If anything, you were too good at playing the part of a lady. All the men dancin' with you, or just tryin' to dance with you, sure thought so. Now tell me just exactly what happened with Josh and I'm sure you'll see no one can fault your manners."

MaLou sighed dejectedly, not really wanting to talk about the scene she could not seem to erase from her mind. Reluctantly deciding maybe she did owe Lance an explanation since he had spent so much time trying to help her, she finally turned back toward him. "The first time he asked if I'd like to go outside and talk I said I'd rather dance, so we did. By the next time he asked me to dance I was getting tired. There didn't seem to be anything to drink but beer and I didn't want that. I just wanted to sit down for a minute and rest, so I asked him if he'd still like to talk a while."

"You asked him that?" Lance whispered hoarsely, thinking the pretty girl had not the slightest bit of sense where men were concerned.

"Yes, go ahead and tell me that was stupid, but I thought Josh was my friend and I didn't even suspect I wouldn't be safe with him."

Lance reached out to take her hand and gave it a comforting squeeze. "You should have been safe with him, too. Now tell me what happened next."

"He suggested we sit in the buggy to talk, but the minute he got in he grabbed me and . . ." MaLou stopped there, too embarrassed to continue.

Lance did not press her for the details he could so easily imagine. "It sounds like Josh needs lessons not only in manners but also in how to kiss if he upset you so badly." While he had tried to make his remark sound teasing, he was getting angry all over again. "I'm glad you bit the bastard, MaLou. It served him right for gettin' fresh with you."

"I know it does," MaLou agreed softly. "But what happens now? The whole town laughed at me before. They'll never stop making fun of me now."

The moonlight provided her fair curls with an enchanting sparkle, giving her such an angelic appearance Lance's sympathetic concern swiftly became tinged with desire. He dared not draw her into his arms, but raised her hand to his lips and kissed her wrist lightly. "What will happen, little lady, is that Josh will be far too ashamed to tell that story, so I doubt anyone will ever hear it unless you repeat it yourself."

"But I'd never do that!" MaLou exclaimed, wondering why Lance's kisses were so wonderfully soft and sweet while Josh's had been absolutely horrid.

"Of course not. Now tomorrow is Sunday and I expect he'll come callin', so you ought to wear one of your other new dresses and be ready for his visit."

"Oh no," MaLou moaned in despair. "You don't really think he'll come to see me, do you?" She could think of nothing more embarrassing than having to face Josh again after he had treated her so rudely, and she could not suppress a shiver of dread.

MaLou looked so terrified Lance wondered if Josh had tried to do a lot more than just kiss her. "MaLou, just what exactly did Josh try to do?" When she averted her eyes quickly, he made her a promise. "If you'd like me to watch for him tomorrow, I'll gladly stop him before he reaches the house and throw him off the ranch. It would be a real pleasure, in fact."

While his offer was certainly a wonderfully exciting one, MaLou could not accept it. "I doubt Josh will have the nerve to show his face here, but if he's got enough sense to know he should apologize to me, then I'll let him do it." As she glanced down at their hands, MaLou thought, as always, how very pleasant Lance's touch was: light and yet endlessly reassuring. "I don't know what I can possibly tell my father though. He wants me to marry Josh, but I would not even consider that now."

Lance knew he should keep his opinions to himself. He knew it, but he could not seem to take his own advice. "I doubt Josh will be your only caller tomorrow, MaLou. There were too many other men who wanted to spend their time with you tonight, and I'll bet quite a few of them will show up here."

MaLou sighed dejectedly, remembering the smiling faces of her partners and wondering which ones had actually been so smitten with her they would come calling. That prospect only provided an additional problem. "It was easy to avoid talking while we danced, but if a man's sitting in my parlor, what am I supposed to say to him?"

"MaLou"—Lance spoke her name with a low chuckle, but he really did not want to be the one to give her advice on how to amuse other men—"if a man thinks enough of you to come callin', then he'll be tryin' to impress you. All you need do is listen attentively until you wish to make a comment on somethin' he says. Then say what's on your mind. Isn't that what you've always done anyway?"

"Well, yes, I suppose it is, but you're always telling me I say the wrong things. Besides, I don't think it's even possible to pretend to be a lady and say what's on my mind at the same time."

"Well," Lance mused thoughtfully, "I never realized women worried so about impressing men, but now that everyone's had a chance to see how pretty you are, I think you'll get lots of practice entertainin' callers. In fact, if two or three men come by tomorrow afternoon, then you can just let them talk to each other while you sit, smile sweetly, and decide which one you like the best. Since pretty young women are so scarce in Tucson, you ought to have your pick of the men."

As he continued to offer encouraging hints, MaLou thought only of how much nicer Lance was than Josh. He was not only better looking and more intelligent, but a whole lot more considerate too. It was painfully obvious he had no interest in her, however, or he would not have been telling her how to please other men with such unabashed enthusiasm. That hurt, too, when she doubted she would ever meet a man she would find more appealing than him. What difference did it make who came calling on her, when the only man she wanted to see would not be among them? She knew none of their conversations ever ended on a happy note, but in the last week he had been so sweet to her she could not help but wish there could be far more between them than the stilted relationship between a charming tutor and the reluctant pupil he was trying to turn into a lady. When he paused, she turned their conversation to a new direction. "I know you're trying to make me feel better, but it's no use, Lance. Do you remember the time you kissed me and then just walked away? I didn't know what I was supposed to do, but it was obvious I hadn't done it. Then tonight when Josh kissed me, I hated it so much I did the only thing I could to make him stop. You're right, there's a lot more to being a lady than just knowing how to dance, but I'm afraid I'll never get it straight when I don't even know how to kiss a man so he won't either just walk off or try to climb all over me. There's got to be something in between, but I don't even know what it is."

Lance could see the sparkle of unshed tears glistening upon the tips of her long lashes and could think of only one way to reassure her now. Nature provided most girls with a gradual transition from pretty child to stunning young woman and it was not surprising MaLou had not been able to bridge that tremendous gap in less than a week's time. She had apparently never played games with boys and exchanged the sweet kisses of childhood that held the promise of love, so it was no wonder Josh's passion had both shocked and appalled her. He himself had made the mistake of thinking his kiss had not affected her in the slightest and to learn now she had not understood why he had not wanted more tore his heart in two.

They were seated very close and he needed only to incline his head to reach her slightly parted lips to steal another kiss. Just as the first time he had kissed her, this was an impulse too strong to ignore. It was simply what he wanted very much to do and he did it. Her lips were soft and resisted the pressure of his for only a fraction of a second before yielding and then returning his kiss. He drew back then, hoping she would smile, but she looked more confused than ever and he knew the fault was still entirely his. They argued constantly because he would not give in to the attraction that had always existed between them, while she was so naïve she did not seem to recognize that delicious magic for what it was.

The night was warm, the moonlight's luminous glow seductive, and the charming innocence of his lovely companion so enchanting he ceased to provide himself with the excuses that had forced him to treat her in a brotherly fashion and drew her into his arms. He trailed feathery kisses from her damp lashes to her temple, then down her cheek to her throat before returning to savor again the honey-sweet taste of her lips. His embrace remained very light so as not to frighten her. Despite the hot temper he knew her to possess, she suddenly seemed very fragile to him. She was incredibly lovely, but as delicate as the wildflowers that provided the desert with a glorious blanket of color each spring. She responded very shyly at first but soon lifted her arms to encircle his neck, drawing him close as she began to enjoy his kisses as greatly as he enjoyed hers. It was then Lance realized he was as great a fool as Josh, for his passion for her would be just as impossible to control.

MaLou had no idea what she had said to turn her maddeningly detached companion into so tender a lover, but her fears about her own imagined feelings melted away as he enfolded her in his arms and she asked no questions about his startling change in mood. Instead, she snuggled against him, molding her gentle curves to the hard lines of his muscular frame. When he traced the outline of her lips with the tip of his tongue, she understood what he wanted and opened her mouth, no longer considering such an action in the least bit revolting. She had not known people could kiss so deeply but thought Josh an even greater fool than she had earlier for not knowing how to make it as pleasant as Lance did. She ran her right hand down the buttons on his shirt, opening it to his waist so she could slip her hand inside to caress his bare skin. His flesh was warm and the dark curls growing over his broad chest provided a provocative texture, but she did not stop to think what her touch was doing to him. She slid her hand beneath his arm to reach his back, tracing the muscles that flexed as he changed position to pull her across his lap. He had propped his foot on the front of the buggy to fashion her a comfortable backrest and she lay completely relaxed in his arms, returning each of his slow, sweet kisses with delicious ones of her own.

Since she had not asked permission before touching him, MaLou did not complain when Lance slipped the puffed sleeves of her gown off her shoulders. His mouth left hers then to trail teasing nibbles down her throat. She ran her fingers through his jet black curls as he lowered his head and was surprised by their softness. His hair was thick and glossy but as fine as her own. She traced the shape of his ear with her fingertip, then the curve of his cheekbone. His beard had not had time to grow and his skin still held the artificial smoothness a sharp razor leaves in its wake. When he shifted her position slightly, she realized he had loosened the bodice of her gown to expose her breasts. That she had not even noticed struck her as wildly improbable, but her only concern was that he was slowly stripping away her clothes while he had discarded no more than his tie. That simply wasn't fair. As he lowered his mouth to her breast, she whispered in his ear, "Take off your shirt. Please," she added as an afterthought.

Barely distracted by her request, Lance peeled off his shirt and coat as though they were one garment and again buried his face between her fragrant breasts. Her skin was not only lightly scented with the fragrance of gardenias, but he swore she tasted as sweet as nectar, too. Lost in his own dreams, he teased the pale pink tips of her breasts to flushed peaks before he drew one flavorful bud into his mouth. She was a lovely young woman and he intended to enjoy each facet of her delicate beauty while the night was theirs alone to share.

MaLou continued to consider Lance Garrett a remarkable man in all respects. That she had known so little about making love appalled her, but her curiosity would not allow her to ask him to stop, although she was certain they had gone way beyond the limits of propriety now. She did not dwell on that shocking fact when his gentle loving was so marvelous it seemed she would never have her fill. She felt his hands moving down her back. He had already loosened her gown and now he unlaced the corset he had insisted she wear, but she did no more than recline in his arms, languidly wondering what he would do next. She was having such a wonderful time simply holding him in her arms, she could not imagine anything any better than what he had already shown her about being a woman.

Lance had made love in a carriage upon occasion, but never in a buggy. It annoyed him to have so little room in which to move when he wanted the freedom to lavish kisses on every inch of MaLou's delectable body. With masterful ease he removed her gown, then continued to cast away the layers of her lace-trimmed lingerie until at last she was clad only in her sheer silk camisole and pantaloons. Although petite, her proportions were exquisite. Her legs were long, her hips narrow, her waist tiny, and her breasts delightfully full. Her hands were small but seemed never to be still and her touch, while soft upon his bare skin, was as seductively warm as the desert wind. Why he had wasted so much time talking about how a lady should behave when it was so much more enjoyable simply to show her how a woman could please a man he did not know. He felt as though all he had done was waste time where she was concerned, and he intended to remedy that sorry situation immediately.

Lance pulled her camisole off with an anxious tug, then held MaLou close as he covered her face with light kisses. Her breasts were still wet from the caress of his tongue, the nipples teased to hard knots, and as he crushed her supple body against the muscular planes of his chest, the pain he caused the flesh he had made so sensitive was achingly sweet. Her lips were swollen from his kisses, she was breathless with excitement, and now a flickering flame of desire had begun to warm her belly with a new and even more compelling sensation. She pressed closer still, thinking if she could just hold him more tightly, the gnawing need he had awakened within her would be satisfied, but she found that precisely the reverse was true. Her joy in his tender affection had warmed to desire and now burned with a passionate fury every bit as hot as his.

Lance loosened the ribbon tie on MaLou's pantaloons, then slipped his hand underneath the waistband. His fingertips brushed her dimpled navel, then with a lazy caress combed through the triangle of blond curls nestled between her thighs. She rubbed against him then, inviting him to deepen his slow exploration of her lithe body's abundant charms and he did not hesitate to respond. A warm, sweet wetness flowed over his fingers providing a slippery path to its source and he traced it eagerly, at the same time cursing the cramped seat of the buggy, which made each of his actions impossibly awkward.

MaLou gasped sharply as Lance's fingers dove deep within her, for his boldness served only to increase rather than to ease her consuming need for release from the tormenting sensation he had created within her. Her senses reeling from the splendor she had never even imagined existed much less experienced, she had to muffle the sounds of her sobs against his shoulder, but she had no desire to take a bite out of his gorgeous hide. She wanted to beg him to stop his fiendishly erotic touch at the same time she felt her traitorous body grinding against his hand pleading for more. In the very instant she was certain she would lose both her virginity and her sanity simultaneously, a tumultuous climax shuddered through her loins, finally freeing her from the raging madness of unquenched desire. That ecstasy washed over her in thundering waves, at last leaving her trembling in his arms when the rapture he had created receded to mere ripples of pleasure that left her warmed clear through by its luminous afterglow. Of all his lessons, she was certain this one would prove to be the most valuable, but she was too blissfully content to thank him just yet.

Lance did not know how he had managed to come to his senses in time to abandon his own mindless quest for pleasure in favor of protecting the virtue of the beautiful creature in his arms. His hand still rested lightly on his belt buckle. He had meant to pull her across his lap and bury himself so deeply within her she would never want another man, but at the last instant he had remembered MaLou was a virgin and while undeniably a most passionate one, she did not deserve to be initiated into the art of making love in her father's buggy. Lord Almighty! he swore silently as he tried to think of some clever way to talk himself out of the mess he had just gotten himself into, even if he had avoided carrying his passion for her to the limit. What he had done was awful enough and he knew her father would be well within his rights to demand he marry her immediately, and that thought was as welcome as a hangman's noose. He hugged MaLou tightly and felt her heart return to its normal rhythm long before his stopped its frantic pounding. He sensed this was one night he would never get to sleep.

When MaLou felt calm enough to speak coherently, she asked the only question she wanted answered. "Why did you stop before you'd taken your own pleasure?"

Still feeling like a condemned man trying to talk his way out of taking a walk to the gallows, Lance cleared his throat nervously before he offered what he hoped would strike her as a reasonable excuse. "I lost my head, MaLou, but not so completely I thought making love to you in this tiny buggy would be a good idea."

"It's only the buggy then and not me that caused you to stop?" MaLou wrapped her arms around his neck and nuzzled his throat with playful kisses, determined to get the truth out of the handsome man for once.

"MaLou!" Lance grabbed her wrists to pull her off him and forced her hands down into his lap, but she responded to this bit of discipline by rubbing her thumb up the side of his still-swollen manhood and he had to lace her fingers in his to make her stop. "Damn it, MaLou, I'm trying to treat you the way a gentleman treats a lady. Don't make it impossible for me."

"Isn't it far too late to worry about behaving like a lady and a gentleman?" MaLou purred sweetly. He had pushed her pantaloons down to her knees so that she was as good as nude in her opinion, and she thought a discussion of manners ludicrous considering her state of undress. She did not want the delicious intimacy they had just shared to dissolve into the aloofness he so often displayed, and when he did not respond, she tried again to keep the mood of love alive. "I think I fell in love with you the day you came to the ranch, but I never dreamed you felt the same way about me until tonight. You needn't be afraid to ask me to marry you, because I'll say yes."

Lance wound his fingers in her flowing curls and cradled her head upon his shoulder, knowing he would never get out of this mess alive. "Oh, MaLou, you don't even know what love is, so how could you possibly love me?"

It was not simply his question but the despair in his voice as he asked it that alarmed the pretty blonde. She struggled to sit up so she could look him in the eye while they talked, since the subject was so very important. "I know enough to be certain when a woman tells a man she loves him he shouldn't argue with her about it. Just what is it you're really trying to say, Garrett—that you don't love me and never will?"

Lance closed his eyes to shut out her tormented expression as he shook his head. "No. I'd fall in love with you in an instant if I'd just let myself, but I won't, since that would be disastrous for us both. I've got nothin' to offer you, MaLou, not one damn thing. I'd just break your heart and I refuse to do that to someone as dear as you."

Rather than considering her pose to be one of loving abandon, MaLou suddenly felt utterly ridiculous. She scrambled off his lap, yanked her pantaloons into place, and hastily tied the ribbon at the waist. "My clothes are scattered all over. You'll have to help me find them because I sure as hell can't go home looking like this," she managed to mumble before she choked on her tears.

"Oh, MaLou, don't cry. Please don't. You've got no reason to be ashamed. This was all my fault."

"I'm not ashamed!" MaLou cried out angrily, for truly she was not. Her feelings for him were very real and she saw nothing wrong in revealing them or in enjoying them as they had. He was the one who ought to be ashamed if his loving tenderness had been no more than a sham. She began sorting through the heap of lingerie lying at her feet, but it was in a hopeless tangle. "If you'd just get out maybe I'd have enough room to dress!" she scolded sharply, tears still rolling down her cheeks in miserable profusion.

"MaLou . . ." Lance knew he had hurt her, and deeply, but he felt far worse about what had happened between them than she did. He reached out to touch her shoulder, but she shoved his hand away.

"Don't you ever touch me again," MaLou responded in a vicious whisper. "Don't even speak to me! All you ever do is lie, so I wish you'd just keep your damn mouth shut!"

Finding her camisole, she pulled it on, then tried to find her corset. How she would get it laced up in the state she was in she did not know, but she vowed not to ask Lance to do it.

Giving up his efforts for the moment to make her see his side, Lance climbed out of the buggy with his shirt and coat in his hand. He put them on, buttoned up his shirt, took the tie from his pocket, and tied it as neatly as he could without the benefit of a mirror. MaLou was still cursing and tossing her clothes about so he spent his time pacing beside the wagon while she got ready, hoping by the time she was dressed she would have calmed down enough to listen to reason. He ached all over and it was not simply because he had not satisfied his desire for her. It was his conscience that was inflicting the worst of the pain and he knew he deserved every insult she was heaping upon him now. Finally he could stand no more of his own abuse and lashed out at her. "I'm no liar, MaLou. Just because I've got sense enough to know we'd never be happy together doesn't make me a liar!"

"You are so a liar, and a coward to boot!" MaLou replied, her outrage far too bitter to allow her to be still.

"How can you possibly call me a coward?" Lance shouted in return. "I'll stand up to any man and you've seen me do it too!"

Somehow MaLou had managed to wiggle into her corset and slips and now she pulled her dress on over her head. "Facing death isn't anything for you. I know that. It's living that has you scared witless!"

Lance stared at her, his hands clenched tightly at his sides. "You don't know a damned thing about livin' either, MaLou MacDowell, so I'll thank you not to give me advice!"

"You needn't worry. I'm not even speaking to you!" MaLou reminded him. "I can't find my combs," she remarked absently. She stood up and felt along the leather seat, but she could not find them. "They were in my hand. I must have dropped them when . . ." When she had put her arms around him, she realized, but she could not bring herself to speak the words. Surely there was nothing more humiliating than telling a man you loved him and having him reject that love as coldly as Lance had. Knowing there could never be any betrayal worse than what she had suffered that night, she sank down into the seat, covered her face with her hands, and wept openly over the wretchedness of her fate.

Lance raised his eyes to the stars, hoping for some inspiration to help him dry the lovely young woman's tears, but he saw nothing in their sparkling beauty to help him. He walked around to her side of the buggy, reached in, and felt around on the floor, being careful to avoid MaLou's tiny feet. "Here are two combs. How many did you have?"

MaLou grabbed them from his hand without answering and sitting up very straight, she coiled her curls atop her head and secured them with the two combs. "Take me home," she demanded with an icy calm, and after brushing away the last of her tears, she was ready to go.

Grateful she had not taken the reins and driven off without him, Lance walked back around the buggy and got in. "We didn't decide what we'd tell your daddy," he reminded her softly.

"I'll tell him the truth," MaLou informed him swiftly. "I don't want to see Josh, or any other man, as long as I live!"

Lance had not known it would be possible to feel any worse, but he now did. He could not blame MaLou for despising him. He had shown her the incredible beauty a man and woman could create together out of love and then had snatched it from her grasp with a cruelty he had not suspected he possessed. He had been worried about breaking her heart. Well, it was painfully obvious he already had. He had given her the confidence to make love to him with all the emotion a woman could possess and then he had refused the far more important gift of her heart. "You mustn't hate all men just because I disappointed you so badly, MaLou. You've got both beauty and spirit, and I won't destroy you by takin' your love when I can't return it."

"Love is a gift, Garrett. It's not something you can demand, or refuse," she added angrily. "Now let's go home. The dance must be over by now and my father will be expecting us."

Lance studied her expression in the moonlight and was surprised by its hardness. "Did you ever pick wildflowers, MaLou? Do you know what happens to them if you try to bring them home and put them in a vase?"

"They just wilt and die," MaLou replied flippantly, still not understanding his point.

"Well, someday you'll be grateful you waited for a man who can return your love rather than wasting it on a reckless drifter who'd destroy your very soul as casually as some men pick wildflowers."

While MaLou understood that wildflowers could not be picked without destroying their beauty, she did not think his romantic analogy applied to her. She was far tougher than a flower and was certain loving him would not kill her, even though he had hurt her so badly death did not sound in the least bit frightening that night. Love had warmed his kisses and heated his touch to a searing flame and she was certain that it had not been only her imagination. He loved her all right, but he was just too damn proud to admit it or to explain why he was so reluctant to do so. Well, she had her pride, too, and she would not beg him to declare the love he wanted to hide.

When they reached her door, MaLou laid her hand on Lance's sleeve. "You just see to the horse. I'll tell Dad how badly Josh behaved and blame the way I look on him."

How she looked was even more beautiful than she had appeared when they had left the ranch hours earlier. Her tears had made her eyes sparkle and darkened her lashes, while her fair skin was still flushed from the excitement of making love. "He's sure to ask me what happened tomorrow, but I won't tell him anything other than what happened with Josh," Lance promised softly.

"Good. I wouldn't want to force you to lie to him as well as to me and yourself. Good night."

She had slammed her door before he could respond to her insult, but he knew he had not lied to her when he had said he could not fall in love with her. He just would not do that to her and that was no lie, yet his conscience did not seem to believe him any more than she had and would not stop tormenting him with what he had done, not only to her but to himself, by refusing her love.

Chapter VIII

Thomas had dozed off, but he tossed his book aside and leapt from his chair as his only child came through the front door. "How did it go?" he asked sleepily as he tried unsuccessfully to stifle a wide yawn.

MaLou licked her lips, then wished she had not, for they still tasted of Lance's intoxicating kisses and made it nearly impossible for her to reply. "The dance was very nice until Josh got too forward and Lance knocked him out. Outside of that it was a nice evening." She quickly yanked her combs from her hair before her father could notice it was not styled as it had been when she had left. She shook her head, sending the curls cascading down about her shoulders and hoping they would partially hide her face, for she was afraid her expression would give away far more than she cared to reveal in words.

"But I thought Garrett understood how much you like Josh," Thomas complained with an exasperated sigh. "I didn't want him fighting with him."

"Josh made a complete fool of himself and deserved it, Dad." MaLou swept past him, hoping to escape to her room before his questions became any more difficult to answer, but he reached out to stop her.

"You look so pretty, baby. I'm sure Josh couldn't help forgetting his manners so don't be too hard on him."

MaLou looked down at her father's hand, which rested lightly upon her arm. His touch was as loving as Lance's, while Josh had had such a confining grasp she had not been able to bear it. "Lance is certain Josh will apologize to me. I don't know whether or not he'll be ready to do it by tomorrow, but I think he probably will come by soon."

Greatly encouraged by this prospect, Thomas positively beamed at his lovely daughter. "Good. If he comes by tomorrow we'll ask him to stay for supper. It's high time you were married, baby, and you couldn't do any better than Josh Spencer."

MaLou was not even remotely tempted to tell him how violently she disagreed with his opinion. "What about you, Dad? Don't you think it's time you and Candelaria were married?"

Thomas moved away to turn down the lamp. "Neither of us wants to get married, MaLou. I wish I could make you understand that."

"Did you ever ask her?"

"No, of course not. I told you I don't want to get married again." Thomas was too tired to argue and gestured to hurry her along. "It's late. Let's get to bed."

"Wait a minute. How do you know she wouldn't like to get married if you've never asked her?" MaLou was beginning to feel women were at an awful disadvantage having to wait for the men they loved to make up their minds when surely something as important as marriage ought to be a joint decision. A woman could always say no, of course, but how did she inspire a man to propose so she could tell him yes? "Well, how do you know how she feels?" she asked again.

Thomas was used to MaLou's moods and was not surprised she had taken such an intractable stand, but he had never thought she had wanted to see him remarry. "Why are you so damn curious tonight, girl?"

MaLou replied with the most reasonable excuse she could offer. "If I marry Josh, surely he'll want me to live on his ranch rather than come here to live with us. I don't want you to be left all alone."

That she was at least considering marriage delighted Thomas so greatly he reached out to envelop her in an enthusiastic hug. "Don't you worry about me, baby. When you get yourself settled with a husband, there will be plenty of time for me to decide whether or not I'm lonely."

"That's true, but will you do something about it?" MaLou inquired perceptively.

"I just might, but you'll have to wait and see." Thomas walked her down the hall, gave her a good-night kiss on the cheek, then went to his room thinking he would have to find some way to reward Lance Garrett for doing such a fine job of turning MaLou into a lady.

MaLou closed her door and leaned back against it, relieved her father had been so distracted by her questions he had not taken a good look at her. She had to gather her courage before she dared take a peek in her mirror, but she was surprised none of her inner turmoil was readily apparent in her reflection. "Dear Lord, what an awful night," she exclaimed. She kicked off her slippers, peeled off her silk stockings, then removed her dress. She tossed the lacy slip over her chair, unlaced her corset, and wiggled out of it. It was then she discovered she had donned her camisole inside out, for the pretty ribbon trim was now next to her skin. "It's a damn good thing I don't have a maid," she whispered softly to herself, but despite her bitter argument with Lance, she did not feel guilty for having shed her clothes without uttering a single word of protest. Even with her hair down, in her camisole and pantaloons she looked somewhat boyish and she stepped up to her mirror to examine her features more closely. Lance was a gentleman, she supposed, or she would no longer be a virgin. She looked different though. The gleam that brightened the green of her eyes was even more cynical than usual and she knew she would have to be careful or her father would suspect he had not heard the whole story about her evening. It was at times like these that she wished she had a mother in whom to confide, for surely another woman would be able to offer better advice than a man like Lance gave.

She sank down on the edge of her bed as she remembered her brief trip to visit her mother. She would not have been tempted to confide in that shrew even if she still lived with her and MaLou dismissed Lily MacDowell from her mind. Perhaps some women were cut out to be mothers and others were not. If that was true, she doubted she would have the capacity to love a child either. Of course, she would have to marry to have a child and marriage seemed an even more unlikely possibility than it had before she had met Lance Garrett. She was startled to realize that although her thoughts had strayed to her mother, they had swiftly come full circle, right back to Lance.

He had described himself as a reckless drifter. Maybe he would be gone before Josh got around to proposing. The thought of Josh touching her the way Lance had made her shiver with disgust, and she got up to get a nightgown. She wanted to take a bath, to wash every trace of him from her body but knew she would not heat water and bathe in the middle of the night without making her father suspicious and she dared not risk that. She would just have to wait until morning to get clean. As she climbed into bed, she decided she would wear her pink dress and be ready to greet callers, but since she had never had any she could not really believe she would have some the next day either. When she closed her eyes, the memory of Lance's rakish smile taunted her anew and she wondered how long he would have to be gone before she would begin to forget him.

Every bit as distraught as MaLou, Lance wanted to pack his belongings and clear out before dawn, but he could not get the feisty blonde's voice out of his mind. She had called him a coward and surely running out on her in the middle of the night would be a cowardly act. He would have to hang around a while longer to see what happened between her and Josh, just to satisfy his curiosity if for no other reason. He sure as hell wouldn't go to their wedding, even if they invited him, which he doubted they would. The thought of MaLou snuggling up to Josh as she had to him turned his stomach, but he knew if he left he would always wonder about what had become of the pretty girl. Noticing the bunk across from his was stripped of its bedding, he turned to Manuel Ortiz, who had the bunk next to his. "Where's Charlie?"

Manuel had just left a game of cards at the far end of the bunkhouse and stretched lazily before he replied. "MacDowell fired him. I heard him yelling about whitewash and the next thing we knew Charlie was gone."

Even in his present rotten mood, Lance could not help but laugh. "I'm sorry I missed seein' that."

Manuel sat down on his bunk and leaned forward as he dropped his voice to a conspiratorial whisper. "That is not the best part. Later I heard the boss tell Nathan that if anything ever happened to you he'd hold him responsible and fire him too."

"What?" Lance was disgusted now. "I can take care of myself," he protested with an angry frown.

"Yo sé. So do the others, but many things can happen to a man when his back is turned. If you should suffer some unfortunate accident, it might be difficult to prove who is to blame. The boss is a cautious man. I do not blame him, for Nathan's made no secret of his dislike for you."

That was another good reason to stick around, Lance told himself. He would not give Nathan the satisfaction of thinking he had run him off. Charlie had not been bright enough to think of throwing whitewash on him himself, so it must have been Nathan's idea. It would be a pleasure to give that bastard another beating. He doubted he would have long to wait before the man pulled another stupid stunt, but he would take care of it himself rather than go to MacDowell about it. He folded up his suit and got ready for bed, knowing he would not sleep a wink when devising solutions for his rapidly multiplying problems would keep him occupied until dawn.

Early the next morning Thomas knocked on MaLou's

door, then peered inside. "MaLou, honey, there's a Corporal Anderson here who wants to take you to church. I have no idea what to tell him. Do you?"

MaLou opened one eye and rolled over to look at her father. "Corporal who?"

"Anderson. He says he met you last night at the dance and he's come to escort you into town for church." Thomas waited at the door, only slightly less befuddled than his daughter, who was obviously still half asleep. "What am I going to tell him?"

"Tell him to go straight to . . . no, wait a minute." Realizing how rude that would be, MaLou sat up and pushed her hair out of her eyes as she tried to think how a lady would handle an unexpected caller at such an early hour. She would not tell the young man to get lost when she knew firsthand how rejection hurt. She would try instead to do the proper thing. "Why don't you give him some breakfast and tell him I can't possibly be dressed in time to get to church. Then heat me some water for a bath, please. I'll be out as soon as I can get ready."

"You're sure you want him to stay? He seems like a nice boy and all, but—"

"Yes. If he's come all the way out here to see me, then I want him to stay," MaLou insisted as she threw back her covers. "Unless of course missing church will upset him."

"You know he's just come to see you, baby. I doubt he'll care if you aren't dressed in time to make it to church."

When her father closed her door, MaLou got out of bed and gathered up the clothes she had left lying carelessly about the room when she had come home. When she had finished straightening up, she made her bed, then laid out the clothes she wanted to wear that day. Her mother had insisted that the house be built with a separate room for bathing. Located between the bedrooms, it held a washstand and tub. Conveniently, there was an outside door so water could be brought from the kitchen without its having to be carried through the house. With company there, MaLou was grateful she would not have to walk through the parlor to reach the kitchen and bathe in there.

Her father rapped lightly upon her door when he had carried the hot water to the tub and she hurried into the small room to prepare to meet her guest, though it was not until she had walked into the parlor and saw him that she recalled which man he was.

"Good morning, Corporal," she greeted him warmly as though she was frequently awakened by eager young men. "Since my hair is still slightly damp, do you mind if we go outside on the porch and sit in the sunshine until it dries?"

"Not at all, Miss MacDowell." Andy had leapt to his feet when she had entered the room and now rushed to open the front door for her.

"Please call me MaLou, and may I call you by your first name too?" she asked as she stepped outside.

"Oh yes, please do. I'd like that," the attentive corporal responded with a lopsided grin.

MaLou looked up at him, waiting for him to supply his name, but when he did not she had to ask him what it was. The question embarrassed him so badly his whole face turned bright red.

"My name is really Leonard, but everyone calls me Andy," he explained in a breathless rush.

MaLou thought Andy Anderson a fine-looking young man. Fair haired and blue eyed, he was so good-natured she could not help but like him. She remembered dancing with him only once, and obviously he had been far more impressed by that casual encounter than she had been. There were two chairs on the porch so she chose the smaller one and took care to smooth the skirt of her pink gown over her knees to strike both a modest and attractive pose. "I'm sorry I wasn't dressed when you arrived. It was very thoughtful of you to want to take me to church. My mother used to attend services regularly, but I'm afraid my father and I seldom make that effort. I hope you're not disappointed I wasn't dressed in time to go." Actually, she thought he had been very clever to think of a way to be the first to arrive at her door.

Andy was still blushing as he shook his head. "No, I'm not disappointed at all. I think you're even prettier this morning than you were last night."

"Why, thank you." MaLou smiled, hoping he would have something more to say, but when the silence between them grew awkward she knew Lance had been wrong and she would have to be the one to keep their conversation flowing smoothly. "I know you're not from Tucson. Where's your home, Andy?" At that question the young man's expression grew thoughtful and he began to talk not only about his home in Minnesota but about his family and friends, all of whom he missed dearly. MaLou found his story so interesting she had no time to be self-conscious. She soon discovered she could keep the young man talking by occasionally offering a sympathetic word or two and she wondered if such a simple technique would work with other men as well.

Lance searched the buggy thoroughly that morning, found two more combs, and put them into his pocket to give back to MaLou. He had found several chores that kept him working near the barn and main corral so he could keep an eye on the house. If Joshua Spencer had the nerve to come calling, then he definitely wanted to be around to see how he was received and how long his visit lasted. He was not at all pleased to see MaLou chatting happily on the front porch with a soldier. From the looks of him, he was not much older than she and could not have fought during the war, but he still found it difficult to look at a man in a blue uniform and think of him as representing the United States Cavalry rather than the cursed Union Army. That was the only thing he disliked most about the Arizona Territory: it was too damn full of cavalry troops for his taste. He took off his hat and wiped the sweat from his brow with his shirt-sleeve as another man rode up and joined MaLou and the corporal on the porch. He did not recognize this fellow either and went back to work, just biding his time until Josh appeared.

* * *

At noon the MacDowells had to borrow enough food from Jake to serve Sunday supper to half a dozen young men, but that Joshua Spencer was not one of them annoyed Thomas no end. MaLou's male guests were all polite young fellows, personable and bright, but he had his heart set on her marrying Josh for so long he could not even consider anyone else. The soldier he dismissed immediately, even though he found him likable enough. The other five were men he knew at least by name if not personally, but none of them were good enough for his little girl either. It was nice to see her finally getting some attention from Tucson's bachelors, but he was pleased to see that while she treated her guests politely, she did not appear to be overly fond of any of them. That kept him hoping Josh was still her favorite. At the close of the meal he left the house to escape MaLou's talkative guests and when he saw Lance by the barn he walked over to him.

"MaLou told me about what happened last night. Suppose you give me your side of it, Garrett."

Since the man was not carrying his shotgun, Lance knew MaLou surely could not have told him much. Since there was nothing he cared to admit, he provided a brief explanation of his fight with Josh, then shook his head sadly. "I was certain he'd come by today to apologize to MaLou, but I guess he just doesn't have the courage to face her."

"I'm real disappointed in him, too," Thomas agreed, "but maybe he just wasn't up to it." He chuckled then and turned his back to the house so there would be no chance MaLou would overhear their conversation. "I never thought I'd see the day when MaLou could talk with a man for more than five minutes without starting a fight, but today she's been so considerate to her guests she doesn't even seem like the same person. Is that your doing too?"

Lance swallowed hard, afraid he had hurt MaLou so badly she was merely numb rather than consciously making an effort to be pleasant. "I've always enjoyed talkin' with your daughter, sir. She's bright as well as pretty. I don't think she'd fight with a man unless she had a good reason."

Thomas glanced back at the house. MaLou and her guests were all back out on the porch laughing about a joke one of the men had told. "Looks like you're right. There's just one thing, Garrett," he remarked as his expression became more serious.

Lance braced himself for the worst. "What's that, sir?"

"If you ever have another occasion to punch Josh Spencer, just don't hit him so damn hard!"

"Let's just hope he's learned to behave himself," Lance replied with a wicked grin, thinking he would make it a point to wallop Josh every chance he got. MacDowell seemed satisfied with his answer and went strolling off looking for Nathan, but Lance kept his eye on the porch, musing that if he ever had a daughter as pretty as MaLou he would not let her out of his sight.

While Lance had no idea MaLou had noticed his almost constant comings and goings that day, she most certainly had. He seemed always to be carrying a bridle or harness, but she did not recall ever having seen him repairing such items before. Quite a few of the men were handy with leather work, but she had not known he was one of them, nor had she noticed that their equipment was in such desperate need of attention. It was difficult enough to force him from her mind without the constant reminder of his presence, but he had obviously decided to clean out the whole tack room and she would not leave her guests to tell him to go do his work elsewhere.

"Miss MacDowell?"

"I asked you to call me MaLou, Andy," the pretty blonde reminded him with an engaging smile, hoping her lapse in attention had not been too obvious. She was pleased when he returned her smile, then one of the other men spoke and she tried to listen more attentively so she would know how to respond if expected to do so. They were a pleasant group and kept the conversation flowing amongst themselves, for which she was truly grateful, but both her mind and her glance kept wandering to Lance Garrett, who seemed to be every bit as restless that day as she was.

It was nearly sundown before the last of her guests had departed. She thought she would be able to relax by herself that evening, but she had been inside no more than ten minutes before there was a knock at the front door. Her heart leapt to her throat. Praying it would be Lance, she went to open it before her father could rise from his chair.

Feeling very foolish, Josh gripped his hat tightly as his eyes wandered hungrily up and down MaLou's stylishly attired figure. To see her so nicely dressed two days in a row was more than he had dared hope. "In pink you look even more like an angel than you did last night, MaLou."

His chin was badly bruised where Lance had hit him and her teeth marks were clearly visible on his ear, but his compliment seemed so sincere she hoped he had not seen her disappointment when she realized it was he at her door. "Thank you, but isn't it rather late to be paying a call, Josh?"

Hearing the long-awaited young man's name, Thomas quickly got up to invite him to come inside. "Nonsense, MaLou. Josh knows the way home and he won't get lost after dark. Come on in and sit a spell. I was just going outside for a stroll myself, but I'll say good-bye to you before you go." With a sly wink only MaLou could see, he went out the door as Josh came in, considering himself exceedingly clever for thinking of a way to leave them alone.

MaLou was astonished her father had not demanded an apology from Josh and promptly sent the battered young man on his way. That he had not done so made it all too obvious Josh could do no wrong in his eyes. Infuriated by that thought, she left the door standing ajar and did not bother to invite him to sit down. "If you've come to apologize for last night, I think you'd better start talking real fast."

Thinking she must not have told her father what had

happened between them, Josh mistakenly assumed she had already forgiven him. He had counted on his considerable personal charm to impress her and had not spent more than a few minutes working on a clever apology. "I'm sorry, MaLou. I really am. When you were a little girl I used to give you hugs and kisses all the time. I guess I was so happy you were finally old enough to return them I got carried away. I promise it won't happen again."

"It better not," MaLou informed him coldly, but neither the seriousness of her expression nor the icy tone of her voice had the slightest effect on the width of his grin. She had spent the whole day listening to half a dozen men trying to impress her and they all had been a whole lot nicer to her than Josh had been. It was Josh's father who owned the ranch bordering theirs though, and Josh whom she had always expected to marry. Where her mind had been all those years she did not know, but he now seemed so terribly shallow she did not care if she ever saw him again, and marriage was absolutely out of the question. She could not announce that since he had not asked her, but she made no great haste in stifling her yawn. "I'm sorry, Josh. It's been such a long day. Was there anything else you wanted to tell me before you go?"

Josh had never been dismissed so abruptly from a young lady's home and immediately balked. He gestured toward the settee and then reached out to take MaLou's hand. "I know you're mad at me and you've got every reason to be, but since I went to the trouble of riding over here I'd like to stay a while longer. Please?" he added, again relying on the brightness of his smile to charm her into agreeing to his request.

It now seemed to MaLou that she had never really known Josh, but thinking her father would expect her to entertain him for a few minutes at least, she reluctantly agreed to let him stay. "Would you like some coffee or tea?" she asked rather absently, thinking she would need something to stay awake and would have to offer him some too.

"No thanks, but I'd welcome a brandy if your dad has

some." Josh walked over to the settee, tossed his hat on the adjacent table, sat down, and made himself comfortable while he waited for her to fetch it.

MaLou put her hands on her hips, wondering where the arrogant young man got the colossal nerve to order her about like a servant. She was about to tell him precisely what she thought of him when there was another knock at the partially open door. Not really caring who it might be, she flung it open wide but was astounded when Lance strode right past her into the front room.

Hoping to look completely at home in her parlor, Lance took her combs from his pocket, reached for her hand, and laid them in her palm as he leaned down to kiss her cheek. "You forgot your combs, darlin', and I didn't want them to get lost." He then turned to Josh as though he had just noticed him. "Evenin', Josh. I'm surprised to see you here. Carl thought you were dead, but I can't say I'm sorry to see he was mistaken."

Enraged by his comment, Josh bounded up from the settee. Like a charging bull he lowered his head and aimed his right shoulder at Lance's midsection, hoping to plow right over him. MaLou screamed as she hurriedly spun out of the way, while Lance nonchalantly sidestepped Josh's blow, grabbed him by the belt and the seat of his pants, and hurled him right out the door. Thrown off balance, the young man stumbled as he tried to catch himself, then with a horrified shriek he toppled off the porch. He landed flat on his back in the dirt, his position not very much different from that of his last encounter with the Southerner.

Hearing the commotion, Thomas MacDowell came running up in time to offer Josh a hand to help him to his feet. "Can't I leave you two alone for more than a minute, girl, without you stirring up trouble?"

That her father would blame her when Josh had started the fight was more than MaLou could bear. It had been Lance's fault really, since his insult had started the brief brawl, but she was wise enough to keep that opinion to herself. "This is the second day in a row that Josh has behaved like an ill-mannered oaf and he has only himself to blame that he's gotten whipped for it twice."

While MaLou exchanged murderous glances with her father, Josh tried to brush off his clothes and regain what was left of his dignity. Lance, however, was having a great deal of difficulty containing his laughter. Thoroughly disgusted with both her father and Josh, MaLou left them briefly, then returned with Josh's hat. She tossed it to him as she bid him a hostile farewell. "I'll thank you not to come back until you've learned how to behave as a gentleman should, Mr. Spencer."

"What makes you think I want to come back?" Josh replied gruffly.

"Now you just wait one minute, Josh," Thomas cautioned him sternly. "You two have been friends far too long to stay so angry with each other. I'm sure you can tell MaLou good night a lot more politely than that." When Josh made no effort to do so, Thomas gave him a helpful nudge. "Tell her good night, son. You'll be real mad at yourself in the morning if you don't."

Josh first gave Lance an evil stare, then swallowed his pride and said good night to MaLou. "Maybe next time I come to see you we won't be interrupted," he added as he turned toward his horse, and without so much as a backward glance he rode away.

"You go on inside, baby. Mr. Garrett and I have a piece of unfinished business to discuss."

"I'm not going anywhere," MaLou protested angrily. "Josh took one look at Garrett and went wild. Rather than allow the maniac to bust up all our furniture, Lance tossed him out the door. You've got no cause to be angry with him." Yet MaLou was still so angry with Lance herself she did not dare look at him as she spoke to her father.

"I'm not mad at the man, MaLou, but our conversation just doesn't concern you, so please go back inside," Thomas ordered calmly.

MaLou knew that was a flat-out lie, but since Lance could obviously defend himself if need be, she left the men to finish their conversation without her. She was in no mood to go to sleep now, though, and went into the kitchen to heat some water for tea.

"Come on, son, I'll walk you over to the bunkhouse." Thomas was still frowning, and uncertain just what to say, he waited until they had nearly reached it before he spoke.

"I'm real grateful to you for getting MaLou into a dress. That was a big accomplishment in itself. Then today she managed to talk sweetly the whole damn day through to half a dozen young men who thought her so charming I'm afraid they're going to be back again next Sunday. The problem is that Joshua Spencer is the only one worth marrying and I can't have him getting beat up every time he comes to call. Do you understand me, Garrett? If you two can't stand the sight of each other, then I want you to make yourself scarce whenever he's here. He's never going to have the chance to ask MaLou to marry him if he spends all his time fighting with you."

Lance shoved his hands in his hips pockets as he gave the only reply he possibly could. "Josh isn't half good enough for her and you know it."

Taken aback by his remark, Thomas nevertheless had a ready retort. "Well, you sure as hell aren't either."

"I didn't say that I was," Lance informed him coolly. "But you ought to stop pushin' MaLou toward Josh and let her make up her own mind about him. She can certainly think for herself."

"Yes, she can, but it doesn't hurt to point out that a man with a fine ranch and plenty of money makes a far better husband than a good-looking cowhand who'll give her nothing but a dozen kids and a whole lot of heartache." When this opinion met with stony silence from Lance, Thomas took another tack. "Now suppose you tell me what you were doing up at the house just now."

This was easy enough for Lance to explain. "I saw you leave and was afraid MaLou wouldn't be safe with Josh. I went to the door just to ask if she felt comfortable being alone with him and, well, you know the rest."

Since he could hardly criticize the man for caring about what happened to his daughter when he had hired him specifically to help MaLou, Thomas did not quite know what to say. "All right, I'll admit to being a bit overeager where Josh is concerned, but I'd never force MaLou to marry a man she doesn't love and I know she's always loved him. Next time he comes over I'll sit on the porch. Then if he isn't real polite I'll be there to toss him out myself. You just go on about your business and let me handle him from now on."

"Fine," Lance agreed. "I didn't mean to sound like I was tellin' you how to go about bein' her daddy, but I was concerned about her."

"And I appreciate that too," Thomas responded. The two men parted company on an amicable note, but Lance was far more pleased with the way the evening had ended than he would admit to Thomas MacDowell, or anyone else.

Chapter IX

MaLou found only dust in the bottom of their long-empty tea tin and slammed the lid back on the decorative canister as she made a mental note to buy more tea. She could not recall the last time she had wanted a cup of tea, if ever, but the fact that there was none was as horribly frustrating as her father's refusal to allow her to take part in his conversation with Lance. She settled for a glass of water, which she carried into her bedroom to sip, since she had no desire to speak with her father again that evening. Sitting down on the edge of her bed, she tried to regain enough of her usual composure to review the day in a lucid manner, but a long while passed before she grew calm enough to make such an attempt. To have had six of the young men with whom she had danced come to see her had been immensely flattering and she had to admit they had been so charming she had been genuinely interested in their conversation. While none of the topics they had discussed had been particularly deep, most had been amusing. After her initial awkwardness with Andy Anderson, she had not felt like she was merely acting a part, either. Her callers had seemed so eager for her company it had been a simple matter to please them with little more than a polite smile and a few leading questions. Perhaps being a lady was not going to be nearly as difficult as she had always feared it would be. Or at least it would not be difficult with men who had been as taken with her as her gentlemen callers had obviously been. She kept reminding herself that there were so few single women in Tucson, the competition for her affection was naturally quite keen, and she hoped that if she continued to view her popularity in that light she would not become as spoiled as pretty young women were usually thought to be.

In sharp contrast to the other men, Josh had set her on edge the moment he had arrived. Had he deliberately waited until so late in the day to come see her so he would not have to compete with any other callers she might have had? Or was he so conceited he had wanted to make her wait, mistakenly believing she would be sitting there pining away, her daydreams filled with romantic thoughts of him? "That's probably closer to the truth," she murmured softly to herself.

When it came to conceit, she considered Lance Garrett no better. She still did not understand why he had chosen such an inopportune time to return her combs. That he had kissed her and called her "darlin'" after the way they had parted was ridiculous too. That whole scene had probably had nothing to do with her. It was more likely he had just wanted to start another fight with Josh. Why he had taken such an intense dislike to the young man she did not understand, but the longer she considered the antagonism that existed between the two men the more jealousy seemed the underlying cause. "But why would Garrett be jealous?" the distracted blonde mused aloud. She had said she loved him and would be happy to marry him, but he had turned her offer down cold, so why would he act like a jealous fool the next day? Such erratic behavior made no sense at all to her. If the man did not want her for himself, why would he deliberately start a fight with a man who had made it no secret that he did want her, and badly?

She straightened her shoulders proudly then, vowing it would be what she wanted that mattered, not what some drifter who could not make up his mind from one day to the next thought should happen. Perhaps as Josh had said, it was simply his sudden realization that she had grown up that had made him behave so impulsively. If that was the case, then she would have to forgive him and hope he would conduct himself in a more gentlemanly manner at their next meeting. She had been tired that night, and Josh's mood could not have been all that good either after the beating he had taken the previous evening. Their visit might have gone poorly even if Lance had not interrupted them. On the other hand, they might have been able to talk in a civilized fashion, but that was something she would never know now.

Certain she was only becoming more confused, MaLou rose, set her empty glass upon her dresser, and began to undress for bed. When she had bathed that morning she had been in such a great hurry she had given the graceful contours of her body no thought but had concentrated solely upon scrubbing herself clean. Now, as she peeled away her clothes, her thoughts were flooded with the memory of how easily Lance Garrett had undressed her. He had been so wonderfully sweet to her, his touch gentle, his kiss adoring, and nothing they had done had seemed wrong. She could not help but wonder what would have happened had Josh shown her such consideration and patience. Would she then have responded as readily to his touch as she had to Lance's? She caressed the tip of her left breast and shivered as the pale pink tip grew firm beneath her fingertips, afraid her body might swiftly betray her again were she to meet another man with Lance Garrett's tenderness. She had never thought herself so lacking in character, but perhaps that was only because she had never before had the opportunity to discover such a flaw. If she could not control her desires, then she would have to be far more careful. She did not dare go anywhere without a chaperone ever again.

Frightened by the possibility she possessed such a terrible weakness, MaLou stood in front of her mirror lightly tracing the path of Lance's meandering caress, and the same delicious warmth he had created within her began to flicker then glow with a dangerous heat. It was true then, she realized with an anguished cry of guilt.

Perhaps Lance had considered her so easy to seduce he did not want her for his wife. All she knew was that she could no longer trust the emotions that had guided her all her life, for not only her heart, but her body as well, had betrayed her the first time she had been alone with a handsome man. She was terrified she might someday fall prey to her own uncontrollable passions. She would then disgrace not only herself but her father as well and undoubtedly end up a whore on Maiden Lane. Horrified by such a ghastly prospect, she slipped on her nightgown, crawled into bed, and, using her pillow to muffle the sounds of her sobs, cried herself to sleep.

All Lance saw of MaLou the next morning was a flash of brown and white as she sped by on her pinto mare. She was clad in her buckskins, her long hair flowing free as she whipped past him. He had missed straying into her horse's path by the barest of margins and was still staring after her when Manuel reached his side.

"Do not say that I did not warn you about that one, *amigo,*" the wiry Mexican reminded him. "She would make a better bride for a Chiricahua brave than any white man."

"That's not a fate I'd wish on any woman," Lance interjected with a sullen frown. He knew little about the Apache bands that roamed the Southwest other than what he had learned of those who raided along the Mexican border, and none of that information had been complimentary. "Why would you even suggest such a thing?"

Manuel shrugged. "I know their maidens marry men of their own choosing. I am afraid MaLou will not be so lucky."

While MaLou had not really proposed to him, she had been the one to bring up the subject of marriage, while he had quickly scuttled the idea. His throat suddenly felt uncomfortably tight at that memory and he coughed to clear it. "You needn't worry about MaLou. She won't be forced into anything, let alone marriage, but I doubt she'd choose an Indian."

"I have a cousin who's married to a Chiricahua," Manuel confided as they continued toward the cook house.

"You're not serious," Lance scoffed, thinking his friend was teasing him.

"No, it is true. Many Mexican women have been stolen on raids and I have yet to hear of one who wished to return to her family after having been a Chiricahua's wife."

"Well, that's probably more out of fear of how they'd be treated if they tried to go back home than due to any great love for the Indian way of life. You know they'd be shunned if not spit upon and their children would be called half-breeds."

"A Chiricahua brave always keeps his children, Garrett, if not his wife. Just like MacDowell, they do not let their babies go."

They had reached the cookhouse and Lance turned to look down at his friend. "Are you sayin' that's where he got the idea to keep MaLou?"

"*Quièn sabe?* I was not here then and I do not know."

Lance had seen no signs of Indians on any of his many rides over the broad expanse of the MacDowell ranch, but recalling some of the more gruesome tales of the atrocities the Chiricahuas had committed upon hapless settlers, he felt his flesh begin to crawl with a sudden sense of foreboding. "I haven't seen any Indians near here, but do you think MaLou is safe goin' out ridin' alone?"

Manuel scuffed the toe of his boot in the dirt as he tried to give an honest opinion. "They move over the land with the freedom of the wind. That we saw none yesterday does not mean they are not out there today. They would never kill so pretty a woman, but they would not let her go either, and as you say, she might not have the courage to leave them even if given the chance."

That was all Lance needed to hear. "Tell Nathan I've gone after MaLou if he asks for me. I learned a long time ago not to ignore my hunches and I'm afraid somethin' is very wrong today."

Manuel did not argue, for he knew Lance Garrett to be every bit as stubborn a man as MaLou was a woman. "A fatal combination," he remarked aloud, chuckling to himself. Hoping Jake had fixed flapjacks for breakfast, he hurried into the cookhouse and took his place in line.

Lance saddled Amigo in a minimum amount of time and swiftly set out at a gallop on MaLou's trail. Forced to squint into the rising sun, he soon discovered she had gotten such a good head start he could catch no sight of her. Discouraged, he drew Amigo to a halt to give the horse a rest while he made up his mind what to do. The rich grass that covered the fertile valley of the Santa Cruz River provided excellent grazing land for cattle, but the herd roamed over a wide expanse and none of the stock was visible in the area through which MaLou had ridden. In some respects that was a good sign, for any Indians hoping to rustle a few head of cattle would obviously be elsewhere. Still, there might be hunting parties out searching for game and who could say where they might be? That MaLou went riding alone had always bothered him, for it was dangerous in addition to being downright improper for a young woman to put herself at risk so needlessly. He was doing no good to either himself or her, though, when he had no idea where she had gone. Hoping the distant mountain range had been her goal, he tapped Amigo's glossy flanks with his heels and resumed the chase.

From her perch at the rocky base of the Santa Rita Mountains, MaLou had at first been curious, then grew increasingly alarmed, as she watched a lone rider approach. Her apprehension did not lessen when she recognized the swift black stallion as Amigo. She could not imagine why Lance had followed her, but she doubted his motives could possibly be good. She wiped her hands on her thighs, drawing comfort from the softness of her buckskins before reaching for the Colt she had strapped to her hip. She doubted she could shoot the handsome man even if he had come looking for the affection she would swiftly refuse to give, but she did not want him even to suspect that. She had every right to hate him, so she would just have to make him believe that she did. She remained atop an outcropping of rock, which, cushioned by several layers of dirt, provided a comfortable bench. Shaded by the spindly branches of an acacia, she tried to behave as though he were a stranger who had just happened by.

That MaLou had not hidden from him pleased Lance enormously, but her expression was so far from welcoming that after he had leapt down from Amigo's back he kept his distance. "Mornin'!" he called out with a friendly wave.

"Good morning, Mr. Garrett," MaLou responded without a trace of a smile. "I come up here because I like to be by myself to think, so I'd appreciate it if you kept right on riding."

While he knew the young woman must have no end of pressing problems to contemplate, he would not deny he had his share as well. "What a coincidence. I was just lookin' for a good place to think too." He did not bother to ask if she would mind if he joined her, since she had made it quite plain that she would. He dropped his reins so Amigo could graze near her mare, and picking out a spot where the rocks provided a comfortable backrest, he sat down to work out his own dilemmas.

Appalled the man would not leave when she had told him to go, MaLou called out to him, "Do you plan to sit there all day?"

"Please, I'm trying to think and I don't like to be interrupted any more than you do," Lance teased, grateful she could not see his smile from where she sat. He was counting on her curiosity as well as her feisty temperament to make it impossible for her to ignore him, but he began to worry he had misjudged her when a long while passed before she spoke again.

"My father hired you to work, not to sit idle and think, Garrett. Didn't you tell me you prided yourself on giving a good day's work for your pay?"

"That's true," Lance agreed, but he did not even budge, let alone make the effort to leave.

He had cocked his hat down low over his eyes and he looked so relaxed MaLou wondered if he might soon fall asleep. If he did, then she would be able to slip by him and leave without having to argue about who was bothering whom. Still it was plain he had followed her and she wanted to know why. "Do you plan to follow me every day, Garrett?" she challenged abrasively, not caring if she insulted him.

Lance opened his mouth to give her another smart retort, but then decided the truth would fit the situation far better. First he shifted his position so he would not have to look over his shoulder when he spoke with her. They were at the foot of the mountains and the pine trees growing far above them looked so inviting he was sorry they could not take advantage of their refreshing shade. Where they sat the warm air was very still, the rocky terrain dotted by scrub brush and deserted except for a few lizards sunning themselves on nearby rocks. Trying to speak with the clarity of the morning light, he began his explanation. "I don't think it's a good idea for you to go out ridin' alone, MaLou."

The defiant blonde's reaction to his opinion was so hostile she simply refused to discuss the point. "That's not your decision to make, Garrett. Besides, you've already made it more than plain you don't care what happens to me anyway."

"I never said that!" Lance denied instantly, yet he could not deny that that was precisely the message his actions had conveyed.

MaLou had found it a lot easier to direct questions to his back, for now that they were facing each other it was nearly impossible to focus her attention elsewhere and maintain control of her temper. Although they were seated some distance apart, separated by five or six yards of rocky hillside, she was certain he saw far too much with his piercing blue gaze. The vibrant color of his eyes was as bright as the cloudless sky, and unable to return his steady stare, she shaded her eyes with her hand as though avoiding the glare of the sun and looked out over the valley. "Some things you don't have to say, Garrett." His presence imparted a warmth far different from that of the day, and while she tried unsuccessfully to suppress its effect, she grew increasingly uncomfortable. Unfortunately, she found she did not have to look at Lance to feel the torment of desire, and that provided shocking proof of the weakness over which she had shed so many tears. While her traitorous body longed to again be enfolded in his loving embrace and savor the marvelous taste of his kiss, her agile mind rebelled violently against those feelings as though desire in itself were the same as surrender. The result of that highly charged conflict was a smoldering rage, which swiftly flared out of control. Picking up a loose stone, she hurled it at him, crying, "Get out of here! Go on, get!" While she scarcely needed to reemphasize her need for privacy, she grabbed another stone and sent it flying toward his head.

Lance ducked the first missile, but the second bounded off his shoulder, leaving a painful bruise. "Hey, cut it out, MaLou!" he shouted as he raised his arms to protect his face, but that only prompted her to launch still more stones with a surprisingly deadly accuracy. Never one to back down when faced with a fight, Lance gave no thought to escaping her vicious assault by staging a retreat but instead grabbed up several of the rocks that had landed nearby and lobbed them back at her as he scrambled up the hillside bent on taking her position.

MaLou had expected Lance to turn tail and run, but when she realized he was coming after her she dodged behind a large boulder and gathered up still more stones to use as ammunition. She was so angry now she wanted him dead and had no objection to killing him off herself, but as she rose up to hurl another rock, Lance was so close he reached out to grab her wrist and with a savage yank pulled her right over the top of the boulder and down into the dirt at his feet. Before she could scramble away, he dropped down upon her, neatly pinning her beneath him while he held her hands above her head in a firm grip. Her hair flew about whipping his cheeks as she struggled to break free, but he was far too strong to be affected by her actions no matter how desperate.

"You bastard!" MaLou screamed, choking on the dust they had kicked up all around them.

The green of her eyes glowed with such fierce light that Lance half expected her to summon the strength of a demon, but when he realized she could not escape him he used a brutal kiss to muffle the string of insults she had begun to yell. He felt her writhing beneath him, unconsciously arousing not only his anger but his passion as well, and as long as she fought him he refused to lift his mouth from hers. Had he tried to wrestle a dozen rattlesnakes into submission his task would have been no less a challenge, for MaLou possessed not only a furious anger but considerable stamina. She continued to fight him by twisting and turning, wiggling and shoving, until finally the salty taste of her blood brought him to his senses. He raised his mouth from hers then, but his glance was still dark as he stared down at her ravaged lips. She was gulping for air but did not beg him to release her when she finally caught her breath.

"I hate you!" she shrieked. "Get off me, damn you. I hate you!"

Lance watched in rapt fascination as a tiny rivulet of blood continued to trickle from the gash his teeth had sliced in her lower lip. She had every right to despise him and yet hatred was the last emotion she stirred within him. Ignoring her hoarsely shouted insults, he leaned down and with the tip of his tongue licked away the bright red blood flowing from the cut. While she was still too startled by his action to object with words, he kissed her very gently, as though he were attempting to convince a small child a kiss would make the pain of an injury go away.

MaLou's anger had been fueled by Lance's confining embrace. When his manner suddenly became tender, her mood turned first to confusion and, then, much to her shame, again became desire. Her heart now began to pound with that frantic beat rather than anger, and no longer able to think clearly enough to struggle, she lay still. Lance held her so tightly she could feel every delicious inch of him through the soft fabric of her buckskins. The weight of his muscular body pressed her down into the sandy soil, the contours of their bodies fitting together perfectly despite their disparity in size. The earth beneath her held the comforting aroma of the land, but she could also smell the spicy scent of the soap Lance had used to shave that morning as well as her own faint fragrance of gardenias. The sun overhead blinded her with shimmering waves of light, which at the same time surrounded Lance's jet black curls with a radiant halo. When his lips again caressed hers, her battle was fought solely within herself, and her stubborn refusal to respond inspired him to show her still more of the sweetest expression of affection in hopes she would give him the same in return.

MaLou closed her eyes tightly in a futile attempt to shut him out, but that served only to bombard her other senses with the weight of his hard-muscled body, the intoxicating taste of his kiss, and the sharply masculine scent of his skin. Overwhelmed by his presence, she finally lay relaxed in his arms and when he felt confident her response would no longer be hostile, he released his hold upon her wrists but did not end his kiss. MaLou was faced with an agonizing choice now. She knew right from wrong and this was clearly wrong: the wrong time, the wrong place, and from what Lance had insisted, the wrong man. Yet enveloped in the warmth of his embrace, she felt none of it wrong in the innocent depths of her heart. She knew better than to speak of love to him again, however, and instead raised her arms to encircle his neck as she slid her tongue between his lips to return his kiss. She felt him shudder then, as though his surrender were even more difficult than hers. She wanted to hear him talk of love in his seductive drawl, to learn the secrets of his past and share his dreams for the future. Her kiss was filled with love and his with a gentle tenderness, but while she held him tightly in her arms, she knew she had touched only his handsome body, not his well-protected heart, and that was not nearly enough. She combed his curls slowly with her fingertips as she realized she was still in control of her emotions, for surely love involved far more than merely the heated madness of desire and she wanted it all.

Lance felt the change in MaLou's mood and while her kiss was no less luscious, she had withdrawn from him in some subtle way and he wanted to know why. He kissed her one last time as his fingertips traced the smooth swell of her breast, and then he leaned back so he could study her expression. She was regarding him with such a wistful glance he knew she was near tears, and again hugging her tightly, he buried his face in her tangled curls as he tried to decide how best to apologize. Then he realized she was the one who ought to apologize to him since she had started the fight, though he doubted she would agree with that reasoning, and after giving her another sympathetic hug, he moved away from her. He leaned back against the boulder she had used for cover, bent his right knee to strike a comfortable pose, and rested his arm across it. "I came after you because I was worried about you. I don't want you to think that just because I can't let myself care for you that I don't care what happens to you."

MaLou rose up on her elbows, certain she must look like she had just been trampled by a stampede, but in no mood to worry about her appearance, she simply disregarded it. "You're making no sense at all, Garrett, as usual." He looked so remorseful she struggled to sit up and then gave him a comforting slap on the knee. "What awful thing would happen if you fell in love? I'm not saying you ought to fall in love with me, I'm just asking because I'd like to be able to understand you better."

Lance noticed his hat lying in the dirt and reached over to pick it up. He then brushed it off before slamming it down on the back of his head. "There's not enough left of me to understand, MaLou. I swear to God there isn't."

"Don't try to tell me the war left you impotent, Garrett,

because you've held me too close for me to believe that."

That MaLou would even know that word struck Lance as hilariously funny and he could not keep himself from laughing. He raised his hand, silently pleading for patience until he finally got his laughter under control. "No, there's nothing physically wrong with me. It's just that, well . . ." He seemed to be searching for the correct word for a moment and then shrugged. "It's too long a story to tell."

MaLou was not about to let him get away with that excuse. "I'm not going anywhere," she stated bluntly, "and I think you owe me the truth for a change."

"I haven't lied to you," Lance insisted, but he found the pretty blonde's disheveled appearance so disconcerting he had to look away. He had not raped her. That was something he would never do to any woman, let alone to one he cared about, but that she looked as though she had been assaulted hurt his already troubled conscience further. "I never talk about myself," he objected stubbornly.

"I could have drawn my gun and shot you instead of throwing rocks, Garrett," MaLou cautioned with a rapidly rising temper. "Don't tempt me to start putting holes in you now."

Knowing MaLou, Lance was certain she was as good a shot as he was, though he did not care to provide her with a target. "All right, but if you get bored and fall asleep, don't complain I didn't tell you my life's story."

"I won't get bored," MaLou assured him, thinking as always how much she enjoyed hearing him talk. "Were you born in Georgia?" she encouraged.

Lance nodded, then after a long pause he began to put his memories into words. "It is a beautiful state, MaLou, very lush and green, with magnificent forests and wide rivers. My family had owned the plantation where I was born for three generations and I never questioned our way of life. We owned slaves to tend the cotton just as all our neighbors did, but we never abused them. Now I think just sellin' one human being to another is abuse in itself, but the issue of slavery wasn't the only cause of the war. The needs of the people in the North and South were so different it seemed like we never agreed on anythin' and we'd be better off on our own." He hesitated, then gave her a teasing grin. "I still think that although we failed to convince the Union, they should let us go. There's a lot I could tell you about, like the fun I had growing up or about my family and friends, but it's pointless since the war changed it all."

"Tell me anyway," MaLou insisted. She crossed her legs to get comfortable, not realizing her position was totally unladylike, and swept her hair away from her eyes, obviously eager to hear whatever he wished to tell.

Lance shook his head, his expression growing stern. "No, thinking about the past only makes the present all the worse." He swallowed hard then, wishing he had not agreed to her demand. "I was eighteen when the war began. My fiancée was seventeen and her parents sent her to England thinkin' the war would last only a few months and she'd be safest livin' there with relatives."

"Your fiancée?" MaLou asked with an astonished glance. "Well, tell me a little something about her at least."

Lance responded with a disgusted sneer. "She was a pretty blonde named Madeline who loved me so desperately she promptly forgot we were engaged and married an earl who promised her not only wealth but a title as well. I have no idea whether they have a happy marriage or not, but I've always hoped she's been thoroughly miserable."

"That's all she deserves," MaLou readily agreed, hoping he did not still love the heartless bitch. How could any woman desert the man she loved when he had gone off to war? Unable to stand her curiosity, she blurted out her question. "Do you still love her? Is she the reason you can't love anyone else?"

"No, losing Madeline was very painful at the time, but now I can't even remember what she looked like," he confessed sheepishly. "That was merely the first in a long string of tragedies."

MaLou sat quietly waiting for him to continue, wondering what else had happened. "Were you ever wounded?" she prompted sympathetically.

"Not even once." The day was bright and his companion attentive, but Lance felt increasingly uncomfortable, almost as though he were suffocating, and he quickly unbuttoned several buttons on his shirt. Wanting to get his tale over with as rapidly as possible, he plunged right into the worst of it. "I saw far too many of my men killed though. My father died in a Union prison camp. My mother and younger brother burned to death when General Sherman torched our home on his cursed march to the sea. There wasn't even enough of them left to bury. I went back there only once. There wasn't a buildin' left standin' nor anythin' growin' on the land. There was nothin' but a blanket of ashes as far as the eye could see. The war might have lasted only four years, but it seemed like a hundred to me. I lost everyone and everythin' I'd ever loved and it took me a good two years to get far enough above that sorrow to laugh again. I can still remember that day. I was workin' on a ranch in Sonora and one of the other *vaqueros* was tellin' a story about this woman who—" Lance stopped abruptly then, realizing the tale was a totally inappropriate one to repeat to MaLou. She was staring at him, tears overflowing her thick lashes, and, embarrassed he had again been the cause of her anguish, he quickly looked away. "You see why I never tell that story? It doesn't lessen my pain to share it and I don't want your pity."

"Pity?" MaLou whispered hoarsely, for that was not what she felt for him at all. "It just seems like such a senseless waste, Lance, when there was no way the South could win the war. Everyone said so at the very beginning."

"If you're tryin' to make me feel better by sayin' I lost everythin' that ever mattered to me in a senseless war we were doomed to lose, I suggest you try somethin' else!" Infuriated she would be so insensitive, he rose to his feet, then leaned down to offer her his hand and hauled her up. "You look like hell," he scolded angrily as if the sorry state of her appearance were her fault rather than his.

"Lance, I . . ." MaLou reached out to touch him, sorry she had been unable to provide the comfort he obviously craved.

Lance turned away to block her caress and started down the rocky hillside. "I have water in my canteen so we can wash your face, but I don't know what we'll do about your hair."

MaLou stared after him, hurt that while she had finally convinced him to reveal something about himself his attitude toward her had remained unchanged. To add to her dismay, she had the uncomfortable suspicion that regardless of what she might have said to him he would have reacted just as badly. He had given her only a brief glimpse of what she knew must be nearly unbearable grief, but then he had again shut her out of his life. How he could do that she did not understand, for the more she knew about him the more she wanted to know. When he came back with his canteen and offered his handkerchief, she brushed by him. "I don't want to trouble you. I'll just say I fell off Flor." She turned back then. "Oh, I didn't tell you I've finally named my mare. Flor Silvestre is too long, so I'm simply calling her Flor, but you'll know exactly what I mean."

Lance watched her ride away with the same reckless haste he had witnessed earlier that morning, while her parting words continued to echo in his mind. He had tried to make her understand she was precious to him, but she had thrown his words right back in his face. *Flor silvestre* were the Spanish words for "wildflower," and had he seen one growing nearby he would have crushed it beneath his heel, though the violence of that gesture would not have made his heart feel one bit lighter.

Chapter X

Fortunately for MaLou, her father was nowhere about when she arrived home. She unsaddled Flor, brushed the mare hastily, then returned her to her stall. Walking nonchalantly rather than running to the house so as not to attract any attention to herself, she was greatly relieved to find it empty. She put water on to heat for her bath, then went into her bedroom, where one look in her mirror convinced her Lance's description of her appearance was an apt one. She did indeed look like hell and then some. Though she knew a bath, shampoo, and change of clothes would improve her looks tremendously, there was still the cut in her lip to explain. Her mouth was now so swollen she knew her father would be sure to ask what had happened to her, and despite what she had told Lance she would say, she would hardly have landed on her face had she been thrown from her horse. It was not until she had begun to bathe and lather up her gardenia-scented soap that she got the inspiration to say she had slipped while getting out of her bath and had cut herself on the edge of the copper tub. It was a plausible excuse and since she had never before lied to her father he would have no reason to doubt her word. That caused her a stab of guilt, but it was only a small one.

Even soaking in the soothing warmth of the tub, MaLou found it impossible to think of anything pleasant. She simply could not forget how greatly Lance Garrett had suffered. While his expression had been grim, he had sounded matter-of-fact as he had described the tragedies that had beset him. The Civil War had cost him the lives of his parents and only brother but a whole way of life as well. Her father had told her he had been an officer in the Confederacy, a major as she recalled, and he had been remarkably young for so much responsibility. Lance had mentioned his men too, so she knew their deaths still weighed heavily on his mind. His losses had clearly extracted not only a staggering but a lingering toll. If two years had passed before he could laugh again, how long would it take his heart to heal sufficiently to allow him to fall in love? According to Lance, the damage was irreparable, but she refused to believe that was true. She was certain someday he would fall in love again; the problem was it most likely would not be with her. That was a difficult thing to accept, but if he continued to lead such an aimless life he would move on soon and their paths might never again cross.

She sank down into the water to wash her hair, her tears mixing with the bubbles as she wished she were not so totally lacking in feminine wiles. Madeline had undoubtedly been an adorable flirt who could make men's hearts melt just by batting her eyelashes. In her opinion Lance was better off without the fickle young woman, but she believed that despite his insistence that he had forgotten her, he truly had not. He must have loved her, and dearly, to have wanted her for his wife. Maybe if Madeline had waited for him, he would have stayed in Georgia and rebuilt both his home and his life. It was ridiculous to be jealous of a woman she had never met and never would meet, but MaLou could not help but envy the young woman who had won Lance Garrett's heart since the feat had proven to be an impossible one for her.

Thomas MacDowell was a perceptive man. He paid close attention to everything that transpired on his ranch and little of importance eluded his notice. His rebellious daughter had taken to wearing dresses almost too easily, but her mood was no longer the carefree one he loved. She seemed always to be preoccupied and while he had tried to draw her out she had refused to confide in him. So he now had a daughter who dressed attractively and could entertain young men politely, but her bright sparkle had been dimmed by concerns she would not reveal and he wondered if he had made a serious mistake in trying to make a lady of her. MaLou's perplexing change in personality was not his only problem, however. Nathan was as edgy as a cat, always cussing out one man or another, and he was tired of hearing complaints from his foreman about the laziness of the hands, or from the men about Nathan's high-handed attitude. At least there had been no more trouble between Nathan and Lance, for which he was grateful, though he sensed it was still brewing. He feared the bad feelings between the two men were boiling just below the surface and would eventually erupt again in violence. When at the end of the week it came time to send more cattle up to Camp Grant, he decided to put Lance in charge to buy himself a week or so of peace, at least on one front.

Lance nodded agreeably as Thomas described the brief trip. He understood that the sale of beef to the military for the purpose of luring Chiricahuas to a peaceful way of life on a reservation was highly unpopular with most of Tucson's citizens, but he had no objection to driving the cattle to the fort. "I don't see how anyone thinks they have the right to tell you to whom you can sell your beef, sir. Just give me the directions and I'll make certain there are no problems on the way."

"I know I can count on you, Garrett. The fort's located about fifty miles northeast of here, where the Arivaipa Creek joins the San Pedro River. That's way too close to assemble a band of Apaches, according to some of our more prominent citizens, but I guess they've got a right to their opinion just as I have the right to hold mine."

"Yes, sir," Lance agreed, although he was certain a correct opinion inherently held far more value than an incorrect one.

"Cut fifty head out of the main herd and leave first thing in the morning. I'll send Manuel and three others who have all been up there before so there will be no danger of your getting lost, but I'll let them know you're the trail boss." He broke into a wide grin then. "If anyone tries to stop you, you have my permission to stampede the cattle right over them."

Lance could not help but hope someone would prove foolish enough to try to interfere with them, but he doubted the townspeople who would prefer to see the Indian starve, if not worse, had the courage to do more than merely talk tough or send irate letters to the newspaper. "I'll do that," he assured his employer with a wicked grin, welcoming the idea of the trip and hoping it would indeed prove exciting. MaLou had again retreated behind a wall of polite indifference, so their conversations the last few days had consisted of no more than an exchange of stilted greetings at breakfast. He was not pleased with that either, but not knowing how else to behave with her, he believed some time spent apart might help them both put their friendship into a better perspective. Even the word "friendship" hurt him, but he knew that was all he could ever allow to exist between them. Hoping their present conversation would provide a logical excuse for his question, he asked his boss about his daughter's morning rides. "Do you think MaLou's all right goin' off by herself the way she does? I'd hate to see someone try to influence you by harmin' her."

Startled by that possibility, Thomas needed a moment to reply. "I can see how letting her go out on her own might strike you as reckless, but she's as safe as any man on the ranch. I told you I made the mistake of raising her like a son, but at least she knows how to shoot and ride so she can take care of herself. Why, the worst thing that's happened to her lately is that she cut her lip when she slipped getting out of the bathtub. I think she's probably safer out on the range than she is at home," he confided with an amused chuckle.

Lance did not argue, but he was still worried, for he knew how MaLou had really cut her lip even if her father did not. If he could follow her, then so could Josh, or any other man who took a liking to her, but he was afraid he would not be able to convince Thomas of that danger without giving away his own guilt. After a few more minutes spent discussing the journey to Camp Grant, Lance went to the cookhouse to tell Jake to prepare enough food for them to take along. The group was too small to take a chuck wagon and cook, but he did not enjoy cooking himself and hoped one of the others would.

When she did not see Lance in the breakfast line Friday morning, MaLou panicked, terrified he had left the ranch without bothering to tell her good-bye. When she noticed several others were also missing, she quickly asked Jake where they had gone and was relieved when he mentioned Camp Grant. Her father had said he was sending more cattle to the Cavalry outpost, but he had not told her which men would be going. Had Lance assumed she had known he would be leaving and wondered why she had not told him good-bye? Damn! she swore softly to herself. He had been the one leaving so he should have been the one to come say good-bye to her. That he had not spoken more than a word in passing since the morning he had followed her to the mountains had not only confused but hurt her feelings as well. It had taken considerable restraint on her part not to go to him and tell him she thought his criticism of her remarks was totally unjustified. She knew her attempt to offer sympathy had been sincere, even if her words might have been more tactful. Now the weekend had nearly arrived and she did not see how she could possibly entertain another group of callers when she was so disgusted with Lance she could think of little else but him. The cut in her lip was almost healed, but the damage to her emotions provided a far worse scar.

Josh Spencer had not told anyone about his run-in with Lance Garrett after the dance, let alone their brief confrontation at MaLou's home, but somehow it seemed to be common knowledge that the handsome Southerner had beaten him not only at cards, but with his fists as well. Not one to take the ridicule he enjoyed heaping on others, he became all the more determined to impress MaLou favorably. He found out which men had gone to see her and decided that none offered him much in the way of competition, but since he wanted it understood that MaLou was his girl, he made it a point to tell them all so. He could not find the corporal to inform him, but he knew he would run across him sooner or later. That the pretty blonde had gone to a dance with one of her father's ranch hands was difficult to explain, but he merely laughed off the question and said that the next time she attended a party it would be with him. On Saturday morning he got cleaned up and put on a new green plaid shirt that gave his hazel eyes as emerald a cast as MaLou's, and, satisfied he looked his best, he rode over to see her.

Josh swept off his hat as he gave her a courtly bow. "Good morning, MaLou. I was planning to ride into town this morning and I thought I'd come by and see if you have some shopping to do and would like to come along." While she was dressed in her buckskins, he thought she looked so attractive he did not suggest she might like to put on a dress.

MaLou was surprised by his invitation, but she considered any distraction preferable to remaining at home when she had no hope of catching even a glimpse of Lance Garrett. She had done little all week but review their last conversation in her mind and because she was thoroughly depressed by that endless repetition, the prospect of going into town was a very tempting one. She doubted Lance could possibly return in a more considerate mood, so there was no point in staying home while she awaited his return. He certainly had not asked her not to see other men. If she was ever to have a husband it would most likely be Josh and she knew the sooner she accepted that fact the happier she would be. His smile was the charming one she had once admired, the light in his eyes sparkling with a teasing warmth, and she saw no reason not to agree. "Why yes, there are a few things I wanted to get, some tea and a couple of items of clothing if you have the time to wait while I try them on."

"I'll make the time," Josh assured her. "Do you want me to drive your buggy or will we need the buckboard?"

MaLou doubted she would ever be able to ride in the buggy without her memories of Lance betraying her feelings for him. Besides, she had no desire to repeat the scene she had played in it with Josh either. "No, I won't buy so much that we'll need either. I'll just saddle my mare and ride."

Josh was disappointed in her choice, as he had hoped for a chance to kiss her at least once and that would be damn near impossible on horseback. Thinking he might be able to make her reconsider, he apologized again for his brutish behavior. "I am truly sorry I let my emotions get so out of hand at the dance, MaLou. You needn't worry I'll be so . . . well, so impatient ever again. I can wait for you to want to kiss me." He flashed his most engaging grin then, hoping it would lessen the wait. "At least I hope I have that much patience."

His attempt at humor gave MaLou's spirits a much-needed lift, for it was a delight to have a man trying to impress her rather than having to watch each and every word she spoke in fear she would insult him. "I'm sure you do, Josh. I'll tell Dad I'll be gone for a few hours and then we can go."

Josh spoke with her father too, but all the while he kept a lookout for Lance Garrett and was glad when the man failed to appear before they left. As they rode along into town he studied MaLou's profile, finding her delicate features so pretty he could not understand why he had not noticed her long before the previous Saturday night. She had charmed him as a child, but somehow he had forgotten her and he was sincerely sorry he had made that mistake. "I want to tell you something, but you've got to promise me you won't laugh at me if I do."

MaLou was too curious to learn what he wished to

confide not to agree. "All right, I won't even smile. What is it?" She patted Flor's neck and smoothed out her mane rather than look at him, for she was afraid that despite her promise she might be so amused she would laugh anyway.

"When I joined the Army and left to fight in the war there were a lot of things I missed. I used to have such vivid dreams about my mother's cooking I'd wake up swearing I could smell it. We weren't fighting all the time, and when we weren't I used to pass the hours daydreaming about my family, my friends, and there was one pretty little girl I recalled quite fondly. Do you know who I mean?"

For some reason MaLou thought instantly of Madeline, for surely a Southern belle would smile seductively and say, "Why, Mr. Spencer, surely you don't mean little ole me?" She almost laughed out loud then, but at her ridiculous mental image rather than at what Josh had said. "I was only ten or eleven when you went off to the war, Josh," she reminded him shyly, not even tempted to flirt with him as she knew Madeline would.

"Closer to ten, I think it was, but I was just seventeen. By the time I got home I felt like I'd been away ten years at least, and I was hoping that, well . . ."

When he seemed too embarrassed to continue, MaLou prompted him a bit. "What were you hoping? I've already promised not to laugh, so you needn't worry that I will."

A sheepish smile tugged at the corner of Josh's mouth, for he was still afraid she might think him a fool. "I was hoping that you would have changed as much as I had."

"Changed?" MaLou asked with a puzzled frown. The war had certainly changed Josh. She had noticed that the first time she had seen him after he had come home. He had left Arizona a gangling youth and had returned a handsome man, making the seven-year difference in their ages seem like a chasm that could never be bridged. Now that they were nineteen and twenty-six, however, that seven-year span no longer seemed so wide.

"Well, I don't really mean changed. I guess what I mean is that I'd hoped you had grown up too," he explained hesitantly.

"You weren't gone nearly long enough for that, Josh."

She was right, of course, but still her comment was hilariously funny and Josh was the one to burst out laughing. "I'm sorry, MaLou, but I'm not the one who promised not to laugh." He kept right on laughing too, until tears filled his eyes and he had to use his shirt sleeve to wipe them away. "Yes, sir, if the war had only lasted a few more years I'd have come home and found you all grown up."

At first she was confused, then insulted, but finally MaLou saw the humor in her remark too. "I didn't mean that, Josh!" she protested with a bright blush. "The war was much too long as it was."

Josh leaned over and gave her arm a squeeze. "I know what you meant, sweetheart. I know."

MaLou felt very foolish, but somehow making a fool of herself in front of Josh was not all that bad since she had seen him doing the same thing so often of late. "Are you sure you're grown up now, Josh?" she asked impulsively.

"Yes, I sure am," Josh assured her, thinking her delightfully childlike still. "And since you are too, I think we should definitely do something about it."

Fearing he was going to propose to her right there on the road to Tucson, MaLou widened her eyes in alarm. She gripped her reins nervously, not knowing how to respond if he did. Since she could not have Lance, she supposed she ought to marry Josh, but she did not want him ever to suspect he was her second choice. Still, she doubted she could accept his proposal with the enthusiasm he deserved.

Josh saw instantly by the abrupt change in MaLou's manner that he had frightened her and he had not meant to do that. He would have to slow down even though that was the last thing he wanted to do. He was not used to having to work so hard to impress a young woman in the first place, let alone one with her charming innocence. "What I mean is I'd like to come calling and be your escort whenever there's a party. My folks are thinking of hosting one themselves next weekend and I want you and your father to come." That would be news to his parents, but it was about time they gave a party and he knew they would be happy to do it if he told them he needed their help to impress the MacDowells.

MaLou slowly began to relax as he continued to talk about coming concerts and social gatherings. That was precisely what they needed, she reasoned, time to grow close, and perhaps they would eventually fall in love. She looked toward him and smiled. "That all sounds very nice, Josh, really it does. I would have welcomed your invitations last year, or the year before too." She caught herself then, realizing that sounded as though she were criticizing him for moving too slowly when just the opposite was true. Still, if he had proposed to her when she was seventeen she would have been ecstatically happy to become his bride. Then she never would have fallen in love with Lance and that would have spared her a lot of pain.

"I'm right sorry I didn't pay more attention to you two years ago, MaLou. The time just got away from me, I guess, but I won't disappoint you again. I promise you that."

MaLou thought fate had been very cruel to make Josh fall in love with her just as another man had stolen her heart. She could not control her own emotions, let alone influence anyone else's, though. "I used to daydream a lot about you too, Josh," she confessed, but the smile that lit his face at her revelation failed to warm her heart.

At one time Lance had welcomed the drudgery of a cattle drive as the perfect release for his tortured soul, but he no longer found the mental as well as physical fatigue nearly so appealing. As trail boss he constantly circled the herd while Manuel rode point. He had assigned two men to be flank riders who rode at each side, while the fourth was a drag rider bringing up the rear. Fifty head were no challenge at all to manage and they made fifteen miles a day easily. Unfortunately, none of the men had shown any talent for cooking so they had shared the task, each thinking the others could do better. None of their meals was anywhere near as good as the ones Jake prepared.

Determined to bring the drive to a swift end, Lance kept the cattle moving at a brisk pace. They set out at dawn each morning, stopped at noon to let the herd graze while they ate, then changed horses. He rode Amigo each morning, then chose a fresh mount for the afternoon so the stallion did not become as tired as his rider. At sundown the herd was "thrown" off the trail to graze, then forced in close so they would lie down for the night. That was not the end of Lance's day, however. He took his turn at watch with the others, slowly circling the sleeping herd while he hummed or sang softly to himself. As cattle drives went, this one would be short. He had ridden on others where he had been in the saddle for eighteen hours a day for four months straight. Driving a large herd was grueling work, for the problems were constant. There were the dangers presented by the land: rivers which had to be crossed or deserts where lack of water drove man and beast alike nearly mad with thirst, uneven terrain that caused accidents to the chuck wagon or cost them good horses. Then there were the dangers caused by man, whether cattle thieves or Indians hoping to help themselves to a few head. Add to that the weather, which could be unbearably hot or so rainy the cattle were in danger of drowning, and it seemed neither an easy nor pleasant way to earn a living. That cowhands earned precious little only added to their misery, though most men who had chosen the occupation were not suited to anything else. Lance, however, was a talented man who had been born for a far better life.

The hardships of the trail did not concern him, but had the trip been longer than a week he knew he would have quit. When he had told MaLou he had no ambition to be more than he was, he had meant it and would have argued all day that he did, but now as the miles separating them grew more numerous, he became increasingly dissatisfied with his lot. Always before when he had gotten these same restless feelings of discontent they had been vague and he had cured them by moving on, but she had forced him to face the fact that he was trying to escape the demons he carried within himself, which was impossibly foolish since it could not be done. It was time to stop running, but why he had discovered that when there was no one around to tell he did not know. MaLou was the only person he knew who would care about his change of heart, and that he could not stroll up to her house after dinner to chat frustrated him no end. She had always demanded the truth from him, but finally being compelled to admit it when there was no way to do so was doubly agonizing.

"Mañana," Manuel offered encouragingly, hoping to lighten his friend's pensive frown. "Tomorrow we will be there. We have never made this trip so quickly, but you have set a brutal pace."

"Hardly brutal," Lance argued. "If the fort needs beef, they shouldn't have to wait the whole week to get it."

Manuel had watched Lance's mood go from sullen to dark to morose, and while he was certain MaLou was the cause, he thought he would keep his advice to himself for a change since his friend had always ignored it. "They have a good cook at the fort, or at least they did when last I was there."

"Well, let's hope he's not on leave," Lance joked, knowing they could all do with a good meal. He tried to keep that thought in mind as they approached the fort the following afternoon, but at the first sight of the cavalry troops' blue uniforms he felt so sick to his stomach the last thing he wanted was food.

First Lieutenant Royal E. Whitman had arrived in Arizona about the same time as Lance Garrett. A New Englander, he had served in the Union Army, rising from the rank of sergeant to that of temporary colonel during the years of the Civil War. Following its end, he had found civilian life no longer to his liking and after two years had reenlisted in the Army. A serious and responsible man, at thirty-seven he had assumed command of "H" Troop of the Third Cavalry at Camp Grant and was doing his best to run the isolated outpost efficiently.

Lance knew as Thomas MacDowell's representative he should make the effort to put forth a presentable appearance, but he cared so little what the Army thought of him he did not bother to clean up or shave. Still covered with the dust of the trail and sporting a four-day growth of beard, he introduced himself to Lieutenant Whitman and waited impatiently as the man filled out the necessary paperwork to secure payment for the cattle.

Whitman had difficulty hiding his smile, for he knew precisely what was on Lance Garrett's mind. His speech and distant manner gave him away for what he was: a Southerner who had never come to grips with surrender. "You're a long way from home, Garrett," he mused out loud.

"It's no more than fifty miles," Lance contradicted curtly.

"I wasn't referring to Tucson," the lieutenant explained without looking up.

"Well, that's my home," Lance insisted even though he felt as though he would never again have a place that held the warmth of a real home for him.

"We're no longer enemies, Garrett. Don't treat me like one."

He had not issued that as an order but in such a friendly tone Lance was instantly ashamed he had been rude. "I'll try to remember that," he offered with the beginnings of a smile.

"You'll all join us for supper, won't you?" Whitman invited graciously.

"Just give us some time to clean up."

"Take all you like. Our facilities, while spartan, are at your disposal. Please tell Mr. MacDowell his continued support of our efforts here is greatly appreciated. I know his stand is an unpopular one and I admire his courage. It's far easier for the people of Arizona to demand that the Army annihilate the Apaches than it is for them to understand President Grant's desire to bring them peacefully to reservations."

"It's far easier to be on the Indians' side from where he's sitting in Washington," Lance pointed out perceptively. "The settlers are here and they've got every reason to be afraid."

"Come take a little walk with me," Royal invited. "Have you ever met an Apache?"

Lance had had occasion to shoot at quite a few while in Mexico, for they had raided Don Ricardo's herds frequently. That could not be called a proper introduction, however. "Can't say that I have." He followed the lieutenant outside, thinking the outpost could not have occupied a more hot and barren stretch of land, but he had learned its location was perfect from a strategic point of view. It sat at the intersection of four vital routes of Indian travel. To the south the San Pedro Valley could be followed all the way to Sonora and the Apaches used it frequently to raid Mexico. Ten miles to the north lay the Gila River and the trail the Kearny Expedition had taken to California. To the east the Arivaipa Canyon cut through the Galiuro Mountains, providing access to the upper Gila and Sulphur Springs valleys. To the west, along the route Lance and his men had come, lay the thriving city of Tucson.

"General Stoneman believes the Indians can be supervised at feeding stations until permanent reservations can be established. From the success we've had here, I agree. The Chiricahuas you see living here have surrendered and in exchange we've promised to keep them supplied with rations."

As they walked about the camp, Lieutenant Whitman called out greetings by name, apparently having made it a point to know each of his charges on sight. The braves instantly impressed Lance, for they were both fit and handsome. While they were of no more than average height, they had lithe yet muscular builds with well-proportioned limbs and broad chests. Their hair brushed their shoulders, making their posture seem all the more proud. They wore only buckskin breechcloths secured at the waist by a belt and moccasins that reached nearly to their knees, but they had a quiet dignity that made their scant clothing seem more than adequate. The women wore skirts and moccasins, but their raven black hair was worn long and veiled their bare breasts so they too seemed adequately clothed. The expressions of these Chiricahuas were pleasant as they returned Whitman's greetings. They seemed a remarkably good-natured lot. The men were scattered about talking with each other while the women were all actively engaged in some useful task, whether it was weaving baskets, minding small children, or tending their cooking fires. Their tepees dotted the landscape, forming a village that appeared both contented and well ordered.

"Well, what do you think?" Whitman asked when they had returned to his headquarters. "Can these people live in peace or not?"

As they had walked through the camp, Lance had been aware of the dark eyes focused upon them. Sparkling, restless, they observed far more than the casual observer would note. "I think that's somethin' we'll need more time to tell," he replied noncommittally.

"You're a cautious man, aren't you?" Royal replied with a ready grin.

"I wouldn't be alive if I weren't."

"Well, maybe after a few more trips out here you'll be ready to offer an opinion."

Lance nodded thoughtfully, uncertain he would be in Thomas MacDowell's employ long enough to make another such trip. "Thanks for the tour." He offered his hand and smiled when Royal took it. "Now I'll go and tell the men to get ready for supper. We'll be leavin' early tomorrow mornin', so if I don't see you then I want you to know your hospitality is appreciated."

"You're welcome. I know you must be in a hurry to get home."

"Yes, we are." As Lance turned away he realized he did want to go home, but only because MaLou was there and he had missed her more than he had thought possible.

Chapter XI

Lance lunged to the side, ducking his head as he heard a rifle bullet ricochet off the rocks to his left, but before he could return the fire he was splattered with blood as Manuel, who had been riding on his right, was hit. Suddenly going as limp as a rag doll, his friend slid from his saddle, then lay still, in grave danger of being trampled to death by his own horse. "Take cover!" Lance shouted to the other three men who, stunned by the surprise attack, had drawn their horses to a halt and had become targets as tempting as sitting ducks. Lance leapt from Amigo's back, slapped Manuel's mount on the rump to send the frightened horse out of the way, then hauled the injured man away from the trail so he would not be hit again. They had expected that if there was trouble, it would overtake them while they made the journey to Camp Grant, not on the way home. They were only a few hours from the ranch now and they had all been laughing together, the men looking forward to a trip into town on Saturday night, and Lance knew that none of them had been as alert as they should have been. He blamed himself for not heading off the attack though, since he was in charge and should have anticipated trouble in time to prevent it.

The shots had come from someone lying in ambush on the bluff up ahead, but when no more rounds were fired Lance thought it likely whoever had shot at them had turned tail and run. He kept down though, in case the bastard was still lurking nearby hoping to get in another shot. Manuel's left sleeve was drenched with blood, but as he ripped away the damp cloth he was grateful to find the bullet had passed clear through his shoulder. If it had nicked the artery there would be nothing he could do to save his friend's life, but, hoping the wound was not as grave as he had at first feared, he began applying pressure. "Jaime, come here and help me!" he called to the nearest man. With his help they soon slowed the flow of blood to a mere trickle. As soon as they had bound the wound tightly with strips of cloth torn from an extra shirt, Lance left Manuel in Jaime's care. He drew his Colt and began inching his way toward the spot where he was certain the shots had come from, using what cover he could find until he had worked his way around to the rear of the rocky bluff, but it was now deserted. After climbing up to the summit, he shouted to his companions that the danger had passed. He then peered down at the trail, lining up imaginary shots from a variety of angles, but each time his conclusion was the same: he had been the intended victim rather than Manuel, but the assailant had apparently not been an expert enough shot to hit him. The first bullet had been aimed at him but had gone wide and hit the rocks to his left. The man had then over-corrected his error and his second shot had gone too far to the right and had hit Manuel. They had all scattered then and apparently the culprit had fled rather than stuck around hoping Lance would again move into his sights.

Confused by his frightening discovery, Lance sought a small patch of shade, sat down, removed his hat, and wiped his forehead on his sleeve. What had prompted someone to shoot at him? He knew he had made enemies in Tucson. There were the Hatchers to begin with, Nathan was not fond of him either, and Josh flat out hated him. It was unlikely the Hatcher brothers would have known he would be traveling that way, though, so he crossed them off the list. It was also doubtful Josh would know his schedule, but Nathan would have known he would probably be coming down that trail that day or the next and it would have been a simple matter for the foreman to sneak away and lie in wait for them. That was going to be a difficult accusation to prove, however, and since Nathan undoubtedly knew there was wide opposition to the feeding station at Camp Grant he would have plenty of townspeople to blame. The soil was too rocky and dry for him to find any tracks, and, discouraged he had found no substantial clues to the assailant's identity, Lance rejoined the others.

"Did you see him?" Jaime asked excitedly.

Lance shook his head. "No, he got away clean." He knelt down beside Manuel and, taking hold of the injured man's wrist, was encouraged by the steady beat of his pulse. "Gather what branches you can find and we'll make a *travois* like the Indians do and get Manuel home as best we can. We can't give him any more care than we already have so there's no reason to stay here any longer than we have to."

Readily complying with his order, the three men roamed about the area while he remained with Manuel, and although it took them a long while to find two branches sturdy enough to use as poles for the *travois*, they at last found them. They lashed the ends to Manuel's horse and stretched a blanket between them to form a platform upon which he could rest. They considered it a blessing that he had not regained consciousness, for they had to make the trek home at such a slow pace it would have seemed an eternity to a man writhing in agony from a gunshot wound.

It was nearly sundown on Friday when they reached the ranch and it was MaLou rather than Thomas who reached the men first. "Why didn't you send someone ahead so we could have come out to get Manuel with the buckboard?" she cried out as she knelt by the Mexican's side ready to help them carry him into the house.

"I didn't want to provide the bastard who shot him with

another target," Lance replied coldly, in no mood to hear criticism from anyone, least of all her. She looked up at him briefly, her glance as dark as his, and he realized with a shudder of dread that MaLou went riding alone every day and it was just possible she might have been the one who had tried to kill him. Her reason was as good as anyone else's for wanting him dead, but that she could hate him so intensely caught him by surprise. He heard her calling his name, but it took him a moment to respond.

"Lance? Are you all right?" MaLou asked again, thinking he looked far from well. "There's blood all over your shirt. Is it Manuel's or yours?"

She rose and reached out toward him, but Lance recoiled instantly and stepped aside. "It's all his. Are you sure you don't want him in the bunkhouse?" he asked to distract her.

MaLou had not dreamed he would find her touch so objectionable, but Manuel's health was her chief concern now. She did not tell Lance what she thought of him for leaving without saying good-bye and greeting her so coldly upon his return. "We've a spare bedroom. Carry him in there," she directed the others before running ahead to hold open the door.

Thomas MacDowell came out to join them then and hastily dispatched a man to bring a doctor from town. Manuel was not only a good worker but such a friendly soul he was one of his favorite ranch hands, and he, just like his daughter, wanted him to have the best of care. When they had laid Manuel on the bed in the bedroom that had once been his wife's, he made certain the man was breathing easily, then sent away everyone but Lance.

"Tell me what happened. If you have any idea who did this I'll see he's arrested tonight."

"Help me undress him while you talk," MaLou requested matter-of-factly. "Manuel will be far more comfortable without his clothes."

Complying with his daughter's request, Thomas reached for the Mexican's boots and yanked them off.

"Well, Garrett, what do you think? Do you know who did it?"

Lance could not believe the man was going to allow his daughter to undress Manuel, but when she reached for the unconscious man's belt buckle Thomas merely grabbed his cuffs and got ready to remove his pants. "I couldn't track him, or her," he added for MaLou's benefit, "but whoever it was was gunning for me and Manuel just happened to be in the way."

"You're sure about that?" Thomas asked skeptically.

"Yes, sir, I am," Lance insisted, then explained why the angle of the shots had convinced him of it. "I can't very well go around accusing people when I have no proof of their guilt, but there aren't many who knew where I was going and when I'd be coming back." Much to his dismay, MaLou and her father nonchalantly continued to remove Manuel's clothing until they had stripped him naked. They then covered him with a blue and white quilt as though they had often shared the same chore, and for all he knew they had.

Thomas walked around from the foot of the bed to touch the injured man's forehead and seemed pleased when he found it cool. "Everyone here knew where you were and you know you're not real popular with some folks."

"Yes, sir, I know that." Lance kept his eyes on MaLou, but his heart fell when her expression filled with fright. "What's the matter, MaLou?" he asked pointedly. "You look more upset than I do about the fact that someone tried to kill me today."

MaLou smoothed out the quilt over Manuel's thighs as she searched her mind for a lucid reply to his comment. When she found none, she told him the truth. "Josh wanted to buy back his ring. I told him you probably wouldn't be back until tonight or tomorrow, but I just can't believe he'd try anything so desperate as murder just to get even with you."

"Do you know where he was around noon?" Lance inquired calmly, wondering why MaLou would defend the young man so staunchly.

The pretty blonde shook her head. "No, I haven't seen him today. They're having a barbecue at his ranch tomorrow and he told me he'd be busy getting ready for it."

"That ought to be easy enough to prove," Thomas murmured with a distracted frown, "although I don't relish the thought of asking him to provide an alibi."

"What about Nathan?" MaLou suggested anxiously. "I didn't see him at lunch, did you?"

Thomas shook his head. "No, baby, I didn't, but I warned him if anything happened to Garrett it would mean his job and I know he believed me."

Lance continued to observe MaLou, for her expression mirrored his own doubt and confusion. He could not help but wonder what she would do if he went after Josh. Was she protecting him because she had decided she did love him after all, or because she knew Josh could not possibly have fired the shots because she had?

Thomas shivered. The bedroom in which they stood had not been used in years, and although Lily was not dead, he felt as though her ghost were looking over his shoulder. "There's still a good possibility this had nothing to do with you personally, Garrett, even if they did aim for you. The shooting could simply have been a warning not to send any more beef to Camp Grant. Before we go around accusing anyone of attempted murder, I think we ought to give that angle more serious thought."

"I wouldn't make an accusation I couldn't prove," Lance assured him.

"I know you wouldn't." Recalling their earlier conversation about MaLou's safety, Thomas had to admit Lance had been right. He turned to his daughter and gave her a firm order. "I don't want you out riding alone until this matter is cleared up, MaLou. If you want to go riding with Josh, that's fine; if not, then take Garrett here with you."

Lance opened his mouth to point out that if someone was gunning for him he was the last person who ought to accompany her, yet if it had been MaLou who had tried to kill him, she could not make a second attempt while everyone knew they were together. Since he could not decide which of them would be in the most danger, he kept quiet, but he thought the situation ironic in the extreme.

"But, Dad—" MaLou began to argue, seeing that Lance appeared no more pleased than she was about his edict.

Thomas raised his hand to silence her. "Not another word, MaLou. I don't want you leaving the house unless either Josh or Garrett is with you. That someone took a shot at him isn't the only reason. We've had cattle missing more than once lately and I don't think they're just strays we'll eventually round up."

"You think someone's rustling our stock?" MaLou asked in dismay. "Why didn't you tell me about this?"

"Because I didn't want to worry you. Nathan's been doing his best to keep it quiet at the same time he's trying to gather clues. I'm sure if we asked him where he was today he'd say he'd been trying to track the rustlers."

"And we couldn't prove that he wasn't," Lance pointed out with a sigh of regret. He was tired and dirty and the sight of the one true friend he had made there at the MacDowell ranch lying on the bed deathly pale did not help his mood any. This was not the first time he had been covered in another man's blood and he could not wait to get out of his badly stained clothes. "I want to wash up, then I'd like to come back when the doctor gets here. If he thinks someone ought to stay up with Manuel tonight, then I'll do it."

Even though she had told herself constantly that her situation was hopeless, MaLou had been looking forward to seeing Lance again, and that his homecoming had proven to be such a shocking one had only added to her depression. She had wanted him to shout her name and gather her up in his arms with a loving hug, though he obviously had no intention of doing that, ever. "Of course, we can take turns if you like."

"If you're going to Josh's barbecue tomorrow, you don't want to be up all night," Lance reminded her.

How he had managed to make such a considerate

remark sound insulting MaLou did not know, but rather than argue she showed him to the door. "Do you really think a woman might have shot Manuel?" she asked as he stepped out onto the porch.

"Yes, ma'am, I think it's a good possibility," Lance replied without hesitation.

"But who?" Then she realized from the darkness of his gaze he had meant her. "Oh no, you couldn't think that I'd do such an awful thing. You just couldn't believe that."

Since she had decided to confront the issue he saw no reason to back down. "You had the opportunity and a damn good motive, MaLou. Just where were you at noon?"

"But you heard my father and me talking about it! I was in the cookhouse helping Jake serve lunch. Everyone saw me, so if you expect me to provide witnesses I have plenty of them."

"Good for you." Lance turned away and walked toward the bunkhouse wondering why he had been so anxious to see her when all they ever did was argue.

MaLou did not know which was worse, that someone had tried to kill Lance, or that he had thought that someone had been her. His suspicion was so totally unjustified she sat in a stunned silence until the doctor appeared. His name was Sean O'Reilly and he was the nephew of the doctor who had brought her into the world. He had been out of medical school a scant two years, but he had had plenty of experience with gunshot wounds since he had gone into practice with his uncle. He explained that the prompt attention Manuel had received had undoubtedly saved his life. He stitched up the two wounds in his shoulder and assured them the feisty Mexican would awaken soon.

"Make sure he takes plenty of fluids and keep him in bed until he can get up and walk around on his own without getting so dizzy he'll risk a concussion if he falls. I'd hate to see him trade one injury for another. Besides, if he gets too rambunctious he'll rip out his stitches and I charge double every time I have to do my work twice," he teased with a broad grin.

Lance thought the red-haired man's sense of humor probably saw him through a great many trying situations, but he found it difficult to laugh with him. "I'll be happy to cover your bill," he offered as the young man packed up his bag.

"You'll do no such thing," Thomas insisted. "Manuel works for me and I'll take care of all his expenses."

"You've still got my money in your safe, sir. I don't mind using it to pay Dr. O'Reilly."

"That's enough, Garrett. The expenses are rightfully mine and I don't want any more argument about it."

Lance shrugged, understanding his boss's point, but he had no use for the money and thought Manuel's medical expenses a worthy cause. When the doctor bid them good night, Lance again volunteered to sit with his friend. "I'd like to stay here with him if you don't mind."

MaLou reflected that while her father had no objection to his offer, she most certainly did. "You've been riding all day and you'll never stay awake. Dad and I can take turns and keep an eye on him by ourselves."

"No, I want to stay," Lance insisted in a slightly louder tone. "If you won't let me pay the doctor's bill, at least let me do this for him."

While his request was a generous one, Thomas could not agree. "MaLou's right, Garrett. You'll be in worse shape than Manuel is if you don't get some sleep. Go on to bed and you can keep him company tomorrow while we go to the barbecue. Come over right after breakfast and that way whichever one of us takes the last shift can get a nap before we leave."

Lance shifted his weight apprehensively, not wanting to leave his friend even though he was certain the MacDowells would take good care of him. "All right," he reluctantly agreed. "I'll see you after breakfast then. Good night."

MaLou did not dare turn to watch him go, for she knew the hunger in her eyes would spark her father's curiosity and she had no wish to arouse his suspicions where Lance was concerned. "Why don't you take the first shift, Dad? Then I'll take the last. I'll go to bed right now and then relieve you at two."

Thomas agreed, thinking she ought to be the one to take a nap before they left for the party at the Spencers'. He pulled a chair up to the bedside and made himself comfortable. "Just put the coffee pot on to boil and bring me the paper before you go to bed and I'll be fine."

MaLou kissed her father good night, then filled his requests before she went to bed, but she found it impossible to fall asleep when she could not forget Lance's bitter accusation. She had proof aplenty that she had not been the one to shoot at him, but if she had wanted him dead, she would not have missed. Chilled by that thought, she snuggled down in her covers and at long last drifted off to a troubled sleep.

The next morning Lance finished his breakfast quickly and walked over to the MacDowells' house. He knocked softly at the door, then, thinking they might both be in the bedroom with Manuel and unable to hear him, he tried the doorknob. Finding it unlocked, he let himself in. The house still held the chill of the night air, although the sun was up, and he moved quietly through the parlor and down the hall to the bedroom where his friend lay.

MaLou had been sitting close to the bed, then unable to stay awake she had rested her arms on the side and propped her cheek upon them, thinking that if Manuel stirred, she would instantly awaken. She was clad in a white flannel nightgown, the high ruffled neckline, long sleeves, and floor-length hem of which covered her lovely figure completely.

Lance had not expected to find her either asleep or in such a graceful pose and he remained leaning against the doorjamb while he tried to decide what to do. Her hair lay spilled over the bed and it took him a full minute to notice that Manuel was awake and slowly sifting the end of a soft blond curl through his fingertips.

"Cómo estás?" Lance called softly as he approached the bed.

Manuel smiled slightly as he opened his eyes. "Don't wake her," he pleaded in a hoarse whisper, "for I'll never have another chance to hold her in my arms."

Touched by Manuel's poignant request, for it was unlikely he would ever hold her again either, Lance turned away to pull up another straight-backed chair and sat down on the opposite side of the bed. "She makes a poor nurse," he responded with a smile, glad to see his friend was at least feeling well enough to enjoy the company of a pretty woman.

Manuel still looked pale and weak, but he had his usual spirit. "No, *amigo,* she is a very good one since she is so pretty to look at."

"She is that," Lance agreed. MaLou's expression was so sweet he was dreadfully sorry he had given voice to his suspicions. He had been tired and so worried about Manuel he had not been thinking all that clearly or he would have considered the fact that she had far too much courage to shoot someone from ambush. That still left Josh and Nathan as suspects. For a long while they sat in companionable silence. Manuel was obviously enjoying MaLou's company, but Lance found it impossible to look at her without a confusing mixture of anger and desire, which was too painful to continue. Rising slowly to his feet, he walked around to her side of the bed. "I think I should carry her into her room."

"If you must," Manuel agreed philosophically, giving her curls a final pat.

MaLou sighed softly as Lance gathered her up in his arms, but she did not awaken as he carried her down the hall. He was not certain which room was hers, but finding the door ajar at the one to his right he peered inside. Her buckskins were tossed over a chair and the covers on the brass bed turned back so he was certain that was where she belonged and he carried her through the door. He doubted she weighed more than a hundred pounds and she fit so snuggly in his arms he stood for a moment, just holding her and enjoying the soft scent of gardenias that clung to her flowing curls. Then remembering that her father was likely to come walking down the hall at any minute, he leaned down to lay her on the bed, carefully pulled the covers up to her chin, then tucked her in. He could not resist the impulse to kiss her and brushed her lips lightly with his own, but as he started to straighten up her eyes fluttered open momentarily and she spoke to him.

"Oh, it's you, Lance," she murmured with a contented sigh and as she fell back to sleep a blissful smile graced her lips as she whispered, "I love you."

Lance stood frozen in place, not knowing whether she had been awake or asleep when she had spoken, but, as before, her words filled him with nearly unbearable sorrow. When he was certain she was fast asleep he bent down again to kiss her tangled curls and whispered the reply he truly wanted to speak out loud but could not. "I love you too."

When MaLou awakened two hours later she was embarrassed to find herself in her own bed but assumed her father had carried her back to her room when he had come to relieve her. She yawned as she stretched languidly, then, concerned about how Manuel had fared, she got up and brushed out her hair. She planned to bathe and dress nicely for the Spencers' party but donned her buckskins now to visit their patient. When she saw Lance talking quietly with Manuel she was delighted to find him awake. "How are you feeling?" she asked cheerfully as she entered the bedroom.

"I'm fine, thank you." Rocking back in his chair, Lance responded to her greeting with a cocky grin.

"I was speaking to Manuel," MaLou corrected him. "Not that I'm not pleased to hear you're well too, but it's Manuel I'm most worried about." She stepped between the two men so she would not have to face Lance while they talked. She enjoyed his teasing no more than his aloof disdain.

While he knew the pretty blonde did not realize it, Manuel saw a great deal in the brief glance she and Lance had exchanged. Their affection for each other was obvious and he could not understand why each of them fought it with such vigor. Had she cared for him, he would have enjoyed her love to the fullest. But, alas, he knew that unlike Lance, he would never win the heart of a young woman like MaLou MacDowell. "I am so grateful to be alive I will not complain about how I feel," he replied in answer to her question, but it was plain he felt far from well.

MaLou touched his cheek and was glad it was still cool. Like most of the men, he did not bother to shave often, but he had such a light beard it mattered little. "Have you had something to eat?"

"*Sí,* Jake sent over some breakfast."

"We have several novels you might enjoy reading, or listening to Lance read if you like. They're in the bookcase in the parlor."

"I am fine," Manuel insisted shyly, not wanting to be a burden either to the pretty girl or his friend.

"He's been tryin' to talk me into helpin' him walk over to the bunkhouse," Lance confided.

"What? Well don't you dare take him over there." MaLou turned to face Lance briefly as she gave that order, but she could tell by his sly smile that he had no intention of letting Manuel out of bed and relaxed. "Garrett has a lot more sense than you do, Manuel," she scolded the injured man. "The bunkhouse is far too rowdy a place for you to be, so just forget the idea of going back there until you're well. Jake can send over your meals and we'll take turns keeping an eye on you so you don't grow bored. Now if there is anything you need, anything at all, just let us know."

Manuel nodded slightly. "*Sí, señorita,* I will."

MaLou leaned down to kiss his cheek lightly. "I really am glad you're doing so well and I'll come back to check on you later." She was surprised to see him blush, for she had not thought her kindness would embarrass him so, but rather than prolong his discomfort she left the room and went to heat the water for her bath. Having the two men in the house would make things difficult if she wasn't careful, but she regarded Manuel as a friend even if Lance was not. When she and her father were ready to leave for the barbecue, she stopped by to tell Manuel good-bye and found Lance reading to him.

"I won't interrupt the story. I just wanted to let you know we're leaving."

Lance turned the book over on his lap to keep his place as he looked up at her. She was wearing a lavender print dress trimmed at the bodice with white eyelet and purple ribbons, which complemented her fair beauty and slender figure to perfection. It looked brand new and he wondered when she had bought it. That she would be with Josh rather than him for the rest of the day was almost more than he could bear, but he tried to be gracious about it. "You needn't rush home. We'll be fine," he assured her, but he failed to keep the mocking tone out of his voice.

MaLou stared down at him, not understanding why he would be so sarcastic, but unwilling to allow him to insult her again, she quickly patted Manuel's hand and left the room. Her father planned to drive their buggy to the Spencers' ranch, but he had told her he would be happy to let Josh drive it home. Because she did not want to disappoint him by refusing even to consider that option, she decided to wait and see how the evening turned out before she worried about who would drive the buggy home. "Thanks for carrying me back to bed this morning. I tried to stay awake, but I guess I didn't make it."

Thomas gave his daughter a skeptical glance. "I didn't carry you anywhere, baby. When I got up you were already back in bed and Garrett was helping Manuel eat some breakfast. Do you suppose he did it?"

MaLou's cheeks flooded with a bright blush at the thought. "I sure hope not. I was probably just so tired I don't remember going back to bed."

"Well, as soon as we get home I'll be sure to tell him to stay out of your room. I'm going to put a stop to that right now, no matter what his excuse was."

Horribly embarrassed, MaLou objected strenuously. "No, please don't say anything to him. I must have been half asleep and took my own self back to bed. If you mention it, he'll think I'm accusing him of something that never happened and I don't want to look like a fool."

"Neither do I, baby, but we can't have Garrett or any of the other hands strolling in and out of your bedroom. How would that look to Josh?"

"Josh will never hear about it in the first place, so let's not borrow trouble worrying about what he'll think. Now tell me when you first suspected someone was rustling cattle." MaLou slipped her arm through his and kept their conversation focused on the ranch for the rest of the ride to the Spencers'. She was certain in her own mind Lance had carried her back to bed and she wished she had not been sound asleep so she could have enjoyed it.

Knowing what MaLou planned to wear, Josh had put on a pale blue shirt, hoping the colors of their clothes would blend handsomely. He liked to wear pastel colors, since they made his tan seem darker at the same time his hair looked all the more blond. He felt as though he had greeted half the population of Tucson before he finally saw the MacDowells' buggy pulling up in front of the house. "I was beginning to worry something might have happened over at your place," he teased as he helped MaLou climb out of the shiny conveyance.

"Something sure as hell did," Thomas blurted out as he handed the reins to the Mexican lad who was watching the horses during the party. Like MaLou, he could not believe Josh had had anything to do with the incident and saw no reason not to describe what had happened.

Josh frowned deeply, appalled when he had heard the whole story. "I warned MaLou something like this was bound to happen if you kept on sending beef to Camp Grant. Better keep real quiet about that while you're here today because most of our guests agree with me rather than you."

MaLou studied Josh closely as he and her father continued to talk about the ambush, but she could not detect even the slightest trace of guilt either in his expression or manner. He seemed as shocked by what had happened to Manuel as they had been, but when they were alone together later in the evening, she brought up the subject again. "In spite of what my father told you, there's a possibility the men returning from Camp Grant weren't ambushed by someone who wants to discourage the sale of cattle to the Army."

They had spent a relaxing afternoon, talking with friends, listening to the joyous music of the *mariachis* his father had hired, and finally sharing one of the best barbecued-beef dinners he had ever eaten. Josh had considered his efforts to entertain MaLou a wonderful success and he wanted to talk about their future rather than anything else. That was why he had invited her to take a stroll through his mother's garden. They were already holding hands and he stopped walking and pulled her around to face him. "Who else would have had a reason to shoot at them, MaLou?" he asked with scant interest, hoping only to hurriedly advance the conversation to far more personal topics.

The sun had set, but the evening was still warm and the roses that surrounded them fragrant. Despite the romantic nature of the setting, MaLou wanted to hold a serious discussion. "Lance thinks it was someone trying to kill him. I know you don't like him, but—"

Instantly Josh took offense. "Hold on a minute, MaLou. You don't think I had anything to do with this, do you?"

MaLou swallowed hard, fearing she was making as big a mess of things with him as she always did with Lance. "No, I don't, but if something were to happen to Lance, your name would be one of the first ones mentioned."

The sparkling light of the stars danced brightly in her eyes, making their marvelous clear green shimmer seductively, but he still did not understand her point.

"Just who are you worried about, MaLou, him or me?"

"I don't want anything bad to happen to either of you, Josh," she assured him sweetly, not realizing her reply told him nothing he wanted to hear.

"I don't want to talk about Lance Garrett or ambushes or anything else. All I want to talk about is you and me," he confessed in a breathless rush.

MaLou knew what was coming and the only way she could think to stop him from proposing was to lift her lips to his. "Let's not talk," she whispered softly and he kissed her with such wild enthusiasm she was afraid he had misunderstood her desperate invitation for passion. As before, his bruising kiss simply frightened her and she struggled to break free.

"Damn it all, MaLou! What's gotten into you now?" Josh complained bitterly.

"Nothing, but can't you . . . well, can't you kiss me just a little bit more lightly?"

Josh sighed impatiently, for he wanted to show her how much he cared for her and he did not think the shy, soft kisses she apparently wanted were any measure of his love. He took a deep breath and then tried again. "Like this?" he asked.

As his lips met hers MaLou tried to enjoy their touch, but she was so dreadfully nervous she felt as though her insides had been tied in knots. She liked Josh, truly she did, but she did not love him and it pained her conscience terribly to mislead him about her feelings. That she might have to live out the same wretched pretense for the rest of her life brought tears to her eyes, for she knew she would never be able to do it. "Josh," she whispered as she tried to draw away.

In no mood to stop now, Josh cradled her face tenderly between his hands, and when she opened her mouth to protest he slid his tongue between her lips for a slow, sweet kiss he did not end until finally he felt her relax against him. He lowered his hands to her waist then and hugged her tightly. "You see, I can be as gentle as you want, honey."

MaLou pressed her face to his shoulder, thinking this was the worst torture she would ever have to endure. Recognizing the lively strains of a dance tune, she stepped back and reached for his hand. "Let's go back to the party. I'd like to dance, wouldn't you?" she asked as she began to pull him along toward the music.

Josh shook his head, sorry she had not wanted to kiss him more than once. She had kissed him though, and grateful for that small surrender, he broke into a wide grin and agreed. "Only if I can dance with you."

MaLou laughed impishly, delighted he had not gotten mad or argued, and they spent the rest of the evening dancing until the *mariachis* were so tired they could not play another note.

Chapter XII

By the time MaLou was ready to leave the Spencers' party, her father was so tired of being accused of siding with the Apaches rather than his own kind he was in no mood to let Josh drive his daughter home. He grabbed her hand, helped her up into their buggy, and with no more than a wave to their hosts drove off. While she knew they had both had a difficult time of it, if for two entirely different reasons, MaLou had no more interest in reviewing the evening than he did and respected his silence by keeping her own. When they arrived home she entered the house while her father drove Buck around to the barn. As she passed by the spare bedroom, she paused a moment before knocking at the door, but hearing low chuckles she was too curious not to peer inside.

It was impossible to tell which of them was more drunk, but both Lance and Manuel returned her inquisitive glance with sheepish grins. Looking very much like small boys who had been caught in some devilish mischief, they abruptly ended their conversation as she entered the room. Feeling he owed her an explanation, Lance struggled to his feet and immediately began one. "Manuel's shoulder was hurtin' him so much I knew we had to give him somethin' for the pain and whiskey was all we had."

Since Manuel was obviously feeling no pain now, MaLou chided them both. "A drink or two for medicinal purposes is reasonable, of course, but what's your excuse,

Garrett? Were you in pain too?"

"No, ma'am," he assured her with a wicked grin. "I was feelin' fine and I still am."

"I can see that. Do you need anything, Manuel?" MaLou inquired sweetly, her far more pleasant tone of voice in sharp contrast to the one she had used with Lance.

"No, *señorita*. Good night."

"Good night." MaLou gave Lance a firm order as she turned to go. "He'll be all right alone tonight, Garrett, so you can go on back to the bunkhouse where you belong."

Lance left the nearly empty quart bottle of whiskey on the table beside the bed so Manuel could reach it himself if he needed another drink later. *"Hasta mañana,"* he called softly to his friend before following MaLou out into the hall. "How was the party?" he asked in a teasing drawl.

"Marvelous," MaLou replied flippantly. "It was one of the best I've ever attended."

So she would not escape him until he was ready to let her go, Lance reached out to rest his left hand against the wall and his arm effectively blocked the way to her bedroom. "Did you remember my warning not to go off alone with Josh?"

That she had not even recalled his advice, let alone followed it, startled MaLou, but she told him the truth. "Josh can be very charming when he wants to be and I wasn't afraid to go for a walk with him."

The light in the hallway was dim and Lance's vision not all that clear, but he could see that MaLou's hairstyle and appearance were as neat and proper as when she had told him good-bye. If Josh had again tried to have his way with her, she had obviously survived the encounter quite well. He had not wanted to see her embarrassed or hurt, but that she would regard him with such a coolly superior attitude annoyed him no end. "So I belong in the bunkhouse, do I?" he inquired in an abrasive snarl. "I thought you expected better from me."

"It doesn't matter what I expect, Garrett. You're the one who has to live your life, so the choices are all yours." Infuriated he would be so obnoxious, MaLou retorted with a tone as sarcastic as his. The fact that even drunk she found him so irresistibly appealing she longed to throw herself into his arms only served to enflame her temper several more degrees. Recalling how he had reacted the last time she had tried to touch him, however, she kept her hands clenched tightly at her sides.

The word "choices" struck an oddly discordant tone in Lance's numbed mind. Had he ever had any real choices to make or had he always done what he had to do without questioning the cost to himself? Thinking the choice now was an easy one, he reached for the wall with his right hand, deftly capturing MaLou between his outstretched arms. He leaned down and kissed her lightly upon the temple, then trailed tender kisses across the soft curve of her cheek to her mouth. Her lips were set in a furious pout that begged him for teasing nibbles.

His abrupt change in mood had caught her by surprise, but MaLou stood rigid in his embrace for only an instant before slipping her arms around his waist and drawing him close. She then returned his playful kisses with a desperate abandon that both shocked and thrilled him, but before he could even begin to respond with the lavish affection he wished to show her they heard the front door close and she pushed him away with a frantic shove.

"You're drunk, Garrett," she whispered angrily, as though she had just discovered that fact. "Get on out of here before my dad has time to notice. Well, go on, get!" MaLou ordered emphatically.

Lance heard Thomas's footsteps as he moved through the parlor and knew he would be upon them in the next instant, but he could not seem to make his own feet move. He could do no more than stare down at MaLou wondering why she had kissed him as though they would swiftly be parted for all eternity. He shook his head hoping to clear it, but when he opened his eyes she was gone.

Mistakenly believing Lance had just closed the door of the spare bedroom, Thomas slapped him on the back as he brushed by him. "'Night, Garrett. I'll look in on Manuel later."

"'Night, sir," Lance called out after him, but it took all his willpower to leave by the front door rather than follow MaLou into her bedroom to finish what she had begun. He might have had far too much to drink, but the invitation in her kiss had been unmistakable. Still, he could not spend the night in her bed and not expect her daddy to greet him with a shotgun and a preacher at dawn, and MaLou deserved a lot nicer wedding than that. He chuckled as he tripped going up the bunkhouse steps and collapsing across his bunk fell fast asleep still fully clothed.

MaLou, however, had not even begun to undress. She might have kept Josh from proposing that night, but what could she do if he asked her to marry him the next afternoon? She could not ask him to give her a year or two to consider it, but clearly it was going to take Lance Garrett at least that long to make up his mind. Why had he kissed her again, if, as he had said, there could never be anything between them? Had he just wanted his kiss to be the last she tasted before she went to sleep or had he been so drunk he would have kissed any woman who happened by? Afraid that was the truth, she finally began to undress, but the sight of her elegant new lingerie only served to make the sweetness of Lance's kisses that much more impossible to forget.

Sunday afternoon Josh arrived to find Corporal Andy Anderson seated with MaLou on the front porch. They were laughing together as he rode up and as he tied his horse's reins to the porch rail he was disgusted he could think of no clever way to quickly get rid of the man. He mounted the steps two at a time, crossed the porch, then bent down to give MaLou a hug and a kiss. "Thanks again for last night," he remarked with a teasing wink, hoping the corporal's imagination would supply the erotic details he could not.

Since MaLou understood precisely what Josh was attempting to do, she gave Andy's knee a comforting pat.

"Don't pay any attention to Josh. He's just trying to make you jealous."

"Which he has every reason to be!" Josh exclaimed with a ready chuckle. He sat down close to MaLou, then rested his arm protectively upon the back of her chair.

While Josh continued to laugh and tease, MaLou found his brazen effort to show Andy she was a piece of property he had staked out as his own totally ridiculous. She sat forward to keep her shoulders from brushing against his arm, but although she reassured Andy often by both her words and glance that she enjoyed his company, she could tell the impression Josh was making was the far stronger one. When Lance suddenly strode up to the porch, she had to shade her eyes with her hand to see his face, for he had his back to the sun. After her initial delighted surprise, she was sadly disappointed to realize he had not come to see her.

"Are you looking for me, Josh?" Lance called out in a challenging tone.

Andy took in Josh's astonished expression, then Lance's menacing stance, and fearing he was about to be caught in the middle of a fistfight if not far worse, he leapt to his feet. "I think I ought to be going now, Miss MacDowell. I forgot to check the duty roster this morning and I don't want to end up in the stockade if my name is on it."

MaLou rose with him, sorry Josh and Lance had frightened him away when he was a sweet boy whose company she truly enjoyed. Besides that, with him present she would not have to be alone with either of the other two men. "I'm sorry you have to go, Andy." She sighed regretfully, wishing she could escape as easily as he what was surely to be an unfortunate scene.

Lance waited until the overly anxious corporal had mounted his horse and turned toward the road before he repeated his question. "Well, Josh? If you wanted to see me, here I am."

Josh rocked back in his chair, bringing it precariously close to toppling over as he replied. "Yeah, I've been looking for you. I want to buy back my ring and I've brought the money."

Lance stood with his thumbs hooked in his gun belt, his feet apart to provide the balance a gunfighter needs. "The price is six hundred dollars," he informed him coolly.

Astounded, Josh brought his chair down on all four legs with a loud clatter. "Six hundred? But I only lost five to you!"

"Next week it will be six-fifty. Better buy it back now."

Josh looked to MaLou for some help but found her frown as deep as his own and twice as noncommittal. "I only brought the five with me," he explained, hoping he could charm Lance into being more reasonable.

Lance turned away, as though he saw no reason to continue their discussion. "Look for me when you get back with the rest."

"Wait a minute!" Infuriated by the cowhand's belligerent attitude, Josh turned his back toward him as he spoke with MaLou. "Lend me the money, honey. You know I'm good for it."

"Sorry, Josh, but I haven't got a hundred dollars," MaLou responded truthfully.

"Well, your father must!" Josh argued. "Go get it from him. You know he'll lend it to me."

That much MaLou did know. Her father was so partial to Josh he thought the young man could do no wrong. "I think you'd better talk with him yourself because it won't look right if I'm the one borrowing the money when you're the one who needs it."

Exasperated that he had to borrow money to buy back a ring he ought not to have wagered in the first place, Josh yanked open the front door of her house and called out her father's name as he stepped inside.

Afraid Lance had only just begun toying with Josh, MaLou hurried down the steps and rushed toward him. "We told Josh about what happened to Manuel and he assured us he had nothing to do with it."

Disgusted she would be so gullible, Lance whispered a rebuke. "What did you expect him to do, confess?"

Lance's threatening glance made him look not only

hard, but mean as well, and MaLou marveled at the memory of his gentle kisses, for surely this defiant stranger could never display such tenderness. He had obviously come looking for a fight and she had no desire to witness another brutal exchange of blows between them, although she realized Josh was always on the receiving end. "No, I didn't expect him to confess! Don't be absurd. But if he had done it I'm sure he'd have given himself away somehow. He's not all that clever, you know."

"Yes, I know that, but I didn't think you'd noticed," Lance teased, the faintest trace of a smile curving across his lips.

"Must you be such an insufferable bully?"

"If you don't like the way I'm handling this, then go on back in the house and stay out of it, MaLou."

"I will not! You think I'm going to let you beat him up again?" The feisty blonde put her hands on her hips as she stepped in front of him. "When he hands you the money, just take it and go."

"You mean this is good-bye?" Lance asked melodramatically. "I hadn't planned on leavin' your ranch just yet."

"Damn you, Garrett!" MaLou screamed as she lost all patience with him.

Josh did not just leave the house. He slammed the front door shut so hard it nearly splintered. He did not like seeing MaLou with Lance Garrett again. For some strange reason the fact that they were having such a heated argument bothered him as greatly as if he had caught them kissing. He wanted to be alone with MaLou and since the corporal had left he wanted to get rid of Lance in a hurry too. He walked up to him and handed over the money. "You needn't count it. It's all there," he assured him confidently.

Ignoring his boast, Lance counted the worn bills slowly, tugging on each one as though he wanted to make certain it was genuine. When he was satisfied Josh had indeed given him six hundred dollars, he removed the young man's gold ring from his finger and dropped it into his outstretched hand. "There you are. Maybe wearin' it will remind you not to bet more than you have ever again."

Insulted that he would dare to offer him advice, Josh slipped the ring on quickly, wondering how deep a gash it would make in Lance's cheek if he were to double up his fist and hit him as hard as he could. That thought was so tempting he could barely contain it. "I had nothing to do with the shooting, Garrett. I hadn't hoped to pull this ring off a dead man."

Lance was surprised Josh had had the courage to mention the ambush to him and decided that MaLou might be right about his innocence. "That's a real comfortin' thought, Josh. Let's just hope nobody's plannin' to take it off you that way either."

Stepping back slightly, Josh put his arm around MaLou's waist and pulled her close to his side. The arrogant Southerner was as difficult to beat with words as he was with fists, but Josh vowed that someday soon he would get the better of him. "Let's go for a little walk, honey, so Garrett can get back to work."

While he did not enjoy being dismissed as though he were a lowly servant, Lance stepped aside. He touched the brim of his hat in a jaunty salute, then winked at MaLou, knowing by the brightness of her blush she had remembered he had warned her not to go off alone with Josh, but she sauntered right by him as though the blond man were the most well-behaved escort she could ever hope to have.

As soon as they were out of earshot, Josh began a vigorous campaign to have Lance fired. "I don't like that man, MaLou. Your father may have hired him because he's good with a gun, but his kind are far too dangerous to have around."

"Only in your opinion," MaLou chided. "My father would see right through any objections you have to the man, so don't bother to speak to him about Lance. You'd just be wasting your breath. Besides, whether it's rustlers we're up against or townspeople who want us to stop sending cattle to Camp Grant, a dangerous man who knows how to shoot is exactly what we need to protect ourselves." The clever blonde was amazed at how practical she had made Lance's presence sound when her reasons for wanting him nearby were all purely emotional in nature.

Josh fumed silently, knowing that what the petite blonde said made sense. "All right, I won't say anything to your dad, but I still don't like the man. He's too . . . well, too damn slick."

"Slick?" MaLou repeated his word with a lilting giggle. "Lance isn't a phony, Josh, if that's what you mean."

"Well, I say he is," Josh insisted stubbornly. "He's after something and I'd just like to know what it is."

MaLou licked her lips pensively, wishing with all her heart that she was what Lance was after but all too aware that he had too many problems of his own to devote any time to anyone but himself. "This is a pretty day, isn't it? We're having a lovely autumn this year."

Sensing by her abrupt change of topic that his attractive companion wished to keep their conversation light, Josh did so, but that took considerable effort when what he really wanted to do was propose and demand that MaLou set a prompt wedding date.

The morning sky was overcast, the breeze chilly, but MaLou wanted to go riding anyway since the solitude of the open range provided a constant source of comfort to her. When she found that Lance had already saddled Flor, she hastened to thank him, but his response both surprised and disappointed her.

"I'm sure you haven't forgotten your daddy said you weren't to leave here without either Josh or me by your side. Since I don't see him anywhere about, I figure I'll have to be the one to go along with you this morning."

Since she had not invited Josh to go riding with her, MaLou thought it highly unlikely he would suddenly appear to be her escort. Had Lance's words or expression held the slightest suggestion he looked forward to riding with her she would have been delighted to have him along, but clearly he considered it a tiresome duty he would just as soon avoid. "I don't need to be watched like a child, Garrett," MaLou responded impulsively. "I appreciate your concern, but I'll be fine on my own."

Lance shook his head as he flashed a knowing smile. "I won't take any risks where you're concerned, darlin', so stop arguin' about it and let's go."

He had saddled Amigo too and MaLou watched with a disgusted glance as he swung himself up into the stallion's saddle. "I am most certainly not your 'darlin',' Mr. Garrett, so I'd appreciate it if you didn't call me that. Besides, Josh isn't here to get jealous and that's the only reason you're nice to me, isn't it, just to infuriate him?"

"No, ma'am, I'm just tryin' to please you," Lance declared with uncharacteristic openness.

That he would tease her struck MaLou as being unbelievably cruel, but when she tried to escape him by setting out at a gallop, he drew right along beside her and held Amigo's pace to the one Flor had set. The pinto mare had not only speed but endurance, and ignoring her companion, MaLou gave Flor her head until they had almost reached the mountains. She slowed the horse to a walk then but continued to pretend she was alone.

Lance liked everything about MaLou, especially her proud posture when she rode. She was definitely a lady at heart, even if she had again dressed in her buckskins. There were a great many things he wanted to discuss with her, but not when she was in such a dark mood. He rode a long way in silence, giving her the opportunity to accept his presence, no matter how grudgingly, before he finally spoke. "I've been givin' a lot of thought to our last few conversations," he began hesitantly, taking care not to insult her again.

MaLou held her breath, afraid he would mention the way she had kissed him when she had come home from Josh's party. Since she had no excuse for such wanton behavior, she did not relax until she was certain he would not speak of it. Then she wondered if he had been so drunk he had forgotten all about that night, although she certainly never would. "I can recall several arguments rather than conversations. Just which ones did you mean?"

"I'm talkin' about the fact that our conversations, or arguments if you prefer, keep goin' in circles. It's my fault rather than yours, and I've decided it's high time I did somethin' about it."

MaLou turned to get a better look at him, but his preoccupied frown revealed little of his inner thoughts, though they were what intrigued her the most. "You needn't say it again, Lance. I understand you've been through a great deal. That you'd rather not become involved in my life is understandable. I'm just sorry I insulted you when I was trying to be sympathetic. I didn't mean to do that."

"I know you didn't so you needn't apologize." Lance flicked the ends of his reins against his thigh as he struggled to put his thoughts into words she would more readily understand since it was plain she had no idea what he was talking about as yet. "What I'm tryin' to say is that I was wrong when I told you I'd never want more than what I have today, because I suddenly find I want a whole lot more. Since you're responsible for my change of heart, I'd like to thank you for it."

"I am?" MaLou's eyes widened in surprise. "In what way?"

Lance could not help but laugh until he realized she was not just fishing for compliments; she was genuinely confused. "I've just been driftin' from one ranch to another for the last five years. It's not a rewardin' life, but it was the only one I'd found that didn't cause me more pain than I already had. But that was before I met you."

MaLou did not see how meeting her had changed anything, but since he had just told her it had she thought she owed him the courtesy of hearing him out. He seemed far more relaxed than she had ever seen him. When he turned to look at her, his smile was so warm she swore she could feel it all the way to her toes. He looked content, at peace with himself, but she felt just the same: miserable.

"You never asked for anything but honesty, but I couldn't give you that until I'd finally become more honest with myself. It's time I let the past go and while I won't forget the life I once lived, I'll not mourn its loss any longer."

MaLou nodded, thinking she at last understood what he was trying to say. Somehow she had inspired him to be the successful man they both knew he could be. That meant he would be leaving, and soon, for the ranch had little to offer a talented young man with the ambition he had finally rediscovered. She would not beg him to stay. If it was time for him to seek his destiny, then she would not stand in his way, but it was difficult to smile when she was heartbroken by the thought of telling him good-bye. "I'm real happy for you, Lance. I know you'll be a success at everything you do."

MaLou's mood was so downcast Lance wondered what had happened to the wonderful honesty she had always displayed, for she obviously was not giving voice to what was on her mind now. Before he could ask what was troubling her, a bolt of lightning parted the dark blanket of clouds veiling the mountaintops just ahead. Its bright flash blinded them momentarily and was swiftly followed by a near-deafening clap of thunder. "Damn it!" he swore angrily. "We're goin' to be awfully wet by the time we get home!"

MaLou stood up in her stirrups for a better view of what lay ahead. Huge raindrops were falling all around them now, leaving dark circles on the dirt as they landed with an audible plop. She had paid scant attention to their surroundings as they had begun to talk, but the horses had wandered into a *barranca* and she knew that was no place to be when it rained in the mountains. "Come on, Garrett," she yelled as she turned Flor around. "We've got to get out of here. If there's flooding, a wall of water will come rushing down this gully and we'll be washed all the way to Mexico!"

Lance knew what flash floods were and what horrible damage they could do. It would not have to rain long in the mountains before the water trickling down the hillsides gathered sufficient momentum to become raging torrents that swept away everything in their paths once they reached the valley below. He was as startled as MaLou to realize how dangerous their present location was and wasted no time in digging his heels into Amigo's flanks to wheel him around. "Let's go!" he shouted into the wind, hoping to swiftly reach the end of the dry wash where they could make a dash for higher ground. Sensing his master's urgency, Amigo ran with a powerful stride, but each time Lance looked back for MaLou she seemed to have fallen further behind. Her little mare was swift, but would she be swift enough? The rain continued to fall, splashing off the brim of his hat and cascading down in front of his eyes, but far more frightening was the faint rumbling in the distance. As the sound grew louder he recognized it for what it was: water churning down the *barranca,* gathering speed and strength as the rain continued to fall. How he could have been so careless about the direction in which they had ridden he did not know, but while he was counting on Amigo to have the power to outrun the flood he realized with a sudden horror that Flor did not.

He pulled Amigo to a halt then, and the terrified stallion reared with a piercing neigh, calling to the pinto mare, exhorting her in his own way to run with the speed of the wind to escape the watery peril that was rapidly gaining on them. When at last Flor drew alongside, Lance reached out to grab MaLou from her saddle, for Amigo could easily carry them both to safety, while the mare, relieved of her burden, could keep pace with the larger horse. The *barranca* twisted and turned, its erratic path slowing the progress of the flood, but Lance had no sooner reached a place where he could send the massive black stallion scrambling up the steep embankment and out upon level ground than the waters raged past them with an earsplitting howl. Leaping out of the wash only inches behind them, Flor was thoroughly drenched and upon reaching safety shook herself like a dog to fling the water from her brown and white coat, but Amigo stood quietly waiting for his master and MaLou to dismount before he followed her example.

Lance quickly untied the blanket rolled up behind his saddle and taking MaLou's hand in a firm grasp sprinted toward a tree-covered rise to their left. They would be safe there and with the blanket drawn tightly around them they would be reasonably dry. They sat huddled together, too badly frightened by the fate they had so narrowly escaped to have any interest in continuing their conversation. Gradually the rain began to lessen in intensity. The sun's fiery rays fought to pierce the clouds and at last broke through, sending broad streams of golden light shooting across the desert floor. The storm had ended as abruptly as it had begun, but still MaLou and Lance clung to each other, neither wanting to be the first to draw away.

Snuggled in Lance's arms, MaLou was grateful he had taken her into his confidence and knew she should ask if he had had time to make any plans, but it was impossible to think of anything other than how good it felt to be cradled in his embrace. She rubbed her cheek against his arm as his lips began to caress her nape with light nibbles. The moment was such a perfect one she longed to savor it into eternity, for it was rare that they shared such blissful accord. She arched her back, languidly aligning her supple body against the hard muscles of his chest. His lips were warm, soft, and smooth as they slid down her throat and she could not suppress a shiver.

"Cold?" Lance murmured softly as he tightened his embrace.

The chill had been brought on by the delicious nearness of him, not by the dampness of her clothing. "No," she replied as she turned to look up at him and instantly his eager mouth covered her shy smile with a kiss that grew progressively deeper and more intense until he had laid her across his lap where he could ravish her mouth in a more comfortable position. To MaLou, the change in her companion was astonishing, for without warning his mood had gone from considerate sweetness to the dizzying heights of passion. Demanding, searching, searing, his tongue slid over hers, threatening to steal her very soul before he lifted his mouth from hers and spoke in a hoarse whisper. "I want you, MaLou. Lord, how I want you."

It was not a question that required a response but a statement of fact she did not debate, for the strength of her desire was a match for his. She had been willing to give herself to him after the dance, and despite the strain of the past week, she felt no differently toward him now. She wanted him too but did not waste any time replying in words; instead she reached up to lace her fingers in his wet curls and pulled his head down to hers as she opened her lips invitingly. She was his for the taking, her surrender so complete he did not doubt that the gift of her innocence was freely given.

"Let me help you with your clothes. We'll drape them over the bushes so they'll be dry when we're ready to leave," Lance offered helpfully.

MaLou saw no need for such a convenient excuse as she reached for the buttons on his shirt. Clothing was clearly in the way when she wanted to feel the warmth of his skin pressed against her own. Hurriedly each peeled away the other's clothes, flinging the wet garments aside between long and fevered kisses. Finally, with a savage tug Lance removed the last of MaLou's lace-trimmed undergarments and laid her down tenderly upon his damp blanket. He then stretched out beside her and weaving his fingers in her wet curls cradled her face tenderly between his hands as he began to kiss her again. The bright rays of the sun warmed his back while the beauty of the dear young woman in his arms inflamed his blood with a far more primitive heat. She had given him a reason to again regard life as precious and he could never thank her enough for restoring his belief in the future. It was going to be a glorious future too—he was certain of it—and it was one that he intended her to share.

MaLou ran her fingertips over the curve of his hip before wrapping her arms around his waist to hug him tight. His deep kisses demanded the fervent response she readily gave, but while she had expected him to take her swiftly, he moved very slowly, making each kiss and tender caress a perfect expression of love in itself rather than a mere prelude to something more.

Lying nude in his arms, MaLou was exquisite in her delicate blond beauty, but while his mind overflowed with compliments, he lacked the breath to give them voice. Her pale golden skin invited the exploration of his lips and hands while the memory of how close he had come to making love to her in the cramped confines of her father's buggy flooded his mind with the limitless possibilities they could enjoy that day. Inspired by that delightful prospect, he slid his cheek along the fullness of her creamy smooth breast, then took the firm pink nipple between his teeth. His tongue teased the sensitive nub, then sought its twin for further play. He could feel MaLou's hands upon his back, holding him close as he covered her breasts with adoring kisses. There was not the slightest shyness in her kiss as his mouth returned to hers while his hand slipped between her thighs to begin a slow, sweet caress that encouraged her to share still more of herself.

As before, MaLou's lithe body swiftly betrayed her desire for him, but she no longer felt such weakness a flaw. She wanted only to give him pleasure as intense as that he provided so willingly for her. His intimate touch teased her senses, luring her emotions steadily toward fulfillment as he invaded the last of her lissome body's secrets, then demanded an intimacy of an even more erotic nature. She felt his loving kisses slide from her breasts to the smooth hollow of her stomach, but as he moved between her legs she grew frightened and tried to pull away.

Lance put his hands around her waist so she would not escape him. There was no way he could avoid hurting her, but he wanted that pain overwhelmed with such heady pleasure she would recall only the joy of making love and shed no tears. "It's far too late to change your mind, MaLou. You're mine now," he assured her with a deeply satisfied smile. He kept his eyes on her confused expression until he was certain his face was indelibly imprinted upon her heart and mind. He lowered his head then, spreading light kisses over the triangle of fair curls between her thighs before sending his tongue sliding along the fragrant cleft. He heard her call his name but ignored that breathless plea to delve ever deeper into the warm, moist recess that slowly opened before him like the soft petals of an exotic flower. His tongue continued to caress her tenderly as he savored the flavorful essence her body had so thoughtfully provided to welcome his. Sweet, and yet with the faintly salty taste of tears, he thought it delicious.

MaLou was certain she had descended to the depths of madness, for surely a woman ought not surrender herself with such total abandon. The joy of his shocking kisses flooded her veins with a rapturous heat at the same time her cheeks filled with a bright blush of shame. When they had yet to exchange any words of love, how could they make love with a passion to rival the gods? How could their bodies seek a closer union than their constantly warring spirits had ever achieved? Her mind was tormented by doubts, but the ecstasy Lance had created within her won out as wave after wave of exquisite pleasure shuddered through her graceful body, leaving her dreamily drifting upon a cloud of such incredible beauty she did not ever want to open her eyes and again look upon the harsh face of reality.

Certain he had pleased her most thoroughly, Lance moved swiftly to make his possession complete, his first deep thrust putting an end to the only resistance her slender body would ever provide. She was truly his now and he sought her lips, still hungry for her kiss as the ecstasy he had given her echoed again and again through his powerful frame. She had given him not only the thrill of love but also the gift of perfect peace, and he held her cradled in his arms as he kissed her long sweep of dark lashes and tiny ears. So delighted was he to have been the one to teach her the greatest of life's mysteries, he could not stop smiling.

Just as he had intended, the warmth of his passion had minimized her pain, but MaLou was so desperately afraid he had been telling her good-bye she could not bring herself to speak that word to him. She simply clung to him, the flood now threatening her life one of unbridled emotion. She longed to speak of love again, but she had learned her lesson too painfully on that score ever to mention her devotion again and remained silent. When Lance's flurry of tender kisses again grew insistent, she realized with delighted surprise he wanted to make love to her again. She had not the slightest hesitation this time, for she wanted all the beautiful memories she could possibly gather to bring her the lingering warmth of love when he was gone.

Chapter XIII

"Did you ever make love to Madeline?" MaLou asked as she rose up on her elbows so she could study Lance's expression closely as he replied.

"MaLou!" Lance cringed visibly at such a personal question, certain the pretty girl would never learn the proper limits of curiosity. "That is not the type of question a woman ever asks a man, and most especially not after they've just made love."

"Yes or no, Garrett?" MaLou asked persistently, ignoring his patronizing frown. "You owe me that much since you told me so little about her." She ran her fingertips over his bare chest, parting the black curls as she traced a graceful swirl. His deep tan would cover him completely if they laid out in the sun much longer, but she thought that would only make his muscular build all the more handsome.

Lance considered it a real challenge to phrase an answer diplomatically, but since he doubted she would be still until he told her what she wanted to know, he finally answered her question. "No, I did not. That's not to say I didn't want to, but . . . well . . . well, the truth is she was a manipulative little bitch who used her virtue as bait for a trap. Once I'd gotten over the shock of her leavin' me for the earl, I've never been sorry I lost her. I think the truth is I was damn lucky not to have married the woman."

MaLou was enormously relieved by his reluctant

confession and her whole expression lit up with a happy glow. "I think you were lucky, too, for if she didn't see what a fine man you are she must have been stupid indeed, and no man needs a stupid wife, no matter how pretty she is."

While he could not argue with that, he thought she ought to apply the same rule to herself. "Madeline's plantation adjoined ours. It wouldn't have been a marriage, but a merger of agricultural interests. She'd been thrust at me since I was old enough to notice there was a difference between boys and girls, but just because something strikes two sets of parents as advantageous to them both doesn't mean it will be a good thing for their children."

He had grown quite serious as he had shared that bit of wisdom and MaLou thought she knew why. "Are you speaking about you and Madeline or about Josh and me?"

"Both," Lance explained. "You don't need a stupid husband any more than I needed a stupid wife."

MaLou looked away, unable to meet his steady blue gaze when his words caused her such terrible distress. Surely it was far more rude to give advice about a woman's future than to inquire about a man's past. Josh would at least pretend that he loved her and maybe he really would, while Lance had made love to her without offering any pretty promises at all. Suddenly she was ashamed she had ever thought she could be satisfied with memories of physical pleasure, when that prospect now seemed so empty. While she knew this day would live in her mind forever, rather than a consolation, she now feared it would be a curse coming between her and every other man she would ever meet. She sat up, reached for her camisole, and drew it over her head. Looking up at the angle of the sun, she realized with a stab of alarm how late it was. "We've got to get back. It's way past noon and I never stay out this long," she told him anxiously, hoping he would think she was concerned solely with the lateness of the hour rather than with his failure to speak of love.

"MaLou?" Lance reached out to touch her arm before

she could move away. She had changed so abruptly from a loving confidante to an aloof stranger and he wanted to know why. "You're not sorry about what happened between us, are you?"

Sorry did not even begin to describe how she felt. She loved him and she always would, while all he would say to her was that she should not marry a man as lacking in brains as Josh. Well, just what choice did she have when he had not given her even the faintest glimmer of hope he would one day ask her to be his wife? Just as before, it seemed all the choices were his and he consistently made the wrong ones as far as she was concerned. "No, I'm not sorry," she assured him as she hastily gathered up her clothes. Her buckskins were so well tanned they were still soft and supple even after getting wet. She borrowed his handkerchief and used water from his canteen to wash as best she could, but even with that delay she was dressed and ready to go several minutes before he was.

Lance knew they had gotten ahead of themselves, but he had expected the delicious closeness they had shared while making love to last and MaLou's suddenly withdrawn mood both surprised and saddened him. He wanted to take her in his arms and kiss her until the light of desire again turned the green of her eyes to molten gold, but she seemed so anxious for them to be on their way he shoved such romantic thoughts aside. "We can use the storm as the reason for our being late. No one will question that excuse."

MaLou knew her father trusted him, which caused her a sharp pang of guilt. She had been with Lance, so he would not have worried about her, but she hoped he asked no questions she would have to answer with lies. "Let's hope not." She gave Flor an encouraging pat, then headed back toward the ranch at the same furious gallop with which she had left it. When she saw Nathan walking toward the barn, she hoped her expression would not betray her emotional turmoil and tried to greet him with her usual sunny smile. "Did it rain here? Lance and I got caught in an awful downpour near the mountains," she explained as she leapt from Flor's back.

"Did you now?" The foreman eyed her suspiciously before turning to scan the horizon for some sign of Amigo. Sighting the black stallion and his rider swiftly approaching, he relayed the message he had been given. "Your dad went out to look for you more than an hour ago. He told me if you came back before he did to have you stay right here."

"Why would he have done that?" MaLou asked nervously. "Didn't he know Lance had gone with me?"

"Well now, I reckon that might have been exactly why he was so worried, Miss MacDowell." With a smile that closely resembled a smirk he took Flor's reins and led the horse into the barn. His knowing glance left MaLou blushing so brightly her cheeks were still flushed when Lance reached her. "Dad went out looking for us," she told him hurriedly, her long-lashed eyes bright with fright.

Lance chuckled slyly, grateful his usual good luck had held. "Well, since he didn't find us you needn't look so guilty, darlin'. He'll probably be back soon, so why don't you go on in the house and find somethin' useful to do?"

What MaLou urgently wanted to do was take a bath in the hottest water she could stand to wash away every last trace of him. Splashing cold water on herself out on the prairie had not left her feeling nearly clean enough. "I understand. If I just follow my usual routine he won't become suspicious."

"That's right." Lance was disappointed she seemed so apprehensive when he did not think they had done anything wrong. "We got distracted and didn't finish our talk, but I've got lots more to say to you tomorrow," he promised with a teasing grin.

MaLou was afraid the kind of talking he was interested in doing required no words, but she did not want to argue with him when Nathan might reappear at any minute. "I've got to go," she whispered breathlessly and sprinted toward her house with a long, graceful stride.

* * *

When her father still had not returned by suppertime, MaLou went to the cook house to find Nathan. "Did my dad say anything about dropping by the Spencers' or going anywhere else?"

Lance never ate his meals at the same table as the foreman, but he overheard MaLou's questions and could not help but want to be of some assistance. When she walked by him on the way out, he stood up and followed her outside. "MaLou? It'll be dark too soon to start a search for him tonight, but if he's not home by mornin' I'll go lookin' for him first thing."

"That's what Nathan said too." MaLou twisted her hands nervously, certain something dreadful had happened to her father. "Where could he be, Lance? He knows this ranch like the palm of his hand and he couldn't have gotten lost."

Lance took her hand in a gentle clasp to walk her back to the house. "No, I'm sure he isn't lost, but his horse could have gone lame and left him without a mount. It won't be too cold tonight so he'll probably just sit tight and wait for us to find him in the mornin'."

"I hope you're right," MaLou prayed aloud, but still she could not shake the horrible feeling of foreboding that had plagued her thoughts all afternoon. "Did you want to visit with Manuel for awhile? I'm afraid he's felt rather neglected today."

"I'll sit with him an hour or two. Then, if you'd like, I'll visit with you," Lance offered graciously.

MaLou's lashes nearly swept her brows she was so shocked by his suggestion. "Oh no, I don't think that would be wise. We can't risk starting any gossip."

"Who's gonna be doin' the gossipin', MaLou, your ranch hands? Don't you think they've got more respect for you than that?"

"I don't honestly know," MaLou confessed shyly. "I just wish Dad would get home."

"That he's late is just an unfortunate coincidence, MaLou. I'm sure it has nothin' to do with us," Lance tried to reassure her again. It annoyed him that she seemed to be stricken with remorse when he felt elated still. If her father did not return home, then he would make it a point to stay with her, but he did not put his offer into words since he was afraid she would again promptly refuse it. When they reached the house he left her pacing the parlor while he went to see Manuel.

"Is the *patrón* home?" the Mexican asked as Lance came through the door.

"No, not yet." Lance pulled up a chair close to the bed and got comfortable while he tried to think of something cheerful to say to his friend, but Manuel appeared nearly as upset as MaLou about Thomas's extended absence.

"I do not like this, *amigo*. What if he has been shot?"

Manuel's question had a decidedly ominous ring and Lance made no attempt to soothe his worries as he had MaLou's. "Taking shots at ranch hands is one thing, Manuel. Gunning down Thomas MacDowell is quite another."

Manuel nodded, but he was still not convinced. "I have been in this bed too long. Help me get up."

"All right, but if you get dizzy you're goin' right back under the covers." Lance rose to his feet and shoved his chair aside so Manuel would not trip over it. He helped his friend into a sitting position, then eased him over to the side of the high iron bed. The Mexican was so short in stature his feet dangled several inches from the floor. Lance put his arm around Manuel's waist to help him stand, then waited a minute to be certain he would not simply collapse in a heap when he released him.

It took the injured man a moment to get his balance, but then he felt well enough to take several steps before returning to bed. "There, you see, I knew I could do it. I will walk a few more steps in the morning and go back to the bunkhouse in the afternoon."

"You don't like my hospitality, Manuel?" MaLou called from the doorway.

"But of course I like it!" the wiry man exclaimed. "But you have spoiled me and soon I will never want to get well."

"I thought you two might like some coffee. I didn't

mean to interrupt your visit," MaLou offered by way of apology for having disturbed the two men.

"I'll come help you," Lance volunteered. "We'll be right back, Manuel." As he stepped out into the hall, Lance took the distracted blonde's arm. "Come and sit with us. We're not talkin' about anythin' you can't hear and it will help to pass the time."

Grateful for any diversion, MaLou accepted his invitation and joined the two men until Manuel began to yawn widely. "We're tiring you. Come on, Garrett, it's time we said good night." The slender blonde took Manuel's coffee cup as well as her own and carried them into the kitchen. When she turned around, Lance was standing right behind her and she was startled. "Oh, Lance, I didn't realize you'd followed me so closely!"

Lance reached out to encircle her waist and drew her into his arms. He pressed her cheek against his chest and rested his chin atop her curls. "We have so much to talk about, MaLou. You're so nervous you'll never be able to sleep so you might as well stay up and talk with me."

MaLou was so comfortable in his arms she did not step back as she questioned him. "Just what is it you want to discuss, Lance? Your plans?"

"Yes. Aren't you in the least bit curious about what they are?"

"Yes, of course I am, but I don't want to pry," she admitted sadly, certain his plans did not include her, and no matter how exciting they were to him, she did not really want to hear them.

"Come on." Lance took her hand as he led the way into the parlor. The settee provided ample room for them both and as soon as she was seated he took the place at her side. "I told you this mornin' that I'm tired of livin' in the past—sick to death of it is closer to the truth. I don't want to go from bein' a bitter young man to bein' a bitter old man with nothin' in between. I want a chance at bein' happy again. Now I know when I speak with your daddy tomorrow he's not goin' to be pleased, but—"

"Lance!" MaLou squealed in horror. "You're not going

to tell him about us!"

She looked so terrified Lance could not help but laugh. "I'm talkin' about askin' his permission to marry you, darlin', not lettin' him in on secrets I won't share with anyone but you."

"You want to marry me?" MaLou mumbled in surprise, no less confused than she had been by his previous announcement. "But I thought you said—"

Lance leaned forward to silence her question with a lingering kiss. He wound his fingers in her soft curls and did not release her until he was certain she at last understood him. "I know what I said, MaLou, and I was wrong. Now you told me you'd say yes if I asked you to marry me. Have you changed your mind?"

His proposal was so completely unexpected, MaLou did not know whether to laugh or cry. She felt like jumping up and down while she screamed "Yes!" over and over again, but since he had worked so hard to teach her how to be a lady she thought she should try acting like one now. "Wait a minute," she began sedately. "This morning you said you were tired of just drifting from one ranch to another. Are you planning to go back to Georgia?"

Lance shook his head emphatically. "No, there's no point in doin' that. That's part of the past and I'm done with it. I'm also smart enough to know I can't marry you and take over the runnin' of the ranch when your daddy is still so active. Too many people would be suspicious of my motives and neither of us deserves that kind of gossip goin' on behind our backs. Thanks to Josh Spencer I've got eleven hundred dollars locked in your daddy's safe and I can use that to make a lot more. Since Tucson is growin' so rapidly I'm sure I can find a business opportunity or two that will suit my talents."

MaLou frowned slightly, uncertain just exactly what those talents might be. "Are you talking about gambling, Lance? About using the money Josh lost to you to win enough to go into business on your own?"

It was the way she had spoken the word "gambling" that warned Lance to choose his words with more care.

"You know what your daddy pays his hands. That's not enough for a man to support a family and save somethin' aside for the future. If we're to have a home of our own, I'll have to earn the money in whatever way I can. I'm not askin' you to marry a gambler, MaLou, because I don't intend to earn our livin' by playin' cards. I'll be a respected member of the business community within a year. You can count on it."

"You don't want to get married for a year?" MaLou whispered dejectedly, for that seemed like a lifetime to her.

"No, I'd like to marry you tomorrow. The problem is goin' to be convincin' your daddy that's a good idea. He'll point out that Josh will inherit his family's cattle ranch while all I've got is my good looks. Now if you were my daughter I'd tell you to follow your heart, but I don't think that's what he'll say, do you?"

"I don't care what he says, Lance," MaLou insisted with a determined calm. "You're the man I love and nothing will ever change that. I don't see why you have to go out on your own, though, when there's more than enough work for all of us here. Dad can never keep his accounts straight and I'll bet you're real good with figures, aren't you?"

"Yes, and I'll be glad to help him if I can, but I still want to earn our livin' in my own way. I won't just be Thomas MacDowell's son-in-law for the rest of my life."

MaLou considered that prospect highly unlikely since he was such a strong-willed man. "I know you're not marrying me for my money, Lance, and anyone who might think you were would soon see he was wrong," she insisted proudly.

"I'll not have anyone sayin' it in the first place, MaLou. Let's not argue about this. Tomorrow I'll tell your daddy I'm quittin' my job here and that I plan to make you my wife just as soon as I can support you. I can't promise you anythin' but love tonight, but I won't let you down."

MaLou was certain he would not. He was a proud man and she knew he had every reason for that pride, for he had intelligence and a ready wit in addition to the good looks he had so casually mentioned. "Do you absolutely have to leave the ranch?" she asked wistfully.

"Yes, ma'am, but not until tomorrow," Lance pointed out with a wicked gleam brightening the blue of his eyes.

MaLou understood his unspoken question and could not bear to tell him no. She gave him her hand as she rose to her feet. "Let's make sure Manuel is asleep first."

Lance had not really expected MaLou to agree to letting him spend the night in her bed, but since she had been so sensible he saw no reason to argue with her decision. They found Manuel sound asleep, snoring very softly, and closed his door before going across the hall to her room. "Don't light a lamp," he warned her. "It wouldn't be proper of me to let you stay alone in the house with Manuel, but no one need know just where I spent the night."

"There's a room for bathing at the end of the hall. It has an outside door, so if you have to leave quickly, go that way." MaLou began to unbutton his shirt, still numbed from the shock of his proposal. "On second thought, you stay right here. If my dad finds us together he'll make you marry me immediately, whether or not you can afford to have a wife, and I wouldn't object to that."

With a careless shrug Lance let his shirt slip off his shoulders, content to allow her to undress him before he returned the favor. "No, I want you to have a proper weddin', MaLou. Every bachelor in Tucson is goin' to cry his eyes out because he let such a beautiful woman get away, and I for one am goin' to enjoy handin' out handkerchiefs."

MaLou doubted anyone would be crying at her wedding, but the idea was such an amusing one she could not help but laugh. "I doubt anyone but Josh will be moved to tears and I think that will be mainly because he's lost this ranch rather than because he's heartbroken he's lost me."

She had put on her pink dress that night and as he helped her remove it Lance recalled the first night he had seen her in it. She had been lovely, but without the smallest shred of confidence that she was the beautiful woman he and her father had thought her to be. "We've both changed a great deal since we met, MaLou."

"For the better?" she asked shyly.

"Oh yes, definitely for the better," he assured her. He wrapped his arms around her narrow waist and lifted her clear off her feet as he kissed her with the same conviction that rang in his words. Since no one had ever paid her the compliments she deserved, he made his extravagant. "I love everything about you." He carried her over to the bed as he continued to lavish praise on her fair beauty. "Your figure is perfection and your skin is softer than moonlight. When we're out in the sun your hair shines with the beauty of spun gold. I have never met another woman with more glorious eyes and—"

MaLou raised her fingertips to his lips to interrupt him. "You are going to make me very conceited, Mr. Garrett."

"Every beautiful woman should be a bit spoiled. It makes them all the more attractive," he assured her.

"Really?" MaLou asked with a playful giggle, loving the way he spoiled her.

"Really." Lance ran his hand down her side, enjoying the lithe curve of her figure as well as the smoothness of her skin. He considered her a rare treasure and one he would never give up. That she had invited him into her bed so readily thrilled him all the more, for it made it plain her love was as unrestrained as his. "I love you," he whispered hungrily, as eager to possess her as he had been the first time, and he knew if he lived to be a hundred he would never have his fill of the bewitching creature in his arms.

MaLou snuggled against him, glad she at last knew what to expect but certain that making love with Lance would always be exciting. "Every time I've told you I think you're handsome you've scolded me for being too forward. Do I dare pay you compliments now?"

Lance hesitated a moment, as though he were giving her question serious thought. "There are many advantages to bein' tall and good-lookin', and one of the best is hearin' women tell me about it. Now that you've promised to become my wife though, I'll try not to be as modest as I was."

MaLou did not know whether the charm was in his teasing words or his marvelous accent, but she loved hearing him talk, especially now that he had finally relaxed and shown her how fun-loving he could be. "I think I am the lucky one, Mr. Garrett, and the people crying at our wedding are all going to be women."

"You're the only woman I care about," Lance insisted as he nibbled her earlobe playfully. "Let all the others cry."

MaLou sighed contentedly as his hands moved over her, working a subtle yet irresistible magic. His gentle caress lured her senses tenderly toward the most exquisite of pleasures. While she knew each of his gestures would lead to one increasingly more intimate, every one was a delight in itself, making the journey toward total intimacy as enthralling as the destination. She lay languidly enjoying the smoothness of his touch and the delicious flavor of his kiss until her curiosity made her wonder if he would be as responsive to her caress as she was to his. He was lying on his side and she traced the path of the dark curls that tapered to a thin line as they crossed the flatness of his belly. When he did not brush her hand away she continued her explorations with a tantalizing grace. That the tip of his manhood would have the softness of velvet while the shaft was both smooth and hard intrigued her all the more. "What would happen if I kissed you here?" she asked in a seductive purr. "Or is that another question a lady never asks a gentleman?"

Her caress was not hesitant but a knowing motion that slid around and over him in intensely pleasurable waves, making it difficult for him to analyze her question, let alone answer it. "Just do it," he whispered hoarsely, amazed by the incredible speed with which he had gone from being her loving teacher to her adoring pupil. What she lacked in experience she obviously made up for in imagination and he could not have been more pleased. She did not simply kiss him but caressed him so lovingly with her lips and tongue he could take very little of such exquisite torture. Her name was slurred as he called to her in an incoherent plea, but he managed to draw her up beside him. Resting her knee upon his hip he entered her while they still lay upon their sides, grateful to find her welcoming wetness eased his way. He had meant to be patient, to teach her slowly and tenderly so the joy they would share making love would be infinite, but he had never expected the petite blonde to have such a passionate nature. She moved into his arms, timing the motion of her hips to the frantic rhythm of his in an ageless dance that quickly brought them to the shattering heights of a stunning climax, then left them dreamily adrift on rapture's silken wings. Lance had never had a more magnificent partner than the slender beauty in his arms and he thanked her with both his well-muscled body and flattering words until the first light of dawn had filled the eastern sky with a rosy glow and sleep finally overtook them where they lay.

When MaLou awakened later that morning she was certain the width of her smile would leave her with no secrets. Her father would take one look at her satisfied grin and know exactly how she and Lance had spent the night. While he had left her bed, the sheets still held a faint trace of his scent and she snuggled down into them, drinking in that subtle fragrance with unabashed glee. Lance was the most fascinating man and she prayed her father would agree he was the perfect choice for her. The bliss of that thought was swiftly replaced with guilt as she remembered he had undoubtedly spent a cold and hungry night. Since the dear man deserved far better, she left the warmth of her bed, dressed with her usual careless haste, then hurried over to help Jake serve the men breakfast. The talk that morning was centered about one topic—locating her father as rapidly as possible—and MaLou was grateful she could count on the men for their enthusiastic help.

When the meal was over, they all gathered outside the cookhouse, where MaLou began giving Nathan directions for making up search parties. "Lance and I would have seen Dad had he ridden toward the mountains, so there's no point in searching in that direction. Let's divide up into two groups. One can move to the north, the other the south. Whoever finds him can fire three shots and we'll all meet back here. Which area do you want to supervise, Nathan, the north or south?"

"I'll take the north and leave the south to you, Miss MacDowell." The foreman's sardonic grin was as taunting as his words, but MaLou pretended not to understand his insult.

"Fine." The efficient young woman divided the men into two equal groups and quite naturally took Lance with her. "Dad was riding Buck and the fact that the horse didn't come back to the barn alone is a good sign. Let's spread out and see if we can't bring them home before noon." She glanced toward Lance then, a shy look cast through her thick lashes, which he met with a teasing wink. When they had ridden out far enough for the men to be widely scattered, she moved Flor to Amigo's side. "Dad is sure to be in an awful mood. I think you ought to wait a day or so before talking with him about us."

Lance nodded, deciding her point was well taken. "All right, I'll wait, but no more than two days, MaLou, and that's my absolute limit. The sooner I leave, the sooner we can get married, unless, of course, you've changed your mind?"

"After last night?" the petite blonde inquired with a saucy toss of her long curls. "I'll never change my mind about you, Lance Garrett. Never."

Lance looked around quickly, and seeing no one close enough to be watching them he leaned over and kissed MaLou soundly. "Now come on, let's be the ones to find your daddy so we can get back to ridin' strictly for pleasure."

Since she knew precisely what pleasure he meant, MaLou tapped Flor's flanks with her heels and the lively mare began to run with such a fluid beat she and her mistress seemed to be sailing upon the wind.

That splendid mood of elation had long since disappeared when, three hours later, they heard the faint echo of gunfire far to the north. By then they were both hot, dusty, and tired.

"Oh, damn it!" MaLou complained loudly. "Why did it have to be Nathan's group who found him?"

He had long known she was an intensely competitive young woman, but Lance felt this was no time for rivalry. "You should have known the north would win, darlin', since they always do, but all that matters is that they found him."

"Yes, I know. I didn't mean to sound ungrateful." Still, MaLou was disappointed she had not been the one to find her father herself. They raced back to the ranch, then had to wait nearly thirty minutes for Nathan's search party to appear. "I don't see him. Do you?" MaLou relied upon Lance's greater height to provide him with a better view than she had as she strained to make out the faces of the men approaching.

What Lance saw chilled him clear to the bone, for Nathan was leading Buck and he was certain the blanket-draped body slung over the buckskin's saddle had to be her father's. "Go on in the house, MaLou," he ordered sternly.

"But why?" MaLou needed only one glance at Lance's stricken expression to understand, but rather than run toward the house she ran straight toward the approaching riders. Nathan saw her, pulled away from the others, and drew his horse to a halt. Eager to return to the barn, Buck neighed a loud protest at the delay but stood quietly when MaLou reached him.

Nathan had hoped to find Thomas MacDowell, but not as he had, and feeling no sense of triumph he explained his gruesome discovery in his usual taciturn style. "There are about fifty head missing off the north range. Your pa must have caught the rustlers red-handed. He never had a chance."

Despite her anxiety the previous afternoon, MaLou had never expected their search to end in such a horrible tragedy. Lance had followed her and she turned to face him. "Alex Spencer was my father's closest friend. I'll need you to ride over to his place and ask him to come help me plan the funeral. I wouldn't even know where to begin."

"I don't want to leave you," Lance confessed readily, not caring what meaning Nathan read into his words.

MaLou simply stared up at the handsome young man wondering how she would ever be able to look at him without remembering they had been making love when her father had gone looking for them and met his death instead. If that guilt were not a heavy enough burden, she had then spent the night in his arms while her father's body had grown cold and stiff out on the prairie. She felt like a ghoul, like some horribly evil monster who had feasted upon the joys of the flesh while her father had died a horrible death all alone. Surely Thomas MacDowell had deserved far more loyalty from his only daughter. "When I tell you to do something, Garrett, you do it! Now stop wasting time. Get on over to the Spencers' place and tell Alex I need him!"

Lance could not have been more shocked had MaLou accused him of her father's murder, but knowing how badly she was hurting inside he forgave her for striking out so angrily at him. "Yes, ma'am, I'll do that right now." As he turned away Lance could not forget MaLou's haunted stare. She had been looking right through him, not at him, when she had spoken so sharply and he was appalled to think she would blame him for her father's death, though clearly that was exactly what the grief-stricken woman had already done.

Chapter XIV

The only consolation Lance had was that it was Alex rather than Joshua Spencer MaLou relied upon for advice in planning her father's funeral. While slightly more than twenty years separated father and son, they could easily have been mistaken for brothers. Alex had maintained his trim build, still had a full head of wavy blond hair, and had decided a mustache enhanced his rakish smile long before his son had discovered its value. There was also a Mrs. Spencer, a rather prim, willowy brunette by the name of Constance, who seemed surprisingly ill at ease in the company of either her husband or son. Lance was certain she must have had property, for she and Alex seemed too poorly matched to have married for love. They had only the one son, and the Southerner was too fine a gentleman to allow himself to speculate on why they had not been blessed with more children.

He had thought it best to keep his distance for several days and observe MaLou's reactions, but when she gave no sign that she even recalled his name, let alone loved him, he realized he had made a serious mistake in not stepping forward immediately to take his place at her side. All three of the Spencers hovered about, as well as many other well-meaning family friends he had not met who had brought their home-baked delicacies and visited for several hours, leaving him with no opportunity to speak with the distraught blonde alone. Not wishing to intrude upon her grief, Manuel had returned to the bunkhouse, so he no longer had his friend as an excuse to visit the house.

On the morning of the funeral, Lance rode into town with the other cowhands since they had all wanted to attend the service, but by the time they arrived they found the adobe church full and had to stand in the rear. Thomas MacDowell was described in the eulogy as a fine man who had been cut down in his prime and a friend to all, but Lance did not think the cleric went nearly far enough in calling for the capture of his murderers. Cattle rustlers were vermin in his view, and any who would stoop to murder were even worse. He had ridden out to see where Thomas's body had been found, but by then there had been so many horses trampling the scene he had been unable to track the culprits. He knew bringing to justice the men who had killed her father would not bring the man back, but still he was determined to do it. Even if it proved nothing to MaLou, it would prove something important to himself.

As they began to file out of the church after the service, Lance felt a light tap on his shoulder and he slipped his hand under his suit coat to the ivory handle of his Colt before he turned to see who wished to speak with him. "Mr. Cordova." He greeted the dark-eyed man by name but had no interest in chatting with him. "I'm sorry, but I need to get right back to the ranch."

"I understand, but first I have a favor to ask," Jesse confessed in a hushed whisper. "May I please have a few minutes of your time?"

The man was as elegantly attired as he had been on the two previous occasions when Lance had seen him. Perhaps in deference to the occasion he was dressed in black, but there was nothing somber about his suit. The short jacket had been expertly tailored to flatter his lean physique while his flared pants were elaborately decorated with black satin embroidery and bright silver buttons that matched those on the jacket. The snowy whiteness of his shirt contrasted sharply with his deep tan, making the dark brown of his eyes shine all the more brightly.

However, it was his expression that impressed Lance rather than his fancy clothes. He was not flashing his usual ready grin and Lance thought his request might actually be a sincere one. "All right, let's just step back into the church."

Jesse nodded in agreement and when the last of the mourners had left they took seats in the back pew. The handsome Mexican cleared his throat several times, as though his subject were a difficult one to approach. "My aunt, Candelaria Delgado, was a very dear friend of Mr. MacDowell's. It's possible MaLou has never heard of her, but she would like to call on her and offer her sympathies. We would both be grateful if you would make a discreet inquiry so my aunt might send written condolences should a personal visit not be welcome."

Lance thought Jesse's flowery request most unusual considering the circumstances of Candelaria's friendship with Thomas. "Unfortunately I have no influence whatsoever with MaLou, so I think you should be making your request directly to her. I do know that she knows who your aunt is and precisely what her relationship was with her father, but I haven't the vaguest idea whether or not she'd wish to see the woman."

His expression mirroring his dismay, Jesse was clearly shocked by Lance's revelation. "She knows about my aunt? Are you certain of that?"

"Yes, they argued about her one time in my presence. She was Thomas's mistress, wasn't she?" Lance was in a hurry to end their conversation. He wanted to get back outside in the sunshine, for the dank chill of the candle-lit church depressed him terribly.

"My aunt will be most distressed to hear this. She is a widow, Mr. Garrett, and wealthy in her own right. Such a fine woman would never be any man's mistress, let alone Thomas MacDowell's."

"I'm merely repeatin' what MaLou told me since you wanted to know her opinion. If her father and your aunt were never lovers, then—"

Jesse raised a well-manicured hand as he interrupted.

"You misunderstood me. I did not say they were not lovers, only that she was never his mistress. A mistress is a woman who is supported by a man in exchange for her sexual favors, is she not?"

"A fine point," Lance admitted reluctantly.

"It is not!" Jesse exclaimed. "In one case we are talking about mutual esteem, regard, and love; in the other, no more than a financial arrangement. The difference is immense!"

"Frankly, I'm surprised you can make that distinction," Lance blurted out angrily.

Jesse stared wide-eyed at the usually polite Southerner, unable to comprehend what he had done to insult him. "Forgive me if I have somehow offended you. It was not my intention."

"When you offered me a job in your so-called saloon, why didn't you tell me it was on Maiden Lane?" Lance asked accusingly.

Jesse straightened his shoulders proudly as he replied, "I have yet to open the saloon I mentioned, but it will be located on Congress, not on Maiden Lane. I would not insult you by offering you employment in a brothel. How can you think such a thing?"

Lance sighed as he leaned back in the pew, his thoughts a hopeless muddle. "You do own an establishment on Maiden Lane, don't you?"

Considering the site of their conversation sacred, Jesse looked toward the altar and crossed himself quickly before replying. "Yes, I do. How did you learn of it?"

"MaLou told me," Lance admitted quite frankly.

"You have spoken to her about such things?" Clearly Jesse could not even imagine such a gross breach of etiquette.

"MaLou is a delightfully straightforward young woman. She knows all manner of facts about Tucson and doesn't mind sharin' them with me. Now I really must be gettin' back to the ranch."

Uncertain whether or not Lance had agreed to grant his request, Jesse stood and followed him out the door. "You will ask Miss MacDowell if she'll receive my aunt, won't you? Candelaria and I both would be most grateful if you would."

Lance was about to refuse when he realized Candelaria's request would provide an excellent excuse for him to speak with MaLou and, regrettably, he feared she would not talk with him without some credible reason for the conversation. "All right. I'll do it, but it might take some time for me to get the reply back to you. Where can I reach you?"

Jesse turned away to hide his smile, then broke into the wide grin Lance had remembered. "My office is in the Silver Spur. Any of the hands on your ranch will know where it is."

Lance knew without asking it would be on Maiden Lane and wondered why the man had been so reluctant to admit he had business there when it was obvious he was extremely successful. Since he did not have the time to ask such a question, he dismissed it from his mind. Most of the carriages were still parked in front of the church since Thomas was being buried in the adjoining cemetery and he hoped his absence had not been noted. "If you want to visit the grave, go without me. I've seen more than my share already."

"I understand." The elegantly clothed Mexican took the path leading to the cemetery and as Lance watched him go he was surprised to find that he had grown very curious about what sort of woman Candelaria Delgado might be. If she was anything like her nephew, then she would be both beautiful and well mannered. That was precisely the type of woman he thought MaLou should have for a friend, but he had no idea if she would agree.

While MaLou understood her father was dead, she could not truly believe she would never again see his friendly grin, hear his booming laugh, or feel his boisterous hugs. He had been so full of life, always ready to lay aside whatever task he had to spend time with her. She was certain he had been the very best of fathers, and that he had died in such a senseless fashion was far too ghastly a circumstance for her to accept calmly. Had he been out looking for rustlers, he would have been well armed and have had plenty of men with him, but he had gone to find her. That horrible truth echoed endlessly in her mind: he had gone looking for her and found a hideous death instead.

She had mumbled a distracted "thank you" when Constance Spencer had brought over a black dress for her to wear to the funeral. They were almost the same size so she had adjusted the hem for her more petite stature and considered the fit adequate. She did not really know Constance all that well, but the shy woman had done her best to ease her grief and MaLou was grateful she had made the attempt. Alex had been wonderful. He had seen to the many details of the funeral and notified all of her father's friends of the tragedy. Josh, however, had seemed as numb as she was, neither able to share her sorrow nor lighten it. Had she been seriously considering marrying him, his embarrassed aloofness would have given her real doubts about the wisdom of their marriage, for she was certain tragedy should bring a couple closer together, not drive them apart.

She knew she could not avoid Lance forever, but she was not ready to face him again either. The mere sight of him brought too gruesome a reminder of where she had been when her father had met his death. She knew it would be irrational to blame Lance for what happened, but that failed to lessen her own deeply painful sense of guilt. It was her own desire that had betrayed them both and had had such tragic results. She felt no differently about Lance—she loved him still—but now that love was tinged with such deep sorrow she feared the future he had promised her could never be a happy one when it would always be haunted by the grim specter of her father's murder.

* * *

Lance knew MaLou would have plenty of sympathetic company for the first few days after the funeral. Then everyone would be anxious to get back to their own lives and she would be expected to deal with her problems on her own. She was only nineteen, however, and despite her stubborn independence, she was naïve in many ways. Lance knew that knowing how a ranch runs and running it were two entirely different things. He had the advantage over Josh in that he was there and he meant for her to see that accepting his help was more a practical necessity than a romantic one. As for their love, he planned to make certain it survived her father's death rather than becoming another casualty of the rustlers' guns. When no one had arrived by ten o'clock on the Monday following the funeral, he decided he had waited long enough to see her, strolled over to her house, and knocked on the front door.

Expecting another visit from the self-righteous women who had never considered it proper for a man alone to raise a daughter in the first place, MaLou braced herself as she opened the door. When she found Lance waiting to see her, she was both relieved and apprehensive. "I can't stand being cooped up in here another minute. Do you mind if we talk out on the porch?"

While Lance did indeed mind since it meant he would have to keep his distance, he shook his head. "No, out here is fine." She was still wearing the borrowed black dress and as she moved past him it seemed she had grown smaller somehow. Perhaps she had lost weight despite the abundance of food he had seen carried into the house by callers. When she had taken a seat, he moved opposite her and leaned back against the rail. "I intend to help you, MaLou. You're a strong-willed young woman and I know if you want to run this ranch yourself you'll do a fine job of it. I just want you to know I'll help you all I can."

Unable to focus her gaze upon his face, MaLou looked down at her hands. They seemed very pale and white, a pampered lady's hands rather than her own. Even with Lance she felt the same curious sense of detachment she had experienced since her father's death. She felt as though she were merely a spectator watching two strangers talk, not like one of the participants in an important conversation. "I know you want to leave and I don't want you to think you have to stay on here on account of me. It will be far easier for me in the long run if I don't come to depend on you but instead learn how to do everything on my own."

"No," Lance responded immediately, his tone demanding though his voice remained low. "Too many people will be eager to take advantage of your grief and inexperience. You need somebody to protect you from those vultures. Nathan has neither the experience nor the brains to do it and Josh has too much at stake himself to put your interests first. Your dad gave me a job when I needed one and I figure I owe him this. I'd like to stick around until you have the ranch runnin' smoothly on your own. You're a bright girl and it won't take long, but I'd like to stay here until then."

MaLou frowned slightly as she considered his words. "There's sure to be gossip about us, Garrett."

Lance was tempted to point out that it could not be considered gossip since any rumors circulated about them would most definitely be true. Moving forward, he knelt down by her side so he could look into her eyes as he whispered, "I love you, MaLou. I know you're too unhappy now to plan a weddin', but I still want you for my wife."

Huge tears welled up in MaLou's eyes as she realized he would no longer have to get her father's permission for them to marry. She did not have to answer to anyone now, but that newfound freedom brought not the slightest sense of pride. "Oh Lance, if only—"

Lance interrupted her with a stern rebuke. "Stop it, MaLou! No man can escape his fate and nothing we could have done that day would have changed what happened. I intend to get the men who killed your daddy—every last one of them—but I won't spend a minute being sorry for what happened between us because his murder wasn't our fault!"

MaLou understood he was trying to ease her conscience, but his words failed to have any effect. "Had we been back on time, my dad would not have been out looking for us, Lance. It's as simple as that."

Disappointed she would cling to such a guilt-ridden view rather than accept his far more enlightened interpretation of the facts, Lance rose slowly to his feet but remained at her side. Knowing they would be unlikely to ever reconcile two such opposing points of view, he dropped the discussion of blame and abruptly changed the subject. "Candelaria wants to come see you. I imagine she's as heartbroken as you are over your father's death and it would be very kind of you to allow her to call."

"You've met her?" MaLou asked with a puzzled frown.

"No. Jesse Cordova approached me for her at the funeral. I don't know whether or not she was there."

"She was there," MaLou informed him coolly. "She was dressed in black and heavily veiled, but she was there." The idea of speaking with her father's mistress was surprisingly appealing to the distraught blonde. "Yes, I would like to see Candelaria, for I know she loved my father even if he put off marrying her until too late. Please let her know I will be happy to have her call on me whenever it is convenient for her."

Lance was certain he had failed to accomplish anything of value in their brief conversation. Not only had MaLou not requested his help, she had tried to refuse it even after he had insisted upon giving it. She would make a remarkable wife, but he feared a man would need more patience than he possessed to wait for her to set a wedding date. "You mentioned your father had difficulty keepin' his accounts straight. Would you like me to take a look at his books?"

Since that was a chore she had been dreading, MaLou readily agreed. "Would you please? He had his own system of bookkeeping, but I think you can figure it out."

"I'm sure I can," Lance promised confidently, glad he had found something he could do to help her. "In fact, what I'll do is study them thoroughly and then I'll explain them to you. Now if anyone should approach you with any sort of business proposition, you can tell them I'm managin' your accounts and you'll need my advice before you make any decisions. If they object to that, then you'll know their offer wasn't a legitimate one."

MaLou nodded thoughtfully, thinking it would be best if they kept a strictly business relationship for the time being. "Dad used the room off the parlor for his office. I think my mother had meant it to be a library, but Dad never put in the bookshelves."

"MaLou, does your mother know what happened?"

The lithe blonde had just risen to her feet and reached out to grip the back of her chair to steady herself. "No one has even thought of her. Oh dear, I suppose I'll have to write to her about Dad today, but I have no idea what to say."

"I'll write the letter, then you can copy it in your own hand so she'll think it came from you," Lance volunteered graciously, knowing everything he did for her would give them a further opportunity to be together.

"Oh Lance, I can't ask you to do that."

"It is a small thing," he explained. "Besides, I've had far more practice notifying relatives of tragic deaths than you will ever have."

MaLou understood he was talking about writing to the families of men who had been killed during the war. "That must have been a horrible job, to write and let someone know a husband or son had been killed."

Lance shook his head. "No, the real horror was in watching the men die. I always made them sound like heroes in my letters, every last one, so the people who remembered them would be proud."

MaLou was surprised he would admit to embellishing his letters in such a fashion, but she thought his generosity commendable. "Perhaps I should wait until after the reading of the will to write to her. There might be something Dad wanted her to have and I could send it with my letter."

"And when is that to be?"

"Wednesday morning. The Spencers offered to accompany me, but I told them I'd rather go alone."

"I'll take you," Lance insisted firmly, not making an offer but issuing a command. "If I'm going to handle your father's books for the time being, then I should know exactly what his resources are. Besides, it's far too dangerous for you to ride into town alone."

MaLou knew exactly to what danger he was referring, and that threat brought a wave of revulsion that made her physically ill, but she did not want to get sick in front of him. "I'd like to go in and lie down now. Maybe if you have some time after supper you'd like to look at the books then."

"Are you all right?" Lance had seen her fair complexion pale and was worried she was making herself ill with her twin burdens of grief and guilt.

"I'm just tired," MaLou apologized weakly.

"Well, take a long nap and I'll see you later."

"Yes, thank you, Lance. Until later then."

Lance smiled to himself as he left the porch. Perhaps he had taken the wisest approach possible. If he put his mind to it, there were undoubtedly many other tasks he could handle for the young woman he loved. Nathan would object, of course, but he felt secure enough to offer the help he knew MaLou would need. He wanted her to get used to being around him, to feel comfortable with him again, and he was certain their love would be stronger than ever when she was ready to enjoy it once again.

Jesse bent down to kiss his aunt's cheek as he greeted her. "MaLou will be happy to see you whenever you wish, *tía*. It is a shame you and she were not friends while Thomas was alive, but perhaps you can remedy that situation now."

Candelaria's long sweep of dark lashes hid her tears as she raised a black lace handkerchief to her eyes. "He loved her so dearly, Jesse. That is all I wish to tell her, that her father loved her very, very much. I hope it will bring her some comfort to know that."

Jesse had always considered his aunt one of the world's

most beautiful women. That she had lived her whole life in Tucson where so few people had the opportunity to appreciate that beauty had always saddened him. She was a remarkable woman, for she had not only beauty but resilience and an inner strength he also admired. "MaLou is very pretty. With your help she could be exquisite."

Candelaria regarded her nephew with a suspicious glance. "Are you interested in her for yourself?"

Jesse considered the question seriously for a moment, then shrugged. "Perhaps, but she has several other suitors already."

"And she will have many more now that she owns such a fine ranch, but you are no coward who would be frightened off by a little competition, Jesse. If she has impressed you, then I'm certain you can impress her most favorably in return."

"This is scarcely the time to begin courting her, *tía.*"

"Nonsense, it is an excellent time since she will mistake your calls as gracious attempts to extend sympathy rather than merely being in your own interest. You knew Thomas, so it would only be polite for you to extend your condolences. It is the perfect excuse to visit her, and if she intrigues you then by all means use it."

"No, *tía,* the girl's life is too complicated already. I will wait and see what the next few weeks bring, then if I think I have a chance to win her heart I will make the effort."

"You are a fool, Jesse!" the lovely woman exclaimed. "You are so spoiled by your stable of whores you do not even know how to court a woman of quality. Just because the result is uncertain is no reason not to present yourself at her home. Her surrender will be all the sweeter if the contest for her affection has been a lively one."

Knowing she was undoubtedly correct in her opinion, Jesse did not argue, but it was not the bother of competing with other men that made him hesitate to call on MaLou MacDowell. It was the thought of Lance Garrett's speed with a gun.

* * *

It took Lance a good two hours to figure out how Thomas MacDowell had kept his books. By then MaLou's distracted pacing had become so annoying he gave up all hope of doing any more work and went out to the parlor to join her. "I've discovered the pattern in your father's notations, but it will take me several more nights before I'll be ready to teach his system to you. There are names he mentions frequently, probably the owners of businesses he patronized. Perhaps you'd tell me who they are."

"Of course. Do you want me to do that now or—"

Lance interrupted quickly, knowing he would be wise to leave before his presence made her any more nervous. "No, I've had enough for tonight. I should be getting back to the bunkhouse, where I belong."

He was gone before MaLou could scream at him for teasing her at so inopportune a time. "You're impossible, Lance Garrett," she muttered under her breath as she closed the front door. She was sorry he had left so quickly since the house now seemed dreadfully empty. As she walked through the rooms, her memories of far happier bedtimes were difficult to suppress. Now her footsteps echoed with a hollow ring, for the house was as empty as her heart. While Lance had been there the loneliness had not seemed so bad, but without his presence she again felt adrift in a meaningless void. The black dress had become too depressing to wear and after she removed it she set it aside to launder before she returned it to Constance.

MaLou had always thought of herself as self-sufficient, but as she lay upon her bed, surrounded by darkness, she realized that was because her father had always made everything easy for her. She had helped to serve meals but had never sat with Jake while he planned his menus or ordered supplies. She had never paid any bills or worried about where she would find the money to do it. While her father and the men were involved in the unending work the ranch required, she had simply gone out riding, using her imagination for company rather than tackling any of the problems her father surely must have faced. Rather than assuming responsibility on the ranch, with her father's blessing she had unconsciously avoided it. Well, those days were definitely over. It was high time she learned how to manage the ranch before the vultures Lance had mentioned tried to do it for her. That there were people who would call him one of those vultures pained her, but that type of gossip would be kinder than the truth.

Rather than pacing in the parlor, MaLou was so eager to learn she sat beside Lance on Tuesday night. "I see what you mean. Dad did use names, like James Lee's. Lee operates the mill, so that must be the amount we spend each month for flour."

While Lance was surprised by MaLou's sudden burst of ambition, he considered it a great improvement over the previous day's gloom. With her help he quickly sorted into categories the amounts required to cover each month's expenses. "There's one last entry here. Isn't your mother's name Lily?"

"You mean he was sending her money?" MaLou leaned close to read her father's neat printing. "It just says, 'Lily, five hundred dollars.' That has to be my mother because the whores down on Maiden Lane don't charge nearly that much."

Lance bit his tongue to keep from reminding the willful blonde to show more manners, but he felt her inquisitive gaze sliding over him and knew she expected a reprimand. That made him all the more determined to ignore the remark. "It isn't uncommon for a man to support his divorced wife, but you needn't continue to send her money now that he is no longer able to do it."

"I'd tell you what I think of the woman, but you'd probably wash out my mouth with soap." MaLou did not realize her defiant expression spoke volumes in itself.

Lance thought it unlikely, but did not say so since he hoped it would work to his advantage to have her think he just might do it. "Regardless of what you think of her, she's still your mother."

"Well, she's no longer on the payroll as far as I'm

concerned," MaLou vowed emphatically.

"I don't think we need mention that in your letter," Lance advised diplomatically.

"Maybe I should be the one to write that letter after all."

"No, you'd better let me do it."

MaLou did not argue, since she knew no matter what he suggested in his letter she could send her own version and he would never know what changes she had made. "How do the books look? Is the money going to hold out until we sell the cattle next spring?"

"Your father got a good price for his beef last year so there's plenty in the bank. I wouldn't advise you to think of yourself as an heiress and make plans to tour Europe, but you shouldn't have any financial worries that I can foresee."

MaLou leaned back in her chair, grateful for that news at least. "It will be interesting to see what William Oury has to say tomorrow. He was Dad's lawyer and unfortunately one of the many men who want to see the Apaches at Camp Grant slaughtered rather than fed. He'll be sure to give me a lecture on Dad's politics."

"That's why I'm going along, MaLou. If the man says anything in the least bit rude to you, I'll grab him by his tie, yank him right over the top of his desk, and insist he apologize." Lance wasn't boasting, merely stating what he considered to be a sensible plan.

MaLou was still too depressed to laugh, but she did manage a faint smile. "Oury is something of a living legend. He was born in Virginia, fought with Austin in Texas, and if Travis had not sent him for reinforcements, he'd have been killed at the Alamo. He was a Texas Ranger, fought during the Mexican War, then went to California for the gold rush in 1849. He just happened through Arizona on his way back to Texas in '56 and stayed on. He's handled my father's legal business for years and I guess Dad didn't consider their current disagreement over the treatment of the Indians a reason to find someone else to represent him."

"What about you?" Lance inquired softly.

"I'll let him read the will, but that's it. Oury might be one of the best lawyers in town, but I'd feel as though I were betraying Dad's principles if I hired him. If I ever need an attorney, I'll look for someone else."

"I think that's wise. From what I saw of the Chiricahuas at Camp Grant, they want peace worse than we do. I think we ought to let them have it."

The lamp illuminated the desk with a bright circle of light, but the corners of the room lay in shadows. The setting in which they had worked so easily suddenly seemed seductive and MaLou was all too aware of the intensity of Lance's deep blue gaze. She knew what he was doing. He was waiting for her to again invite him into her bed, but as long as her nightmares continued she could not do it. Ever since her father's death her dreams had been vicious reenactments of the hours she had spent in Lance's arms. Rather than pleasure, the twisted images presented a horrible parody of what should have been the most beautiful of memories and each morning left her filled with unbearable remorse. Try as she might, she could not separate her love for Lance from her guilt over her father's murder. She felt tears again well up in her eyes as they had so often of late but made no attempt to brush them away.

MaLou was dressed in her buckskins, so it was a simple matter for Lance to scoop her up into his arms and cradle her gently upon his lap. He combed her long curls with his fingers and nuzzled her throat softly. "Cry as long as you like, darlin'. I won't leave you." He rubbed her neck and continued to murmur reassuring words until she had fallen asleep. He then carried her into her room, placed her on her bed, and pulled off her boots. After covering her with a quilt, he blew her a kiss. Then, making sure all the lamps were out, he left the house.

Nathan quickly rose from the steps as Lance closed the front door and he issued a menacing challenge. "You're not going to be satisfied until you own this spread, are you, Garrett?"

Whether the foreman had a knife or a gun in his hand Lance could not tell, but he would not make the mistake of turning his back on him and stood his ground. "If you've somethin' to say to me, then just come on out and say it, but I'm not answerin' any of your fool questions."

"Because you can't!" Nathan declared, spitting on the ground for emphasis.

Lance did not bother to argue. He let Nathan think he would take the insult, but as he drew along beside him he made a sudden lunge, grabbed the man's right wrist, and twisted it so cruelly the foreman dropped his knife. "Comin' after me with a knife was the stupidest thing you've ever done," he remarked sarcastically. Then with shocking ease he broke Nathan's arm. When the terrified man began to wail, fearing his neck would be next, Lance clamped his hand over Nathan's mouth and shoved him along in front of him as he strode to the bunkhouse. "Jake can put a splint on that unless you'd like to ride into town to see a doctor. Of course it might be kind of difficult for you to explain how you got a broken arm tryin' to put a knife in my back! Maybe you'd rather say you fell down some stairs."

Nathan nodded frantically, readily agreeing to tell that lie since he correctly guessed it was the only chance he had to escape from Lance Garrett with his life.

Chapter XV

Since she had already laundered Constance's black dress in order to return it, MaLou put on her own blue gown and considered herself properly dressed to visit William Oury's office. That Lance had chosen to wear his suit rather than his usual more informal attire pleased her, for it made the fact that he was handling her father's books for the time being seem indisputably legitimate. As she climbed into the buggy, she reflected that they made an extremely handsome couple, then, ashamed she had let her thoughts stray in that direction, she promptly distracted herself by mentioning Nathan's plight. "I found it difficult to believe Nathan could have fallen down the bunkhouse steps and broken his arm if he had been sober. He insists he was, but I told him I couldn't afford to have a foreman who was either a drunk or so clumsy he had such foolish accidents and if he didn't take better care of himself he could start looking for work elsewhere."

Lance nodded as he tried to keep the width of his smile from giving away his part in the unfortunate man's "accident." "You may not have realized it, but the men are all pretty badly upset about your dad, MaLou. It isn't surprisin' Nathan was so distracted he fell."

"Well, even if it isn't surprising, it's not going to happen again," MaLou insisted emphatically. "I don't want the men thinking they can take advantage of me. I expect them to continue to work as hard for me as they did for Dad."

"I'm sure they will," Lance assured her confidently, for he had never heard any of the men speak about MaLou except in the most affectionate terms. The day was cool and he was glad she had brought a knit shawl. Slipping his arm around her waist, he drew her close to his side. "It looks like the autumn weather is about to give way to winter. I don't want you to catch a chill."

"I'm never sick," MaLou insisted proudly. Despite the boast she remained close, though her posture was somewhat stiff rather than yielding to Lance's unspoken invitation to cuddle up next to him.

"That's good, neither am I." Lance glanced down at her, marveling at the cool detachment she displayed that morning. She had been so nervous when he had taken her to the dance she had bounced up and down the whole way into town. That memory brought a smile to his lips, for she had been adorable, even if she had been unable to sit still. A great deal had happened since that evening, however, and it was no wonder she had changed so completely, yet he took her outward calm as a good sign.

MaLou made no effort to begin a conversation and was grateful when Lance understood she was in no mood to talk and did not pester her with leading questions. When they reached the lawyer's office, she took Lance's arm, and trying to forget Oury's politics, she hoped she could behave like a lady for at least long enough for him to read her father's will. "Good morning, Mr. Oury," she greeted the attorney politely before introducing her companion. "I'd like you to meet Lance Garrett. He's helping me put father's books in order and I knew his presence would be helpful today."

William Saunders Oury was a stern-faced individual with a lean build and piercing gaze, whose readily apparent toughness of spirit had enabled him to survive the many daring adventures MaLou had described. He shook Lance's hand with a firm grip as he dismissed her excuse for inviting him there. "I've heard of you, Mr. Garrett, and I think it's a wise decision for Miss

MacDowell to employ you as her bodyguard. If you can also keep Thomas's books, so much the better."

"Surely I don't need a bodyguard, Mr. Oury." MaLou thought his assumption ridiculous since she could outshoot any man.

"Until we put a stop to the raids those murdering savages out at Camp Grant are so free to carry out, none of us is safe, my dear. That your father wished to help tame those same Indians makes his untimely death deeply ironic."

MaLou frowned slightly, certain she did not want to hear what the man had to say, though she did not want to misunderstand him either. "Just exactly what do you mean, sir?"

The lawyer shrugged, his point clear to him, even if not to her. "It must have been Apaches that killed your dad, MaLou. He caught the thieving renegades helping themselves to his stock and it cost him his life."

"There was absolutely no evidence he was murdered by Indians," Lance contradicted sharply. "I've been to Camp Grant and the Chiricahuas I met there didn't strike me as being so stupid they'd raid the ranch of the man providing them and their families with beef. No sane man would do that."

Surprised to hear Lance speak out so enthusiastically on the Apaches' behalf, William Oury nevertheless failed to moderate his views. "I don't know anybody worth his salt who would claim those heathens are sane."

MaLou saw Lance's posture stiffen at the insult and spoke quickly to keep their discussion from growing any more volatile. "I'm certain those responsible for my father's murder will be apprehended, Mr. Oury, and then we'll see whether their skin is red or white. Now, rather than spend any more time debating that issue, would you please just read my father's will so Mr. Garrett and I can be on our way?"

Lance was delighted to see MaLou still had her old spunk, while he could tell Oury was merely astonished. The attorney had the will lying out on top of his massive oak desk, and while it was obviously difficult for him to stick to business rather than to continue espousing his bigoted views, he cleared his throat several times and began to read Thomas MacDowell's will out loud. He paused frequently to explain the terms in his own words. "Your father wrote his will several years ago, my dear, after you'd returned from the East. Under the circumstances it is a bit unusual, but it was his hope that someday you and your mother would grow close."

MaLou glanced over at Lance, who, knowing her feelings for Lily, gave her a reassuring smile. "That was very sweet of him, but what has that got to do with the will?" she asked bluntly, still trying to hurry the lawyer along.

"It has everything to do with it," Oury announced emphatically. "In his will, your father divided his ranch between you and your mother. You and she are now equal partners."

"What?" MaLou shrieked the word, certain the attorney could not possibly be telling the truth. "You must have misunderstood him. Surely he did not mean to leave her half of the ranch she deserted! She despised Arizona and turned her back on both my father and me more than fifteen years ago!"

"I haven't forgotten the details of your parents' divorce, MaLou, but your father sincerely hoped he could bring you and your mother together when he dictated the terms of his will. It was his wish that the two women he loved most in the world would come to love each other."

"I'd sooner love a Gila monster!" MaLou snapped angrily.

Lance reached out to take MaLou's hand in a comforting clasp as he again joined their discussion. "Does MaLou have any grounds to contest the will?"

"Absolutely none," Oury insisted. "Thomas was not insane, nor under any duress when he made out the document. It was his sincere wish that MaLou and Lily share the ranch."

"Well, it was also unbelievably stupid!" MaLou

shouted angrily. "I will not share so much as a scrap of bread with that bitch! I won't do it!"

Shocked by the young woman's furious outburst, the attorney raised his hands in a plea for silence. "Please, my dear, I know this is a dreadful shock. It is extremely unfortunate that your father failed to discuss his will with you. I advised him to do so, but clearly he did not. Since you know your mother is not fond of Arizona, why don't you make her an offer for her half of the ranch and buy her out?"

MaLou looked to Lance for advice, but he shook his head to warn her to be still. "Mrs. MacDowell has yet to be notified of her ex-husband's death. It would be foolish to offer her money for her part of the ranch when it's possible she may want to make a gift of her half to MaLou."

Oury looked surprised by that possibility since it was something he had not considered, but he did not argue with it. "Of course, there's a chance she might do that. Would you like for me to contact her on MaLou's behalf?"

"No, she'll do it herself. After all, Thomas had hoped to bring the two women together and this will be a good place to start. I hope we can trust you to keep this whole matter confidential, Mr. Oury. It would be best if everyone just assumed MaLou is the owner of the ranch and we'll make that a reality as soon as possible."

"But of course," the attorney assured him, not realizing how deftly Lance had taken over their conversation. "I do not gossip about my clients' affairs."

"Good." Lance bid him good-bye with a curt nod, and, grateful MaLou had kept her thoughts to herself for once, he escorted her from the opinionated lawyer's office. "Just keep still until we're well out of town," he whispered under his breath.

Keeping still was the last thing MaLou wished to do when she was so furious with her father she could barely draw breath to scream her complaints. "Why would he do such an incredibly stupid thing, Lance? Why?"

"Hush!" Lance insisted hoarsely and this time MaLou fell silent. He smiled politely at the people who waved at them, for, as always, the streets of Tucson were congested with visitors, freight wagons, and livestock. He waited until they were well out of town before he pulled off the road and drew the horse to a halt. Wisely, he had not hitched Buck to the buggy but a chestnut mare named Babe. First he loosened his tie, then he turned toward MaLou, whose delicate features were still drawn up in a murderous pout. "I agree with you. While your father may have wanted to see you and your mother become friends, he chose a totally improper and impractical way to accomplish that goal. I don't blame you for being angry. You have every right to be."

"You can save the sweet talk, Garrett. I know what you're trying to do," MaLou shot right back at him.

Amused he had been so transparent, Lance decided to play along. "Just what is it you think I'm doin'?"

MaLou toyed distractedly with the fringe on her shawl, knowing she would never be able to maintain her anger if she looked directly at him. He was simply far too handsome and much too charming for his own good, to say nothing of hers, but she would not play right into his hands. "You're trying to make me calm down, but that's useless because I never will!"

"I'd like for you to calm down so we can decide what to do. I was serious about what I said in Oury's office. I think we can write such a pathetic letter your mother will make you a present of her half of the ranch. It's worth a try at least."

"Dad was sending her six thousand dollars a year, Garrett. Do you honestly think she'll kiss that money good-bye as well as a stake in the ranch? It will never happen. Talk about vultures. Believe me, that's exactly what she is, with well-sharpened claws."

"And yet your father still loved her?" Lance whispered softly, wondering how the woman still had such strong appeal after she and Thomas had been divorced more than a dozen years.

"Dad was in love with a memory, Garrett. He still thought of my mother as a pretty eighteen-year-old girl and conveniently forgot what a selfish woman she'd become."

"I still say you should go slow on this. First write and tell her your father was murdered and how difficult it will be for you and her to run the ranch cooperatively with her livin' in the East. If she hated Arizona as much as you think she did, she won't be eager to come back out here."

"I know you're a betting man, Lance. I'll write as pitiful a letter as I can, but I'll bet you she responds with a wire asking for cash."

"That's not a bet I'd enjoy winnin', MaLou, so I won't take it. Now I want you to promise me you won't breathe a word about your father's will to anyone—not to the Spencers or anyone else. We can't afford to let anyone think your position is less than secure."

"Yes, I understand. There will be plenty of people who'll think a woman can't run a ranch in the first place. If they suspected there was some question as to my ownership, they would never give me any peace."

"Unfortunately, that's exactly right." She was talking with him quite easily now, but her expression was still a hostile one. "Did you want to do some shopping? I just hurried you out of town without asking if you wanted to visit the shops. We could go back if you like."

"No, thank you." MaLou looked away, thinking her situation had gone from bad to worse when she had not even thought that was possible. When Lance called her name in a seductive whisper, she could not ignore the desire in his deep voice any longer. Turning back toward him, she tried to smile but had little success with the attempt.

Lance wanted to promise MaLou he would set everything right, but he knew she would only argue that it was her responsibility, not his. Instead, he made no promises at all but pulled her into his arms. Her lips trembled slightly as they met his, but then she ceased to fight the powerful attraction that existed between them and welcomed the deep kisses they had been without for so many long and miserable days. She clung to him then, her mouth a willing prisoner of his. As she relaxed in his embrace her tongue caressed his with a captivating abandon, luring his emotions into a breathtaking spiral of desire at the same time his generous affection was sweeping away her sorrow. They did no more than kiss, but the longing that swelled within their hearts could not be denied. Rather than risk losing all control of his emotions, Lance forced himself to pull away and reached for Babe's reins. "Once a man and woman have made love it's impossible to stop with kisses, MaLou, but this is no place to take our love for each other any further."

Knowing he was right, the distraught blonde sat up primly and smoothed her curls back into the neat swirl atop her head. "We'd better get back home. It will take me hours to write that letter to my mother and the sooner I start the sooner I'll get finished."

"Yes, ma'am." Lance clucked his tongue to encourage Babe and swiftly had the buggy rolling again. He put his arm around MaLou's shoulders and this time she snuggled against him. "I love you, darlin'."

"How many women have you told that to, Garrett?"

"MaLou!" Thoroughly exasperated, Lance yelled her name before he heard her lilting giggle. She was teasing him and he had fallen for it. "At last count, four hundred and eighty-five!" he answered with a ready chuckle.

"My goodness, is that all?" MaLou gave his arm a loving squeeze, and, while the trip into town to see William Oury had provided more problems than solutions, her spirits soared as though the trip had been a complete success.

Lance had considered their predicament all day, but he could see no way out of it. He had planned to make something of himself so MaLou would be proud to call him her husband, but now it seemed merely selfish to leave the ranch when her life had become so complicated. Yet if he stayed on, he knew they would not be able to keep the intimacy of their relationship a secret for long and he did not want that sort of gossip to damage her reputation. As they worked on the letter to her mother, he found it nearly impossible to concentrate on the task at hand. Fortunately, MaLou had taken his initial suggestions without argument and had written the bulk of the letter herself. They had gone through several revisions, trying to make the wording civil as well as informative, but they were not yet completely satisfied. "Read it to me again," Lance asked with an encouraging smile.

MaLou had not changed her clothes. Still clad in her blue dress, she held the paper upon which she had made her notes and looked very much like someone preparing to deliver an important speech. "Dear Mother," she began, her tone clearly indicating what she thought of the woman.

> It is with heavy heart that I send you the tragic news of Father's death. His murderers have yet to be brought to justice, but I assure you they will soon be hanged for their crimes. It was Father's wish that you and I share equally in the ranch. Since I am here and able to manage our interests, I will continue to do so. Please let me know if you'll be returning to Tucson or if you'd prefer to carry on our partnership through letters. Your daughter, MaLou.

She laid the sheet of stationery upon the table and folded her hands in her lap. "Well, how does it sound?"

Lance frowned slightly. "It's still a little cold, but since you and she have never corresponded before, I'm afraid anything more affectionate would sound forced. Since that letter says all that must be said, do you want to use that or keep revising it?"

MaLou pursed her lips thoughtfully, uncertain whether she was pleased with her efforts or not. "I'm sure we could do better, but I don't really think it matters what I say to her. It's going to be her response that will be the most important. Since she's been getting six thousand a year, she's sure to ask for at least that much."

"Maybe she'll surprise you and not be as mercenary as you think."

"That's impossible." Rather than argue, MaLou straightened up the desk. "I'll write the final copy tomorrow when the light's better."

As she looked up at him her emerald gaze was both seductive and questioning, leaving Lance feeling even more ill at ease. He desperately wanted to make love to her again, but at the same time he did not want to start a pattern that would quickly lead to scandal. "The last time I spent the night here, we both thought I'd be leavin' the next day. I can't go sneakin' into the bunkhouse every mornin' one step ahead of dawn like I did last time either. We're goin' to have to be a lot more discreet, MaLou, and—"

As if she sensed where his hesitant words were leading, MaLou moved off her chair and onto his lap. She put her arms around his neck and snuggled against him as she whispered, "You're the one who said we can't go back, Lance, and I know you're right. Why should we concern ourselves with what others might say about us when we know the truth? My father always did what he felt to be right, whether it was supporting the Confederacy or sending beef to the Chiricahuas, and I'd be a poor excuse for a daughter if I didn't follow his example."

Lance did not know if it was the subtle fragrance of gardenias clinging to her glossy curls, the petal-soft sweetness of her lips, or the determination gleaming so brightly in her eyes that made her views sound so sensible. All he did know for certain was that he wanted her too much to argue that it was not in her best interests to take him as her lover. That point seemed totally irrelevant to him now. Still cradling her tenderly in his arms, he rose to his feet and with a wicked grin carried her into her room. "If we leave the lights on in the parlor each night, someone would have to peek in the windows to see we aren't sittin' there chattin' politely about the weather."

"Any man I catch peeking in my windows is going to find himself out of a job real fast," MaLou vowed confidently as she slipped from his arms.

When she began to untie her sash, Lance reached out to do it for her. "Wait, let me undress you first tonight, and if you ask me how many women I've undressed before you, I will simply strangle you and be done with your impudent questions once and for all."

"Before or after?" MaLou purred sweetly.

"Before or after what?" Lance asked with a puzzled frown.

"Do you plan to strangle me before or after we make love?" the stunning blonde inquired with a teasing giggle.

Lance drew her close and nuzzled her throat with eager kisses as he slipped her gown from her shoulders. "After, of course. I want you very much alive now."

"Why thank you, but that would be a touching farewell." MaLou stood quietly in his arms as he continued to peel away her clothing, wondering why their conversation did not strike her as being ghoulish when it most certainly was. Finally she thought of a way to put an end to her questions that would satisfy them both. "I don't care how many women you've known before you met me, Lance. I know I'm not your first, but I must be the last."

"You must?" Lance asked in a mocking tone, knowing he would not have taken that request calmly from any other woman. From MaLou, however, it was not an ill-tempered demand, but a statement of fact. "You are not only the last, *mi última amor*. You are the very best I could ever have hoped to find."

He sounded so sincere, MaLou knew he had never said those words to another woman and never would. "I love you," she whispered as she reached up to kiss him, certain he was the finest man who had ever lived.

Since they dared not light the lamp beside her bed, Lance not only had the challenge of removing what seemed like unending layers of lingerie, but also had to do it without appearing clumsy in the dark. "I love seein' you in pretty dresses, but damn it, they are a real chore to get off!"

"Do you want my help?" MaLou asked as she reached

for the buttons on his shirt. She loved the feel of his bare skin next to her own and was as impatient as he to disrobe. "It's not nearly so difficult to undress a man in the dark."

With her hands moving over his chest, her light caress promising the delights she had given the last time he had shared her bed, Lance was sorely tempted simply to rip the last of her garments from her lithe frame. Since they had been presents from him, he restrained his enthusiasm and treated her delicate silk lingerie as gently as he had always treated her. When she at last stood nude in his arms, he was so grateful he sank to his knees and covered the satin-smooth flesh of her stomach with lavish kisses. His hands moved lightly over her calves, then up her slender thighs, parting them slightly to make it easier for him to explore her body's most enchanting secrets, for he wanted to know her more completely than he had ever known any other woman.

MaLou laced her fingers in his ebony curls to press his face close, as always too pleased by the marvelous sensations he created within her to be shocked by the way he made love. She wanted to share so much with him and her body was only the beginning. His hands caressed the sleek flesh of her thighs before his fingertips wandered higher to fondle the blond curls nestled between them. His touch, while loving, was knowing, drawing forth the most exquisite sensations before he raised his hands to grip her waist and let his lips and tongue pursue their own quest to possess her.

His searing kiss made the ecstasy he had created within her loins deepen until the pleasure he gave was nearly pain and she called his name in a fevered cry, begging for release. Always a considerate lover, Lance swiftly brought his erotic sport to a stunning conclusion. As tremors of rapture roared through her veins, the beat of MaLou's heart echoed in her ears with such fierce rhythm that had Lance not been holding her so tightly she knew she would never have been able to remain on her feet. When he lifted her into his arms and carried her to her bed, she knew she would never have been able to walk even that short distance on her own, so drunk was she with pleasure.

Lance was as intoxicated with love as his charming companion, but somehow he managed to remove the last of his clothes before joining her in bed. He covered her face with adoring kisses, straying over her thick fringe of lashes to trace her high cheekbones before nibbling her delectable ears. At last he found her mouth and tarried there. His tongue playfully caressed hers as his fingertips brushed over the lush fullness of her breasts. She was the most fascinating creature and he brought their bodies together slowly, savoring her response as deeply as his own. She had both fire and grace, making each of their unions unique and yet ever more meaningful, more loving. That he could not remain with her until dawn broke his heart, for he never wanted to leave her side.

MaLou sat up as Lance got dressed. "Kiss me good-bye, please," she asked almost too sweetly, fearing when he left her the horrid dreams would come again.

"If I start kissin' you again I won't be able to leave!" Lance replied, trying to keep his chuckle low.

"I said please," MaLou reminded him.

This time Lance caught the frantic note of worry in her voice and sat down on the edge of the bed. "Is somethin' wrong?"

Since everything was wrong, MaLou did not even know how to begin to answer his question, so she did not try. "No. I just love you and I want you to kiss me good night."

"My pleasure, ma'am." Lance leaned forward as he raised his hand to caress her throat. He kissed her very deeply and gently before pulling away. "Good night."

"Good night." MaLou waited until he had gotten to her door to call his name. "Lance?"

"Yes?"

"Good night," MaLou whispered again.

"'Night."

Once he was gone MaLou lay back down and tried to find a comfortable position in which to sleep, but the bed seemed enormous without him to share it. For a moment she had been tempted to tell him about her dreams. That impulse was quickly overcome once she realized there was no way she could describe them. How could she explain nightmares in which the delicious sensation of making love to him ended in the blood-chilling horror of finding he was not the one in her bed but that his place had been taken by Death himself instead? Just thinking of that hollow-eyed visage made her shiver with dread, and while she tried only to think of how dearly she loved Lance as she fell asleep, it was Death again who came to make love to her in her dreams.

Since the MacDowell ranch was a considerable distance from town, Señora Candelaria Delgado had sent word ahead so MaLou would be expecting her call and would be ready to receive her. Such a courtesy merely distressed the already distracted young woman, who was certain she would manage the visit poorly. "If only you would stay here with me, Lance."

Lance shook his head at the same time he gave her an encouraging grin. "You needn't be so nervous. I'm sure you'll think of many interestin' things to discuss, since she and your father were so close." Yet MaLou did seem nearly beside herself with anxiety. For the past week they had spent each evening together, but while he had left her house quite early, she did not appear to be getting nearly enough sleep and he was very concerned about her. "Think of Candelaria as another ally, not an enemy."

"Yes, I know I'm being very foolish." They were standing on the porch waiting for the woman to arrive. MaLou had dressed in her lavender dress and had baked small cakes to serve, and, thank goodness, she knew she had plenty of tea. "It's just that when the others came after Dad died there were so many of them they could all talk to each other and I didn't have to worry about what I said."

"Just smile sweetly and let her do all the talkin'. Frankly, I'm so curious about the woman I think I'll hang around and talk to her driver just so I can get a look at her."

"She's very beautiful," MaLou confided easily. "And you were wrong. I was never jealous of her."

Seeing a wisp of dust on the horizon, Lance gave her hand one last squeeze and went down the steps where he could wait out of the way and still have a clear view of Candelaria when she left her buggy. Her driver had set such a brisk pace he did not have long to wait. To his surprise, the widow was younger than he had thought she would be, or perhaps, he reflected, she merely appeared far more youthful than her actual years. She was dressed in black as was the custom of widows of fine Mexican families, but the dark satin of her gown was very becoming. She was of medium height with a slender figure, and her jet black hair was neatly drawn back in a chignon and covered with a delicate black lace *mantilla.* Her olive skin seemed to glow with an inner radiance, and without doubt she had the most beautiful brown eyes Lance had ever seen. When she glanced in his direction he thought instantly of the fawns he had seen each spring in the forest near their plantation, for her gaze held the very same serene curiosity as those splendid animals. She radiated a gentleness and refinement he had not seen since before the war and he knew anyone who met her would instantly recognize her as a fine lady. How such a woman had even met Thomas MacDowell, let alone loved the man, he could not begin to guess, but even stranger was the thought that Thomas had still been in love with his ex-wife when Candelaria was the alternative. In an attempt to make himself useful, he stepped forward to offer her driver refreshment as MaLou showed her into the house.

"It is so sweet of you to allow me to visit you, my dear. My friendship with your father was a long one and he spoke of you frequently and always with abundant love. That is the reason I wished to meet you now, to tell you that I feel as though I already know you and I hope you'll come to me should you ever have need of a friend."

MaLou poured their tea and watched with growing admiration as her guest sipped hers daintily. She was trying her best to display the fine manners she knew she was supposed to have but truly did not. "Thank you. I'm certain I shall have need of many friends in the months to come."

Candelaria glanced about the parlor, thinking the stark room lacked a woman's touch and wondering if MaLou would make any changes. "It will be difficult for you to manage here all alone. Forgive me if I sound forward, but I know it was your father's hope that you might marry Joshua Spencer. While marriage might seem an attractive alternative to you now, I hope you'll not rush into something you might later regret."

While she would have rebelled upon hearing that advice from most people, MaLou found Candelaria's sweet voice and gentle presence so soothing she was not in the least bit offended. "Yes, I know Josh would have been my father's choice, but since I'll be the one who'll have to live with him I've always thought I'd marry the man who pleased me."

"I wish I had been that wise," Candelaria confided softly.

"I know you are a widow, but your marriage was not a happy one?"

The Mexican woman found MaLou's frankness delightful and responded truthfully. "Luis Delgado was closer to my father's age than my own. He was a generous man who left me very well provided for, but the five years of our marriage were most uncomfortable for me. Unfortunately our only child, a daughter, did not survive infancy."

The woman spoke of that tragedy with a calm MaLou could tell was born of rigid self-control. "Forgive me if this sounds like none of my business, but I often told my father he was a great fool not to marry you."

Rather than be insulted, Candelaria set her teacup aside so she could laugh without fear of dropping it. "How very young you are, MaLou," she finally said with a charming smile. "You have the same delightful ability to make me laugh that your father had. Marriage was not something our friendship required to sustain it. We each had our separate lives and were happy apart as well as together."

When MaLou considered the joy she had found with Lance, she did not understand why her father and his beautiful lady had not wanted to be together all the time rather than just occasionally. "Would you like more tea or another cake?" she asked politely, rather than offering another opinion on her guest's friendship with her father.

Candelaria took another cake. "These are delicious. Will you bring me the recipe when you come to call at my home?"

Of the many women MaLou knew, most were like Constance Spencer and greatly overshadowed by their husbands. Candelaria was very different, however, a woman who had made her own life for herself, and she knew she would like to get to know her better. "I would love to come see you the next time I'm in town."

"Good. I'll look forward to it. Now tell me about that handsome young man I saw outside. Is that Mr. Garrett?"

MaLou's cheeks flooded with color as she nodded. "Yes. Did my father tell you about him?"

"Yes, he mentioned him a time or two," Candelaria admitted readily, but she dared not tell MaLou what her father had said. From the lovely way MaLou was dressed and was behaving, she was certain hiring Lance Garrett had been the wisest investment Thomas had ever made, but she would not reveal the details she had been told. "When you come to visit me, I will introduce you to some of my nephews. If you like handsome men, then you are sure to like them."

"Yes, I'm sure I will," MaLou agreed sweetly, but she knew Lance was the only man she would ever need.

Chapter XVI

MaLou spent Sunday afternoon with the Spencers as she had done nearly every week since her father's death. While nothing had ever been said, it was obvious in their generous hospitality that they expected her to wed Josh after a suitable period of mourning had elapsed. It was not an assumption she wished to encourage, but she had little choice in the matter since Lance had insisted she continue to see Josh in order to keep anyone from speculating on the depth of her relationship with him. They had received no reply from the letter to Lily, and, certain the reason was that the woman had failed to receive it, MaLou had sent another. Until the ownership of the ranch was totally in her name, she knew she could do little about her personal life, but it was becoming increasingly difficult to keep Josh at bay.

"You didn't hear a word I said, did you?" Josh asked accusingly. He slapped the reins down on the horse's rump and the speed of the buggy increased slightly. "I don't know why I even bother trying to talk with you on the way home. You never listen to me."

"Of course I'm listening," MaLou contradicted calmly, for indeed she always made it a point to listen closely enough to catch his subject if not the nearly endless detail. "The finest ranch is the one with the finest bulls. You've told me that many times."

Josh frowned sullenly, disappointed he had been

unable to catch her at being as inattentive as he knew she truly was. "I'm sorry. I know you're not interested in talking about ranching anyway."

"Why, of course I am. If I can learn something from you my father forgot to teach me, then I'll be that much better off."

Josh knew exactly what he wanted to teach her but that would have to wait until after their wedding. That thought was so exhilarating he blurted out a hasty proposal. "Let's get married at Christmastime, MaLou. That way we can consolidate the stock on your ranch and ours by the spring roundup."

MaLou could not imagine a less romantic approach, but no matter how he might have phrased his proposal she would have rejected it. "It's really much too soon for me to consider marriage, Josh. The first Christmas without Dad is bound to be an unhappy one and no honeymoon should be marred by that sorrow."

"The spring then?" the young man suggested instead.

"Please, Josh, there's no way for me to know how I'll feel until spring arrives." MaLou wished with all her heart she could tell Josh the truth, but since that was impossible, she made the most generous offer she could. "Why don't you start seeing other girls too, Josh? I won't mind since I know any of them would be more fun for you than I am."

While that was definitely true, Josh could not agree, for he had told all his friends MaLou was his girl and had threatened them harshly in order to keep them away from her. He could not parade other women through town or MaLou would soon be surrounded by men who figured he had moved on. "No. That's sweet of you to make such an understanding offer, but you're the only woman I want to see."

They had reached her house and MaLou knew she would have to kiss him good night. She was grateful that the fact they had no chaperone always prevented her from having to invite him to come inside. "Please thank your parents again for me for another wonderful day. I always enjoy their company."

"But not mine?" Josh asked defensively.

MaLou did not want to play childish games with words. "I meant for you to thank them for me, Josh, while I intended to thank you myself." She leaned forward then, now used to his good night kisses, although she never enjoyed them. He might try to kiss her as tenderly as Lance did, but all too often he bruised her lips with his brutal enthusiasm. She broke away as quickly as she dared, then kissed him lightly on the cheek and climbed down from the buggy. "Good night, Josh. Thank you again for the nice day."

"Good night," Josh called back with a dejected sigh, clearly depressed she had not accepted his suggestion that they marry soon. She remained on the porch, and when he was well on his way she wiped her mouth on the back of her hand, as disgusted about the way the evening had ended as he, but for an entirely different reason. The days were growing short. It was already dusk, and chilled by the night air she hurried inside, built up the fire in the stove, and put on the tea kettle to boil. When she had brewed a flavorful cup of tea, she carried it into her bedroom, but as she set it down to light the lamp Lance stopped her.

"You won't be needin' that," he called out with a devilish chuckle.

Startled, MaLou responded sharply. "Have you no shame at all? How long have you been stretched out on my bed as though you owned it?"

"When you're not here, what's the difference?" he replied in the lazy drawl that fascinated her still.

The weary blonde sat down on the edge of the bed and reached for her teacup. "I can't take much more of this, Lance. The Spencers have been so nice to me and this is no way to repay them."

"And just why are they so nice to you, darlin'?" Lance inquired with more than a hint of sarcasm.

MaLou took a soothing sip of the steaming hot tea before she replied. "I know. They'd like to see our two ranches combined to make the largest spread in the Arizona territory. But married to Josh I'm certain I'd be no happier than poor Constance appears to be."

"Well, I don't think there's anythin' we can do for that woman, but we're doin' all we can for you, MaLou. Do you think it's any easier for me to see you ride off with Josh each Sunday than it is for you to go? When I want so much for you, to be able to give you so little is tragic."

Since he had had far too many tragedies in his life, MaLou certainly did not want to provide an additional one. Setting her teacup aside, she rose and began to disrobe. "We decided in the beginning that we understood each other and that was all that mattered. Eventually everything will work out in our favor. I'm sure of it. Sundays are just difficult for us because I have dinner with the Spencers. We won't have to worry about them once we're married though. Lord knows, they'll probably never speak to me again after that."

The light in the room was very dim, but Lance knew the contours of MaLou's slender figure so well now his imagination as well as his eyes provided his vision. She removed her clothes with a casual disregard for the garments, draping the layers here and there about the room. At his urging, she had bought more gowns in fabrics suitable to Tucson's winter climate, but he still preferred seeing her in her buckskins to anything other than her beautiful bare skin. "Did he kiss you again?"

"Josh?" MaLou asked flippantly as she removed her silk stockings.

"Who else?" Lance replied, hoping there were no others worth mentioning.

"I have tried my best to teach him, but he refuses to learn how to kiss as well as you do."

Rather than his being flattered, Lance's expressive features formed a grim mask of fury. "Don't tease me the way you tease him, MaLou, or you'll be real sorry."

"I don't tease Josh in the first place, and how can you accuse me of teasing you when you share my bed each and every night?" Now completely nude, she moved atop the bed and crawled over him. He was still dressed, and straddling his hips, she unfastened his belt buckle.

"Answer me that, Mr. Garrett. When have I ever teased you?"

Try as he might, he could not recall a single instance in which she had coquettishly promised affection she had not freely given. He reached up to cup her breasts lovingly in his hands, his thumbs slowly circling the pale pink tips until they became tender buds. "I've never been jealous because I've never cared enough about a woman to have a reason."

MaLou leaned down to kiss him and her fair curls tumbled down around his face like a silken veil. "You have no reason now, my love. None at all."

As the tip of her tongue slid between his lips, Lance's powerful body shuddered with the force of the desire that had smoldered all afternoon and he lost all interest in arguing the question. He wrapped his arms tightly around her waist and, rolling over, pinned her beneath him. Only when he held her that securely did he really feel their love would have a bright future. Perhaps he had been a rogue too long, spent too many years detached from all involvement in the lives of those he had met to ever give his love as freely as she gave hers to him. Even crushing her in his loving grasp he still felt alone, as though he had fallen into a bottomless crevasse, and while he tried to catch hold and save himself, the icy sides ripped his hands to shreds and left him plummeting headlong to his doom.

MaLou was stunned by the ferocity of Lance's confining embrace. She had always considered him a passionate man, but the flames of that passion swept over her now with a blinding heat. It was not the sweetness of love she tasted in his demanding kiss but the unbearable pain he had borne alone far too long. It was the most horrid of her nightmares come to life, for he had unleashed the worst of his personal demons and she could escape neither their fiery breath nor grasping claws. For the first time he did not bother to undress, but merely shoved his clothes aside and took her swiftly, satisfying his own savage hunger but leaving her with barely enough strength to fill her lungs to breathe. His forceful thrusts had not hurt her, but he had given her none of the intense pleasure she had recalled whenever she spoke his name. She felt simply drained, as though somehow he had consumed her very soul to sustain his own. Totally abandoned by the man she adored, she felt as horribly alone as he. "Surely that was not making love," she whispered weakly when he finally moved away. Hot tears were rolling down her cheeks, but she lacked the energy to wipe them away.

Lance sat on the side of her bed, still so dazed he could not explain what had happened even to himself, let alone to her. "I think I love you too much," he apologized regretfully. "Way too much."

That the power of that love had overwhelmed them both brought a faint smile to MaLou's lips, for she had felt only Lance's stark terror, not his love. After she had taken several deep breaths she began to feel more like herself. While still trembling slightly, she moved behind him, rested her cheek upon his shoulder, and gave him a warm hug. He reached up to pat her hands but offered nothing more in the way of explanation for the strange violence of his behavior. When she realized he was as deeply confused as she, MaLou slid off the bed. She kissed him as she began to unbutton his shirt. "You can't go back to the bunkhouse like this or you'll be the one to fall down the steps and break your arm, or worse." She continued to talk to him in a soothing whisper as she peeled away his clothes and helped him into bed. "Just stay with me tonight and everything will be all right in the morning. I know it will."

With his head cradled tenderly upon MaLou's breast, Lance did not feel like arguing any more than he had before, and as soon as he closed his eyes he was fast asleep.

MaLou, however, was still wide awake. She stared up into the darkness, her fingers moving lazily through Lance's thick curls as she realized he had taught her a valuable lesson that night. Before, he had always put her pleasure before his own and she had not known that without that loving tenderness she would feel nothing but an aching emptiness rather than the incredible beauty of fulfillment. Remembering Josh's brutish kisses, she could easily imagine what it would be like to make love with him: simply humiliating rather than enjoyable. Since he was so much like his father, Alex was undoubtedly just as self-indulgent in his affection, leaving his poor wife feeling only used rather than adored. It was no wonder Constance was so terribly shy around her husband if that was what her life had been.

What was the word Candelaria had used to describe her marriage? "Uncomfortable." That did not even begin to explain how a woman felt when a man simply satisfied himself at her expense. "Torture" was a far more descriptive term and MaLou vowed that Lance would never again treat her so heartlessly. She would not make the mistake of getting into bed with him again when he was angry, but surely he was at fault for what had happened, not she. She loved him dearly, but there was still so much she did not understand about him, as the harshness of his actions that night had just proven. They had so little time to spend together and he was always so reticent to discuss his past that she had given up her attempts to encourage him to confide in her. That had obviously been another mistake, and a serious one.

Unable to come to any conclusion other than that she loved a man who could not escape the torment of his past, MaLou realized he presented only one of her problems. She owed it to her father's memory not only to keep operating the ranch successfully, but to hunt down his killers. The Chiricahuas had somehow become her responsibility too, but she was positive they had not killed him. Lance, the ranch, the rustlers, the Indians—they all began to spin around slowly in her mind, creating a muddled blur. It was now painfully obvious Lance had yet to free himself from the horror of his past. There seemed to be no way to convince him she would be proud to call him husband now, and she could only pray that what was best for him would prove to be the best for them both.

When several hours later Lance began to stir, MaLou was still awake. "Ever since Dad was killed I've had the most horrible dreams, but none of them was ever as bad as what you did to me tonight. That was a glimpse of hell I don't ever want to see again."

After several hours of reflection her voice was very calm, as though she were merely commenting upon some point of mutual interest, but Lance understood exactly what she meant. "Did I hurt you?"

"Not physically, no, but had you treated me with such total indifference the first time we made love I'd never have made love to you again, nor to any other man for as long as I lived."

Appalled that he had abused her so cruelly, Lance pulled her into his arms, but this time his embrace was the gentle one she had grown to expect. "I had been thinkin' ever since I saw you ride off with Josh that I had no nice home to which to take you, no family who'd welcome you, no way to entertain you in a respectable fashion. The only reputation I have in Tucson is the dubious one I earned for shootin' Randy Hatcher. The only thing that comes naturally to me is trouble, MaLou, and maybe I've caused you more than enough."

MaLou's response to that opinion was immediate and hostile. "If that was supposed to be an apology, it was pathetic!" she replied as she slipped from his arms. Infuriated, she grabbed her pillow and bashed him right in the face with it.

"MaLou!" Lance whispered hoarsely as he tried to ward off her repeated blows. "Stop it!" Finally in self-defense he yanked the feather pillow from her hands, tossed it aside, and grabbed her wrists. Forcing her down upon the bed, he easily subdued her attempts to escape him. "If it's an apology you want, I can think of only one way to give it."

As his lips brushed hers lightly, MaLou ceased to struggle. "I couldn't bear to lose you, Lance. Please don't ever frighten me like that again. Please don't."

That was a promise he knew he could not make. He knew only one way to control his emotions and that was to deny them, but he could no more stop loving her than he could stop breathing. "You'll have to take me as I am,

MaLou, the bad along with the good."

"No," the delicate blonde protested softly as his lips again covered hers, but all too swiftly his magical caress turned that defiant response to surrender. This time he filled both her lithe body and innocent heart with a rapture so perfect that when she awakened the next morning the sorrow of their first passion-driven encounter was no more than a half-remembered dream.

Jake brought home the long-awaited letter from Lily after one of his treks into town for supplies. MaLou thanked him for remembering to check for mail, then carried the letter inside to open. It was hours until she would see Lance and she knew she would never be able to stifle her curiosity that long to read it with him. She paced the parlor restlessly for a few minutes, building up her courage, then she ripped open the envelope and hastily read her mother's reply. The woman had not even bothered to offer her sympathies. She merely instructed MaLou to sell the ranch immediately and come to Boston to live. Since she had no intention of choosing either of those totally unattractive alternatives, MaLou was tempted to rip the letter to shreds but thought she should wait until Lance had had the opportunity to read it with his own eyes since it served to prove her claims of her mother's selfishness.

When Lance entered the house that evening, MaLou handed him the letter and stepped back. "What do you suggest now?" she asked caustically.

Lance read the letter through twice, then took MaLou's hand and led her over to the settee. "I think I'm finally beginning to believe your description of what sort of woman your mother is," he mused thoughtfully as he tapped Lily's elegantly embossed light blue stationery against his palm. "Since you're of age, you needn't do anything she says."

"I didn't intend to either!" MaLou snapped angrily, then feeling guilty she apologized. "I'm sorry. I don't mean to yell at you, but the woman is simply a witch and I've had all afternoon to think about how evil she is!"

"All right, I agree," Lance began with a teasing smile, knowing MaLou always suspected his motives when he agreed with her. "All you need do is tell her you've no intention either of sellin' the ranch or goin' to Boston. Remind her you're fully capable of runnin' the ranch successfully and that you've been doin' just that. Then she'll have to decide if she wants to continue the partnership, give you her half, or ask you to buy her out."

MaLou's dark glance readily revealed her disgust. "I don't need to wait for her answer to know what she'll want: she'll insist I buy her out."

Lance reviewed the letter another time. Lily's handwriting was filled with elegant swirls, but nowhere was there the slightest trace of affection or warmth. "You'll make the bulk of your money in the spring. We'll just stall the woman until then."

"You've seen Dad's books. The sale of cattle brings in a sizable sum, but it's not equal to a half interest in the ranch."

Not ready to give in, Lance offered a possible solution. "You can send the woman twenty percent a year for five years. Offer whatever terms you like. Don't forget you've got the advantage of being here in Tucson. She'll have to take your word for what the ranch is worth and accept your terms or go to the trouble and expense of comin' here herself."

"Oury's not the only attorney in town, Garrett, and she could hire another man to represent her. Since we've made a habit of providing beef to Camp Grant, I'll bet there are a lot of people who'd be only too happy to help my mother sell the ranch right out from under me."

Lance took a deep breath and leaned back to get more comfortable while he considered the likelihood of that happening. Unfortunately, it appeared quite good. "I doubt she'll take such a drastic approach immediately. Let's see how she responds to your second letter before we start worryin' about money."

"We?" MaLou asked skeptically, but seeing the hurt in his eyes she reached out and took his hand. "I'm sorry, Garrett. I know we're in this together. I know that."

Lance watched the worried frown furrow MaLou's usually unlined brow and vowed he would find her whatever money she needed to buy out her mother. It would make a nice wedding present, in fact, and tossing Lily's letter aside he pulled MaLou down across his lap and kissed her until she was giggling and gasping for breath. "You've got to learn to trust me, little lady. No one's ever goin' to take this ranch away from you while I'm here to prevent it."

The man never lacked confidence, but MaLou found it so easy to believe him she reached up to lace her fingers in his curls to pull his mouth down to hers and ceased to worry about her mother's greed.

The rapidly approaching Christmas season left MaLou feeling like an outsider, for although she received several invitations in addition to the one from the Spencers, she had no interest in attending parties. Her father had always loved Christmas and made it such a joyous celebration she found his absence doubly distressing. Finally Candelaria insisted she join in the party at her home on December sixteenth.

"Since you have lived in Tucson all your life, you must know that Mexican families celebrate the holidays beginning with December sixteenth and continuing until we exchange gifts on January sixth. I give wonderful parties, and I insist that you attend."

MaLou licked her lips nervously, trying to make her request sound too reasonable to refuse. "Whenever I come into town I always bring Mr. Garrett with me so I don't have to travel alone. He usually takes care of buying supplies while I'm visiting you, but if I were at a party, there would be nothing for him to do."

Candelaria had had several opportunities to observe MaLou and she had found that while admirably straightforward about some things, the young woman was conveniently noncommittal about others. "Tucson provides many amusements for single men, MaLou. He could simply bring you here, find a diversion for himself, and return for you in the morning."

MaLou considered the woman a wonderfully warm and sympathetic friend, but she had no desire to reveal the secrets of her private life to her. "I could scarcely suggest the man spend the night in a whorehouse, Candelaria."

The charming woman could not help but laugh then. "My darling, you needn't be so terribly blunt with him. Surely the man has been into town and knows how to keep himself amused, whether it's with cards or women, or both. He would undoubtedly appreciate the opportunity to spend a night here on his own."

MaLou had never asked Lance if he had been down on Maiden Lane and she never would since that was something she did not want to know. The thought of him being with another woman sickened her so thoroughly she could barely suppress a revealing shudder. "How Mr. Garrett wishes to amuse himself isn't really the question here. I'd like for him to be invited to your party too. Since you've told me it's to be a large family celebration, surely one more guest won't matter."

Candelaria was a perceptive woman, but she did not wish to believe what she feared might be true. "I will invite him if that's your wish, but you must be careful not to become overly fond of him, MaLou. He's already been on your ranch longer than your father thought he'd stay."

"He discussed Lance with you?" MaLou knew her father had at least mentioned him, but she had thought he had most likely simply related his gunfight with the Hatchers and little more.

"Very casually, of course," Candelaria disclosed before offering more tea. "He's very attractive, but you're a wealthy young woman and must be on your guard against handsome drifters whose motives can never be fully trusted."

Candelaria spoke with such conviction MaLou could

not help but argue that Lance did not deserve to be put in such an insulting category. "You'll have a chance to talk with him at your party. I think then you'll see he's a sincere man, a true gentleman in every respect."

"I certainly hope so, my dear." Since Thomas was dead, the attractive widow decided, she would have to take it upon herself to see that Lance Garrett did no more than the job for which he had originally been hired.

Dressed in a green velvet gown that made her eyes sparkle with the fire of emeralds, MaLou was ready to leave for the party when Lance came to her door. She had expected him to be wearing his suit, but surprisingly he was dressed as a Mexican gentleman in an elegantly embroidered black *charro* outfit decorated with shiny silver buttons. The short jacket enhanced his broad shoulders and ended at his trim waist, showing off the attractive curve of his narrow hips, while the flaring pants made his above-average height all the more impressive. "I thought you were Mexican the first time I saw you until I got close enough to see the color of your eyes. Where did you get that suit? It fits so beautifully it has to have been tailored for you."

"Do you like it?" Lance could already see by the width of her smile that she did, though he had evaded her question by asking one of his own.

"Like it? I love it! It's perfect for a Mexican party." She walked around him slowly, then stopped in front of him and put her hands on her hips. "But we are not leaving until you tell me where you got it."

Lance chuckled slyly. "What does it matter if it fits well and you like it?"

"Come on, Lance, out with it. Tell me the truth," MaLou insisted once again.

"Jesse Cordova knew I'd been invited tonight and suggested I might like wearing this. He's doing his damnedest to get me to come to work for him. I've owned these suits before and since I've always liked them I took it, but whether or not we'll ever do business together remains to be seen. Now does that satisfy your incessant curiosity?"

"Isn't it unethical to accept such a bribe from him?"

"It was not a bribe, it was a gift," Lance corrected her. "Now do you wish to stand here and argue all night or attend Candelaria's party?"

"Cordova's a fool or he'd know he can't buy your loyalty with gifts."

"Thank you." Lance bent down to kiss her cheek. "I doubt anyone will notice what I'm wearin' when you're so very pretty."

Still embarrassed by his praise, MaLou turned away to get her shawl and went to the door. "I think we'd better leave before we get carried away with compliments, don't you?"

Lance did not agree. "No. I plan to tell you what a beautiful woman you are all the way there."

"I shan't listen," MaLou teased with a toss of her fair curls. At his insistence, whenever she wore her hair up she left the wispy tendrils he adored falling free.

Delighted her mood was such a good one, Lance helped her up into the buggy and whistled happily as they started into town.

A high wall surrounded Candelaria's home, but it was far from forbidding. It enclosed a large patio awash in light from hundreds of candles, where a sizable crowd had already begun to gather. Since her family was a large one, there were guests of all ages, from toddlers to a frail gentleman who seemed to be called grandfather by everyone. They were welcomed warmly, but it was Jesse who reached them before their hostess did.

"Good evening, Miss MacDowell, Mr. Garrett." Jesse gave a slight bow as he greeted them. He was dressed in a suit similar to Lance's and was very pleased his new friend looked so handsome in his. "Do you think there is a resemblance between us, Miss MacDowell?" he asked as he stepped to Lance's side.

MaLou studied the two men with a critical glance, as though Jesse's question had been a deeply serious one. They each had handsome builds, although Lance was the taller and she was certainly the stronger. Each had black hair, but Lance's had more curl. The color of their eyes was different, but their features were really quite similar and the bronze tone of their complexions was exactly the same. "You are both so handsome it is nearly impossible to look at you and think at the same time," she finally replied, giving Lance a teasing wink. "While I doubt anyone would ever mistake one of you for the other, you do look very much alike."

Candelaria joined with them and she needed no more than a single sweeping glance to understand why MaLou was so taken with Lance Garrett. While her nephew's good looks were a source of great pride to him, after a few minutes' conversation it became obvious to her that Lance gave no thought at all to his remarkably handsome appearance. He was so respectful in his manner and remarks she hoped she would not offend him, but she still planned to speak with him privately before the evening was over. "I am so happy you could join us tonight. Perhaps you already know we call the parties we have before Christmas *Las Posadas,* which means 'the inns.' As soon as everyone has arrived, we'll have a procession. I always let the children carry the little figures to form the Nativity scene we'll create when we return and give the adults the candles. We'll sing carols and act out Joseph's attempts to find lodging at an inn, but of course no one will let us in until we come back here where everyone will be invited to come inside for the party."

"Do you have a *piñata* for the children?" MaLou asked as two little boys scampered by. She was well acquainted with the customs Candelaria had described, but this was her first opportunity to actually take part and she was looking forward to it.

"Oh yes, a very pretty one shaped like a star. Then we'll have what I hope you'll consider a marvelous dinner and you can dance until dawn if you like. Now please excuse me while I see if we're ready to begin the procession."

As his aunt left them, Jesse again began to chat, his manner a very informal one. "I know MaLou does not come from a large family, but what about you, Garrett? Did you have a gathering like this one to celebrate the holidays?" He favored them both then with one of his most charming smiles.

MaLou saw Lance's expression freeze for an instant before he responded that he had never attended any parties quite so enthusiastically celebrated as this one. MaLou knew better than to ask such questions of him, but she wondered if Jesse would ever be perceptive enough to realize Lance's past was a book he seldom opened. She found the friendly Mexican's company somewhat tiresome, but he walked along beside her during the procession and while his voice was not quite as pleasant as Lance's, she enjoyed hearing them sing together. She knew the words to most of the carols herself, but fearing her voice would make more people wince than smile, she kept still. After they had strolled through the neighborhood they returned to Candelaria's patio, where the servants had hung a *piñata* from the limb of an olive tree. As their hostess had promised, it was shaped like a five-pointed star. Decorated with brightly colored paper and long streamers, it contained a clay pot filled with candy and small gifts for the children. As the children were blindfolded one by one to take their turns to attempt to break the treat-filled star with a long stick, the *piñata* was raised and lowered to make that feat all but impossible until each child had had at least one turn. The crowd encouraged each participant by shouting instructions to swing higher or lower, which invariably proved to be not of the slightest assistance but added to the overall hilarity of the event.

While MaLou was as absorbed as the other adults in the children's game, Candelaria stepped to Lance's side. "Would you come with me for just a moment, Mr. Garrett? I need a bit of help."

Lance glanced down at the attractive brunette, wondering if that politely worded request wasn't actually a command. Deciding that it definitely was, he knew exactly what she wanted, and hoping to get it over with quickly, he agreed. "Of course." He followed her inside the house where she led him into a small library and quickly closed the door.

Pretending complete ignorance of her purpose, he scanned the book-lined shelves. "Is there a book you'd like me to reach for you?" he offered helpfully.

"Please forgive me for that small lie, Mr. Garrett. I wish only to talk. As you know, Thomas was very dear to me and in the short while I've known MaLou I've become very fond of her."

"She enjoys your company as well, Señora Delgado," Lance replied politely, taking a perverse pleasure in interrupting her with the compliment.

"I'm so pleased to hear that. She is a lovely young woman, but a very unworldly one. I know Thomas asked you to help him teach her the things he could not. From what I've seen, you've done a beautiful job of inspiring her to become a lady. All I'm asking is that you do not carry your instruction too far."

"Do you think it is possible for her to become too ladylike?" Lance asked with a perplexed frown, apparently having no real understanding of her request.

Candelaria was not nearly as naïve as Lance had believed. She placed her hand on the doorknob as she replied, "What I am saying, as you well know, Mr. Garrett, is that if there is ever the slightest hint of scandal concerning you and MaLou it will cost you your life."

As she opened the door, Lance placed his hand above hers and slammed it shut. She was delicate and lovely but suddenly reminded him of a deadly spider, and he had no intention of getting caught in her web. "You seem to have a very convenient set of morals, *señora*. MaLou knows exactly what you were to her father and if you make the mistake of tellin' her to stay away from me she'll laugh in your face just as I'm doin'. Save yourself that embarrassment. Now the next time you make the mistake of threatenin' me, I'll forget that you consider yourself a lady and treat you like the bitch you are!" With that bitter retort Lance left the room and slammed the door in her face. He moved back through the crowd on the patio and took his place at MaLou's side, which was precisely where he planned to stay. And just as he anticipated, Candelaria dared not ask him to leave.

Chapter XVII

As Candelaria had promised, the dancing did last nearly until dawn. While she was not expected to know any of the traditional Mexican dances, MaLou still apologized each time she missed a step. She was always forgiven and soon discovered the men at the party were so eager to teach her their favorite dances she had no shortage of partners despite her lack of expertise. She was not surprised to see Lance swiftly master the few dances he did not already know, for he was bright and his coordination superb. She preferred dancing with him to dancing with any of the other men, for he was not only graceful but also wonderful fun. Since she dared not reveal he was her favorite, she allowed him to partner her for only a few numbers. She was careful that while everyone would surely know they had arrived together, there would be nothing in their actions that would cause undue curiosity about the nature of their friendship.

By the time the guests began to depart, MaLou was so exhausted she thought her hostess's invitation to stay the remainder of the night a most attractive one. Uncertain how Lance would feel, she approached him to ask.

It was obvious to the handsome Southerner what MaLou wanted to do. While he had given her no indication he had not been as warmly received that evening as she had, there was no way he would spend the night under Candelaria's roof. Before he could refuse, however, Jesse provided a reasonable alternative.

"Why don't you come home with me, Garrett? You will find my hospitality even warmer than my aunt's."

"Is your home nearby?" Lance asked the man who had seldom left his side, but his eyes were still focused upon MaLou's. If the man lived in a private apartment at the Silver Spur, he wanted no part of his invitation.

"Yes. It is no more than a five-minute journey. We all live within walking distance of one another."

Before Lance could respond, MaLou entered their conversation. "I understand you are trying to lure Lance away from my employ, Mr. Cordova," she remarked with what appeared to be a teasing smile. "He is needed far too greatly at my ranch for me to let him go and I can assure you no matter what you offer to pay him I will pay him more."

Jesse was astonished that the petite blonde was aware of his efforts where Lance was concerned and even more so that she would vow to outbid him. "There are other compensations besides monetary ones," he responded slyly.

"None that I can't match or better," MaLou insisted firmly, her point a serious one even if her smile was still beguiling.

Lance began to laugh. "Please, you two, you are embarrassin' me. Since Jesse's home is close by, send word to me in the mornin' when you're ready to go home and I'll bring the buggy."

MaLou had to pause for a moment as she discreetly attempted to cover a wide yawn. "Yes, I will. Good night to you both." She turned away to look for Candelaria then, wistfully wishing there were a way to spend the night with Lance as she usually did.

The gracious widow showed MaLou to the guest bedroom adjacent to her own. She brought her a beautiful lace nightgown, then returned when she had put on her own. "Is there anything else that you need? Something more to eat or drink perhaps?"

"Oh no, please, I've had far too much already." Dressed

in the borrowed nightgown, MaLou shook out her hair, then climbed into the high four-poster bed. "Your furniture is so handsome. Is it all from Mexico?"

"No, most of it is from Spain and quite old." She strolled slowly around the room, her fingertips caressing the dark woods of the beautifully carved furnishings MaLou had admired. She related the history of a few pieces, then in the same casual tone changed the subject completely. "I found your Mr. Garrett a most . . . well, a most unusual man."

"In what way?" MaLou fluffed up her pillow, hoping Candelaria would be satisfied with the vague replies she would have to give about her dashing lover.

"The way he moves and speaks, the elegance of his manners, everything about the man gives the impression of wealth, but what do you really know about him?"

"Precious little actually," MaLou responded truthfully. "Apparently he is from one of Georgia's finest families, or what once was one of their finest. He lost a great deal during the war, as unfortunately many Southerners did, and he hopes to build a new life for himself here."

"Does it not strike you that he's chosen an unlikely way to go about it?"

"No, not at all," MaLou replied with a sleepy smile.

Candelaria was not the type of woman who was easily discouraged if there was something she truly wished to do. Her confrontation with Lance had disturbed her deeply, but it had not changed her mind about what she knew she must do. There were several ways to go about dissolving his relationship with MaLou, but to tell her her father had hired the man to be nice to her would simply be cruel and destroy the confidence the young woman had apparently only recently acquired. That would certainly sever their ties, but at far too dear a price. "The easiest way for an ambitious man to gain wealth is to marry it, MaLou. But I wonder, would you recognize such a seduction for what it truly was?"

"Seduction?" MaLou questioned with deceptively wide-eyed innocence. "Why that sounds positively evil, and Lance is never that," she protested convincingly.

Hoping her warning had at least instilled some doubt in the pretty blonde's lively mind, Candelaria made one last attempt to win her trust. "I value our friendship very highly, MaLou, and I hope you'll confide in me should you ever need a mature woman's opinion on any matter, whether or not it is an affair of the heart."

"Yes, thank you, I will. Good night." MaLou could no longer stay awake and snuggled down under the covers as she paid her hostess one last compliment. "It was a wonderful party."

"Yes, it was, wasn't it?" Candelaria replied as she slipped out the door. Since her questions had not evoked the faintest trace of guilt in MaLou's expression, she hoped her suspicions were wrong, but from the way Lance Garrett had stormed out of the library, she would have sworn they were already lovers. Perhaps, she reflected, she had merely hurt his pride and he was the gentleman he appeared to be after all.

Jesse Cordova's home, like his aunt's, was a sprawling one-story adobe house built around a central patio. Since his servants had long been in their beds, he poured brandies for them himself. "Do you find it difficult to work for a woman, especially one as pretty and headstrong as MaLou MacDowell?"

Lance chose a comfortable chair, leaned back, rested his feet on an ample footstool, and took a sip of brandy before he replied. "MacDowell had his own way of runnin' things and nothin' has changed since his death. The hands all know the routine and the foreman sees they follow it. I'm the only one who's new and I have no problems with MaLou. From what I've seen of the other men, they don't either."

"Interesting," Jesse mused thoughtfully. "Is it loyalty that keeps you with her rather than coming to work for me?"

"I told you, I'm not interested in dealin' cards for a

livin', nor peddlin' whores."

Jesse winced slightly. "Please. I never think of my girls as whores. They are simply beautiful women who excel in showing men a good time. You must have noticed the single men in Tucson—ranch hands, miners, men who drive freight wagons, whoever—greatly outnumber the women. Why should they have to do without feminine companionship?"

"I wouldn't call that companionship," Lance argued before taking another swallow of brandy. It was extremely good, as he imagined everything Jesse owned would be.

"Have you never slept with a woman you felt worth her price?" Jesse asked inquisitively.

"Frankly, I've never had to pay a woman to sample her charms. That would take all the fun out of it." Lance had had a good deal to drink that night and he was beginning to sound drunk even to himself. That Jesse was no more sober made their conversation flow along easily.

"I must introduce you to Carmen. She will swiftly change your mind about the value of paying a woman for her talents since she has so many."

"Keep her for yourself, Jesse. I'm not interested."

Puzzled, the Mexican leaned forward slightly and lowered his voice. "If you prefer pretty boys, I can supply those too."

Lance laughed out loud at his offer. "No thank you!" He continued to chuckle, thinking the Silver Spur must cater to an extremely wide range of tastes. "I definitely prefer women—young, pretty ones—but I keep them all to myself."

"MaLou MacDowell is just such a woman."

Lance looked up, his gaze suddenly as dark as the brandy in the silver snifter balanced between his fingertips. "She is a lady, Jesse. I'm goin' to pretend you never mentioned her name durin' this conversation, but I'll warn you not to ever make the same mistake again. As I see it, my job is not only to protect her, but her reputation as well, and I'd never damage it myself."

Jesse nodded. "Forgive me. I did not mean to suggest

that she is not a lady, Garrett." Yet his smile was a knowing one, for he thought the man had stated his protest far too forcefully. "From what I understand, she will soon marry Joshua Spencer. I am surprised she did not ask that he be invited to my aunt's party, but perhaps she is not as eager for the match as he."

Lance tossed down the last of his brandy, and needing sleep more than conversation, he set the snifter aside. "This chair's more than comfortable. I'll sleep right here if you don't have a convenient bed."

"The house is large, built for the family I've yet to sire. Someday soon I must start looking for a wife for myself." He rose and waited for Lance to get to his feet.

"You have many pretty cousins," Lance replied as they left the parlor. He followed him down the hall, thinking as he always had how stark the immaculate whitewashed walls of Mexican homes were. The rambling adobe brick houses were perfect for the Southwest, their thick walls keeping out the oppressive summer heat, but his idea of home was still the stately mansions of the South. With their classical proportions and colorfully decorated interiors, they could not have been more different from the homes of Tucson. While he knew such elegant structures would be totally out of place in the boisterous town, nevertheless he missed them.

"I did not think you had noticed," Jesse remarked with a delighted chuckle. "Yes, they are all pretty and sweet, but not what I want in a woman." When they reached the bedroom he had chosen for his guest, he opened the door, then entered first to light the lamp. "If there is anything you need, please let me know. My room is across the hall."

There was a good-sized bed and that was all Lance required for the moment. Suddenly curious about his host, Lance asked him a final question as he removed his jacket. "Just what sort of woman would suit your tastes?"

The brandy having supplied more than ample courage, Jesse told him the truth. "I want a blonde, Garrett. A fair-haired beauty like MaLou MacDowell, but I think the competition for her hand is going to be much too keen so

I'll have to keep looking until I find another."

While Lance knew that would be a difficult quest, he merely thanked the man for the fine lodgings and bid him good night. As he stripped off his clothes, he had the same thought MaLou had had, that he did not want to end the evening alone. Silently he cursed the fate that had made that their only possible choice.

When MaLou said she would like to stop by her father's grave before they left town, Lance drove her to the church, but respectful of her privacy he remained in the buggy. He thought perhaps she would shed a few tears, but when she returned to his side she wore a fiercely determined expression rather than a sad one. "I want to catch those rustlers, Lance, but I have no idea how to do it."

"We haven't lost a single head since they killed your dad, so apparently they've moved on. Unless we caught them red-handed with your cattle, it would be impossible to prove that any rustlers we might be able to catch were the ones who did it. By now, my guess is they've driven the cattle down to Mexico, sold 'em, and are long gone."

"Not if they were townspeople just trying to give us a hard time," MaLou reminded him.

Lance read the newspaper each week and knew that public sentiment was still running high against what was widely regarded as General Stoneman's policy of appeasing the Chiricahuas by providing free rations for them at Camp Grant. It was a complicated issue but not one he thought would inspire anyone who knew Thomas MacDowell to shoot him dead. "You know these people a lot better than I do, MaLou, but we can't go accusin' anyone of murder without proof and we don't have one single shred upon which to base a suspicion, let alone a conviction."

"I know, but it's still something I want to do," she vowed in a determined tone.

"Well, so do I. Let's just keep our eyes and ears open. If it was someone from Tucson just tryin' to stir up trouble for your dad who panicked when he got caught, then his buddies were with him and sooner or later one of them will let somethin' slip."

Greatly encouraged by that prospect, MaLou gave his arm an enthusiastic squeeze. "Do you really think so?"

"I know so. Murder is a nearly impossible secret to keep, MaLou. Let's be just a little more patient and see if we don't hear somethin'."

"Well, what if we discover who did it but can't prove it?" the feisty blonde wondered out loud.

Lance looked down at her, his glance as well as expression supremely confident. "Then I will take care of the bastard myself, MaLou. But let's not cross that bridge until we come to it."

That he would calmly vow to avenge her father's murder did not surprise her and she did not doubt that he would do it, either. "Then we would be the ones with the secret to keep."

That thought brought the first hint of a smile to Lance's lips. "We're already real good at that, darlin'."

"Yes, we certainly are." MaLou did not tell him Candelaria had thought it necessary to warn her about his motives, since she knew it would only upset him needlessly. He had warned her that people would accuse him of being a fortune hunter, but she knew he most certainly was not. As they rode home they fell into their usual companionable silence and she did not complain. She planned to know Lance Garrett for the rest of her life and surely that would be long enough to learn all there was to know about him. What she already knew was the most important thing anyway: she loved him, and desperately.

"Do you still have those bad dreams?" Lance asked suddenly, certain she had been far too tired to have had them the previous night.

"What? Why, no. After I told you about them, they disappeared. That's strange, isn't it?"

"Suppose there's a connection?"

MaLou chewed her lower lip nervously, certain there

was. "Probably. Maybe telling you about them was enough to banish them forever."

"But you didn't tell me about them," Lance reminded her. "You needn't do it now, either. I can imagine what they were since I am something of an expert on nightmares, I have so many myself."

"Maybe telling me about yours would make them go away too."

Lance shook his head emphatically. "No, I wouldn't want to frighten you just in hopes I'd make myself feel better. That would be cruel."

"Well, I wish there were something I could do to make your nightmares go away," MaLou insisted sympathetically.

"Oh, believe me, darlin', you already do!" he confided with a teasing chuckle.

MaLou knew exactly what he meant, and while her cheeks filled with a pretty blush, her laughter was as carefree as his.

Each year her father had provided special meals for his ranch hands during the holidays and MaLou continued the tradition. They always had plenty of beef, so for a treat on Christmas Eve Jake baked hams and served them with yams and fresh greens. His corn bread was feathery light and there was plenty of honey to make it sweet. The Mexican hands always managed to produce *tamales* to fill out the menu with their traditional dish for *La Nochebuena* and the meal was always eagerly anticipated and long remembered. MaLou helped Jake serve the food, then took her own plate back to the house to dine alone so the men would not have to worry their language might offend her if their merriment grew too boisterous. She did not mind eating alone since Lance never failed to pay her a visit later, but that night she was so anxious to see him she found it difficult to sit still long enough to enjoy her food. When at last he came to the door, she quickly drew him inside.

"I have something for you!" she exclaimed happily.

"Another present, MaLou? I got the same bonus the other men did and it was more than generous," he reminded her with an appreciative grin.

"I hope you weren't insulted by that. I had to treat you as I do all the others, but I wanted to give you something special too."

"You needn't have done that." Lance seemed genuinely surprised as she thrust a brightly wrapped gift into his hands.

It took MaLou a few seconds to realize he truly was flustered. "Why Lance, didn't you know I'd have something special for you?"

He had not seen her smile so prettily in weeks and was touched he was the cause. "I didn't think about it at all," he admitted shyly.

"Well, open it! I want to see if you like it." She sat down on the settee and patted the place at her side. "Come sit down. Has it been so long since someone gave you a gift?"

Lance frowned slightly as he sat down. "I can't even remember when it was, so it must have been a real long time ago." He tugged at the ribbon, enjoying having the present so much he did not want to hurry opening it even though MaLou was fidgeting nervously at his side.

While she longed to hear him tell how he had spent his Christmas Eves as a child, she did not ask. Christmas held so many memories for her and all of them good, but she could see that that was not the case with him. She watched as he finally unwrapped her package and opened the box.

Lance removed the tooled leather belt and gave a low whistle as he admired the highly polished solid silver buckle. Not even Jesse Cordova owned one as fine as this and he was delighted with it. "Thank you. This is the nicest one I've ever seen."

"Why don't you try it on?" MaLou suggested enthusiastically, pleased to see he truly did like her gift.

"Sure thing." Lance rose to his feet, removed his well-worn belt with its scarred brass buckle, and dropped it to the settee. "This must have been very expensive."

"Yes, it was," MaLou agreed with her usual frankness. "But it will last for years and years and always remind you of the first Christmas we spent together."

"As if I'd ever forget," he teased her with a ready grin. Once he had threaded the belt through his belt loops he fastened the buckle and asked for her opinion. "How does it look?"

"It's not quite as handsome as you are, but it will have to do." MaLou stood, stepped into his arms, and gave him an enthusiastic hug. "I love you so much, Lance. Merry Christmas."

Lance pressed her close, enjoying the soft sweetness of her figure for as long as he possibly could before he finally moved back slightly. "Now I suppose you'll be expectin' me to have a gift for you."

While MaLou had certainly hoped that he would buy her something, she would not admit it. "I bought you a present because I wanted to give you one, not because I expected one in return."

"Then you won't be disappointed if I don't have one for you?" Lance asked skeptically.

"You've given me a great deal already, Lance," MaLou replied sweetly, unwilling to admit just how deeply disappointed she would be.

Lance leaned down to give her a kiss, then pulled a small package from his hip pocket. "You're sweet to say that, darlin', but I wouldn't forget you."

MaLou took the box and shook it slightly, trying to figure out what was inside. It was wrapped in red paper, tied with green string, and rattled slightly when shaken.

"Why don't you open it, MaLou? That's the best way to find out what's inside." Lance took her hand and led her back to the settee so she could unwrap his gift more easily.

MaLou was certain he would not wrap a wedding ring, but truly that was the only thing she wanted from him. At his urging, she tore the paper from the small box and removed the lid. Inside she found a beautiful gold locket suspended from a delicate chain. In the shape of a heart, it had been engraved in fancy script. *"Mi última amor,"* she whispered softly as her eyes filled with tears.

Lance had expected her to squeal with delighted surprise, not cry, and he did not know what he had done wrong. "You don't like it?"

"I love it!" the tearful blonde insisted between hoarse sobs. "I love it."

She looked so miserable, Lance was certain that could not possibly be true. He pulled her across his lap and hugged her tightly. "If you'd rather have something else, just tell me and I'll buy it for you."

"No, this is perfect." She tried to wipe away her tears, but they kept falling, dampening his shirt and making her feel very foolish. "I'm sorry. I just wish I could tell everyone how much I love you."

Lily had yet to reply to MaLou's second letter, but Lance was still anticipating considerable trouble from the woman and he had promised himself he would not leave the ranch until MaLou was its sole owner. He tilted her chin with his fingertips, then kissed her very softly and gently until her sorrow was tinged with desire. He brushed away the last of her tears, then kissed her again when she made a brave attempt to smile. "You won't have to wait much longer, and then if you want to run notices in the paper telling everyone how wonderful I am I won't object."

"I just might do that." MaLou handed him the locket so he could fasten the chain, but when she lifted her long curls out of his way he began nuzzling her nape so hungrily she nearly slid off his lap she was giggling so hard. "Lance, you're tickling me! Stop it!"

"Well, that's a whole lot better than making you cry." Holding the locket carefully, he draped the gold chain around her neck, fastened the clasp, then kissed her nape one last time. "There. It looks as pretty on you as I knew it would." He wondered if she had bought something for Josh but then decided he did not really want to know. "You can wear it when we're together now, and then one day you'll never have to take it off."

MaLou studied his expression closely, thinking that if

he had had only his own interests at heart he would already have married her. Then with a sudden stab of alarm she wondered if maybe it would be even more clever of him not to marry her. What if it took years to settle the dispute with her mother over the ownership of the ranch? Would he delay their wedding until the deed was in her name? She wanted to believe he was protecting her, but what if he was protecting only himself?

"MaLou? What's wrong?" Lance felt her shiver as though chilled and held her more tightly. "Are you cold?"

"No," she assured him, too confused in her own mind to put her worries into words. She remembered then that he had planned to ask for her hand on the day her father's body had been found. Had the dear man lived, then they would already be married, or at least so she thought. Lance would have been able to leave the ranch and go into business, and she was certain he would have been the instant success he was determined to be before they married.

Lance knew MaLou so well he sensed as well as saw her confusion and rightly guessed its cause. "Everythin' will work out for us soon, MaLou. Let's just enjoy each other tonight and not let anythin' come between us." He smiled warmly and soon felt her begin to relax again. He leaned forward to capture her lips in a gentle kiss he waited patiently for her to deepen. She had learned so quickly how to make love and he did not want to delay another minute before savoring the delights of her silken-smooth flesh. "Let's go into your bedroom where I can peel off your clothes and start kissin' you at your pretty pink toes."

"What an enchanting invitation." Eager to accept it, MaLou paid him that compliment as she slid off his lap. Leaving the boxes and wrappings from their gifts to be cleaned up the next day, she extended her hands and pulled him to his feet. "I can't think of anywhere I'd rather spend Christmas Eve than in bed with you."

"I think that's lucky for us both." Lance dropped his arm to encircle her waist as they walked down the hall. While her door was open, the one to her father's bedroom had been closed each time he had been in the house and he wondered if she had ever cleaned out the room. Since it was no time to ask, he did not, but he was curious all the same.

As they entered her room, she reached immediately for his new belt buckle. "I know exactly where I'd like to begin kissing you, but it's not your toes," she whispered seductively.

Lance stood very still, knowing what she was suggesting and not about to object. She was the most uninhibited beauty it had ever been his pleasure to meet and he wondered if that came from the unusual nature of her upbringing. If so, then he would raise every daughter they had as if she were a son until she turned nineteen. What glorious creatures they would be, though he was certain they would never give their husbands more pleasure than their lovely mother continually gave to him. Each touch of her fingertips and brush of her lips was filled with such abundant love he longed as much as she did to end the secrecy that surrounded them. His plan was a good one, however, and not one he would discard in a moment of weakness like the one that overcame him now. She was not so much undressing him as inspiring him to rip off his clothes himself, for he found the hours they were apart each day growing increasingly impossible to bear when he knew the thrills the coming night would bring.

Without a single wasted motion, MaLou undressed the handsome man. First her small, soft hands, then her slightly moist lips, caressed each new area of flesh she exposed, providing a tantalizing preview of the love she planned to lavish upon him. She knew his body nearly as well as her own now, but he fascinated her still. Every part of him had its own appeal. She liked to rest her head on his broad shoulders and feel the strength of his muscular arms as he wrapped them around her. She loved to press against the flatness of his belly while she rolled her hips against his and felt him grow hard with desire. She had found out quite by accident that rubbing against him like that was as pleasurable to her as to him and did it often.

When he was completely unclothed she continued to

move with deliberate grace, seating him on the edge of the bed while she reached for a pillow to cushion her knees before kneeling between his outstretched legs. Resting her arms upon his thighs she was as comfortable as he as she leaned forward to draw the tip of his manhood into her mouth. She found his taste and scent as deeply erotic as he found the sensuous swirls of her tongue. She had needed little in the way of instruction to learn which motions gave him the most pleasure and as he laced his fingers in her long curls to press her face closer still, she was pleased the magic of her loving was still as powerful as his.

By the time MaLou had discarded her own apparel and joined him in the bed, Lance's passion-dazed mind had begun to clear. He swept back the covers to expose every delectable inch of her pale body and, as promised, began placing adoring nibbles upon her toes. His tongue caressed her instep, then her well-turned ankle, before his fingertips circled her calf. His lips strayed slowly up the inside of her thigh, then returned to her dimpled knee to begin their luscious journey once again. He sampled one slender leg thoroughly, then began again at the toes of the other, thinking he would never tire of teasing her senses so playfully when she did the same to him.

While Lance's kisses tickled her feet, a delicious excitement had begun to build within her loins by the time his lips traced the inner curve of her thighs. She held her breath then, waiting for him to plunge his tongue deep within her, but instead he moved away. He stretched out beside her, drew her into his arms, and kissed her lips instead. While surprised at his sudden change in tactics, MaLou returned his deep kisses with several of her own, thinking his loving delicious no matter how he wished to give it. He soon slid down by her side and drew first one flavorful nipple and then the other into his mouth. His tongue caressed her tender flesh as she smoothed back his thick curls and held him cradled in her embrace. He was the dearest of lovers, patient and sweet, and the longings he created within her lissome body swelled like a tide of rapture and flooded her veins with continuous waves of heat. When his lips moved over the flat plane of her stomach she knew this time he would not stop with playful nibbles. His tongue slid down between her legs, caressing her from arousal to fulfillment with an irresistible rhythm that matched the driving beat of her heart. She shuddered as the ecstasy swept through her and a low moan of surrender escaped her parted lips. He slid over her then, clasping her with the entire length of his powerful body as his first driving thrust joined them in a mutual pleasure so deep they plunged to its depths before rising gracefully to the surface, where they floated on the calm sea of a radiant afterglow.

MaLou lay snuggled in Lance's arms, more asleep than awake. The year was nearly over and she knew it was one she would never forget, for it had brought her not only terrible grief, but a love so beautiful it had made even that sorrow easier to bear. Their time together had passed swiftly, but she had savored each and every minute of it. She reached up to grasp her new locket and a slow, sweet smile curved across her lips. "I love you, Lance Garrett," she whispered softly.

Lance stretched, flexing his muscles with a lazy, masculine grace. "And I love you, MaLou MacDowell, more every day."

"Are you certain you don't mean more every night?" she asked with a teasing giggle.

Lance sprang for her then, capturing her in a confining embrace as he muffled his laughter against the elegant curve of her throat. "Yes, my darlin', you're right. Our days don't begin to compare with our nights."

"Well, let's not waste the rest of this one," MaLou suggested softly as she slid her fingertips down his back and over the smooth curve of his hips, and to her immense delight, they did not waste a second of the time they still had to share.

Chapter XVIII

Lily MacDowell's second letter was nearly identical to her first. She again directed her daughter to sell the ranch and come to Boston. While Lance had not thought it possible, the letter was several degrees cooler in tone than the previous one. "Well, this is gettin' ridiculous and we can't write the same response," he advised as calmly as he could. "Let's offer her what she'd have received from your father in five years' time: thirty thousand dollars. That ought to be enough to convince her you've no intention of leavin' Tucson."

"The bitch doesn't deserve a nickel, Lance, not one nickel," MaLou insisted as she did each time they held this same discussion. She sat back in her chair, her arms folded across her chest, her expression a petulant frown.

"Look at it this way, MaLou," Lance explained in a soothing tone. "I'd like to have the issue resolved so I can get on with my plans. You'll have to borrow the money from the bank, but makin' money is no problem for me and I'll see the loan is promptly repaid. You'll not be goin' into everlastin' debt to buy your mother's half of the ranch from her."

MaLou's glance was still murderous. "Why should I have to pay the bitch for what is rightfully mine? This is the worst mistake Dad ever made, but I fail to see why I should have to be the one to pay for it!"

Lance sighed wearily, tired of fighting her anger when he was not the cause. "If thirty thousand seems too high, ask her to make you an offer. Or, don't do anything until I get back from Camp Grant if you like. Just put the problem out of your mind for a week until I come home. I don't want you worryin' about this the whole time I'm gone."

"I could go with you," MaLou offered brightly, a smile now lighting her delicate features with a pretty glow.

Lance shook his head emphatically. "No, MaLou. I'm takin' twice the men, and more than twice the precautions, but I don't want you to be at any risk. The men would welcome a fight and I know you probably would too, but you're far too precious to me to risk so foolishly."

When he leaned over to kiss her, MaLou wrapped her arms around his neck to give him a loving hug. "I'll miss you terribly, but I know you're right. The men would be too cautious with me along, and then someone might get hurt who would otherwise have been safe."

Glad she was at least being sensible about the trip, Lance scooped her up into his arms. "Enough arguin' for tonight, MaLou." He then whispered such an enticing invitation in her ear, she nearly purred with delight.

While they had not decided how to deal with her mother, MaLou always agreed completely with the man she adored whenever he was in the mood to make love. "Don't you think you'd better put me down?" she asked demurely. "What if someone should see you carrying me through the house?"

Lance laughed out loud at her question. "There's not a man on the spread who doesn't know exactly what we're doin', MaLou, even without seein' us."

While she thought that was undoubtedly true, it caused her no sense of shame. They had found such perfect happiness together, she simply did not allow guilt to hamper it. She wrapped her arms around his neck and nibbled his earlobe as he carried her into the room. "You are a devil, Mr. Garrett," she scolded with an accent as thick as his, and he gave her no chance to say anything more.

* * *

Lance had his handkerchief pulled up over his nose so he would not choke on the dust the cattle kicked up. He had paid close attention on his last trip and now had found the route north easily on his own. He had ridden ahead each day, scouting for trouble, but none had appeared. Fearing it might again strike as unexpectedly as it had before, however, he remained constantly alert. That the trip was a brief one was something for which he was truly grateful, but at least this time they had brought along Pablo, the young man who usually assisted Jake, and had had far better meals.

Manuel spurred his mount to catch up with Lance. They could see for miles in every direction, so he knew it would be safe to talk. He had insisted upon making the trip, not to prove his courage to others, but only to himself. "What do you plan for today, another hour or two?"

Lance glanced up at the sun, knowing he was pushing not only the cattle, but the men as well, and making even better time than they had on their first trip to Camp Grant. "Two at least, maybe more," he replied optimistically. "Are you tired?"

Manuel shrugged. "No more tired than the others."

Lance laughed at that show of diplomacy. "Did they send you to ask me to slow down?"

"I may have heard one or two complaints, but that's all."

"Good." Lance's glance swept the horizon again to make certain it still contained no more than scattered scrub brush.

"Of course, none of us has as good a reason to hurry as you," Manuel offered with a knowing smile.

While he knew exactly what the feisty Mexican *vaquero* meant, Lance did not admit it. "Is that so?"

"Oh yes, it is so," Manuel insisted, then with a sudden reckless bravado, he decided to ask the one question they all wanted answered. "Why have you not married her?"

The question itself could have been taken as an insult, but Lance knew that coming from Manuel it was only gentle prodding. "I intend to." The men knew nothing about the terms of Thomas's will and Lance would not reveal them. That apparently William Oury had been as closemouthed as he had promised had come as a welcome surprise. "I'd like to have more to offer than I do now, but it won't be long."

Manuel sighed unhappily, for now that he had brought up the subject of MaLou, he found he was not satisfied with Lance's answers. "Both she and Josh are fair. She'd have no way to explain a black-haired child."

Lance knew instantly it had been a mistake to allow the man to think he would discuss such a personal issue. "She'll have no reason to be makin' any such excuses, Manuel, and neither will I!" With that hoarsely worded vow he turned his horse away and circled the swiftly moving herd to gather up the strays. He did not need to be told he owed MaLou marriage when he already ached to make her his wife. Were she to become pregnant, then he would marry her immediately, since the disgrace of bearing an illegitimate child would be far worse than that of marrying a ranch hand. MaLou was not pregnant, however, and while that seemed to be the one bit of luck they had had, he hoped it continued a few months longer.

When they arrived at Camp Grant, Royal Whitman greeted Lance warmly. He needed only a few minutes' conversation with the Southerner to see his mood was a far better one than that of his previous visit and he was pleased by this. They enjoyed a pleasant supper together, then went out for a stroll. "As you can see, our numbers have grown," he remarked with a sweeping gesture toward the Chiricahua settlement. "We have new arrivals almost daily. That's why I needed more beef."

"Does the government plan to set up a reservation here?" Lance asked curiously, knowing that regardless of what the thinking was in Washington, the citizens of Tucson would never allow one to be built within a week's ride from their town.

"No, this is a temporary location only," the lieutenant assured him with a preoccupied frown. "As you know, I'm on my own here and I have to trust my judgment to be correct."

"As every man must," Lance pointed out with a reassuring smile.

"Yes, of course," Royal agreed, pleased he had found his guest not only intelligent but sympathetic as well. "Let me tell you what's been happening here since your last visit so you'll understand my problems more fully. A while ago some Apache women came to me under a flag of truce. They were looking for a boy they said had been captured by soldiers."

"Was he here?"

"Yes, but he did not wish to leave with them."

Lance nodded, easily understanding how such a dilemma would take a man of King Solomon's wisdom to resolve. "What did you do?"

"I considered him old enough to make his own decision and let him stay. The women then returned to trade with us. Before they left, they asked if their chief might come to talk with me about peace. Naturally I extended such an invitation, since that is our mission here."

As they drew closer to the Indian camp, Lance saw several little boys playing a game of tag. The setting sun glistened brightly on their glossy black hair and his thoughts instantly strayed to MaLou. Since she was blond, it was possible their children would be fair too, but he planned to make her his wife long before their births or coloring would cause any embarrassment. Knowing his mind was wandering shamefully, he forced himself to pay far closer attention. "What did the man have to say?"

"His name is Eskiminzin. He's quite young. He has a band of some one hundred fifty who consider themselves Arivaipa Apaches. They wish to make peace and settle along the Arivaipa Creek. I suggested he go to Fort Goodwin in the White Mountains, but he insisted this is his home and they want no other. Their ancestors raised corn in this valley and they can gather mescal here, which they can't do at Goodwin."

Lance stopped walking then and turned to face the earnest lieutenant. "It is gettin' more and more difficult for me to understand why, if the Apaches agreed to be peaceful, they can't live where they want to when we have that privilege."

"They are where they want to be for the time being. I told them to make their camp here on the creek about a half mile from the post. Since I have no authority to make treaties, I wrote to General Stoneman for further instructions, but as yet I've received no reply. I keep close track of the Indians, issue rations every other day, but until I hear from Stoneman, no permanent arrangements for a settlement can be made."

"Do you ever see copies of the *Citizen*?"

Royal winced. "Their criticism is brutal, and yet when I move among these people, I feel what I'm doing is right."

They had discussed Thomas MacDowell's death before dinner, for the lieutenant had been deeply saddened by it. "Miss MacDowell will continue to supply all the beef the Army wishes to buy. Her father was on your side. So is she."

Since Lance obviously was too, Royal considered himself fortunate to have such fine allies. "We could do it here, Garrett. We could finally bring peace to the Territory, but I can't do it alone."

"I don't think anyone expects that," Lance assured him.

"Well, most days it sure feels that way," Royal admitted regretfully.

They turned back for the fort then, each man hoping the future would be bright for himself as well as the Apaches.

With her evenings spent alone, MaLou found her thoughts straying frequently to her father. He had been such a charming companion and she still missed him as greatly as she had on the day of his death. She had not been in his room since the funeral but decided that since the house would one day belong to her and Lance she could not keep her father's room locked as though it were a shrine. It would be far better to clean it out and redecorate it now than to wait until they needed it for a child's bedroom. Convinced the beauty of her memories did not depend upon keeping her father's room untouched, she gathered all her courage and armed with her broom, dust pan, and dust cloths, she went in to begin its transformation. She knew there were some of her father's things she would want to save, but there was no need to save them all. Beginning with the dresser, she removed all his clothing and arranged it in neat stacks on the bed. She then opened the drawer he had used for personal items and sorted through them reverently. Not only his gold pocket watch was there, but the one that had belonged to his father, a man she had never known. There was an assortment of odds and ends such as loose change and buttons that had fallen off shirts he had worn out long ago. There was also a stack of old letters, and as she withdrew them from the drawer she found an envelope addressed to Lance hidden underneath. The money he had won was still in the safe, so what could this be? she wondered. Too curious to wait for his return to find out what it contained, she was delighted to discover that the envelope had not been sealed. She opened it quickly and took out the brief message.

The sight of her father's neatly penned hand brought tears to her eyes, but she wiped them away and read the note aloud: "Lance, in a few short weeks you've managed to accomplish what I couldn't do in nineteen years. You've made a lady of MaLou. The smartest decision I ever made was to offer you that job. I want you to have this bonus. You've earned every cent of it. Thanks again." Her father had signed his name but apparently had not had time to gather the cash for the bonus he had mentioned.

MaLou sank down on the bed and read the letter again, for its shocking contents had simply stunned her, but the longer she studied it the more dreadful her suspicions became. Was it possible Lance had been hired solely for the purpose that the thank-you note appeared to make painfully obvious: to make a lady of her? Considering his first days on the ranch, that did not seem possible, for their initial conversations had been brief and antagonistic rather than cordial. It had not been until he had offered to escort her to the dance that their friendship had blossomed. Blossomed was hardly the correct word, she realized with a bright blush, when they had come so close to making love in the buggy on their way home. Surely her father would have skinned Lance alive rather than providing him with a generous bonus had he ever found out about that. She reread the letter several more times, her mood sinking steadily lower. Had her father really thought her so pitiful a female no man would ever be nice to her unless he paid one to be? She gave in to the wave of tears that flooded her eyes at that dismal thought and sobbed dejectedly. She could easily imagine the conversations that had taken place between the two men she loved, and she felt far more than merely hurt, for they had betrayed her trust in the cruelest fashion. Had she simply been sold outright it could not have been more humiliating. If her father had still been alive she would have immediately confronted him with her shattering discovery, but since only Lance could provide the answers she needed, she had no choice but to suffer the most agonizing doubts until he returned home.

As soon as he reached the ranch, Lance went to MaLou's door so she would know they had all returned safely. "Give me some time to clean up and I'll give you a full report after supper."

MaLou was dressed in the red-and-white-striped gown, which was still her favorite. She had taken special care with her hair and knew her appearance was as flawless as any lady's could possibly be, even if her mood was anything but ladylike. "I want to speak with you now, Garrett," she ordered calmly. She moved aside to allow him to enter but did not sit down or invite him to take a seat either.

"I've really missed you," Lance revealed readily as he moved through the door, but as he reached for her waist to draw her into his arms she stepped away to avoid his touch. "What's wrong, MaLou? You look so pretty. Are you expectin' company?"

"No, you're the only man I wanted to see today." MaLou had her father's note in her hand and showed it to him now. "I finally got around to cleaning out my father's room while you were away and I found this."

Puzzled, Lance took the thick envelope from her and broke the seal. When he found a thousand dollars in fifty-dollar bills wrapped within a single sheet of stationery, he gasped with surprise. "What is this, MaLou?"

"It's addressed to you. Why don't you read the note?" she replied helpfully.

Lance scanned the letter hurriedly, then frowning deeply he handed the bills to her. "Put this in the safe with your money, MaLou. I don't want it." He jammed the letter back in its envelope, folded it in half, and shoved it deep into his hip pocket.

MaLou had thought a thousand dollars a reasonable reward for his services and was surprised he had refused it. She counted it out slowly, as though she had no idea how much he had handed her. "But Lance, my father must have had a good reason for giving you this. Are you sure you don't want to keep it?"

Lance shook his head. "No, I won't take it, and that's final." When his emphatic refusal served only to make MaLou's perceptive gaze all the more curious, he tried his best to explain in terms that would not insult her. "Your daddy asked me to do a favor for him, which I did, but I won't take money for it."

MaLou sighed softly, the most important of her questions answered, but knowing that he would not accept money for doing the job for which he had been hired did not make her feel any the less abused or ashamed. "Well, that's certainly to your credit," she told him first, but then her fiery temper got the better of her. She reached for his hand, slapped the money into his palm, and folded his fingers down over it. "I don't know which betrayal is the worst. That my father would think it necessary to hire a man to make a lady of me or that you would accept the job, but just as he said, you've definitely earned every cent of this bonus and I insist you keep it!"

Realizing she had read the note made Lance feel as though he had been kicked, for he could well imagine what she thought of him. "It wasn't like that at all, MaLou."

The petite blonde stepped back, folded her arms across her chest, and tapped her foot impatiently. "I know men sometimes take their sons to whorehouses in order to 'make men out of them.' At least my father was more creative. He bought me my own whore. It's a shame he died without knowing just how much you'd taught me about being a lady, isn't it?" she asked with deadly sarcasm.

If there was one thing Lance knew well, it was that when MaLou was in an unreasonable mood it was pointless to try to argue logically with her. Unfortunately, he was tired, dirty, and in no mood to argue in any fashion and his temper flared in response to her insult. "I am no whore!" he denied heatedly.

MaLou unfastened the gold locket he had given her for Christmas, reached out to open his shirt pocket, and dropped it inside. "My father apparently had a different opinion when he offered you the job. Keep the locket, since it's obvious I'm not going to be your last love after all. You can stay the night if you like, but I want you off the ranch tomorrow." Anticipating just such a hostile farewell scene, she had removed the money he had won from the safe and now turned to pick up the envelopes from the marble-topped end table by the settee. "Here's the rest of your money along with your wages. I don't plan to speak to you ever again, so if by some horrible coincidence we should happen to meet on the street in Tucson, I plan to pretend we've never met. I hope you'll be gentleman enough to do the same."

"Have you lost your mind?" Lance asked crossly. "I love you! I thought you loved me. When I left here a week ago we were hopin' we could be married before too much longer, and now suddenly you don't even want to speak to me?"

MaLou stared at him coldly, still thinking him

heartbreakingly handsome and trying with all her might to ignore that fact. "Do you think I'm being too hasty?" she inquired sweetly. "Perhaps you think you deserve a chance to convince me I'm wrong. It needn't be a long, impassioned speech, Garrett. Just tell me the truth. Did my father ask you to teach me how to be a lady or not?"

Lance took a deep breath, stalling for time as he tried to think of some way to explain what her father had asked him to do that would not make her feel worse than she already did. Each sentence he began in his mind got him deeper into trouble, and finally he knew there was no way out. "It doesn't matter what he asked me to do, MaLou. The only important thing is that you and I fell in love."

"You mean you got caught in your own trap?" she asked accusingly.

"No!" Lance countered angrily. "Josh was the one who was supposed to fall in love with you, not me! But you know that as well as I do."

Apparently confused, MaLou mused aloud, "I wonder why Dad didn't just pay Josh to take me off his hands. It would have been so much easier on all of us."

Somehow that cool detachment was as difficult for Lance to take as her undeserved anger. "I'm sorry you ever found out about this, because it makes both your dad and me look like we were just manipulatin' your feelings and—"

MaLou could take no more of his excuses and interrupted with a fiery outburst. "It doesn't just look that way, Garrett. That is the truth! The man hired you to pretend to like me, to be nice to me and encourage me to act like a lady because he was afraid he'd never be rid of me otherwise!"

Lance knew MaLou had adored her father, but since his death she had grown understandably bitter over the fact that he had left half his ranch to the mother she despised. Now she mistakenly believed the man had simply wanted to get her off his hands. Regardless of what she thought of him, he did not want her hating her father. "You're wrong, MaLou. He loved you dearly and he wanted you to have the husband and family he knew you longed to have. Maybe he should have gone straight to Josh since he thought you loved him, but he came to me instead. Treating you like a lady was no work at all since you are one. I never thought of it as a job. I fell in love with you as fast as you fell in love with me, but I was just too big a fool to admit it to myself or you when I first should have."

MaLou had cried so many tears she no longer had any left to weep and her expression was fierce rather than sorrowful. "I don't ever want to see you again, Garrett. I can't look at you without remembering what you and my father did to me. That hurts more than you'll ever know and I can't bear any more of it."

"I'm not walkin' out on you," Lance insisted in just as firm a tone. "I won't do it. I know you're hurt and angry, and that's no time to make such an important decision as this."

Lance had only a dim notion of just how hurt and angry MaLou was, however. "Don't you understand? I don't trust you anymore. If you'd really loved me as much as you're constantly swearing you do, we'd already be married. You wouldn't have wanted to wait to see whether or not I'd be able to keep this ranch. The ranch wouldn't matter at all to you. It would have been me you'd have been most concerned about, not whether I owned a lot of property or not."

"What are you sayin' now?" Lance knew the weather had not been that hot, but the young woman was talking like she had suffered a sunstroke or some other totally unexplained calamity.

"You know damn well what I'm saying!" MaLou shouted right back at him. "I don't want a man who'd take the job of making a lady out of me in the first place. It's obvious your only interest in me has been what you'd get out of it for yourself!"

Lance tried counting backward from ten to one in a vain attempt to control his temper. "You know damn well why we aren't married. I wanted to make something of myself first. I wanted you to be proud to be my wife."

MaLou stared up at him, her brilliant green gaze as cold as death. "I would have been proud to be your wife, Lance. Right up until the minute I found that letter I would have been proud, and not for what you own, but for the man I thought you were. Now I know the man I loved didn't even exist. He was simply hired to play a part and he played it extremely well. Should any other concerned father wish to employ you to tutor his daughter, I'll be happy to write you a recommendation with the stipulation the girl is told exactly what the hell you're trying to do to her!"

"God damn it, MaLou!" Lance was way past anger now. No one had ever dared to question his integrity and he would not let her be the first. He grabbed the front of her bodice and shoved down inside the thousand dollars she had given back to him as well as the gold locket he had given her. "Now I am going to go clean up, have supper, and then come back. Maybe by then you'll have had enough time to realize you're throwin' away what could be the best thing that will ever happen to either of us!"

MaLou did not call out after him as he stormed out of the house. She just slammed the door dramatically and locked it behind him. She went into the room her father had used as an office, bent down to work the combination, and opened the safe. She yanked the crumpled bills from her bodice, smoothed them out, and placed them on the top shelf. The beautiful gold locket she placed in the small box with her father's and grandfather's pocket watches. She knew that while she would never want to wear it ever again, she did not want to see it lost either. It would serve as a valuable reminder of the dire consequences the next time she was even remotely tempted to trust a man, if that day ever came. Shutting the safe, she spun the dial to secure the lock before rising to her feet, but then having nowhere to go, she turned around and sat down on the heavy steel cabinet. She could not even imagine where she would get the courage to face Lance for a second time that day. Just looking at him hurt so badly she wanted to scream, and the sooner he was off the ranch the better. She had been praying that the old saying, "Out of sight, out of mind," would prove true, though it was not her mind she was worried about, only her heart.

By the time Lance returned, MaLou had realized it would be pointless to refuse to admit him, since he would undoubtedly kick down the front door and she knew there was not a man on the spread with the strength, let alone the courage, to stop him. While he looked rested and refreshed, her mood had not improved. She had not eaten any supper and did not offer refreshments. "You were wrong," she greeted him coldly. "I haven't changed my mind. I still want you gone."

Lance flexed his hands tightly at his sides, tempted to wring her pretty little neck, but he knew that would be no solution to their present problem. "I don't want you thinkin' such awful thoughts about your daddy, MaLou. He doesn't deserve that. He wanted only the very best for you and maybe his methods were clumsy, but they were well intentioned."

"Let's just leave my father out of this," MaLou insisted. "The problem is still the same. You're a fraud and I don't want to know you. Now please go."

Lance took a step closer and lowered his voice. "Don't you think you'd better make certain you're not going to have a desperate need for me before you demand I leave? There's no way you'd be able to pass my child off as Josh's and you know it."

MaLou raised her hand to slap his face, but he caught it in midair. "It's a little late for that, darlin'. There's still a chance you're goin' to be needin' a husband before the month is out, and since you've such a high regard for the truth, you know he'd have to be me."

Not about to take his threat calmly, MaLou lowered her voice to match the menacing whisper of his. "Should I find myself in need of a husband, as you so charmingly put it, I'll follow my father's example and hire one with the proper coloring. What do you suppose Jesse Cordova would charge me for doing such a *favor?*"

He did not know if his reaction came from the thought that she would prefer to marry Jesse or from the inflection she put on the word "favor" that made it sound like an obscenity, but Lance could tolerate no more of her high-handed insults, for they were completely unjustified. Before she could escape his grasp, he swept her up into his arms. "All right, I'll leave the ranch tomorrow, but our last night together is goin' to be one you won't forget as long as you live."

As the black light of rage turned the bright blue of his eyes darker than the midnight sky, MaLou's eyes widened until her graceful fringe of long lashes nearly swept her brows. "You wouldn't dare rape me!" she cried out as she made a desperate attempt to squirm free of his confining embrace.

Lance merely laughed at her panic. "Rape is the furthest thing from my mind, darlin'." He had no intention of wasting any more of his time arguing with the volatile beauty when he knew how swiftly she would succumb to pleasure. When they reached her room, he kicked open the door and carried her inside. He sat down upon the bed, gripped her wrists firmly with his left hand, and used his right to undress her. She cursed him in both English and Spanish with words so foul even he was shocked, but he ignored the abuse as he stripped away first the red and white gown and then her many layers of lingerie. Hog-tying a steer was a far easier task, but he was too determined to give up and kept working until he had stripped her bare. "I'm glad to see you've gotten so much use out of the things I bought you, but Jesse ought to be able to keep you in silks and satins too."

"You bastard!" MaLou shrieked, for she understood exactly what he meant to do now and it was no less humiliating than rape. She had never been able to resist his slow, sweet touch, and as his hands slid over her breasts her fair skin began to burn with shame. She shut her eyes tightly, hoping if she forced his image from her mind she would be able to ignore her traitorous body's response to his loving caress, but when his hand slipped between her thighs that gestures proved futile. Her self-imposed blindness heightened her other senses' awareness of him to a dizzying intensity. She heard the rhythm of her breathing quicken in time with his while the tenderness of his touch made her shiver with anticipatory delight. As his lips met hers, his marvelous taste and pleasantly masculine scent enveloped her in a nearly suffocating cloud of desire. He did not demand a response but instead drew it forth so expertly she found it impossible to cling to her resolve to deny him the surrender he craved. She opened her eyes then and found him staring at her quite intently. His gaze was not the love-filled one that had always warmed her clear through, but a troubled glance that reminded her all too vividly of the nightmares she had thought she had permanently banished but now feared would swiftly return.

Lance felt her slender body shudder with the first tremors of the ecstasy he knew how to create so well and withdrew his hand to rest it lightly upon her knee. He knew he had already won, for she would not have fought him if he had wished to press the advantage he now had over her. It had been his own sense of honor that had stopped him. He had suddenly realized he had been doing exactly what he had sworn he had not done: manipulating her feelings quite shamelessly. With the care he would have shown a priceless porcelain figurine, he lifted her gently off his lap and placed her upon the bed. "I love you, MaLou, and I don't ever want to leave you, but I'll go if that's what you truly want."

MaLou made a frantic grab for one of her petticoats to cover her nakedness before she responded, something she would never have done if they had been about to make love. "If this wretched mess has finally taught you to be more considerate of my feelings, then it was not a total loss, but I haven't changed my mind. I still want you to go."

As Lance rose to his feet, his expression hardened into the defiant mask he had worn for so many years before he had met her. "Just don't make the mistake of marryin' someone else to give my babe a name. Promise me you won't do that to me."

While he had phrased his request politely, it still held the unmistakable ring of a threat and MaLou again rebelled. "That you have to make such an insulting demand only proves I'm right in asking you to go," she pointed out quickly, and not wanting to watch him leave, she looked away as he walked out her door for the last time.

Chapter XIX

After leaving MaLou, Lance hurriedly packed his few belongings, saddled Amigo, bid the other hands a hasty farewell, and left the MacDowell ranch. Regardless of what the headstrong young woman might think, he still had every intention of making her his wife, and by the time he reached Tucson he had his plans made.

Just as he had promised, Jesse Cordova had opened a new saloon where games of chance could be played at any hour of the day or night. Paneled in dark wood, it had a comfortable masculine warmth along with nearly indestructible furnishings, which could stand up to the abuse of its rowdy Tucson clientele. Rather than merely a bordello with a few gaming tables like the Silver Spur, El Gallo del Oro, the Golden Cock, was as well equipped a casino as any in the East and its business just as brisk.

As he strode through the door, Lance had no difficulty locating Jesse Cordova, for the elegantly attired Mexican easily stood out in any gathering and especially so in that one. In sharp contrast to the dusty, tattered clothing worn by the miners and ranch hands who were his patrons, his lavishly embroidered pearl gray suit, while tasteful, still loudly proclaimed the wearer's wealth. Lance swiftly made his way through the crowded room to his side. "I'm ready to talk about a job," he announced abruptly, stating the purpose of his visit without bothering with the flowery pleasantries he knew Jesse would have used as a preamble to any business conversation.

The handsome Mexican flashed an amused grin. "It is about time. Let's use my office."

When he had tied Amigo at the rail out in front, Lance had slung his saddlebags over his shoulder. As they entered the office, he dropped the heavy leather pouches near the door, tossed his hat on top of that heap, and took the seat opposite the desk while Jesse moved around to the chair behind it. Knowing he would have to tell the man something, he had a story ready that revealed at least part of the truth if not all of it. "Miss MacDowell turned out to be more difficult to work for than I'd thought. I just lost my job at the ranch so I've come lookin' for a new one."

Since Lance Garrett had turned him down flat on two occasions, Jesse was enormously pleased to find he had now been forced to come to him. He was far too tactful a man to risk insulting the Southerner, however, by reminding him of their previous discussions about employment. "I am sorry to hear Miss MacDowell's judgment has proven to be so unsound. She seemed to think very highly of you before Christmas," he remarked sympathetically.

"Well, sometimes opinions change," Lance replied noncommittally. "Has yours?" His thumbs hooked on either side of his silver belt buckle, his long legs stretched out in front of him for balance, Lance was rocking back in his chair, his pose so relaxed he scarcely appeared to be a man seriously looking for work.

"No, it hasn't," Jesse assured him. "I'll make you the same offer I did several months ago. You can start here as manager and become a partner when you have the money to buy in."

"What kind of money are we talkin' about?"

Jesse shrugged. "El Gallo has been open just a few weeks, but I've taken in far more than I anticipated. The miners have been lucky, the silver is plentiful, and they can't seem to get into town fast enough to spend their earnings. I am only too happy to see that they have a good time while they do it."

Lance had little patience with the talkative man. "How much, Jesse?"

"Twenty-five thousand for a quarter interest," Jesse replied, now growing as serious as Lance, "and you pocket a quarter of your poker winnings."

Lance shook his head. "No, I'll keep all my earnings until I've cleared the twenty-five thousand you want for a partnership, but that amount has to buy half. From then on I'll split my winnin's fifty-fifty with you," he offered with the easy confidence of a man certain he held the winning hand.

Jesse's dark eyes narrowed slightly. "That is an astonishing proposition."

"I meant it to be."

The Mexican opened the bottom drawer of his desk and withdrew a bottle of brandy. "I should have begun by offering you a drink."

"Drunk or sober, those are my terms." As if to prove that boast, when Jesse handed him a brandy he tossed it down in one gulp, then slammed the empty glass down on his desk. "I can drink you under the table any night of the week."

"If that is some sort of a challenge, I'll not accept." Jesse refilled Lance's glass, then leaned back to get comfortable and took a small sip from his own. "I do not think you are in the proper frame of mind to conduct business. Would you like to tell me what really happened with MaLou?"

Lance had always thought the man overly familiar. They barely knew each other and he had no wish to confide in him or in anyone else. "She fired me. There's no more to tell," he remarked with a careless shrug. He picked up his second brandy and downed it as rapidly as the first, but then kept the empty glass in his hand. "I think my proposition is a fair one. You won't need to pay me a salary for managin' the place while I'm earnin' the money to buy in and I'll be the one takin' all the risks when dissatisfied customers need help gettin' out the door."

Jesse pursed his lips thoughtfully, obviously perplexed. "You have always intrigued me, Garrett. As far as I can see, you have little to your name other than a magnificent stallion and a Colt revolver you know how to use extremely well. I generously offered you the opportunity to earn the right to become a partner here, yet you think you can walk into my office and talk to me as though we were full partners already."

"No, I'm not," Lance corrected him with a rakish grin that was nearly as wide as the one he had frequently seen Jesse wear. "I'll manage this place any way you like as long as the games are honest. There will be no question as to who's in charge until I've raised the money to buy my half, then I'll expect an equal say in whatever decisions must be made."

"You are no better than a bandit," Jesse surmised solemnly, his expression growing stern.

Lance set his glass down upon the desk and rose to his feet. "You needn't insult me if your answer is no. Just wish me good luck and I'll go get into one of the poker games. Of course, you'll never get a cut of my winnin's and they're bound to be sizable, but it looked to me like there's enough money bein' wagered for us both to do all right."

"Sit down!" Jesse commanded sharply.

Lance moved no more than a well-shaped brow. "You can't give me orders. I don't work for you, yet."

"I would be deeply gratified if you would please sit down so we might continue our discussion," Jesse spit out in a frustrated snarl.

Lance sat down, resumed his former casual pose, and rocked back in his chair. "I'm glad to see you have a temper," he teased with a hearty chuckle. "It makes you more well rounded."

Jesse had the uncomfortable feeling Lance was merely playing with him the way a sly cat toys with a mouse. "What is it you really want, Garrett?"

"With enough money a man can buy respectability in any town. I happen to think being part owner of this place is a whole lot faster way to earn that money than herdin' cattle or tryin' to dig silver out of the ground."

"Yet when I first mentioned a job you had not the

slightest interest in my offer," Jesse reminded him.

"Let's just say I wasn't nearly as interested in respectability then as I am now." Lance cast a significant glance at his empty glass and Jesse refilled it.

The Mexican was still nursing his first brandy as he watched Lance polish off his third. "Sixty-forty," he offered this time.

Lance was not impressed. "No, it has to be an equal split, fifty-fifty."

"But you're forgetting I have a considerable amount invested here already."

"And you're forgettin' just how much I can increase your profits," Lance reminded him.

Jesse gave his boast a moment's thought before he replied cynically, "That remains to be seen."

Lance knew he was pushing Jesse and it was possible to push such a proud man only so far. Rather than exceed that limit, he softened his terms slightly. "You'll have plenty of time to see just what I can do while I'm gettin' twenty-five thousand together. If you're not satisfied with my prospects as a partner, then we'll call off the deal. I'll walk out the door and I won't come back. You've got nothin' to lose."

Jesse always made it a point to get what he wanted. Right now it happened to be striking a bargain that would be to his own advantage, and Lance had just given him that hope. "Yes, I think a trial period in a business venture of this sort would be wise for us both. We may find it impossible to work together."

"I don't think so," Lance contradicted with a sly smile. "You're the boss for the time bein', and I'm certain you'll find me a valuable employee."

"Perhaps I should ask Miss MacDowell's opinion about that." It was a deliberate provocation on Jesse's part and he watched closely for what effect it would have on Lance. When the remark appeared to have had absolutely none, he was disappointed.

"She'll tell you I'm dependable," Lance lied smoothly, having no idea what MaLou would say about him, though he doubted she would even consent to speak his name.

While Jesse was still curious about what had happened between Lance and MaLou, he readily understood he would find out nothing that night. "Have you a place to stay?"

"I thought I'd try the Hodges Hotel on Main."

"You needn't bother. I will give you the corner room upstairs. That way you'll be nearby whenever there's trouble."

"There isn't goin' to be any more trouble, Mr. Cordova," Lance assured him confidently. "But I'd like a room where I can sleep without bein' bothered by my neighbors."

Jesse opened the top drawer of his desk to remove a set of keys and tossed them to Lance. "You would have that problem at the Silver Spur but not here, although I can provide you with charming company whenever you feel the need," he offered graciously.

Lance again rose to his feet, tossed the keys into the air, then caught them with an agile swoop. "I meant what I said. I don't pay for women."

Jesse got up and walked around the desk to face him. "You're wrong. Women always make a man pay. It is just not always with money."

"We could argue that opinion all night, but it will have to be another one. I'm goin' to bed."

Jesse offered his hand. "I will not expect you to report for work until late afternoon tomorrow."

Lance shook his new employer's hand with a firm grip. While Jesse's skin was equally tanned and his fingers as long and slim as his own, his palm was as smooth and soft as a woman's and Lance released his hand quickly. The man had intelligence and wit, but he made his living by pandering to the vices of others and Lance planned for their partnership to be brief. The stairs to the second floor were adjacent to the office, and the quarters he had been given directly above it. The suite was large, one Jesse had obviously decorated for himself, but his taste was good if far more extravagant than what the Southerner would have preferred.

It had been a long day, and eager for bed, Lance was disgusted when his unpacking was interrupted by a persistent knocking at his door. When he found a raven-haired beauty dressed in a bright red dress of cascading ruffles, he correctly guessed her name before she could introduce herself. "You must be Carmen."

Batting her long lashes seductively, the coy brunette slipped under his arm, then with the dramatic grace of a ballerina turned to face him. Her brown eyes were dancing with mischief. "*Sí*, my name is Carmen, and Jesse told me all about you, Señor Garrett. He said to tell you I am a present and that he hoped we both enjoyed ourselves tonight."

Lance looked her up and down slowly, his apprais-ing glance an insult in itself. "You just go right back to Jesse and tell him that when I said I wasn't interested in his women I meant it."

Carmen's vanity would not allow her to believe that any man would refuse to spend an evening in her arms. She moved close, pressing the fullness of her ample breasts against his chest. "I can give Jesse any message you like in the morning."

Lance looked away for a moment, the memory of Rosalba Lujan's constant attempts to wring an affection-ate word from him bringing a slow smile to his lips. When he spoke, his voice was a low, taunting whisper. "I will give you to the count of five to leave my room. If you're not gone by then, I'll toss you out the window and I'm not goin' to bother to open it first. One, two . . ."

Carmen's eyes filled with terror as she realized Lance was deadly serious. She did not leave his room with the graceful swirl with which she had entered, but at a frantic run that set her ruffles flapping all around her like the feathers of an agitated hen. She made such a ridiculous sight as she ran toward the stairs, Lance could not help but laugh, and he was still chuckling as he closed and locked his door.

By the time he had stretched out on the bed, Lance had

begun to feel the effects of the brandy, but its mind-numbing warmth did nothing to sooth the aching need in his heart. He knew only too well how painful it was to be stripped of all illusions and wished with all his heart he could have remained with MaLou. He doubted she would find sleep either that night, but together they could have more easily tried. He propped his head on his hand and sighed sadly. She was such a dear little thing. He never would have revealed the nature of the bargain that had brought him to her ranch. He would have gone to his grave with that secret rather than cause her the slightest twinge of pain. Clearly, she had been devastated when she had discovered her father's note and she would not have accepted his explanation no matter how creative it might have been. He had never had more rotten luck, but he was banking on the hope that her memories of the love they had shared would prove stronger than her disappointment in the nature of its beginnings. "I love you, MaLou," he whispered softly, for even if she could no longer hear his words, he did not want to forget how to say them.

To his surprise, Lance found running El Gallo del Oro far more diverting than he had believed possible. It was such a lively place, the hours spent there passed quickly. While Jesse had been amused with the way he had refused Carmen's affections, the young woman most assuredly had not, and he had had no more visits from her or any of her kind. He broke up several fights a night, but usually all he had to do was raise his voice to threaten the combatants that he would bar them permanently from the gaming establishment, and they would either settle down or sneak sheepishly out the door. He played poker, but only in the high-stakes games, and he was careful to exclude any man he knew could not afford to lose. Men he had worked with on the MacDowell ranch came in, but while he knew they could have satisfied his curiosity about MaLou, he asked them no questions about her. He missed the pretty blonde terribly, but each morning when he deposited his winnings in the bank, he counted himself one step closer to regaining her love.

His routine was an easy one until the Saturday night all six of the Hatcher brothers came ambling through the door. Rex and Randy made their way to the bar, while the other four spread out around the room, apparently looking for games they might like to join, yet Lance was not fooled. He had been there long enough for word to get around and he was certain the Hatchers, with their combined intelligence still amounting to near zero, had decided to pay him a call. His palm brushed the smooth ivory handle of his Colt as he began to plot some strategy of his own. He was certain they would wait for someone to start a ruckus, or begin one themselves, and while he was distracted either jump him or shoot him in the back. Not about to walk into such an obvious trap, he went over to Randy, who was leaning against the bar, and asked him a direct question.

"The leg give you any trouble?" he asked bluntly.

Shocked to find Lance so bold, Randy choked on his beer and the Southerner pounded him a few times on the back to help him get over his sputtering cough. "You ought to take better care of your brother," he remarked to the unkempt man at his side. If anything, the group looked even sadder than when he had first seen them. Their greasy hair had grown several inches longer and their expanding waistlines had forced them to let out their belts another notch. Their clothes looked no cleaner, nor had any of them taken to shaving more regularly. All in all, they were such a miserable group Lance had a difficult time taking them seriously, but since they were all armed, he knew only a fool would disregard the threat they posed. When Randy was at last able to draw a deep breath, Lance repeated his question. "Well, do you have much trouble with your leg?"

Randy glanced first at Rex, hoping for some sign his brother would have revised the plan they had rehearsed ever since they had heard Lance Garrett could be found at the Golden Cock. When he saw that the confusion in his brother's eyes merely mirrored his own, he let fly with a wide, swinging punch that Lance easily sidestepped. When he then found himself staring down the barrel of the Southerner's Colt, he jumped back so suddenly he slammed into his brother, Rex, sending the heavyset man careening into the next man. That hostile shove moved like a wave down the ranks of the men standing at the bar, then came back as each one shoved his neighbor in return. Standing at the end of that rolling motion, Randy found himself catapulted toward Lance, whose Colt suddenly took on the proportions of a cannon as it jabbed him in the belly. "Don't shoot!" he shrieked hysterically. "Don't shoot me again!"

"We don't like trouble here," Lance informed him coolly. The usually noisy room had grown deathly still as all eyes were focused on Lance and the quivering Randy, whose knees were knocking so loudly the rattle could be heard clear across the room. "Now I want you to walk out of here right now. Take your brothers with you and don't ever make the mistake of comin' back, because the next time I see you boys in here I might not be in such a good mood as I am tonight."

As the Hatchers searched the faces of the others in the room, they saw nothing but the same contempt that showed so clearly in Lance's expression. "Apache lover!" Randy shouted angrily, and, as though that insult would somehow repay Lance for humiliating him again, he turned away and hurried out the door with his brothers following close behind.

"They look like a line of ducks," Jesse joked as he stepped up to Lance's side.

While they did indeed resemble a mother duck with her ducklings trailing in single file, Lance was too shocked by Randy's parting words to reply. He replaced his gun in his holster and, turning, noted that his boss had also drawn his gun. "Thanks for backing me up."

Jesse twirled his revolver before replacing it in his holster, showing off as he always did in every way possible. "While I cannot draw nearly as fast as you, I am quite accurate, and the Hatchers provide so large a target they would be difficult to miss."

"Come back to the office a minute." Lance turned away without giving Jesse the opportunity to respond, and the Mexican first waved to their customers to encourage them to continue their sport.

They shared the office now and without thinking Lance took the chair behind the desk, but Jesse did not object. "Tell me everything you know about the Hatchers," he requested hurriedly as soon as the Mexican had closed the door.

"You know all there is to know," Jesse assured him. "They are cowardly fools who count upon their size and number to help them win a fight. By challenging them first, you called their bluff."

Lance nodded impatiently. "Yes, I know their kind, but what I need to know is more about their backgrounds. That remark about lovin' Apaches was so out of place I can't help but wonder what inspired it. Could they have been the ones who were rustlin' MacDowell's cattle?"

Jesse sank down into the chair opposite the desk, for once at a loss for words. He took a deep breath, then let it out slowly as he replied. "A great many settlers, both Mexican and citizens of the United States, have been murdered by Apaches, so hatred for them is widespread. It would be ridiculous to accuse a man of rustling Thomas's stock just because he despised the Indians. The suspects would simply be too numerous."

Lance waved away the objection. "That I know, but the only reason Randy would have called me an Apache lover would have been because he knew I had driven cattle to Camp Grant. How could he have known that unless he had been watchin' us?"

"Perhaps he didn't, but everyone knows you worked for MacDowell, and he made no secret of his opinions."

Lance yanked open the bottom drawer of the desk and removed the brandy and the two clean glasses that were always kept there. He poured them each a generous amount, then allowed the last few drops to fall into his glass. "You need another bottle of brandy."

"This is your office too," Jesse replied indignantly. "I purchased that one. You must replace it."

Lance raised his glass in a silent toast. He had gotten along far better with Jesse than he had thought possible. The man might be a dandy in all respects, but he was also a man of honor and he trusted him. "Thanks again for backin' me up. That wasn't part of our bargain."

"We will have no bargain if I allow some stupid fool to shoot you," Jesse was swift to point out. "I'll tell you what. Let's decide now in which order we'll shoot the Hatchers if they should dare to show their faces here again."

Lance was surprised to find that Jesse was serious, but before he could respond there was a knock at the door and one of their dealers peeked in. "One of you want to talk to a miner about credit?"

"That would be a brief conversation," Jesse replied. "Just tell him there is none."

"Wait a minute," Lance called out as the dealer turned to go. "I'll talk to the man. Send him in."

Jesse finished his brandy and stood up. "I will keep an eye on things." He had no doubt Lance would give the miner the same response he would have, only in far softer terms.

"This won't take me long."

"Take the rest of the night off." Jesse flashed his widest grin as he went out the door and Lance thought he just might take him up on his offer, although what he would do with his time he did not know. When he heard a hesitant knock at the door he knew it must be the miner and called out to welcome him.

The fair-haired young man clutched his worn hat tightly, nervously rolling the brim as he tried to think how best to introduce himself. From what he had just seen, Lance Garrett was not an easy man to deal with, but he was desperate and had no choice. Fear raised the pitch of his voice, but it did not disguise the drawl. "My name's Christopher Buchanan and my claim's a good one. I've been diggin' out high grade ore and there's plenty more where that came from. All I need is a small stake to stay in the game and I'll be able to pay you back later tonight out of my winnin's."

"Sit down, Mr. Buchanan, and tell me where you're from."

Chris's thin face lit up with an exuberant smile as he recognized the sounds of home in Lance's speech. "North Carolina, sir," he stated proudly. "Nothin's the same since the war though, and I brought my sister out here hopin' to strike it rich. We've no other family, but we're doin' real well. Like I said, I just need a little credit to stay in the game."

"Where's your sister tonight?" Lance inquired politely.

Chris swallowed hard. "Well, she's at home. I built a house for us. It ain't much, but—"

Lance raised his hand as he interrupted him. "How old are you, Mr. Buchanan?"

"Nineteen, but I'm almost twenty. I served in the Confederacy. At the end they let me fight."

He had lost track of how many young men he had met just like Chris, nice-looking farm boys who had left their war-ravaged states hoping to find wealth in the West. "I'm sure you were an excellent soldier," Lance complimented him sincerely. "How old is your sister?"

"We're twins," Chris replied with an embarrassed smile. "She's a real pretty girl and a nice one too."

"I'm sure she is, but do you have any idea what's goin' to happen to her if you keep gamblin' away more money than you can afford to lose?" Lance spoke in a brotherly fashion to avoid offending the earnest young man.

Chris looked down a moment, obviously confused by the question. "The silver's there. It's just that we're a little short of money right now. With what I'll win tonight—"

"Chris," Lance interrupted again. "You haven't won anythin' so far."

"Yeah, I know, but my luck is bound to change soon," he replied optimistically.

Lance got up from his chair, walked around to the front

of the desk, and sat down on top of it. He was dressed in well-tailored black wool pants, a snowy white shirt with a black tie, and a blue satin vest, the color of which came close to matching the vivid hue of his eyes. His boots were highly polished and he knew that to the casual observer he looked as prosperous as Jesse, even though that was still far from the truth. "I am goin' to tell you a very well-kept secret, Chris. When it comes to gamblin', there isn't any such thing as luck. The men who win consistently do so because they have more skill. Now you and I could go back out to the front and play poker for an hour or two and I can guarantee you I'd end up ownin' that claim of yours. Now I'd have no need of your sister, but Mr. Cordova could put her to work over at the Silver Spur. Have you ever been there?"

Chris's deep tan faded to a deathly pallor. "Christina ain't never gonna be no whore! She'd kill herself first!"

"Now that's a real charmin' thought," Lance responded sympathetically, giving him a long moment to think about his sister's plight before he continued. "Most of the men who come in here have no families, so if I take everythin' they own they have no one who will be heartbroken over it but themselves. You tell me you've got a sister, and a pretty one, so you have to be a lot more careful about what you do."

"You're not tellin' me nothin' I don't already know," Chris muttered crossly.

"Then what are you doin' in here tryin' to borrow more money to gamble away?"

"I told you, we're short of cash and I was hopin' to double what I had."

Lance kept thinking of Chris's sister. She would be the same age as MaLou, undoubtedly a blue-eyed blonde like her brother, and probably twice as innocent about the ways of the world. "I'll tell you what. Since you need money, I'm goin' to give it to you, but I have one condition."

Chris was so shocked by Lance's words his mouth dropped open, for he had thought the man was taking a long, roundabout way to refuse him. "I told you, I'll pay it back tonight out of my winnin's," he promised breathlessly.

"Listen to my condition first, Chris, before you get all excited. I'll give you a thousand dollars, but that will make me an equal partner with you and your sister in your claim. If you're a fool, you'll take that money, gamble it away, and have to go home and try to face her with what you've done. If you're smart, you'll take the money, put it in the bank Monday mornin', and use it to support you two until your claim starts payin' what you think it will. Oh yes, you have another choice. You can tell me to go to hell and walk out of here. Maybe by the time you reach home you'll have thought of a way to explain to Christina how you lost what money you had when you came to town."

That was a scene Chris did not even want to imagine. As they had talked he had nearly wadded his hat into a ball, and suddenly noticing what he had done he tried to straighten it back into shape, but it was so worn he had only partial success. "You want me to sell you a third of our claim for a thousand dollars?" he asked incredulously.

"You've told me it's a good one," Lance reminded him.

The young man's eyes filled with tears, for he had no idea whether Lance's offer was a generous one or simply an attempt to cheat him out of what he owned. "I don't know what to do. I just don't know."

"Then count whatever money you lost tonight as the price of experience. Go home and don't come back until you have cash you can afford to gamble and lose without missin' it. I've yet to meet a desperate man who set out to double his stake and succeeded in actually doin' it."

Chris got to his feet and backed slowly toward the door. "If I don't sell you a third of our claim tonight, will your offer still be good later?"

"Of course. Go home and discuss my proposition with Christina. You can bring her here to meet me if you like."

"I couldn't bring her in here," Chris exclaimed hoarsely. "I told you she's a real nice girl."

Lance slid off the desk top and walked over to open the door. "Come into town durin' the week. I'll take you both to lunch at a more respectable place."

Chris nodded. "I'll think about it."

"Good. Just remember what I told you about luck. It doesn't exist, so don't count on it rather than your own hard work." He followed the young miner out to the bar, bought him a drink, and sent him on his way home.

Jesse saw Chris leave with a smile on his face, and, curious as to how Lance had managed to refuse a man credit without insulting him, he asked how he had managed that feat.

Lance just shook his head and laughed. "I can't explain just yet, but I discovered he has a pretty blonde sister. When he brings her into town, I'll make certain you're introduced to her."

"If she truly is blonde and pretty, I will look forward to meeting her."

"I knew you would." Lance rested his elbow on the bar, and looking out over the crowded room, he wondered to how many other men he ought to give the same advice he had given Christopher Buchanan. Deciding few would be smart enough to heed it, he asked the barkeep for a bottle of brandy and took it back to the office to store in the desk so he could give the next man who asked for credit a drink along with a lecture.

Chapter XX

Christopher Buchanan brought his sister into town to meet Lance on Monday. As expected, she was blond and blue eyed, but so painfully shy it was not until halfway through their lunch at the Shoo Fly Café that he really got a good look at the girl. While her brother had a slim build, she was so thin her simple homespun dress revealed not the slightest hint of womanly contours. When she finally did lift her eyes from her plate to look at him, it was for only a brief, furtive glance. She was a pretty girl, but in a soft, sweet way without a hint of the vibrant beauty MaLou possessed. Because she was so thin, her eyes appeared enormous, their pale blue the only touch of color her heart-shaped face would have possessed had she not blushed so frequently, for her brows and lashes were as fair as her hair. The moment Chris had introduced her, Lance had been glad he had made his offer, for even if the Buchanans' claim never produced a profitable return on his investment, the money he had provided would see they both had enough to eat for a good long while.

"My proposition is a simple one, Miss Buchanan. I'd like to buy a third interest in your claim."

"Don't you want to see the assayer's report first?" she asked timidly in a voice so low she could barely be heard above the lively conversations taking place at the tables around them.

"No, I have faith in Chris. If he says it's a good claim,

then I believe him." It would have been smart to read that report, he realized too late, not for what it might have shown about the ore, but to make it appear he was more interested in silver than in handing out charity.

"When our claim starts producing more, will we be able to buy back that third from you?" Christina queried in the breathless whisper that seemed to be her normal speaking voice.

"The more your claim produces, the more my third will be worth, Miss Buchanan, so I won't part with it for a mere thousand dollars. I think you'll find me such an agreeable partner, however, you won't want to be rid of me."

Horribly embarrassed that he would think that would be her purpose, Christina hastened to deny it. "It is only that I would like our claim to belong solely to us, not that I'm afraid we won't like bein' partners with you."

"We've little choice, Tina," her brother interjected with a disapproving frown.

"Hush!" the shy young woman reproached him harshly. "You think he doesn't already know that?"

Lance turned away to hide his smile as the fair-haired brother and sister exchanged barbs. That the girl had the spirit to stand up to her brother was something of a surprise, but a pleasant one. They were seated near the front window and as he looked out at the passersby he was astonished to see MaLou and Josh walking by. She was clinging to his right arm with both hands, looking up at him with such a rapt gaze it made his heart lurch. He hoped they might be on their way into the Shoo Fly, where good manners would dictate he would have to speak to them, but they went right on by. He had gotten only a brief glimpse of the woman he loved, but he had not been prepared for the emotional jolt her sudden appearance would provide. To steady himself he grabbed for his water glass, and wishing it were something far stronger, he swallowed its contents in one swift gulp. Then he noticed his two luncheon guests were staring at him with as intent a stare as he had turned on MaLou.

"Well, have you made up your minds, or would you

rather think some more about takin' me on as a partner?" he asked with the most reassuring smile he could manage when his heart still felt as though it were firmly lodged in his throat.

Chris looked over at his sister, and when after a slight hesitation she nodded, he did his best to return Lance's smile. "We think you're about the best partner we could hope to find and we'll be proud to have you."

"Thank you, and now that the matter is settled, let's have some dessert to celebrate. The pie is very good here." Lance had been encouraging the pair to eat all during the meal, since they looked like it had been months since they had enjoyed a good one.

"My sister is a wonderful cook," Chris bragged shamelessly. "You should taste one of her apple pies."

"I'll look forward to it," Lance replied politely, which only served to deepen by several shades the demure young lady's almost constant blush. Since business at El Gallo del Oro would not pick up until late afternoon, there was no reason to hurry their lunch and he talked Chris into joining him in a second piece of pie before they went to the bank. Lance had both Chris and his sister sign a receipt giving him a third of their claim, then had a thousand dollars transferred from his account to theirs. When the trio walked back to El Gallo, they found Jesse Cordova standing at the doorway and Lance quickly introduced his new partners.

Jesse smiled warmly as he greeted the Buchanans, but when Christina risked looking up to take a peek at him she gasped in surprise. "Are you two twins too?" she asked excitedly with the first real smile Lance had seen from her. It made her far more than merely pretty, but it vanished in an instant, leaving only a faint memory of the beauty he had not realized she possessed.

"No, we are not even brothers, but I am certain we are related somehow, even if we've yet to have the time to discover exactly how," the Mexican responded with his usual cheery enthusiasm and broad grin.

Christina seemed embarrassed by his response and said

no more while her brother shook hands with both men. He announced that they planned to do some shopping now that they could afford to make the purchases they needed, and bidding them farewell, he took the shy girl's arm to escort her down the street.

Lance studied Jesse's expression closely, for as Christina walked away his friend stared after her with far more interest than he had expected the man to show. "She is a blonde, but I did not think she was what you had in mind."

Jesse appeared puzzled that Lance would have formed such a mistaken opinion. "I found her delightful. It is difficult to find such charming innocence in a woman here, but I'm afraid she was not impressed with me."

"Are you serious?" Lance asked incredulously, for he could not imagine a more unlikely pair than the gregarious Mexican and the shy young woman from North Carolina.

Now Jesse was offended. "Of course I am serious! She is precisely the type of woman I want since she is both pretty and modest. Do you think I want to spend the rest of my life with Carmen clicking her heels and dancing around me?"

That was a picture Lance could far more readily imagine than the overly demure Christina Buchanan standing at the flamboyant man's side. "I'm sorry. I didn't mean to insult your taste in women. I liked Christina too, but since she's far too shy for me, I'll give you no competition for her."

"I will not even thank you for that," Jesse replied sarcastically. "Now come back to the office. I have news I know you'll want to hear."

This time it was Jesse who took the chair behind the desk and Lance who chose the one on the opposite side. He could tell by Jesse's expression that his mood was serious and he waited patiently for him to begin.

"I stopped by to see Candelaria this morning. She told me I'd just missed seeing MaLou MacDowell."

"Now wait a minute, Jesse—"

"No, you must wait a minute," the Mexican corrected him sharply. "MaLou told my aunt she urgently needs to borrow some money. It has something to do with her father's estate. She's been to every bank in town and none has enough confidence in her ability to run the ranch to give her the amount she needs. She heard more than once that if she were a married woman applying for a loan with her husband the situation would be different—an opinion which seems to have infuriated her no end."

"It's no wonder she's angry," Lance agreed immediately. "She's running the ranch as well as any man could, if not better."

Jesse shrugged. "I believe there were also a few hints dropped about where she chooses to sell her cattle."

That thought made Lance wince. "Camp Grant, you mean?"

"Precisely. Candelaria was quite upset. She says MaLou has changed so greatly in the last month she scarcely knows her."

"Changed, how? In what way?" Now absorbed in their discussion, Lance leaned forward, eager to know what the woman had meant, and the concern in his expression readily conveyed the depth of his emotions.

"Why have you pretended to care nothing for MaLou when it is so obvious that you do?" Jesse inquired softly, his expression as sympathetic as his tone.

"Just finish your story and we'll talk about my feelings later. Is that all MaLou told your aunt, just that she needs a loan and hasn't been able to get one?"

"No, MaLou is apparently hopelessly confused and can turn to no one else for advice. She told my aunt if the only way she can get the money she needs is to marry Joshua Spencer, then she'll have no choice but to become his wife. That is apparently not an alternative she favors, but as I said, she may have no choice."

"Did she tell Candelaria how much she needs?"

Jesse leaned back in his chair. "Twenty-five thousand dollars. That's an interesting coincidence, isn't it?"

Brushing his question aside as unimportant, Lance

asked a pressing one of his own. "I've only got eighteen set aside. Will you lend me the other seven?"

"But you were saving that money to go into business with me. Do you consider her needs more important than your own?"

"Why yes, in this case they certainly are," Lance assured him confidently.

"Do you think MaLou will accept the money from you?"

Lance took Jesse's reply as a yes to his request and relaxed slightly. "No, she wouldn't take five cents from me. I'll have to ask Candelaria to say she's raised the money. I think she'd do it to help MaLou, don't you?"

"Not if you asked her," Jesse responded bluntly. "When I told her you and I were to become partners soon she seemed somewhat upset, but she would not explain why."

"I called her a bitch, that's why." Lance raked his fingers through his thick curls as he leaned back to get comfortable, knowing their conversation was going to be a much longer one than he had anticipated.

"You did what?" Jesse was certain he could not possibly have understood Lance correctly.

Lance sighed wearily, almost as though he had to force his words from his lips. "I've found you to be a man of your word, someone I believe I can trust, but you must promise me not a word of what I'm going to tell you will ever leave this room."

Jesse reached for the brandy. "I am honored to have your confidence. I will not even whisper your name in the same breath with MaLou's," the handsome man promised with a rakish grin.

"See that you don't." Lance slowly sipped the brandy his friend had handed him as he spun a poignantly romantic tale. He described his first conversation with Thomas MacDowell, their unusual bargain, and the fact that he and MaLou had fallen in love, but he supplied not a single detail of their affair. "When she found that note she felt as though both her father and I had betrayed her trust. She wasn't simply angry with us, she was livid, and she wanted me out of her life forever, or so she said."

"I had no idea." Jesse was sincerely moved by the anguish of Lance's unexpected confession, for the Mexican had an extremely romantic nature. "It is her pride that is hurt, *amigo,* and having more than my share of pride myself, I know just how horribly painful that can be."

Lance gave him a quizzical glance. "I'm sorry, but I can't even imagine such a thing happening to you."

Jesse laughed then. "Yes, I know it seems unlikely, but it has happened. We need not concern ourselves with the most wretched of my memories, however. We must decide what to do to help MaLou."

"If you'll lend me seven thousand, I'll have the twenty-five she needs. Perhaps it would be better if Candelaria thought all the money was coming from you. Would you tell her that, that you'll make the loan, but you want MaLou to think she's giving it to her? It is not that MaLou would object to you, but she would be extremely curious as to your reasons. I'm afraid she might suspect I have something to do with it and refuse to accept it."

"What frightens you more, that she'd refuse the loan, or that she'd marry Josh Spencer?"

"She'll never marry any man but me," Lance vowed dramatically, his gaze growing as dark as his thoughts.

"I envy you. I have never been in love, not even once."

Lance found that difficult to believe too. "Well, when you do fall in love, I wish you a whole lot better luck than I've had. MaLou is not even speaking to me."

Jesse frowned thoughtfully as he tried to think of some way to help both MaLou and his friend. "I have it!" he exclaimed suddenly. "Let's say that Candelaria has decided to lend MaLou the money. She might then come and ask me to deliver such a message to the ranch. Unfortunately, I am unable to go so I will ask my most trusted employee to go in my place."

Lance considered such a scenario for a moment, decided it was plausible, then burst out laughing. "Will you ask Candelaria to write the message this afternoon and I'll deliver it tonight. After all, if MaLou was as distraught as your aunt seems to think, then she'd not want her to continue to worry when there's no need."

"I will go right now," Jesse agreed. He replaced the bottle of brandy in the bottom drawer and rose to his feet. "Since you did not take the night off on Saturday, I still owe you one."

"Well, if I'm out delivering messages for you, that's hardly a night off," Lance pointed out quickly. "I'll be working for you still."

Jesse stopped to rest his hand lightly on Lance's shoulder. "I am sorry our partnership will be delayed. I do not enjoy being your boss when I must work so hard to keep you from outsmarting me."

Rather than offering a jest in return, Lance turned serious. "Thanks, Jesse. I won't forget this favor."

"It is nothing. Just try to arrange for me to see Christina Buchanan again."

"I'm sure I can do that," Lance agreed, still marveling at the fact that Jesse had been so taken with her, since she was so unlike any of the women the man employed. Maybe that was precisely what he did like about her, he realized. She still had the sweet innocence his other women had lost. "Your intentions are entirely honorable, are they not?"

"But of course!" Jesse was still laughing as he went out the door, for he could not imagine any man seducing as delicate a creature as Christina Buchanan for sport.

Lance waited until quite late to arrive at MaLou's home, hoping it would make the urgency of his errand seem more believable. When she opened her front door, he quickly shoved his right boot inside so she would not be able to slam the door in his face without hearing him out. "I know I'm not welcome here," he explained hurriedly. "Candelaria needed someone to bring this letter out to you. Jesse wouldn't trust anyone else with the errand so he sent me. I'll wait and take your reply back to her."

Instantly swept with the same heady rush of emotion Lance had felt upon seeing her, MaLou took the envelope with trembling fingers. "You needn't stand out there on the porch. Come on inside," she invited without looking up. She ripped open the letter and read it hurriedly, but when she realized Candelaria thought she might be able to arrange the loan she needed so desperately, MaLou was so touched by the woman's generous nature she did not know how to reply. She had been pacing distractedly but now went to the settee and sat down to read the affectionate note another time.

Now that he had seen her up close, Lance found the dramatic changes in MaLou impossible to overlook. She had always had a high level of energy, but it had now been translated into a tension so intense her motions seemed frantic rather than fluid. It was obvious she was not pregnant, for there was no trace of the subtle glow coming motherhood would have given her complexion and figure. That realization brought another sharp stab of pain, for he would have loved to have given her a child. She was, in fact, far more slender, and when she looked up at him he realized quite sadly that she no longer had the charming innocence Christina Buchanan displayed. That he had been responsible for that loss and the resulting disillusionment she had suffered pained him greatly, for he had wanted to give her only the very best of love. "Do you want to write her a note or just tell me what to say?"

MaLou had not seen Lance for several weeks. That he seemed interested solely in his errand rather than in her made the aching emptiness his absence had left in her life seem all the more acute. "Do you know what she said in this note?"

Since he had not seen it, Lance could reply truthfully. "No, I don't."

"Aren't you in the least bit curious about it?"

Lance could admit that readily too. "Of course I am, but you needn't tell me about it unless you want to."

MaLou glanced over the letter again, uncertain whether his maddening indifference was real or simply her imagination. She had sent him away and he had gone, but she had given no thought to what she would say to him if he ever came back. "I wrote to my mother and suggested she make me an offer for her half of the ranch. She replied with a demand for twenty-five thousand dollars and said if I couldn't send that much immediately she'd hire an attorney to handle a public auction to sell her half to raise it. I doubt an auction would ever bring in that much, but there's no telling who would be the highest bidder and I have no desire to have a partner in the first place, let alone one not of my own choosing."

"I don't blame you, but what does Candelaria have to do with this?" Lance inquired with the most innocent expression he could affect.

MaLou smoothed the creases out of the woman's cream-colored stationery as though it were precious and something she planned to save forever. "She'd invited me to come to her for advice so I did. The banks have all turned me down, and while I play poker very well, I didn't think I'd be welcome at the Golden Cock." She tried to smile then, but the effort produced only a brittle facsimile of her usual warmth and quickly faded. Suddenly fearing she was rambling incoherently, she ended her explanation abruptly. "Candelaria says she wants to help me and if I'll come to her home in the morning, we'll make the arrangements for the loan."

Lance did not understand why MaLou did not look more pleased. "Well isn't that good news?"

"No, not really. I didn't go to her to beg for a loan. I just needed someone to talk with, a friend. I have no one else," she admitted reluctantly, not wanting her situation to sound as pathetic as it truly was.

She looked so utterly defeated, Lance longed to gather her up in his arms and smother her with kisses, but he remained standing where he was. "Well, if she is your friend, it's only natural she'd want to help you in every way she can."

"You don't understand," MaLou hesitated, seemingly undecided for a long moment, before she continued. "I said I needed the cash to settle my father's estate. She has no idea I need the money to pay off my mother. I can't ask Candelaria to do that. She loved my father and I still think he treated her very badly."

This was a complication neither Jesse nor Lance had anticipated, but now that they had involved Candelaria in their scheme to help MaLou he did not know how they could suddenly reveal the truth. She would only accuse him of lying to her again and he could not risk that. "Since clearly she's interested in helping you, I really don't think she cares what you do with the money, MaLou."

"No, I'm sure she'd object if she knew it was going to my mother."

Lance had wanted to help MaLou out of a different situation, not create an even more impossible new one. "Don't worry yourself sick over this, MaLou. Wait until morning and go see Candelaria about it."

Too anxious to remain seated, the distraught young woman sprang to her feet. "No, I'll go back into town with you now. Can you wait a few minutes while I pack a few things? I know I'll still be welcome to spend the night, even if I can't accept her offer of a loan."

"Of course I'll wait. Take all the time you need." It was Lance who paced distractedly now while he wondered if Candelaria would be able to persuade the headstrong blonde to accept the loan without revealing she was not actually the young woman's benefactor. Why was nothing ever simple where MaLou was concerned? he asked himself. Why was everything damn near impossible to accomplish with her?

MaLou returned in a few minutes' time dressed in her buckskins and carrying a small fabric bag. "If you'll saddle Flor for me, I'll run to the bunkhouse and tell Nathan I'll be gone for the night."

"I'll see to it right now." Lance caught himself before he called her ma'am, but as he strode out to the barn he knew nothing had gone as he had hoped it would, for their brief conversation had been far more awkward than he had thought possible. He had wanted her to be so overjoyed to see him again she would forgive him for what he considered imagined wrongs and welcome him to her home with open arms. Instead, she had been so distant she might have been talking with a stranger. With a disgusted frown he saddled Flor quickly and when he led the pinto mare from the barn, MaLou was standing outside waiting for them. She hooked the handle of her bag over the saddle horn, mounted the lively horse with an agile leap, and when he was also ready to go jabbed her heels into Flor's sides. As depressed as she, he made no attempts to begin a conversation as they rode into town, but as they passed the corner nearest El Gallo del Oro, he saw a crowd milling about out front and called out to her.

"Wait a minute. Somethin' must be wrong and I want to see what it is. It's not much out of our way."

While MaLou knew her way through the town, she also knew it would not be wise to traverse the streets alone that late at night and did not argue. When they reached the front of the saloon, someone recognized Lance and shouted to him.

"Garrett! You'd better get inside quick. Jesse's been shot and it doesn't look like he'll make it."

Lance slid off Amigo, then remembering MaLou, he waited for her to dismount and grabbed her hand as he rushed through the double doors. The popular saloon was still crowded, but people were milling about rather than seated at the tables. Gathered in small clusters to talk over what they had seen, they wore expressions filled with shock and disbelief. When Lance and MaLou started toward the back of the room, all the conversations instantly ceased.

Two of the bartenders were trying to mop up the hallway outside the office, but the elder of the two was crying so hard he could not see where he was mopping. Lance grabbed the man by the shoulders and gave him a savage shake. "Tell me what happened, Vance. Do you know?"

Embarrassed to have been caught weeping, the man wiped away his tears on his apron as he related what he knew. "It was the Hatchers. Two of them snuck in the back door and got Jesse when he came back here to the office. The light's dim. They mistook him for you. He killed them both, but he's shot up something awful. Doc O'Reilly's upstairs with him now."

Sickened to think he had been the intended victim rather than his friend, Lance looked over his shoulder at MaLou. "I'm sorry, but I don't want to leave here now."

"Well neither do I!" MaLou insisted with a show of her old fiery spirit. "Let's go up and see if we can't be of some help."

"You'd better let me go in first," Lance warned as they reached the landing. There were curious onlookers standing in the hall and they could hear a woman wailing pitifully. Lance knew even without seeing her it would be Carmen. Jesse had been carried into the room next to his, but when he hesitated at the door, repelled by the all-too-familiar scent of warm blood, MaLou ducked under his arm and went in. There were half a dozen men watching the scene at the bedside, but none seemed either willing or able to help the young physician.

"How can I help you, Sean?" MaLou asked as she rushed up to the bed.

"Just get that hysterical bitch out of here first, then I'll tell you what to do," the red-haired young man ordered brusquely.

Overhearing the remark, Lance went straight to the end of the bed where the distraught brunette was kneeling. He pulled her to her feet and half carried, half shoved her out the door. "Get all your friends together and go over to the church to pray. You're only going to scare Jesse witless howling like that!"

Carmen nodded, but her loud sobbing did not cease as she hurried away. It simply grew more faint as she moved down the stairs and out into the night. Lance had not even looked at Jesse when he had reached for Carmen and now he had to force himself to again approach the bed. First Manuel, and now Jesse. How many more men were going to get hurt before bullets that clearly bore his name found their mark?

Jesse was propped up on three pillows holding a towel to his right cheek as he watched the doctor's apparently futile attempts to stem the flow of blood gushing from above his left knee. When he saw Lance he tried to smile, but that hurt his face so badly he had to give up the effort. "I killed the bastards," he gasped proudly between near-blinding waves of pain. "They shouted your name as they fired, so that's another one you owe me. The fact we look so much alike wasn't lucky after all, was it? At least not for me."

"Shut up, Cordova!" Sean barked sternly. "Save what little strength you've got left 'cause you're gonna need it."

Not waiting for further directions, MaLou crawled over the end of the bed and taking a place near Jesse's shoulders took the towel from him. "Here, let me do this. I can apply more pressure." She raised the makeshift bandage slightly and found a long gash torn across his right cheek where he had been grazed by a bullet. It would leave a scar and such a bad one she turned to look up at Lance with a fearful glance.

Lance had already made his own assessment of Jesse's wounds. It was a shame about his face, but that was nothing compared to his leg. He had seen more than one man bleed to death and others lose their legs from similar injuries. He did not want either of those dire consequences to befall the man who had become his good friend. "Is the bullet still in there?"

Sean nodded. "It hit the bone and I'm going to have to dig it out."

Lance turned to look at the men who had carried Jesse up the stairs and then had not wanted to leave. To a man they were as pale as ghosts and he doubted they would be of any more use. "I'll help you. Will you need any of these other men?"

Sean looked up at Lance, thinking he would be worth at least three of the others who appeared to be ready to throw up on their boots. He turned around to dismiss them. "Thank you. You may go."

Jesse seemed to be having a more difficult time breathing and MaLou used her left hand to hold the towel in place so she could grip his right hand with hers. "Hold on to me and scream all you like, Jesse. The worst will be over quickly and by sunrise you won't feel half as bad."

Lance closed the door after the last man had stepped out into the hall, then quickly returned to the bed. "She's right, Jesse."

"How many times have you been shot, Garrett?" the wounded man asked through clenched teeth.

"None, thank God, but I know MaLou's right." He smiled at her then, not at all surprised to find she had more guts than most men. He felt sick to his stomach himself, but she was sitting there in the middle of the blood-spattered bed offering a man she scarcely knew the encouragement he would need to survive what would surely be an agonizing ordeal. "What can I do?"

"Come around here and hold his leg still because he won't be able to do it." Sean already had his instruments out, but his attention was focused entirely on the bloody wound, not on the man in the bed.

Lance had seen plenty of doctors make the same mistake and spoke to Jesse before he moved to the foot of the bed. "I should have been here when this happened, but I won't let you down now."

"If I don't make it . . ." Jesse wheezed.

"You will!" Lance insisted.

"If I don't, El Gallo is yours. You hear me, Doc?"

"Yeah, I hear you, but it's too soon to start dividing up your possessions. Now just hush so I can get to work."

Lance walked around Sean, took a firm hold on Jesse's ankle, and as he did the memory of a hundred other wounded men flooded his mind with pain every bit as excruciating as that his friend felt and he was not certain then which one of them screamed. When that sound finally died away he swore he could hear the deafening roar of cannons and his eyes began to sting from their acrid smoke. The visions in his head were far more powerful than the reality that surrounded him and the doctor had to call his name twice before he heard him.

"I'm finished, Garrett. You can let go. Jesse fainted, so he didn't feel most of it, thank God."

"Can you do anything for his face?" MaLou asked softly. "He's such a handsome man."

"I'll do my best," Sean assured her. "But he was damn lucky I didn't have to take off his leg and I'll remind him of that fact every time he complains about his looks."

MaLou remained where she was as Sean cleaned the wound in Jesse's cheek. The bullet had scraped the bone, but he brought the jagged edges of torn flesh together to make the scar as neat as he could. He then bandaged the cheek and went over to the washstand to wash his hands. "I'll sit with him tonight. He's lost a lot of blood, but he's a far tougher man than he looks and I think he'll make it. He won't be getting out of that bed for several weeks though. Do you know someone you could hire as a nurse? That Carmen is as useless as they come."

Thinking of how much Jesse had wanted to see Christina Buchanan again, Lance realized she would be an excellent choice. "Yes, I do know a young woman I think will take the job. I'll talk to her about it in the morning."

"Good. My thanks to you both. You were a great help to me. Most people are so squeamish they can't take the sight of that much blood."

MaLou slid off the end of the bed. She looked down at her buckskins, expecting them to be stained, but they were not, not even the long fringe on the sleeves. She did not know how long they had been there, one hour or two, but it was now far too late to arrive at Candelaria's door. "Maybe I should just go on back home," she whispered as she and Lance left the room.

"No, come with me." Lance took her hand and led her next door, but it was not until he had lit the lamp that she realized the room was his. He saw her expression fill with confusion and moved swiftly to block the door. "You heard Jesse. The Hatchers came after me. He might have gotten two of them, but that means there are still four left who'll have an even better reason for coming after me the next time. Stay with me tonight, and if you still want to leave in the morning I won't stop you."

The whole time she had held Jesse's hand she had thought how easily it could have been Lance lying in that bed. The last time they had made love, she had not known it would be the last time and now she did not want it to be. She was no less ashamed of the way he had entered her life, but for the moment that did not matter nearly as much as how deeply she loved him. Without giving him a verbal reply, she went to the bed and turned down the covers, but before she could pull off her buckskins he had crossed the room and drawn her into his arms. He covered her face with a flurry of eager kisses before his mouth found hers for an adoring kiss that left her feeling more lost and alone than ever, for she could no longer tell what was real and what was the most expert of pretenses.

Lance wasted no time in asking MaLou what was wrong. He already knew what was wrong, but making love to her struck him as the best way to dissolve the doubts that so clearly still filled her heart. As though it were again the first time they had made love, he showered her with the most tender affection he could provide, and while her response was not the enthusiastic one for which he had hoped, it was nonetheless a very dear one. He peeled away her soft suede clothes and the thin layer of silk lingerie she wore beneath to reveal completely the superb lines of her lithe figure. He wanted to trace every delicious inch of her lovely body to imprint once again upon his heart and mind each nuance of her delicate beauty.

Tears welled up in MaLou's eyes, for she so desperately wanted the love Lance showed her to be real. His deep kisses were sweet and his touch still held the same irresistible magic. With a mere caress of his fingertips he heated her blood until it burst into leaping flames of desire that soared to ever greater heights of rapture. He had taught her not only the warmth of love, but also the searing heat of passion, and she had learned those lessons well. She returned the pleasure he gave her in full measure and when at last he moved over her to bring their supple bodies together as one, her shudder of ecstasy was perfectly timed with his. In her mind's eye she saw not only their bodies fuse into one perfect being, but their souls as well. Filled with that heavenly vision, she drifted off to the first peaceful sleep she had enjoyed since they had parted and her dreams were filled solely with loving thoughts of him rather than the hideous screams of her own private demons.

Chapter XXI

MaLou rose up on one elbow, momentarily dismayed by the unfamiliar surroundings. The man sleeping so soundly by her side was Lance, of course, but it was the elegance of the room that had surprised her. The walls were covered in a sky blue silk, which had also been used for the gathered draperies at the windows. The marble-topped dresser was large and elaborately carved, as were the room's other furnishings, but the decor was decidedly feminine and scarcely seemed the proper setting for the man who shared the bed. She leaned over to plant a kiss upon his left shoulder blade, thinking his well-muscled back as handsome as the rest of him, for his perfectly proportioned body had not a single flaw. She had never before awakened to find him still in her bed, and she had not this time either, she realized, since the bed belonged to him rather than to her. It was, however, a very pleasant experience to find him resting so peacefully by her side. Feeling lazy rather than energetic, she lay back upon her pillow to contemplate the surprising turn her life had suddenly taken.

She had heard that Lance was working for Jesse. Josh had made it a point to tell her when he had first learned of it, since he seemed to regard such employment as a long step down from working for her. While he had gloated about it, she had made no comment at all. Now she had spent the night in his room above El Gallo del Oro.

Perhaps the second floor was a brothel. If so, she had just spent the night in one. She turned then to look at her sleeping companion and wondered who usually shared his bed. Since she had no right to ask, she would not, but that fact made her no less curious. Perhaps a more important question was how many people who had seen her enter El Gallo had noted she had not left. She had given little thought to her reputation when she had climbed into Lance's bed, but in the clear light of dawn she could no longer disregard it. If her relationship with Lance became common knowledge, it would cause the most sensational scandal, one which would probably reach all the way to her mother's ears. The thought of that woman's disapproving frown turned her stomach with such a violent lurch she knew that while spending the night with Lance had seemed the best of all possible choices the previous evening, her most pressing problem was still securing a loan in order to permanently remove Lily MacDowell from her life.

Easing herself out of the high bed, MaLou used the cold water in the pitcher on the washstand to clean up hurriedly before she pulled on her clothes. Her buckskins had lain all night where Lance had tossed them, but the comfortable shirt and pants showed no sign of that neglect. Needing her hairbrush, she looked around, wondering what she had done with her bag, and then she remembered she had left it hanging on her saddle horn. "Oh, Flor!" she gasped in alarm, fearing her poor mare had been left tethered to the hitching post out front all night. How she could have forgotten her horse so completely she did not understand, but she knew Amigo was no less dear to Lance and apparently he had not thought of his mount either. The sun was already up, the bustling city of Tucson would soon come to life, and she was certain she had no time to lose if she wished to leave El Gallo without being observed. She used the comb she found lying on the dresser to restore some order to her long curls, left Lance's room, and quietly closed his door. She wanted to make certain Jesse was doing well, and finding the door to the room where he had been taken standing slightly ajar, she slipped through it.

Sean O'Reilly was stretched out in a chair near the bed, but while he was sound asleep, Jesse was awake and tried to smile when he saw her. Not wanting to wake the doctor, she tiptoed across the room to the bed. "How are you feeling this morning?" she asked softly.

"Awful," Jesse admitted belligerently, his usually mellow voice a hoarse croak. "I thought you told me the worst would be over last night."

MaLou reached out to touch his forehead with the back of her hand and found it cool. "You are tougher than you look," she replied with a teasing smile, thinking if he could complain so bitterly about his comfort he had plenty of life left in him. "Shall I wake Sean and ask him for some laudanum?"

"No, thank you. I would rather you went downstairs and got me a bottle of whiskey."

MaLou rested her hands on her hips as she shook her head. "No, not unless Sean says it won't hurt you."

"How could it possibly hurt me when I am already half dead?" Jesse pointed out with a frustrated sigh.

Before MaLou could offer further argument, the door suddenly flew open and Candelaria rushed in. As she called her nephew's name, Sean awoke, and embarrassed to find he had fallen asleep, he leapt from his chair and hurriedly tucked in his shirttail in an attempt to make himself presentable. "I'll allow you to stay no more than five minutes, Señora Delgado. Jesse needs his rest to get well," he announced firmly as though he were in complete control of the sickroom rather than having been caught napping.

The elegantly gowned brunette disregarded his edict with a sweep of her hand. "I will not tire him. Why did no one send for me last night? Why did I have to wait until this morning for one of my servants to tell me Jesse had been shot?" She directed that question to no one in particular as she leaned down to kiss her favorite nephew, but as she straightened up she spoke directly to MaLou.

"Have you been here all night?"

"Why, yes, I have," MaLou responded sweetly. She had at least been in the building and hoped the woman would think she had spent the night caring for Jesse rather than making love to Lance. "I received your note last night and came into town to speak with you. When I saw the disturbance here, I got drawn into the excitement and chose to stay."

Just as MaLou had hoped, Candelaria accepted her explanation without question. "Come with me when I leave and we can discuss my note later in the day, after you've had an opportunity to rest. You must be exhausted if you've been up all night. I only wish that I'd been called." She reached down to comb Jesse's hair back from his forehead with her fingertips, taking care not to touch his bandaged cheek. "Didn't you know I'd want to be with you too?"

Sean spoke up in the injured man's defense. "Don't blame Jesse, *señora.*" He had no idea where MaLou had spent the night, but since she had been right there when he had awakened, he could not swear she had not been there for a long while. "My first concern was to save his life, and then I should have been the one to send for his relatives, but, regrettably, I did not. The oversight was entirely mine."

Jesse did his best to give his aunt a reassuring smile. "You are here now and you can see for yourself my injuries are not serious. I fear I may die of thirst, however, and MaLou refuses to bring me a bottle of whiskey."

"As well she should," Sean agreed. "I do not want to see you drinking anything stronger than tea until you can get up out of that bed."

"Then I will get up now," Jesse insisted, but when he tried to rise up slightly, the agonizing pain that shot up his left leg quickly taught him not to be so foolish. "Damn it! Someone bring me a drink!"

"I will see you have plenty of water, fruit juices, and tea, but absolutely no liquor, Jesse, and that's an order." Sean reached for his patient's wrist and checked his pulse before he turned to Candelaria. "Lance Garrett volunteered to find Jesse a nurse. Would you be so good as to remain here for a few minutes while I see if he's already sent for her?"

"I plan to take care of it this morning," Lance called from the doorway. Hoping to find MaLou with Jesse, he had pulled on the clothes he had found strewn over the end of the bed and combed his hair with his fingers before rushing next door. As he spoke, his glance was focused not upon his friend but upon the pretty blonde standing at his bedside.

MaLou had seen that same dark scowl often enough to know Lance was angry with her, but she could not imagine why. Surely he had not expected her to remain in his bed until someone discovered her there. She tried to return his menacing glare with a sweetly innocent smile that would cause no one in the room to become suspicious, but when she glanced toward Candelaria, she saw the woman had not been fooled. The doctor was regarding her with a peculiar stare too, while the smile that hovered upon Jesse's lips made what he thought of the two of them all too clear. When Lance called her name, she jumped more out of embarrassment than surprise.

"Step outside with me for a minute, MaLou. We need to talk." Lance did not wait for her response but headed straight back out the door.

Rather than attempt to explain his request to satisfy her companions' obvious curiosity, MaLou merely excused herself and went out into the hall. She took the precaution of shutting Jesse's door before she spoke. "Yes, what is it?" she asked in an anxious whisper.

"What is it?" Lance shouted in response, not caring who overheard them, but when MaLou cringed at his outburst he lowered his voice to a far more discreet level. "We have to talk."

MaLou licked her lips nervously. "I agree, but this is an especially poor time for conversation. Candelaria thinks I spent the night at Jesse's bedside and Sean didn't correct that impression." She gestured toward his wrinkled shirt and unshaven face. "It's clear you've just gotten out of bed, but I don't want her or anyone else to think I was in it with you."

Lance stared down at her for a long moment before sighing sadly. Two of the Hatchers were dead and he did not even know which two they were. He had wanted to spend what could well prove to be the last night of his life making love to her, but clearly she was now thinking only of the possible damage to her reputation rather than the very real danger to his life. Perhaps that was his own fault, since he had insisted upon the secrecy an affair demanded rather than the openness the marriage she had offered would have provided them. "Did last night change nothing for you?"

MaLou closed her eyes as she leaned back against Jesse's door. Her lashes made dark shadows upon her cheeks as she searched for the words to express the tumult of emotions that churned within her heart. When she looked up, it was all too apparent nothing had changed for her. "I have never denied that I love you, but I can't forget what you did."

"Can't or won't?" Lance asked in a threatening challenge.

The petite blonde looked away, her expression again filling with the sorrow of the heartbreak he had given her. "Do you suppose someone took care of our horses last night?"

How many times he had been tempted to strangle the maddening young woman he did not know, but Lance had never been as sorely provoked as he was now. "I will go see to your horse, ma'am, since it's obvious you care far more for her than you do for me!"

How he could be so completely mistaken about her feelings when she had just said she loved him MaLou could not understand. Her eyes flooded with tears, but she dug her nails into her palms to force them away, and adopting an expression she hoped would pass for a smile, she yanked open the door and stepped back into Jesse's room.

Christina Buchanan had been astonished when Lance

Garrett had appeared at their door with another of his unusual propositions. Since she had neither the experience that would surely be required nor more than the briefest acquaintance with the injured man, she could not understand why he had come to offer her the job of being Jesse Cordova's nurse. Her brother had then quickly taken her aside and pointed out that the offer was too generous to refuse. Since she had little to keep her occupied in their small dwelling and time often weighed heavily upon her hands, she reluctantly agreed to give it a try, but only for one week's time.

Jesse was so delighted to see Christina again he was determined to be a model patient so that she would have no reason to leave him at the end of her first seven days. "I am very grateful to have your company, Miss Buchanan. I would much rather be in my own home, but Doctor O'Reilly refuses to allow me to travel even that short distance. The thought of lying here alone for several weeks is more than I can bear. I hope we can keep each other entertained."

Christina smiled shyly, uncertain exactly how they were going to do that. The red-haired physician had explained that despite the brave front Jesse was displaying, his injury was an extremely serious one that would necessitate a lengthy stay in bed. She understood how wretched that prospect would be for such a vital young man as Cordova but still feared she would not be of much real use. "What would you like me to do for you?" she finally had the presence of mind to ask.

He was too weak to enjoy what he would truly like her to do for him, but the mere thought of her joining him in the bed brought a bright gleam to his dark eyes. "We do not serve food here, but there is a small kitchen downstairs. Could you prepare my meals?"

"Well now," she pointed out cautiously, "that would depend on what you like to eat."

Jesse could see he definitely had his work cut out for him, for while he had mistaken Christina's demure manner for modesty, he now realized the truth was simply that she was desperately shy. "Why don't you just cook whatever you enjoy preparing and I am certain I will like it."

Christina still appeared skeptical that she could please him as she agreed. "I guess I could do that. Is there someone who can do the shopping for me?"

"Yes, Lance will arrange it. Whenever you need anything, just tell him and he will provide it."

"All right, I will," Christina promised. "What else would you like me to do?"

"Just keep me company," Jesse explained. "We can talk, or read books together, perhaps even play cards. Do you know any card games?"

Christina's pale pink lips were poised in a thin line as she shook her head. "No, my mother did not approve of people wasting their time playing cards."

"Not even when they were sick and could do little else?"

The fair-haired girl now shook her head even more vigorously. "No, she regarded playing cards as a sin, no matter what the excuse."

"I see," Jesse mused thoughtfully. It was no wonder the girl was so timid, for from her brief comments he easily recognized the type of straitlaced woman her mother must have been. He did not want to see someone as sweet as Christina grow so embittered she too would regard every pleasant pastime as a mortal sin. "I'll bet she was opposed to dancing, wasn't she?"

"Oh yes!" Christina agreed quickly, her expression growing far more animated as she warmed to their topic. "She always said dancing led to . . ." She began to blush. "Well, you must know." She looked down at the toes of her shoes then, too embarrassed to continue.

Jesse did indeed know. "Loose morals?" he asked.

"Yes, exactly," the shy blonde admitted softly.

That anyone would ever accuse such a dear creature of having loose morals was such a ridiculous thought Jesse immediately dismissed it from his mind. "Bring a chair over beside me and tell me something of your home. I have never been farther east than New Orleans."

Relieved he had changed the subject from that of morals, Christina quickly moved a chair near the bed. It had been several years since she had spent so much time alone with a man, not since all her brother's friends had gone off to the war from which most had not returned. She spent a good deal of her time with her brother, but he was far too dear to her for her to be self-conscious around him. That Jesse was so handsome and charming bothered her too, for never had any man as dashing as he paid the slightest attention to her. That he seemed to genuinely enjoy her company was something she could not quite understand or accept. "Shouldn't we leave the door open?" she asked nervously.

Jesse had made certain Lance had moved Carmen back to the Silver Spur, but he did not trust the woman not to arrive unexpectedly for a visit. At least if the door were closed she would have to knock first, if she remembered her manners and did so. "I would prefer that it remain closed, since there is no telling who might wander in if we leave it open."

"Oh," Christina replied absently. She did not want to appear foolish, and perhaps it was silly to worry about gossip when Jesse could barely move, let alone get out of bed. Still, she knew she was sitting in a man's room above a saloon. Surely that alone put her morals in grave danger.

As soon as she had seated herself, Christina had folded her hands primly in her lap, but rather than relating any information about North Carolina, she seemed lost in her own thoughts. Jesse waited a moment for her preoccupied frown to vanish, but when it did not he feared his request had been the wrong one. Perhaps she was unbearably homesick and his question had served only to make her sad. "If you'd rather not tell me about your home, we can discuss something else, anything you choose."

Christina was embarrassed she had let her mind wander momentarily. "Oh no, I will be happy to tell you about North Carolina. It is a very beautiful state. Nothing like the Arizona Territory, but instead covered with vast green forests and meadows that fill with wildflowers each spring. I hated to leave."

"Then why did you?" Jesse was pleased to see her expression had brightened considerably when she had begun to describe her home.

Christina shrugged her thin shoulders slightly. "Our dad died during the war, and when our mother died last winter, Chris lost what little interest he had in workin' the farm. He wanted to come out west and he couldn't leave me all alone, so he insisted I had to come along too."

Jesse raised his hand to cover a wide yawn and winced as that unconscious reflex caused his cheek a renewed burst of pain. He had been awake since before dawn, and while he did not usually take *siestas* in the afternoon, he knew he would have to that day. His body ached all over and he still wanted a drink. His only consolation was that he had found Christina's quiet presence immensely soothing. "Didn't you want to come with him?" he asked perceptively, sensing there was more to the story than she had been willing to tell.

"I think leavin' home must be hard for everyone," Christina replied softly.

"Was there a young man you did not want to leave?" Since Jesse regarded her as pretty, he was certain other men would have shared that opinion.

Christina again shook her head. She had wound her hair atop her head in a loose knot and reached up to tuck in a few strands that had begun to stray.

"Let your hair down," Jesse asked suddenly. "Please."

The slender blonde blushed deeply. "Why do you want me to do that?"

"Must I have a reason? I think your hair is very pretty. I'd like to see how long it is. Won't you please show me?"

Reluctantly, Christina rose to her feet. "Well, I suppose it won't do any harm." She reached up to remove her hairpins and her soft, shiny tresses spilled down over her shoulders, falling in loose waves that reached clear past her hips. "You see, it's much too long to wear down."

Jesse stared at the young woman, fascinated by the transformation in her appearance. She had looked so prim and proper until she had released that gleaming cascade of blond hair. Now she looked far more like a fairy-tale princess than a simple farm girl. Lance had told him she was nineteen, but he found it difficult to believe when she looked no older than thirteen or fourteen to him. He was going to make certain she ate well and put on a little weight. She was too thin now to have a womanly figure, but he definitely wanted her to develop one, and soon. "You look very beautiful," he complimented her sincerely.

Christina covered her mouth with her hands as she began to giggle. "Me, beautiful?" Clearly she thought he was teasing her and was very amused.

"Yes, you look very beautiful," Jesse insisted. "Now why don't you take some time to move your things into the room across the hall and plan what you'd like to cook for our supper while I take a nap."

Christina looked at him closely and decided he seemed quite a bit more pale than when she had first arrived. "I think talkin' has tired you too much. I'm sorry."

"Don't be sorry," Jesse replied with as sly a smile as he could manage. "Seeing you with your hair down was worth it." In all his life he had never met such an enchanting young woman. It was not simply her fair coloring that appealed to him, but the gentleness of her nature.

"Thank you," Christina whispered bashfully. She thought him very sweet and as she stepped closer to the bed she raised her right hand to sweep aside her long hair and leaned down to kiss his forehead lightly. "You take a nice nap and I'll see you later."

Jesse was so astonished by her affectionate gesture he did not reply, but his smile was as wide as his torn cheek would allow.

MaLou had left El Gallo del Oro with Candelaria. While she had spent the hours before the midday meal in the same guest room she had used at Christmas, she had not been sleeping. She had spent her time pacing restlessly. Since the room was of more than ample size, she was certain she had walked several miles but felt no more at ease by the time a maid arrived to prepare a bath for her than she had when she had awakened that morning. Her dilemma was a simple one: she could not accept money from Candelaria without revealing it was for her mother, and she did not wish to put the woman in the awkward position of refusing to make a loan for that purpose. She ate little of the excellent *arroz con pollo*, took only a few sips of wine, then followed her hostess into the parlor for what she feared would be a horrible ordeal. She knew she had little in the way of tact, and the ladylike grace Lance had endeavored so diligently to instill within her seemed to dictate only one option: silence.

An astute judge of character, Candelaria had spent the noon meal attempting to analyze the perplexing range of emotions that had played across her guest's delicate features. Knowing MaLou to be a proud young woman, she thought perhaps accepting money from a friend would be difficult for her and hoped to ease her mind. "I am so sorry I did not offer my help immediately when we spoke yesterday. My first thought had been to go to my banker and instruct him to make the loan with my guarantee. It was not until much later that I realized we had no need to bother with outsiders when I can well afford to lend you the money you need myself."

Now that she could no longer avoid the issue, MaLou did not even consider solving her problem by lying to the woman about where the money would go. "I cannot tell you how much your offer means to me, Candelaria. You have proven to be a wonderful friend, but it's impossible for me to accept money from you when it is my mother who will receive it." She had packed a simple dress of light grey wool and smoothed the solt folds over her knees as she awaited the woman's reply.

Candelaria was stunned by her announcement. "I am sorry, my dear, but I don't understand how you could possibly owe her such a large sum."

MaLou licked her lips thoughtfully as she tried to explain without making her father sound like the fool she was certain he had been where her mother was concerned. "I did not learn until after his death that my father had been sending my mother money all these years. In his will he left the ranch to both of us, in an attempt to continue to provide for her, I believe. She has no wish to be my partner, however, and has asked that I buy her out. That's why I need the twenty-five thousand dollars. It's also why I can't take the money from you."

"I see." Candelaria exhibited her usual iron-willed self-control and did not give way to the hysterical tears she would have liked to have shed. "Your father was very generous with everyone. It is not surprising he was so considerate of your mother. She surprises me, however, for she must know you'll have to go into debt to provide such a large amount of cash for her."

"My mother cares for no one but herself, Candelaria." MaLou admitted quite frankly. "I can't ask you to make the loan when the money is for her. I simply can't do that."

"Why not? I think it is a wonderfully ironic touch," the attractive brunette revealed graciously. "You are the one who needs the loan. What you wish to do with the money is your concern, not mine."

"Do you really mean that?" MaLou asked skeptically. "If you'd rather not lend me the money, I will understand. You needn't worry that you'll lose my friendship if you refuse."

"But I have no wish to refuse," Candelaria explained once again. "It will be a pleasure. You are like your father, you know, and I loved him very much. How can I refuse you anything?" Jesse would be proud of her for playing her part so well, but Candelaria had begun to regret that the money they would send to Lily would come from Lance and her nephew and not actually from her.

Overwhelmed with the woman's kindness and generosity, MaLou left her chair, crossed the distance that separated them, and leaned down to give her an enthusiastic hug. "You won't regret this, Candelaria. I'll see

The widow rose to her feet and returned the blonde's fond embrace with equal fervor. "We can arrange for a draft to be sent from my bank to Lily's this very afternoon, but to receive the money she'll have to sign over her half of the ranch to you."

"Yes, I want everything in writing so there will be no arguments later," MaLou agreed.

"Speaking of arguments," Candelaria began with an inquisitive glance, "why was Lance Garrett so upset with you this morning?"

MaLou had been certain the woman would ask that question sooner or later and had a ready reply. She had no desire to reveal the real reason why Lance had left her employ and did not do so now. "He can be foul tempered on the best of occasions. This morning he was merely annoyed that I'd expected him to see to my horse, since he's no longer one of my hands. There really was no argument."

The widow frowned slightly. "You really must be more careful, my dear. I'm certain I was not the only one who thought I was witnessing a lovers' quarrel."

MaLou laughed as though that assumption were absurd. "Nothing could have been further from the truth, Candelaria. Now, if you don't mind, I'd like to go over to the bank. The sooner I put my mother out of my life, the better I will like it."

As Candelaria called for her buggy, she wished Thomas had been as eager to be rid of Lily as his daughter. Perhaps then she might have married him and even given him more children. That his devotion to Lily could have prevented such happiness was such a painful thought she quickly pushed it aside. For the rest of the afternoon she limited their conversation about Thomas's former wife solely to the aspects of the loan. She presented her usual ladylike façade. No one, not even MaLou, suspected the depth of her sorrow, for after the many years they had been close, Thomas had not left her so much as a kind word in his will, let alone part ownership of his ranch. The fact that he had wanted to bestow such a magnificent gift upon Lily caused her almost as sharp a stab of grief as his death.

By the time Lance had a moment to go upstairs to visit with Jesse Tuesday night, Christina had already gone to bed. While feeling tired, his friend was restless and welcomed his company. "I will thank you again for talking Christina into becoming my nurse. I know it must have taken a great deal of charm to convince her to do it."

"No, not at all," Lance assured him. "I just mentioned your name and she was eager to do it."

"That is an out-and-out lie and we both know it," Jesse responded with a hearty laugh that ended in a gasping cough.

Alarmed, Lance leaned forward, ready to go to his friend's aid. "Are you all right?"

Jesse cleared his throat and nodded. "I do not like lying here. The pain in my leg never stops and my face hurts whenever I try to smile. Of course I am all right!"

"Good. Now I want you to listen closely. I talked to everyone who was here last night and the only Hatchers seen were the two who tried to gun you down. I thought it would be Rex and Randy, but I guess the kid stayed at home with the others when Rex and Rad came into town. I'm not even sure which one Rad was."

"Big, ugly fellow," Jesse explained sarcastically.

Amused by his description since it could not be used to distinguish one Hatcher from another, Lance leaned back in his chair and crossed his arms over his chest. "If they'd shot me, I wouldn't be in such a cheerful mood."

"If they had shot you I would not be cheerful either, but until I can get out of this bed, I have little choice."

"They came looking for me, and they are sure to be after you now too. To retain the upper hand, I'll have to go after them."

"No!" Jesse ordered sharply. "You will do nothing for the time being. The Hatchers have tiny minds, but they may have learned something from this tragedy. They have lost two of their number and if they do not come after me to extract revenge I will let them be. I killed the two who tried to kill me, so the score is even unless they start something new."

"Which they undoubtedly will," Lance assured him.

Jesse shrugged thoughtfully. "I won't let you go after them, Garrett, nor will I shoot them in the back when I can go after them myself. I have no wish to wipe out the whole Hatcher clan. Let us leave well enough alone for now. If they have learned their lesson, then we will all be able to lead peaceful lives."

"If that's what you want," Lance agreed reluctantly, but he had posted one heavily armed guard in the hallway and another at the base of the stairs to make certain neither of them were ever caught off guard again.

Jesse glanced over at his friend's dark expression and grew curious. "What are you thinking?"

"That you are too trusting."

"Me, trusting? I trust no one. Well, I have learned to trust you and a few others, but not many. Do not make the mistake of thinking I trust the Hatchers. I am willing to give them a chance to live out the rest of their lives, but only one."

Lance remained seated at the bedside until the injured man finally fell asleep. He could well imagine how desperately Jesse hated being thrust into the role of invalid, for he would not be able to tolerate being confined to bed nearly so well himself. Christina had prepared Jesse's supper and had kept him amused, but he had still needed to call for a man's help when he wished to relieve himself. That was such a sorry situation Lance hoped Jesse's recovery would be far more swift than Sean O'Reilly had predicted.

As Lance went to his own room, he could not shake the nagging suspicion they had not heard the last of the Hatcher brothers. Rex and Rad had proved something by their deaths, however. They had shown themselves fully capable of ambushing a man, and he vowed to keep looking for proof they had been the devils who had shot

Manuel and killed Thomas MacDowell. If none of them were left alive to stand trial for those crimes, it would not bother him one bit either.

His bed looked very empty as he approached it, and recalling how beautifully MaLou's graceful body had filled it, he decided he would see her there again, and soon. That thought brought with it the first trace of a smile that had curved across his lips all day and again made his dreams incredibly sweet.

Chapter XXII

Lance kept close track of everyone who entered El Gallo del Oro and noted Joshua Spencer's presence immediately. The young man greeted several friends, went to the bar for a beer, then sat down to play poker for a couple of hours. He appeared to be in the best of moods and won quite a bit of money. Before he left he approached the tall Southerner with a request.

"Looks like MaLou and I will be getting married this spring. Do you think Jesse can get us some real French champagne?"

"Would you like to order it now?" Lance replied calmly, allowing none of the shock the young man's announcement had given him to show in his expression.

"Naw, my dad will come around to do it." Josh was grinning from ear to ear at the tantalizing thought of marrying MaLou. "How is Jesse getting along?"

"He's doing very well, thank you. I'll tell him you were concerned about him."

"Yeah, you do that." Their brief conversation complete, Josh shoved his hat to the back of his head and gave a parting wave to his friends. He then ambled out the door with the confident swagger of a man who was satisfied with every aspect of his life while Lance stood seething with rage as he watched him go.

* * *

It was past midnight when Lance reached the MacDowell ranch, but a light still shone in MaLou's room. He left Amigo tethered some distance from the house so he could approach it without attracting any notice. He was still so outraged that he had heard about their forthcoming marriage from Josh rather than MaLou that he could barely see straight, let alone reason, but he had come to have it out with her once and for all. It had been a week since they had been together after Jesse had been shot. That had been a harrowing night, but surely it could not have slipped the perverse young woman's mind that her affection for Josh had grown so deep she wished to marry him. It was that oversight that provoked him most. Didn't she owe him the courtesy of telling him she was making marriage plans with another man before she climbed into his bed?

Rather than knock at the front door, he went around to the side of the house to the door she had once told him to use as an exit if he should need to make a quick one. Finding it unlocked, he stepped into the small chamber used for bathing. He waited a moment, listening carefully for sounds that would reveal MaLou was not alone in the house. Instinctively, his hand moved to the handle of his Colt revolver and rested there lightly. If he found Josh in her bed he knew it would take every ounce of self-control he had not to shoot him dead. On the other hand, he did not want to step into her room and take a chance of getting shot at either.

As he left the small room and began to move stealthily down the hall, he instantly recognized the sounds coming from MaLou's room, but they were not the soft, ecstatic cries of a couple making love. What he heard were the pitiful, choking sobs of a woman weeping as though her heart were broken. He reached her room quickly and, looking in, found her stretched out upon her bed. She was clad in a plain muslin nightgown. Her face was hidden by her flowing curls, but her anguish was so clear he did not have to see her expression to understand the depth of her sorrow. He crossed the bedroom with two long strides, sat down on the side of the bed, and laid his right hand upon her back. She had been trembling all over but grew still at his touch and turned to look up at him.

While she was horribly embarrassed, the fact that Lance had so little respect for her privacy upset her far more. "What are you doing here?" she asked angrily.

Her tears had washed away all trace of his anger and Lance replied with a careless shrug, "I just dropped by to pay a friendly call."

"At this hour?" MaLou drew herself up into a sitting position, and after modestly tucking her gown between her legs, she leaned forward to hug her knees. "I thought you'd learned to tell me the truth, Garrett. Have you forgotten?"

Lance watched her wipe away the last of her tears, but her fair complexion was still flushed and her eyes very red. Clearly she had been crying for a long while. "Do you cry yourself to sleep every night?" he asked, deftly avoiding her question.

"What if I do?" she asked defiantly.

Lance could not help but believe he was to blame for her sorrow. Then he suddenly recalled why he had come to see her and his temper flared. "This afternoon Josh asked me about orderin' champagne for your weddin'. If the thought of marryin' him is makin' you this miserable, then don't do it."

MaLou stared at her handsome visitor, as shocked by his words as he had been when he had first heard them. "Josh actually told you that? He said we were getting married soon?"

Lance nodded. "That he did."

MaLou opened her mouth to give him her opinion of the arrogant young man but then hesitated. "Wait a minute." She frowned slightly, wanting to be certain she wrung the truth from his lips this time. "Josh said he and I were getting married, so you decided to come out here in the dead of night to ask me about it? Why?"

"Why?" Lance shouted angrily, but MaLou quickly covered his mouth with her fingertips to silence him before he could scream more.

"Hush!" she cautioned anxiously. "You needn't yell at me. Just tell me why it was so important for you to see me tonight."

Lance scowled angrily, certain his feelings for her were still painfully obvious. "You already know why. You told me only last week that you're still in love with me. I'm not going to let you marry Josh, or anyone else for that matter. You ought to have known that too."

MaLou licked her lips thoughtfully, unaware that her gesture was an extremely suggestive one. "I've given Josh nothing but excuses, so he has no reason to think I'll marry him any time soon. I think he just wanted to get your reaction to such an announcement. Did he actually order the champagne, or just ask about it?"

"He just asked," Lance admitted grudgingly, feeling like a complete fool for having been taken in so easily.

MaLou combed her tangled curls away from her face with her fingers, still embarrassed he had caught her looking less than her best. "I'm always criticizing you for not being truthful while I've simply avoided telling Josh the truth far too long."

"That started out as my idea if you'll recall," Lance reminded her. "You mustn't blame yourself if it got out of hand."

"It doesn't matter whose idea it was. It's time I told him the truth."

"Just what is that?" Lance asked curiously.

MaLou blushed slightly. "Simply that I don't love him and never will. I'd like to have his friendship, but nothing more."

As his glance wandered from her expressive features to the elegant curve of her throat, Lance found it difficult not to reach for the pale blue ribbon that held the neckline of her gown in place. A single tug would loosen the drawstring and allow the loose garment to slip off her shoulders, exposing the creamy smoothness of her skin and the soft swell of her breasts. His thinking came to an abrupt halt then as he realized how intently she was staring at him. Hoping she had not guessed in what direction his thoughts had strayed, he cleared his throat and asked a question that had just occurred to him.

"If you weren't lyin' here cryin' about marryin' Josh, then what was makin' you so unhappy?"

"Surely I don't have to explain that to you," MaLou responded with a sad, sweet smile.

"MaLou," he began, ready to repeat the same plea for sympathetic understanding of his motives she had rejected so violently in the past.

"No, don't say anything. There's no need." MaLou reached out to begin unbuttoning his shirt. He had changed his clothes before leaving El Gallo and was dressed in Levis and one of the plaid shirts he had often worn when he had worked for her. "Now that you're here, you might as well stay."

As her fingertips slid through the thick curls covering his chest, he closed his eyes to savor the exquisite pleasure her touch always gave him. He wanted her to agree to marry him. He wanted to hear her say the words, but he did not want to risk starting an argument that might separate them before they had shared another night of bliss. He reached out to envelop her in a warm embrace, and as his mouth covered hers, he pulled away the bow that held her nightgown in place. She giggled deep in her throat as he struggled to push the garment out of his way without breaking off their kiss.

Finally, he released her for a moment, knowing she could do the job far more swiftly herself. "I'd much rather hear you laugh than cry," he revealed in a voice made husky by desire. "I can't bear to think you've cried yourself to sleep every night we've been apart."

"Neither can I," MaLou agreed softly, "but I have." She slid off the bed, let the simple gown fall to the floor, then stepped out of it. Now nude, she slipped under the covers and waited for him to join her in the comfortable bed. "We weren't together nearly long enough."

Lance flung off his boots before removing his gun belt with far more care. "And whose fault is that?" he asked without thinking.

"Yours," MaLou responded with only a slight trace of bitterness.

Casting off the last of his clothes, Lance decided to remain silent rather than begin that debate again, for each of them had far too much pride to acknowledge defeat. Instead, he got into the bed and drew MaLou into his arms. Nuzzling the hollow of her throat, he whispered hungrily, "I've missed you more than you'll ever know."

"Believe me, I know," MaLou contradicted in a seductive purr. She pressed against him, bringing every inch of their supple bodies together and creating a delicious warmth that swiftly ignited passion's flames. She could not forget how he had tricked her, but neither could she forget how sweet the love they had shared had always been. She wrapped her arms around him, then held him still more tightly as his tongue began to caress the soft tips of her breasts. Her flesh responded eagerly to his lavish attention, forming tender buds that grew hard as he nibbled and sucked upon them. She moved against him then, her hips doing their own very primitive dance in time with the slow, circular motions of his tongue as she entwined her legs in his.

That MaLou was as impatient as he to consummate their reunion thrilled Lance beyond measure and his lips returned to hers for a long, deep kiss. He shifted his position, moving over her as he began to bring their bodies together as one. He moved very slowly and gently, entering her only partially and then withdrawing, though never completely, before easing forward again. As always, her warm, wet sweetness encircled him, inviting him to plunge to her very depths, but he held back. He savored the grace of her surrender until the tiny tremors of beginning ecstasy that throbbed within her made further restraint impossible. He lunged forward then, his thrusts now forceful and deep as he joined her in scaling love's most glorious heights. The rapture they created together seared not only their hearts but also their souls, creating a oneness more glorious than they had ever shared. They clung to each other, lost in that splendor until the last ripple of pleasure had faded away, leaving them bathed in the luscious memory of its fiery warmth.

Lance cradled MaLou's head upon his shoulder as he prayed her mood would now be as loving as his. Nothing was more important to him than making her his wife. He had put his pride before her happiness and that had been the most foolish decision he had ever made. "We're goin' to have to get married, MaLou, and soon. I'm goin' to lose my mind if we don't. I don't have nearly the money I wanted to have first, nor a bit of the prestige, but I was a fool to think those things were more important than our love for each other."

MaLou snuggled against him, thinking his proposal wonderfully romantic. "I've tried to live without you, Mr. Garrett, but you saw for yourself how miserable I've been."

Cautiously optimistic, Lance held his breath as he asked, "Did you just agree to marry me?"

"You were the one who turned me down, remember?"

"That's beside the point," Lance scolded as he gave her a loving squeeze. "I want you to marry me. Now say yes."

MaLou smiled as the word rolled easily off the tip of her tongue. "Yes."

Lance responded with an enthusiastic rebel yell MaLou was certain could be heard all the way to the bunkhouse and well beyond. "Well, that does it. I have no choice but to marry you now," she complained between hearty peals of laughter.

"When? I'd insist upon tomorrow, but I want you to have the best wedding Tucson's ever seen and that will take some time to plan."

"I don't want to wait any longer than you do. Nor do I want an elaborate ceremony that will create the type of spectacle you just described, but I won't have time to make any plans until I get back from Camp Grant."

"Camp Grant?" Since he could not discuss any topic rationally with her in his arms, Lance released her and struggled to sit up. "Why are you goin' there?"

Fearing they were already headed for trouble when their engagement was no more than a few seconds old, MaLou sat up and draped her quilt modestly across her breasts. "Lieutenant Whitman sent word there are nearly three hundred Indians camped there now and they need more beef. I can't send men along a route I'm afraid to travel myself."

"Now, MaLou," Lance bgan in a condescending tone.

"Don't you dare 'Now, MaLou' me. Have you been so busy playing poker you're unaware of what's been happening? The Indians at Camp Grant have been blamed for raids on a baggage train going to the Army station in the Pinal Mountains as well as for the attack on Tubac that left two dead, one of them a pregnant woman. Those senseless deaths have outraged everyone. According to editorials in the *Citizen*, the Apaches are striking at will up and down the whole Santa Cruz Valley. They charge that the Indians are being supplied by the government and then allowed to murder peace-loving citizens. I want to know the truth and the only place to find it is at Camp Grant. If those Indians are responsible for the raids, then I'll have no more to do with them. But if they aren't, if it's just renegades causing all the trouble, then I'll keep on supplying the beef the Army needs to ensure peace."

Lance had to admit he had been so busy he had not kept as close track of events as she obviously had, but he had known about the raids she had mentioned and the resulting bitter resentment they had caused. "You might find the truth, MaLou, and then discover no one wants to believe it."

"Nevertheless, I am going to Camp Grant," the hot-tempered blonde stated emphatically. "You can't stop me, so please don't ask me not to go."

Lance was far too wise to accept her vow as a challenge. He realized his choices were limited and he took what he hoped would prove to be the best one. "You know the trip will be dangerous, but if you're determined to go, then I'll go along with you."

MaLou was amazed he would make such a generous

offer. "But can you do that? Doesn't Jesse need you at El Gallo?"

"Yes, he needs me," Lance admitted readily. "But not as badly as I need you. He's getting along pretty well and there are others who can take my place for a week. No one could ever take your place, though. If something happened to you when I wasn't there to prevent it, I'd never forgive myself."

MaLou was so touched by his words her eyes again filled with tears. "I don't know what to say."

"You've already said you'll marry me. That's more than enough for one night." Lance gathered her into his arms, meaning to make love to her until all the tears she had shed were no more than a dim memory. "I love you," he whispered as he lowered his mouth to hers, and her response was so loving he did not know how he would survive until they could live openly as husband and wife.

Unaware of Lance and MaLou's euphoria, Jesse Cordova was nearly beside himself with worry over his own personal problems Tuesday morning. Christina had been with him for the seven days she had promised to serve as his nurse, but she had given him no hint as to whether or not she would agree to stay with him any longer. She had grown more relaxed around him and she had even learned a few simple card games, but she still seemed so terribly shy he doubted she enjoyed herself even half as much as he did when they were together.

Each morning Sean O'Reilly had come to check on his progress. Christina would wait out in the hallway during the physician's visits, but she always smiled at the young man as if she were happy to see him. She did not return to his room right away after Sean left either, and Jesse was certain they were standing out in the hall talking about him. Or worse, they could be talking about something entirely different and far more disconcerting: themselves. What if the doctor liked her too? Sean was a respected member of the community, while Jesse knew he was envied by most for his wealth and disliked by many because of his heritage. Wouldn't any woman as sweet as Christina naturally prefer to wed an American doctor rather than a Mexican who owned a saloon and a brothel?

That was not Jesse's only concern, however. There were also his injuries to consider. His leg was healing, but very slowly, and he knew when the day finally arrived that he could leave his bed, he would probably have to use a cane to manage a walk that would surely be marred by a pronounced limp. Rather than try to shave with half his face bandaged, he had just let his beard grow. It would never cover the scar on his cheek though. He had not asked for a mirror when Sean had changed the bandage, but he knew the wound was a bad one, although he hoped Candelaria's creams might help. Since he had always taken considerable pride in being handsome, he did not know how he would cope if he no longer were. That thought was even worse than the prospect of walking with a limp.

In his own mind he quickly made Christina's choice for her. While Sean was not handsome, his appearance was at least pleasant. He was a respected man who could walk without needing a cane and look in a mirror without having to quickly turn away. In all respects, Sean had more to offer the gentle blonde than he did. She would make the perfect wife for the physician.

When after a long absence Christina returned to his room that morning, Jesse did not remark upon the fact that her conversations with the doctor were growing more lengthy each day. He had no right to keep her from talking with the man. He had no right to ask anything from her that she did not freely want to give. Such rationalizations did not ease the pain in his heart, however, for he felt as though he had already lost her even though she had never truly been his.

While Christina was a naturally quiet young woman, she had a keen interest in others and her observations were generally accurate. When Jesse turned away as she closed his door, she was certain something was wrong, for he was usually cheerful rather than withdrawn. "Jesse? Is somethin' the matter? If you're hungry or thirsty, I'll bring you whatever you'd like."

"No, you won't," the distraught man replied angrily.

Startled by the hostility in his tone, Christina moved no closer to the bed. "Why do you say that?"

"Because all I've ever wanted is a drink and no one will bring me one!"

"You want a drink at this hour of the morning?" the slender young woman asked incredulously.

"Yes!" Jesse shouted. When Christina turned to open the door, he called out to her. "Wait. Where are you going?"

"To call Sean to come back. If your leg is hurtin' so badly, then somethin' must be dreadfully wrong." Tears welled up in her eyes, for she knew his wound was a bad one and if it became infected he would surely lose his leg. That would be such a horrible tragedy she did not want to take any chances.

The poor girl seemed so badly upset Jesse was furious with himself for yelling at her. "No, wait. There is nothing the matter with my leg. I am not in any great pain. Please forgive me."

Christina closed the door, still certain something must be wrong, even if Jesse would not admit it. She had grown very fond of him and did not want to see him suffer needlessly. He had turned away again as though he would rather be alone, but since her job was to keep him company, she did not know what she should do. "Jesse?" she called softly as she approached his bed.

Jesse did not reply. He could not. But when she reached out to touch his hair, he knew he could not hide from her when he could not even get out of the bed. He looked up at her then, his expression an unusually serious one. "The doctor is a good man. Like most men in Tucson he is a bachelor. Did you know that?"

Christina frowned slightly as she withdrew her hand. Whenever she had an excuse to touch Jesse she did, but that was for her own pleasure because she found him remarkably handsome, not merely an attempt to be an attentive nurse. "I'm sorry, I'm afraid I don't see why that matters. He appears to be a fine physician. What does whether or not he has a wife have to do with it?"

Now Jesse was as confused as she. "He is unmarried and so are you. Don't you find him appealing?"

"In what way?" Christina inquired with her usual naïveté.

"As a man!" Jesse replied far too sharply.

The timid young woman blushed deeply, mortified she had not understood the point of his questions. "Oh," she replied nervously, then realizing she would have to provide some sort of reply, she attempted to give him a reasonable one. "Well, yes, he is nice, but I haven't given any thought to what sort of husband he'd make."

"Isn't a doctor considered a good catch in North Carolina?"

Christina nodded. "Oh yes, I'm sure doctors are highly prized everywhere."

She was displaying so little interest in their subject, Jesse blurted out his next question. "Do you plan never to marry?" He had always thought a good marriage was the dream of every female almost from the hour of her birth.

Christina moved the chair she used closer to the bed and sat down before she replied. "When I was growing up, nearly all of the young men I knew went off to fight in the war. A lot of them were killed. I suppose if there hadn't been a war, I'd already be married and have three or four children by now." She smiled shyly before she continued. "The war changed all our lives and not for the better. That's why Chris was so anxious to come to the Arizona Territory. He wanted to start over fresh somewhere new. He's doin' real well too."

While that had all been interesting information, she had not answered his question. "I am glad your brother is having success, but what about you? Don't you want to have a home of your own rather than just keeping house for him?"

"Why are you suddenly so interested in what I'm goin'

to do with my life?" Christina asked suspiciously.

"I . . . ah . . . well, that is . . . why wouldn't I want you to have a happy life?"

Thinking it odd he would stutter over that response, Christina did not let him off the hook. "Since you have no wife and family, why do you think you can give me advice about marriage?"

She had backed him into a very uncomfortable corner, and Jesse decided to rely upon his charm to get him out of it. "It is a simple fact of life that women usually marry at a younger age than men. I plan to have a wife someday."

"Well, just how old are you now?"

"Thirty-one," Jesse replied with a chuckle. "I am a young man still."

Christina leaned back in her chair to get more comfortable. "I don't think you should wait much longer, Jesse, or your bride will probably be so much younger than you you'll constantly be worryin' about her runnin' off with a younger man."

"My wife would not run off!" Jesse protested dramatically, his dark eyes flashing with anger. "She would love me so dearly she would never want to leave me."

"I hope you're right," Christina responded sweetly. "But if I were you, I'd not waste any time before I took a bride."

Jesse regretted ever mentioning marriage, since his companion was discussing the subject far more dispassionately than he could. "You're right. I have obviously wasted the best years of my life. Now it may prove difficult to find a woman who does not find my appearance objectionable."

"Objectionable?" The man's choice of words continually confused her. "You're very handsome, Jesse. I'm surprised your aunt is the only woman who comes to see you. Doesn't everyone know you were shot?"

"I have had no other visitors because I left orders I did not want any," Jesse hastened to explain. The truth was, the only women who would call on him worked for him on Maiden Lane, and he did not want someone as innocent as Christina to meet them.

"You know what your trouble is?" the shy blonde asked suddenly.

Jesse was almost afraid to ask, since he knew precisely what his trouble was. He had spent a week cooped up in a bedroom with a pretty young woman he could not coax into his bed. "No," he growled defensively. "Just what is my trouble?"

"I think you're feelin' so much better you've gotten bored. Surely it can't be too dangerous to move you to your home now. You'd have more to do there and your own servants to tend you. If you wanted a drink, no one would say you couldn't have one. I think we ought to tell Sean you want to go home tomorrow. Or perhaps we can reach him today and see if he won't agree. Then you wouldn't need me anymore and I could go home too," she explained matter-of-factly.

"But what if I didn't go home? Would you have any objection to staying with me for another week or two?" Jesse asked with the first glimmer of hope she had given him that morning.

"Well, no, of course not, unless you don't want me. But if you go home, you won't need me."

"I cannot possibly go home," Jesse insisted, although that idea was incredibly appealing. "I am needed here." She was right, though. He was feeling better. And while he feared he could not get up without fainting, he was far too restless to enjoy spending his time in bed alone.

"Mr. Garrett seems to be runnin' things real well," Christina pointed out. "In fact, I don't think he's come in here once to ask you how to handle a problem."

While that was true, Jesse certainly would not admit it. "He comes up to see me after you've gone to bed. That's why you haven't heard us discussing business."

"Oh, I see." Christina nodded thoughtfully. "Well, I guess if you're really needed here, then you can't go home. I'm afraid you've gotten very bored with my company though."

Jesse shook his head. "Nothing could be further from

the truth." He enjoyed her company immensely. He loved her shy smile, each of her bashful gestures, and the wistful softness of her voice. He found her wonderfully attentive and he was certain the tender concern she showed for his well-being was genuine. On the other hand, she was so sweet a young woman he was certain she would have been an agreeable companion for any invalid. "I want you to stay with me," he confessed softly.

Before she could thank him for his invitation, there was a knock at the door. She rose immediately to answer the summons and found Lance Garrett with a pretty blonde clinging to his arm. She stepped out of their way and hesitated a moment at the doorway, thinking Jesse might wish to be alone with his friends. When he gestured for her to return to him, she closed the door and went back to his bedside.

Lance quickly introduced MaLou and Christina, then broke into a wide grin. "MaLou and I are gettin' married. Will you be my best man?"

While Jesse was delighted by the news, he gestured helplessly. "How am I to do that when Sean forbids me to leave this bed?"

"We're goin' to drive some more cattle to Camp Grant first, if you'll give me the time off. Then MaLou will need to have a dress made. It will be two or three weeks at the very least before we can be married. You should be up and about by then."

Jesse heard little after Lance mentioned he needed some time off. It would make his argument that he needed Christina to stay with him all the more compelling. "If you feel you must go to Camp Grant, then I am certain your reason is a good one. Of course you may have all the time off you wish. I can handle things until you return."

Lance had not expected Jesse to agree to his request so readily and was somewhat taken aback by it. He would not tell the man he was being too generous, however. "Thank you. We're leavin' tomorrow and we'll be gone about a week. None of the hands will know about the trip until dawn tomorrow, so I hope the word doesn't get out in time for anyone to try to stop us."

Christina's eyes widened in alarm. "Would someone really try to stop you?"

MaLou reached out to touch her arm lightly. "You needn't worry. Anyone who tries to interfere with us will surely get the worst of it."

Amazed to find Lance's fiancée such a determined young woman, Christina smiled slightly and asked no more questions. She thought Lance had made a wise choice in a woman, for MaLou was not only beautiful but obviously quite bright as well. They were an attractive pair, one fair, one dark, and as she looked down at Jesse her cheeks flooded with a bright blush, for she saw that they would present the same vivid contrast as well.

As they left Jesse's room, MaLou whispered a question. "Where did Jesse find the blonde? She's not one of his whores, is she?"

That anyone would mistake Christina for such a woman provided Lance with a good laugh. "No, she isn't. She's one of my partners in a silver mine and I introduced them."

"You've become part owner of a silver mine?" MaLou lifted the hem of her gown so she could walk down the stairs safely. "You've certainly been busy since you left the ranch."

When they reached the landing, Lance pulled her into his arms for a lengthy kiss. "I'll tell you all about it on the way to Camp Grant. We'll have plenty of time to talk when we make camp each night."

MaLou turned back to give him a seductive glance before she continued down the stairs. "If you think we're going to waste our evenings talking, you've another think coming, Mr. Garrett."

"You know somethin'? Jesse asked me how I liked workin' for a woman, but I don't think I adequately explained the advantages."

"You'd better not explain them either," MaLou cautioned him with a lilting giggle. "Besides, you don't work for me anymore."

"That's right, I don't." As they walked through El Gallo and out into the sunshine, he was certain their happiness would never be more complete. He slipped his arm around her waist to draw her close, grateful they no longer had to hide their love from each other, or from anyone else.

Chapter XXIII

Lance had feared a cattle drive might prove to be too strenuous for MaLou, but he soon discovered she thrived on spending long hours in the saddle, breathing dust-filled air, and eating food Jake would have tossed to dogs. They had again brought along Pablo, the cook's helper, but while his fare was better than what the hands could prepare for themselves, it was not nearly as appetizing as their usual diet. MaLou did not utter a single word of complaint about the food, however.

He had always considered her a remarkable young woman, but that she would come along expecting to work as hard as the men had surprised him. That she could actually do it too was even more amazing. She not only had the natural athletic ability that made her so at home on horseback but also had mastered the wide range of skills the men possessed. He had known she would not ask for special privileges due to her sex, even though he and the men would have gladly extended them, but as far as he could discern, she needed no special treatment. In every way, MaLou was an asset to the drive rather than a nuisance to have along, and he doubted there was another woman in all of the Arizona Territory who could have received that same compliment.

While the dozen hands sat near the camp fire as they ate their supper on the first night out, Lance and MaLou sat some distance away. Neither had wanted to keep their engagement a secret, so they had announced it before leaving the ranch. Lance accurately read the men's expressions upon hearing the news. While none stepped forward, as he thought Manuel might, to tell him it was about time, it was obvious that it was a commonly held opinion. He would not waste his breath trying to explain the problems that had beset their courtship now that he and MaLou were so happy, but he hoped the men's loyalty to her would keep their gossip confined to the bunkhouse. They planned to announce their engagement properly when they returned from Camp Grant, but he realized their behavior was still far from conventional and he did not want to flaunt the intimacy of their relationship even out on the trail. Unfortunately, that was a subject he found difficult to discuss with the affectionate blonde.

Lance used his last bite of biscuit to mop up the gravy remaining in his tin plate, then washed down the slippery lump with coffee. His meal finished, he set his plate and fork aside with his cup before he whispered softly to MaLou. "I'll take the first watch," he began.

"I don't mind taking a turn," MaLou volunteered eagerly. "I can keep my eye on the herd as well as the others. I won't fall asleep either."

Lance tried to keep smiling so the men seated nearby would not think they were arguing. "No, I won't ask you to stand watch. What I am tryin' to plan, my dear, is some way for us to be alone together later."

"Ah, yes." MaLou nodded, sorry she had not realized that immediately. "Now I understand. At the end of your watch I could meet you where we've tethered the horses. Then later we can return to the camp separately. How's that?"

Lance gave her a sly wink. "All we can do is give it a try. If the hands see you sleepin' over here by yourself when they go to sleep and find you in the same place at dawn, they'll think that's where you've spent the whole night. I won't tell them any different if you promise not to."

"I won't whisper a word of it," MaLou vowed with an impish giggle. "I think we should have gotten married before we left the ranch. That would have made everything so much easier."

"If a cattle drive is your idea of a honeymoon, then I am goin' to reconsider my proposal," Lance threatened with a wicked grin.

MaLou knew he was only teasing her, but she was not ready to give in. Instead, she looked up at the star-filled heavens as she asked, "You don't think this is a romantic setting?"

Lance did not lift his gaze from her delicate features, for he never tired of looking at the pretty girl who would soon be his bride. "The view is magnificent, I'll agree, but I'd just as soon not bring along a dozen extra men and a hundred head of cattle when we go on our honeymoon."

Until that very moment, the prospect of a honeymoon trip had not even occurred to her, but the thought was enormously appealing. "Oh Lance, could we really go somewhere, take a trip? Could we do that? I was so worried about seeing my mother again I didn't enjoy my trip back East. Then I was so angry with her when I left to come home I didn't see much on the return trip either."

She was such a dear creature Lance wanted only to please her. "You pick a place, any place at all, and if I can possibly manage it, I will be happy to take you there."

MaLou thought a minute, and then came up with what she considered the perfect suggestion. "Could we go to Georgia? Some of your friends must still be living there. I would love to meet them and see the part of the country where you grew up."

Lance was so shocked by her request he simply stared at MaLou for a long moment before he responded gruffly, "I'd sooner take you to hell!" He got up then, grabbed her empty plate from her hands, and returned it, along with his, to the cook's wagon. He paused only long enough to assign three other men two-hour turns at watch before going to saddle a horse to begin his shift. Suddenly the night was filled not with the promise of love, but with long, menacing shadows, and he hoped it would pass swiftly since everything always looked better in the light of day. His gaze dark, his expression a savage frown, none of the men who had gotten a clear look at his face could have mistaken his mood. He knew they would take their turns guarding the herd very seriously rather than risk provoking him.

As several men turned to glance her way, MaLou tried to look as though nothing was wrong, but she did not understand why Lance had gotten so angry with her. She had thought of Georgia because it was his home, but he had made it painfully clear that it had been the worst possible choice. She got up, put down her bedroll, and stretched out on it, using her saddle for a pillow as the men did. She was far too agitated to want to rest, though, and spent her time staring up at the stars. Her father had taught her how to recognize the major constellations and she studied each one in turn. That the stars were older than time was somehow reassuring, but while they provided a beautiful canopy for her outdoor bed, they were too far distant to dispel the chill of fear from her heart.

That night Lance had proven himself to be as maddeningly private a person as he had been when he had first come to the ranch and insisted it was now his home. Surely if she had been more accomplished in the art of manipulating men through feminine wiles, she could have lured any secret from his lips. But all she knew of pleasing a man she had learned from him. She could not ask him to help her solve a problem when he was the very one who presented it. No, she was on her own again, as alone as she had ever been, and it was not a comfortable sensation. She had no hope Lance would modify his behavior after they were married, and she had not the slightest clue as to how to modify her own so she would not upset him as she so frequently did, though none of her insults were intentional.

Tormented by that thought, she listened to the men joking amongst themselves as they made ready to go to sleep. They were being careful not to say or do anything in the least bit disrespectful, but she knew this was creating a strain. When they had set out, she had thought it fortunate the trip would take no more than a week, but now the days stretched out before her in a taunting line. A week's time would seem an eternity if Lance's mood did not improve, and she doubted anything she might say or do would brighten it.

When Lance's temper cooled down, he was dreadfully sorry he had spoken so sharply to MaLou. Her suggestion would have been a good one had there been anyone left in Georgia he loved or wanted to see again. The trouble was, there was not a single soul he wanted to search out and introduce to MaLou, not one. His family was all dead and the few childhood friends who had survived the war had left the South as swiftly as he had. No, Georgia was not a state he would ever visit again, no matter how compelling the reason. Why couldn't he have explained that to MaLou in a rational tone instead of responding like an arrogant jackass? The tragic fact that the home and family he had loved were gone certainly was not her fault, and he had had no right to treat her so harshly.

He hummed softly to himself as he circled the herd, attempting to soothe his own soul as well as to comfort the sleeping cattle. When the next man came to relieve him, he took the bay horse he had been riding back to where the others were tethered and unsaddled him, but he saw no sign of MaLou. He waited an extra ten minutes, then certain she was not going to meet him, he carried the saddle that had been his only companion on far too many nights back to their camp. He knew he had hurt her feelings and he had been willing to apologize, but how could he do that if she would not give him the chance?

He found MaLou exactly where he had left her, sleeping on her right side and snuggled into a tight ball as though the blanket she had drawn up to her chin did not provide nearly enough warmth. He did not know whether or not she had deliberately failed to meet him. Maybe her pride had kept her from admitting how tired she was. Or perhaps she had planned to take only a brief nap while he had been on guard but had fallen too deeply asleep to awaken.

Sound asleep she so closely resembled a pretty child that he did not want her to wake up and be alone. He spread out his bedroll next to hers, removed his gun belt, and yanked off his boots. He then lay down and covered himself with his own blanket. When MaLou did not stir, he moved a little closer. That still did not satisfy his need to hold her, and forgetting his earlier desire for discretion, he pulled her into his arms. MaLou sighed softly but did not awaken. Gradually she relaxed in his embrace until her body had gracefully assumed the contours of his. Snuggled so closely, he knew she would be warm, but that was not really the type of warmth he had planned to provide. Too tired to spend another moment in regret, he fell asleep hoping the next night they shared would be the romantic one they had planned.

Just as the first few travelers were awakening to the coming dawn, the peace of the camp was shattered by the sharp report of Manuel's pistol. Lance sat up quickly but did not complain when he discovered the Mexican had just shot a diamondback rattlesnake that had been coiled in a snug nest at the bottom of the blankets he had shared with MaLou.

"You should take better care of your woman," the man advised with a disapproving frown.

Before Lance could draw a breath to defend himself, the cattle, which had been as greatly alarmed by the sound of gunfire as he, began to move. The rider on the last shift could not hold the frightened animals and the herd turned first in a wide arc, then, gaining speed, bolted right toward the camp. With the ground trembling beneath their feet, the men leapt out of their bedrolls and went scurrying for cover. Lance wasted not a single motion as he got to his feet. He grabbed MaLou's hands to yank her upright, then, keeping a tight hold upon her, sprinted for the shelter provided by the chuck wagon. They arrived at that small island of safety with only seconds to spare before the panic-stricken cattle raced by. The lovers clung to each other as the sturdy vehicle rocked and swayed. It was buffeted again and again by the long-horned beasts, but it did not overturn.

When the dust finally cleared, not only was the herd nearly out of sight, but most of the horses as well. The only sound that filled the air was a hail of violent oaths as the men realized how much work now lay in store. A quick glance about the camp revealed no one had been trampled to death, but the once neat circle of bedrolls and belongings that had ringed the fire had been scattered about so thoroughly the littered terrain now closely resembled the site of a fierce battle.

"Are you all right?" Lance asked MaLou without slackening his hold upon her.

To have found a snake sharing their bedrolls followed so closely by the scare of having to outrun a stampede was more than MaLou could bear calmly. As she looked up at Lance with a shaky smile, she suddenly realized she had fallen asleep before she had decided whether or not to sacrifice her pride and meet him. He did not seem angry with her though. His gaze was intense, but filled with concern rather than hostility. She was too badly shaken to think clearly enough to give him more than a reassuring nod before she turned to speak to Manuel.

"The next time you kill a snake, Manuel, use your knife!" she shouted caustically.

Manuel wore a deceptively sheepish grin as he approached her through the debris of the once tidy camp. "Serpents are clever, *señorita*. Had I come close enough to use my knife, the rattler might have felt my footsteps and awakened. You could have been bitten. I'd not take such a risk when I knew I could shoot the snake dead from a few paces away."

"You have a valid point there," Lance agreed, "however—"

MaLou interrupted impatiently, "That is neither here nor there. Flor has run off, but Amigo didn't stray. If you'll start rounding up the horses, then we can all go after the herd."

Lance thought his sweetheart looked particularly appealing with her blonde curls flying about her head in a careless tangle while her features were still slightly swollen from sleep. However, she was not so adorable he had forgotten who was in charge of the drive. "First I'd like to make certain none of the men are hurt, ma'am," he responded sarcastically.

MaLou turned away, embarrassed she had sounded as though the fate of her ranch hands did not concern her. "Of course, but from all the complaining they're doing it doesn't sound like anyone has suffered any harm." She started back toward her bedroll, where she found that the hapless rattler had been stomped upon by so many hooves his scaly hide was too badly damaged to be salvaged for even a hatband, let alone a belt. As she reached down for the corner of her blanket, meaning to flip the limp carcass aside, Lance stopped her.

"Wait a minute," the tall Southerner commanded sharply. "Let's make certain our visitor didn't have a mate."

MaLou rested her hands on her hips so he would not notice how badly they were still shaking. Then she turned to give him a skeptical glance. "If he had a mate, she'd be as dead as he is by now and probably twice as flat."

"I hope so, but let's just take a second to make certain." Lance leaned down to grab the corner of the torn bedroll and gave it a vigorous shake that revealed no further sign of snakes. The cattle had leapt over the barrier formed by their saddles, but their blankets apparently had not been spared the blow of a single hoof and were nearly in shreds. "The snake must have had a hole close by and been drawn by our warmth. Tonight we'll be far more careful about where we make camp and I'll lay my rope in a circle around us. Snakes won't cross a rope."

"I know that. I just wish we'd remembered it last night," MaLou complained with a shudder.

"Well, I guess we were distracted." Lance picked up what was left of his hat, and after an unsuccessful attempt to restore its shape, he plunked it on the back of his head.

He then buckled on his gun belt, which had escaped mishap beneath his saddle. Glancing toward the rising sun, he remarked meaningfully, "I hope the rest of the day doesn't prove so tryin'."

"How could it?" Taking care to avoid the dead snake, MaLou shook out her blankets, but they were still filthy. While she knew she would not want to use them again, she also knew she would have no choice come nightfall. "You'd better get goin', Garrett. Everybody's fine."

Lance had checked on the men as he had followed her back across their camp. The few who still had horses to ride were now saddling them. "I want you to ride with Pablo in the chuck wagon today."

"Why?" MaLou asked with an incredulous gasp. "I wasn't hurt."

"Don't argue. Just humor me for once and do as I say." Lance picked up his boots and took care to dump them out carefully before he pulled them on. To satisfy his own mind, he then made certain none of the desert's many poisonous creatures had taken up residence in MaLou's boots either. He left her then, hoping they would not have to waste the whole day rounding up stray horses and cattle. His only consolation was that their herd was a small one and would not present too difficult a challenge to reassemble.

MaLou watched Lance saddle Amigo and ride out, then sank down in the dirt and hugged her knees. She knew the snake had not been deliberately tossed between them by one of the hands. It had undoubtedly been drawn to the cozy warmth of sleeping humans, but she still thought Manuel should have used his knife to kill it since the potential danger of a stampede was far greater than the outside chance she or Lance might have been bitten. At least she thought it was, but she would say nothing more to Manuel about his choice of weapons.

Their first day on the trail had gone so well, but she blushed deeply as she recalled how it had ended. At least Lance had not yelled at her for not meeting him. He had been sleeping beside her and surely that was a good sign, but she should have known better than to give him orders as though he were one of the hands. Still, trail boss or not, she did not want to take orders from him either. For her to ride in the chuck wagon all day was too ridiculous a request to consider, however, and as soon as one of the men returned with Flor she saddled the mare and went to work. Her dad had taught her how to herd cattle as soon as she could handle a horse. She had had a horse too; not a pony, but a good-sized horse. Her pretty features wore a determined frown as she set out to prove once again what she was certain they all already knew: that she was as good a hand as any man.

Lance saw Flor's distinctive brown and white coat as MaLou streaked by on her mare, but he did no more than mutter a crudely worded curse under his breath. They had a great deal to straighten out, but the midst of a cattle drive was no place to do it. He pulled off his battered hat and used his shirt sleeve to wipe the sweat from his brow. Why the young woman wanted to do such hard and dirty work he did not know, but he hoped it would leave her too tired to argue with him by nightfall.

As soon as they made camp for the night, MaLou headed for the river to bathe. While the men might grow beards and ignore their sweat-stained clothes, she had far higher standards for her own appearance and clung to them even on the trail. The path of the San Pedro River was lined with *palo verde* and mesquite as well as cactus and acacias, providing a thick screen that would ensure her privacy. The water was too cold to invite a relaxing soak, and after peeling off her buckskins, she remained in it only long enough to scrub herself clean and wash her hair. She had brought along clean clothes and hastily pulled on the pants and shirt. The temperature was dropping steadily as night neared, and she shivered as she hurried to dry her hair on what was apparently the only clean towel left in the camp after the stampede.

Satisfied she was at least clean, if perhaps not all that

refreshed, MaLou wrapped her soiled clothes in the damp towel and turned back toward the camp. When she saw Lance sitting on a boulder at the side of the path, she was both shocked and embarrassed. "How long have you been there?" she called out as she walked toward him.

"One minute, maybe two," Lance replied, but the teasing light in his eyes made such a short span seem improbable.

The handsome young man had also taken the time to change his clothes, and even though the light was now growing dim, MaLou could see he was freshly shaven. Still shivering, she set her bundle aside and rubbed her arms to get warm. "How did you manage to clean up so fast?"

Lance reached out to pull her close. "Come here. I'll keep you warm while we talk." He slid off his rocky perch and wrapped her in a snug embrace before he answered her question. "Pablo was heatin' water to cook and I just helped myself to some. Sure beats tryin' to bathe and shave in the river."

MaLou snuggled against him as she tried to imagine how she could retain any sort of modesty if she were to attempt to bathe with a bucket of hot water in the camp. "That's fine for you, but I don't think it would work for me."

"Well, why not? Since you're so anxious to rope and ride like a man, why not try livin' like one all the time?"

MaLou's eyes blazed with a furious light as she looked up at the man she loved. She saw no point in playing games with words and lashed out at him. "You didn't really expect me to ride in the chuck wagon all day, did you?"

Lance fluffed out her damp curls with his fingertips as he attempted to find a tactful way to respond rather than merely incite further defiance. "I didn't expect you to want to work so hard, darlin'. Just because you're a better hand than most of the men doesn't mean you have to prove it over and over again. I thought you were comin' along to keep me company."

MaLou was surprised to find his mood so calm but nevertheless hastened to point out his mistake. "I had the drive to Camp Grant all planned before you came to see me. You're coming along with me, not the other way around."

"Whichever," Lance replied with a shrug. He again pulled her close and rested his chin lightly upon the top of her head. "What do you intend to do after we're married, MaLou? Do you plan to run the ranch while I handle all our business interests in town?"

MaLou licked her lips anxiously, uncertain what to say. "I don't know. I've never been married before."

Lance tried to stifle the chuckle that filled his throat but failed. "I haven't been married either, but that doesn't mean we can't plan how we're goin' to live. Maybe we can solve our problems now instead of just delayin' them until later."

MaLou closed her eyes for a moment and concentrated solely upon the steady rhythm of his heartbeat. That comforting sound was as soothing as the mellow tone of his voice. Finally she knew exactly what she wanted. "If you don't give me orders, then I can't be accused of disobeying them. I won't order you about anymore either since you're no longer one of my ranch hands. Won't that solve most of our problems?"

Lance opened his mouth to argue, then clamped it shut. She had oversimplified the case perhaps, but basically what she had said was true and he had to agree. "Yes, you're right. You're a very capable young woman and you can make your own decisions as well as I can make mine. Now about last night, I never should have been so rude to you when your desire to see Georgia is a very natural one. It would simply bring back an awful lot of painful memories for me though, and I'd rather not ever go back. I should have taken the time to explain that instead of just refusin' to listen to you. I don't blame you for not meetin' me."

MaLou tried to decide which answer would be best. Should she let him think she had deliberately not gone to meet him or admit the truth, that she had fallen asleep worrying over what to do? "I didn't think you'd want me to meet you," she finally whispered softly. He had confused as well as hurt her, but that was as close as she could come to revealing how dreadfully alone he had made her feel.

Lance ran his hands up and down her back to press her supple body more firmly against his own. "I'll always want you, MaLou. I don't care how heated our arguments get, I'll always want you. Don't ever doubt that."

Surrounded by his loving presence, she found that his words were easy to believe. "Does Fort Grant have a chaplain?"

"I have no idea. Why?"

"I don't want to have to wait until we get back home to get married."

There was a note of desperation in her voice that alarmed Lance as much as her desire to be his wife pleased him. He gave her a reassuring hug, then stepped back and picked up her bundle. "Come on, let's go back and see if Pablo has managed to cook somethin' worth eatin'. Then I'll do my best to explain why even if the fort has a chaplain, I'd rather not have him marry us."

"Oh no," MaLou moaned sorrowfully. "I've done it again, haven't I? You wouldn't want to be married by a Union officer even if I did, would you?"

Lance shook his head. "No, I wouldn't, but that doesn't mean I'm not anxious to make you my wife. I wonder what sort of ceremony the Apaches have?"

"You wouldn't ask an Apache to marry us!" MaLou danced along by his side as they covered the short distance to their camp and by the time they had reached it his teasing had made her mood as playful as his.

Lance found several changes since his last visit to the Army outpost. The Arivaipa Creek had stopped flowing when the weather had warmed in March. The Indians had therefore been given permission to move four miles upstream where water was still plentiful. Lieutenant Royal Whitman was there, but a newly arrived Captain Stanwood was now in command. Stanwood had brought verbal orders from General Stoneman in Tucson to continue to feed the Apaches gathered near the fort as prisoners of war. The captain was so pleased by the way Whitman was handling the Chiricahuas he was preparing to depart for a scouting mission to the southern portion of the Arizona Territory.

Again impressed with Royal's report of how well the Indians were adapting to a peaceful way of life, Lance thought MaLou would like to visit their settlement, for he knew she would find it as interesting as he had. "The Apaches deal with you and your soldiers constantly. Would the presence of a white woman disturb them?"

Royal considered his question a moment, then smiled. "Let me go with you. I would like Miss MacDowell to meet Eskiminzin, but I think we should introduce her as your wife, Garrett, just to keep him from showing any undo interest in her. He has more than one wife, but I understand that's a fairly recent practice brought about by the heavy losses of braves in warfare."

MaLou stared at Royal, then laughed as she asked if he were teasing. "You don't honestly think a Chiricahua chief would think me a suitable wife, do you?"

"Why not?" the friendly officer replied. "You are very pretty and there is no reason to suspect that Indian chiefs do not like pretty young women."

"You needn't worry, MaLou. I wouldn't trade you away for a few horses," Lance assured her with a sly wink.

"You'd better not even try or you'll never hear the end of it!" The thought of being an Indian's wife struck MaLou as absolutely impossible when she had so many problems getting along with Lance. Surely no Apache brave would have his patience and she would probably be swiftly strangled, or worse. Thoughts of Trinidad Aguirre, whose pregnancy had not prevented her recent murder, suddenly made their teasing banter seem in very poor taste and she turned the conversation into a far more serious one.

"You must know there are many people in Tucson who blame the Apaches you're feeding for raids on the ranches in the valley. I hope to learn the truth while I'm here, because I won't willingly feed any man who might kill one of my neighbors next week."

Royal was not surprised by her comment; in fact he had been expecting it. "I spend a great many hours with the Chiricahuas each day. I've been paying them to gather hay for our animals and they've been more than merely industrious. Occasionally I allow parties to go out to gather mescal, but I keep a close eye on how many go out and how much mescal they bring in. I've answered all their questions and made certain they understand our government expects them to be obedient. Runners have been sent to other bands related to Eskiminzin's by marriage and they are preparing to come in. While these people have little of what we'd call education, and nothing in the way of wealth, they place a higher value on virtue than many whites and I can't help but respect them. I'm confident what we're doing here is right. The marauding bands causing all the trouble aren't from here. They just can't be."

While MaLou knew that would be extremely difficult to prove, she was inclined to believe Whitman, just as Lance had been. "Well, I am not certain I will ever trust the Apaches as you do, Lieutenant, but I trust your judgment to be sound. Now I would like to meet Eskiminzin, but I hope he'll have the good sense to be satisfied with the wives he has."

Lance reached out to take MaLou's hand. "Don't give the man another thought. When I say you are my wife, he will believe me."

MaLou knew by the determined light in her fiancé's sky blue eyes that any man, Indian or white, would be a fool to cross him. "Good." With that assurance she quickly dismissed from her mind any thought of the chief's taste in women as they followed the Arivaipa Creek to the Apache encampment.

MaLou had thought only of men, but to her surprise the

braves she saw were greatly outnumbered by women and children. That Apaches had families was something she had not once considered during the years of the Civil War when their ranch, as well as most of the others in the Arizona Territory, had suffered repeated Indian raids. The attacks had been brutal. Many ranchers had been killed or so badly frightened they had left their land rather than risk dying in a futile attempt to defend it. Her father had been too tough to turn tail and run, but it seemed ironic that over the years he had begun to appreciate the Apaches' struggle to regain the land their ancestors had freely roamed. Then again, perhaps it was not unusual for men who had once been bitter enemies to gain a lasting respect for each other.

When she was introduced to Eskiminzin, MaLou found the man's dark glance a bit too curious and kept a firm hold on Lance's hand. The chief had a broad nose and generous mouth, but she supposed he was handsome in his own way and tried to smile and greet him politely. She thought at last she was beginning to understand how Lance must feel on the Army post, for she had fired more than one shot at an Apache brave herself and being in their camp made her feel uneasy, despite the warmth of their welcome.

While they did not remain long, MaLou took the time to note the profusion of dogs scampering about, the children playing happily while their scantily clad mothers tended their babies, and the men who moved about unarmed. It was strangely like standing on a corner in Tucson and watching the people walk by, for while everything she saw was uniquely Indian, it held a touch of the familiar too. Nowhere in all the curious glances directed her way did she see the slightest hint of hatred or malice. The Apaches appeared to be as wonderfully content a group as Royal Whitman had sworn they were. Perhaps he could offer no proof as to the goodness of these people's motives, but she felt comfortable accepting his opinion as the correct one.

"I think you're right, Lieutenant. There is no need for these braves to raid when they are treated so well here.

Surely they would not repay your kindness in such a treacherous fashion."

Royal smiled widely. "I wish there were more people in Tucson who could see things so clearly, Miss MacDowell. Unfortunately, you hold a very unpopular view."

"Well, opinions can always change," she remarked optimistically. Yet MaLou doubted they would where Indians were concerned. "I'm afraid it will take a great deal of time though."

"I just pray that we have it." Royal escorted his guests back to their horses, where they found several braves eyeing Flor. "Do you want to sell your horse?"

MaLou shook her head, then smiled as the men backed away. "No, Flor may look like an Indian pony, but she is mine and I'd never sell her." She glanced up at Lance as they made ready to depart, wondering if he was also thinking that she would have a room at the fort that night where they would not only have privacy, but a real bed. To her immense delight, she could tell by the width of his smile that those were exactly his thoughts too.

Chapter XXIV

Jesse wadded the latest edition of the *Citizen* into a tight ball and hurled it across the room. "Committee of Public Safety! How dare they call themselves such a ridiculous name?"

Christina had been embroidering a delicate floral design upon a pillow slip but knew better than to try to continue that work when her patient was in such a volatile mood. "Why is the name so improper? Shouldn't everyone want the people of Tucson to be safe?"

"Of course," Jesse admitted readily. "But I don't like the way William Oury and Juan Elias are going about their so-called 'safety' campaign. First they demanded that General Stoneman send greater numbers of troops against the Apaches while the man is under orders from President Grant to bring the Indians to peace through kindness. The general can scarcely hand out food with one hand and hold a rifle to the Indians' heads with the other."

"People have been killed," Christina reminded him softly.

"Yes, I know, but the incidents are scattered. Only a few braves have been seen each time there's been trouble. There must be more than a hundred Chiricahua braves at Camp Grant, and if they wanted to raid, why wouldn't they do it in force?" Jesse scowled darkly as he thought of his friends. "I hope Lance and MaLou return home soon. I'd hate for them to get caught in the middle of this damn committee's efforts to promote 'public safety.'"

Christina leaned forward, frightened as well as intrigued. "You think this committee might go after the Apaches themselves since General Stoneman won't?"

"They're working themselves up for something and I don't think they'll be satisfied to write letters of protest to Washington. If they get people mad enough, then something will be done, but I hate to think what it might be."

Christina considered Jesse Cordova one of the brightest men she had ever met. He seemed to know everything worth knowing about Tucson and even from his bed managed to keep up with the city's politics. "I wish you wouldn't worry so about it, Jesse. You're supposed to be restin'."

"Resting!" the irate man snarled. "I am sick of resting." Tossing the covers back, Jesse decided right then and there it was high time he got out of bed. "Will you please bring your chair over here so I can lean against it?"

Alarmed, the soft-spoken young woman began to argue. "Oh Jesse, I don't think you should try to get out of bed unless Sean is here to help you. At least let me call one of the men from downstairs. If you fall, I'll never be able to get you back into bed by myself."

Jesse raised his hand as he tried to allay her fears. "Just bring your chair over here. I won't try to do anything but stand up. If my leg won't hold me, then I'll just sit back down on the side of the bed. You won't have to pick me up off the floor. I promise you that," he assured her with one of his most charming smiles.

Christina had had plenty of experience dealing with headstrong men, since her brother definitely was one. It was readily apparent that Jesse intended to get himself out of bed with or without her help, so she did no more than sigh unhappily before rising to her feet, setting her embroidery aside, and positioning the chair next to the bed. "There you are. Now please take care, because I don't want to see you hurt."

While Christina always provided an abundance of

sympathy, Jesse had yet to receive any indication her feelings for him were any deeper than what she would show for a stray puppy. He had not brought up the subject of Sean O'Reilly since their last conversation about the physician had ended with the shy blonde's giving him the advice to waste no time in taking a wife. Just thinking about that day infuriated him all over again, but rather than giving vent to that anger he forced himself to concentrate upon the task at hand.

He had never worn nightshirts before he had been shot, but with Christina present for most of the day he had had to wear something and the loose-fitting garments were the most comfortable choice. Taking care to move slowly, he eased his legs over the side of the bed. His left leg ached as it always did, but not so much he could not move it. He grabbed the back of Christina's chair with his right hand, and putting all his weight on his right leg, he managed to pull himself upright. While his success was exhilarating, it was short-lived, for he felt too dizzy to remain standing for more than a few brief seconds and quickly sank back down on the bed. "You see," he declared in a breathless whisper, "I told you I could do it."

Tears welled up in Christina's eyes, for she was certain he had hurt himself even if he was too proud to admit it. "Just don't try to get up when you're alone. I don't want to come in some mornin' and find you've spent the whole night lyin' on the floor."

"Believe me, I do not want to see that happen either." Jesse felt better already and decided the best way to regain his strength was to use what little he had. "I think I'll try standing just one more time."

Christina had not felt so helpless since the day she had arrived to tend him. She moved to his left, hovering anxiously by his side. "I wish you'd leave well enough alone," she pleaded with him once again.

Jesse tried to hide his smile, but she had come so close a truly fiendish idea had suddenly occurred to him. If it worked, he might succeed in wringing a tender confession from her lips, and if he failed, well, he would be no worse off than he was already, because he was certain she would not suspect he had tricked her. "You must have more faith in me, Christina," he admonished slyly as he struggled to pull himself upright again. To his surprise, he did not feel quite as shaky, and, encouraged, he decided to see if his left leg would bear at least some of his weight before he played any tricks on his pretty nurse. Keeping a firm grip on the back of the sturdy chair, he shifted his weight slowly to his left side, but the resulting pain to his injured leg was so excruciating he quickly forgot his romantic interest in the young woman by his side. In agony, he lost his grip on the chair and in a frantic attempt to stave off a fall he grabbed for the fragile blonde's narrow waist.

Christina was already leaning toward Jesse, and when his hasty clutch caught her off balance, she could not help him regain his. She gave a strangled cry as her feet slipped out from under her, and her wildly flailing efforts to break her fall only succeeded in pulling Jesse down with her. The back of her head struck the floor first, but while that jarring burst of pain brought tears to her eyes, it did not knock her unconscious. She was far more concerned about the man in her arms than about her own discomfort and did not try to scramble out from under him. "Jesse? Are you hurt?" she asked fearfully.

Racked with pain, the distraught man needed a moment to catch his breath before replying. He had wanted Christina draped gracefully across the bed, not slammed against the floor, and he was mortified his clumsiness might have caused her pain. Rising up slightly, he braced himself on his elbows as he hurriedly began to apologize. "Please forgive me. You were right it seems. I am not strong enough to stand without falling, but I never meant to hurt you." Seeing the tears upon her cheeks, he grew even more alarmed and tried to wipe them away.

"Hurt me?" the disheveled blonde complained. "You damn near killed us both!" She lay still, appalled by the stupidity of the man and at the same time fascinated by the warmth of his body, which covered hers completely, though, strangely, not uncomfortably. She had only seen him standing once before that day and he was taller than she had remembered, but from her current perspective it was difficult to make any other judgments about him. Shyly, she reached up and used her fingertips to comb his thick black hair away from his eyes. "Nurse crushed by impatient patient," she offered with a charming giggle. "That would have made a good headline for the *Citizen*."

The very last thing Jesse had expected her to do was laugh at him and his glance filled first with fury and then with a far more dangerous light as he lowered his mouth to hers. He already had her pinned beneath him and he grabbed for her wrists before she could raise her hands to shove him away. She had no way to escape him then, and his kiss grew increasingly more insistent until at last her lips parted slightly. He seized that opportunity to plunge his tongue into her mouth, savoring the sweetness of her taste as he lost all sense of time and place. He wanted her so desperately he blocked the pain still throbbing within his leg and concentrated solely upon winning the affectionate response he had longed to receive from her almost from the hour they had met.

Rather than adored, Christina simply felt trapped in Jesse's ardent embrace. Not recognizing his passion for what it was, she mistook his sudden outpouring of emotion for anger and shocked by his savage kiss began to tremble in fear. While Jesse might not have been able to stand, his grip felt like steel upon her wrists, and although she rebelled inwardly, she had no way to fight him. She had thought him a gentleman despite his occupation, and to discover so abruptly she had been completely mistaken about him disillusioned her terribly. Tears poured down her cheeks as she tried to think of some way to break free without hurting him, but before an idea occurred to her she heard the door fly open and her brother call her name.

Christopher Buchanan had come running up the stairs, so excited about the news he wished to share with his twin he had forgotten to knock at Jesse's door, but the scene that greeted him readily justified that breach of etiquette. He raced across the room, kicked aside the overturned chair, and grabbed Jesse's right arm to pull him upright. He then slammed his fist into the Mexican's face and threw him back on the bed. "You bastard!" he screamed, ready to beat the hapless man senseless, but Christina scrambled to her feet and pushed him back before he could strike Jesse again.

"No! Don't hit him!" she begged, hanging onto Chris's arm so he could not throw another punch at Jesse. Blood was pouring from the injured man's nose and he looked every bit as horrified as she felt. "Stop it, Chris!" she ordered fiercely. "He didn't mean to harm me. I know he didn't."

Chris stared at his sister, amazed she would take Jesse's side. "Harm you? Hell, he was tryin' to rape you! I ought to just shoot the bastard dead and be done with him!"

Sounds of the ruckus coming from Jesse's room finally reached the ears of the men posted as guards and they appeared at the open doorway with their pistols drawn. "Get away from the bed, Buchanan," the man who had let him up the stairs called out. "I thought you were calling on your sister, not gunning for the boss."

There was blood splattered all down the front of his nightshirt and Jesse was certain he was going to be sick, but he did not want anyone, least of all Christina, to believe for a minute he had been trying to rape her. He had just wanted to kiss her and he knew he had gone about it all wrong, but he could not apologize to her with her brother screaming at him about rape. "Get him out of here," he called to the guards, but when Chris grabbed Christina's hand and yanked her along behind him, Jesse was too weak to insist she remain. He saw her tears as she turned back to look at him, but her expression was filled with fear rather than love. Knowing he would never make a greater fool of himself if he lived to be one hundred, he slumped back against his pillows and lay still, not caring if he bled to death before someone came to help him.

Sean O'Reilly considered the tale he had been told too

fantastic to believe until he had seen Jesse. "This is the first time I have ever heard of a man confined to his bed with a gunshot wound getting in a fistfight over a woman. You've got no blood to spare, Jesse, so you'll have to try harder to stay out of trouble until you're well."

Jesse forgave the young doctor for speaking to him in such a patronizing fashion since he believed it was a common failing in the medical profession. He was not a small boy who should be scolded, however, but a man who was far more angry with himself than anyone else could ever be, including Christopher Buchanan. "Who sent for you? Was it Christina?"

"Nope, it was one of your bartenders. Vance, I believe his name is."

It had taken the young doctor so long to stop his nose from bleeding, Jesse began to wonder if perhaps he truly had come close to bleeding to death. He was so tired he was afraid if he fell asleep he might never wake up. "My nose is broken, isn't it?"

"It sure is, but it's not so bad it will be crooked, despite all the blood. You'll be as handsome as you've always been in a week or two. Just don't look in the mirror, 'cause your eyes will be black, but that won't last either."

Jesse swallowed hard, but the taste of blood made his stomach lurch painfully. "I must see Christina. There's something I have to explain."

Sean pulled up a chair and sat down before he replied. "I'd just as soon not get involved in this if you don't mind. Christina's a real sweet girl, and while I don't know exactly what happened here, if her brother was mad enough to break your nose I tend to think you deserved it."

"Well, I didn't," Jesse denied hoarsely. He turned his face to the wall then, certain the doctor had been the wrong person to ask for help since the young man was fond of Christina himself. "I don't deserve any of this!" he insisted bitterly.

Alarmed by the darkness of his patient's mood, Sean got up and moved the chair aside. "Just be grateful your leg didn't start bleeding again or you'd really have been in trouble. Now try to get some rest and I'll stop by later."

"Don't bother. I will be fine," Jesse vowed stubbornly, but once he was left alone he was overcome with despair. What must Christina think of me now? he asked himself. Before he had been shot he could have whipped Chris Buchanan easily, but now he was so helpless the man could have killed him in his own bedroom! That wretched thought disgusted him completely. He had never given such a poor accounting of himself, and to have been beaten so severely in front of a woman he cared about was too great a humiliation to bear. Christina would never speak to him again—he was certain of it.

When Vance appeared with his supper, he sent the man over to the Silver Spur to fetch Carmen. Since she would do anything for a price, he knew she would make a most agreeable nurse, and that was just the type of company he would need for awhile.

The farther they went from town, the harder Christina cried. When her brother stopped their wagon, she looked up and was surprised to find they were not home. "What's the matter now?" she asked between sobs.

"You haven't heard a word I've said, Tina. The ore I've been bringin' out is so high in silver content we're going to be rich! Can't you understand that? Hell, we're already rich! You don't have to be any man's nurse. We can build a big house, dress in fancy clothes, and buy whatever we want just for the fun of it."

Christina had always believed in her brother, but when he had said they were going to strike it rich, she had not really dared hope they actually would. "Don't forget Mr. Garrett will want his third, Chris. Maybe there won't be enough silver to make us all rich."

"I've already figured his share, Tina, and we'll all be rich. We really will."

The sorrowful blonde nodded, still too stunned by the afternoon's shocking turn of events to grasp the full significance of their sudden wealth. "You shouldn't have hit Jesse. You shouldn't have done that. I don't know what got into him, but he wasn't trying to rape me." She tried to explain how they had come to be sprawled upon the floor, but her explanation made no sense to herself, let alone to her brother.

"Just forget the man. I'm sorry now I didn't put a couple of bullets in him, since that's what he deserved. I don't want any talk goin' around Tucson about you and him. You're a good girl and I mean for you to stay that way."

Christina turned away as her brother brought the reins down upon their mules' backs to get the wagon rolling again. Being rich meant nothing to her. What use would a fine house or fancy clothes be if she had no man to love? Not that she had been in love with Jesse or he with her, but she had liked him an awful lot. She wished he had chosen a better time to kiss her because she would have liked to have kissed him back instead of just being crushed in his arms. A new torrent of tears burst forth at that thought. Maybe he had been trying to rape her and she just had so little experience with men she did not even realize it. Though after what Chris had done to him, it would not matter what he had been trying to do. He would never want to see her again.

"I forgot my embroidery!" she lamented sadly. "We got everything out of the room I was usin', but I left it in Jesse's room. It was almost finished too."

"Forget it then. It's gone," Chris ordered firmly. "In fact, just try to forget you ever met Cordova. He's not half good enough for you and you're far better off without him."

"I never had him, Chris," Christina remarked with a puzzled stare.

"Yeah, I know, and you're far better off that you didn't. You're a decent woman and you don't need a man like that."

"One who owns a saloon, you mean?"

"That's not all the man owns, Tina, but it doesn't matter. You try to forget you ever met him and spend your time thinking about all the pretty clothes I'm going to buy for you."

"You don't have to buy me things, Chris. I'm your sister, not your wife."

"That doesn't matter," the young man assured her proudly. "I can buy presents for my sister if I want to. I'm rich!"

Christina clamped her hand over his mouth. "I think you'd better hush up about that, or all we'll be is dead!"

Afraid she might be right, Chris nodded, but he whistled all the way home thinking about what fun it was going to be to be rich for a change.

When he saw Jesse's face, Lance was glad MaLou had had some shopping to do and had not come upstairs with him to see his friend. Then when he noticed it was Carmen who had opened the door, he was doubly glad she had not come with him. "I need to speak with Jesse alone." Before the heavily perfumed woman could open her brightly painted mouth to object, he took hold of her wrist and with a graceful turn spun her right out into the hall. He then took the precaution of locking the door behind her. Turning back to his friend with a quizzical glance, he waited for him to speak. When Jesse appeared to be too embarrassed to offer a much-needed explanation, Lance first opened a window to rid the room of the last traces of Carmen's sickeningly sweet fragrance and then brought a chair over to the bed and sat down.

"The trip to Camp Grant had its bad moments, but we're all back safe and sound, which I certainly can't say for you. If you don't want to tell me what happened to you, at least tell me why Christina isn't here. I thought she'd agreed to stay with you a while longer. Why did she change her mind?"

It had been Lance's close resemblance to him that had first attracted Jesse's notice. He realized suddenly that after all the misery he had suffered recently, no one would mistake them for brothers ever again. In as few words as possible he related what had happened, then held his breath as he waited for his friend to laugh. Lance, however, did not see any humor in the situation.

"Oh, Jesse," he began sympathetically, "anyone who knows you would never believe you'd try to rape Christina. That's just absurd. I'll ride out to the Buchanans' this mornin' and straighten everythin' out."

"No," the battered Mexican insisted firmly. "Stay out of this. I was a fool to think I had something to offer her when it is so obvious that I have nothing she will ever want or need. She is a sweet, innocent girl and you know what I am."

Lance nodded as his perceptive glance swept slowly over his friend's agonized expression. "I know you're an honest man and a fair one. You were a mite too pretty, but that's one problem you won't have to worry about anymore. Now I think if you want Christina, then you ought to stop feelin' sorry for yourself and go after her."

"I told you what happened when I tried to stand up. I fell flat on my face! Or at least I would have if Christina had not been in the way," he admitted sheepishly.

"If you can sit up in bed, you ought to be able to sit in a buggy," Lance encouraged calmly, not reacting to Jesse's hostility.

"I cannot go calling on Christina looking like this!"

Truly the man did look awful. His nose was swollen and his eyes were ringed with deep purple bruises. His right cheek was still bandaged and his new growth of beard was not neatly groomed. "You have looked better, I'll grant you that, but I think the sooner you speak with Christina the better off you'll be. If she's as miserable as you are about this, I'll bet she's still cryin'."

Such a sad thought overwhelmed Jesse with sorrow, for he had thought the slight blonde hated him and he had not once pictured her weeping over the way they had parted. "I cannot bear to think I have made Christina unhappy, but I don't want to see her now, not when I look even more pathetic than I did. It was never pity I wanted from her."

Lance leaned forward to give Jesse's shoulder a comforting pat. "I'll help you get up and walk around each day until you're strong enough to get by on your own. Your cuts and bruises will soon heal. I'll bet by the time MaLou and I are ready to get married you'll be as fit as you ever were. Since the Buchanans are my partners, they're sure to come to the weddin'."

Jesse studied Lance's sly grin for a long moment before he realized the Southerner was not just making a polite effort to make him feel better. "I don't know, *amigo*. I thought you wanted to be married sometime soon. It might be several years before I look good again."

Lance sat back in his chair and shook his head. "A couple of weeks and you'll be as good as new. I'm certain of it."

While Carmen had assured him of the same thing, somehow those words had not sounded nearly as truthful coming from her bright red lips. He had indeed been feeling sorry for himself and decided that was something he would stop immediately. "Enough of my problems. Tell me what you found at Camp Grant and I will tell you what I know of the mood of the citizens of Tucson."

As the two men continued to talk, MaLou ran her errands. She not only bought supplies for Jake, but also did some shopping for herself. Her mood was a carefree one until she saw Josh's friend, Carl Perry, moving down the opposite side of the street. She had done no more than send the Spencers a note saying she had to make a trip to Camp Grant and would be unable to have supper with them on Sunday, but there was a lot more she had to tell them before they heard about her engagement from another source. The thought of visiting the Spencers with news she knew they would not want to hear depressed her so thoroughly she lost all interest in shopping and returned to El Gallo del Oro to see if Lance was ready to leave.

Lance answered the knock at the door, then stepped out into the hall before MaLou caught a glimpse of Jesse. "If you're ready to go, so am I," he told her with a disarming grin.

MaLou tried to step around him, but he blocked her way. "I'd like to say hello to Jesse before we go. How is he feeling?"

"He's asleep," Lance claimed, and taking MaLou's arm, he guided her back down the hall. He had known without asking that Jesse would rather not be seen by the attractive young woman in his present state and he did not blame the man. When they found Carmen flirting with the guard stationed at the bottom of the stairs, he paused for a moment to scold them both before he escorted MaLou out through the saloon.

"Just who was that woman?" the curious blonde asked as they reached her buckboard. "And don't tell me she is another one of your partners either."

"No, I wouldn't enter into any sort of business arrangement with Carmen." Lance helped MaLou up into the high seat, then circled the buckboard, climbed up on the other side, and picked up the horses' reins. "She's from the Silver Spur, actually, but she's been takin' care of Jesse the last few days."

"Well, it's no wonder that he needs a nap then," MaLou suggested in a teasing whisper. "What happened to the other girl, Christina, the one who owns the silver mine with you?"

"That's exactly what I intend to find out. Do you want to come out to her house with me, or would you rather go home? I'd like you to meet her brother, but if you'd rather not take the time today I'll understand."

Since a visit to his partners would provide an excellent excuse not to pay a call at the Spencers', MaLou quickly agreed. "No, I'd like to go with you. I've been looking forward to getting to know your partners since you first told me about them."

Lance debated whether or not to tell MaLou about Jesse's problems and finally decided to keep the man's troubles to himself. He knew his fiancée would never spread gossip about the wealthy Mexican, but he thought he owed the man a few secrets. He realized his mistake as soon as they reached the Buchanans' modest house, however, for Chris was still so angry about the tragedy he believed he had narrowly averted, he started talking about it as soon as he had been introduced to MaLou.

"I'm glad you came out here today, Garrett, because I wanted to see you and I'll never set foot in the Golden Cock ever again after what Cordova tried to do to Tina. I won't let any man take advantage of my sister. I don't care how rich he is. The fact is, we're rich now too."

When Chris stopped to catch his breath, Lance glanced over at Christina. The young woman looked as wretched as Jesse had, although there was not a mark on her, and he wanted to hear her version of their unfortunate confrontation. "Wait just a minute. I came out here today because I wanted to check up on you two and see how you were gettin' along. I didn't plan to get involved in your argument with Jesse, but since I was the one who asked you to take care of him, I feel responsible for what happened, Christina. Do you think you could tell me about it in your own words?"

"I just told you!" Chris interrupted. "The man tried to rape her!"

MaLou could not believe her ears, and while she was both dismayed and disappointed that Lance had not bothered to tell her she would be walking into a fight if she joined him in calling on the Buchanans, she could not keep still. "There has to be a mistake here. Jesse Cordova is a far too elegantly mannered man to stoop to forcing himself upon a woman. I'm certain he hasn't got the strength to do it now anyway."

When Chris again began to call Jesse vile names, Lance silenced him with a fierce glance and a loudly worded command. "I'd like to hear what Christina has to say, please."

Frightened she would not say the right thing, the shy young woman cringed as though Lance had threatened to strike her. "I don't really know what happened. I swear I don't." She burst into tears then and fled from the small house before her brother could stop her.

"Now look what you've done!" Chris shouted at Lance.

"Why couldn't you have just let her be?"

Flustered by Christina's abrupt exit, Lance turned to MaLou. "Would you go after her? I know you're not friends, but you are a woman and that ought to count for somethin'."

"Of course," MaLou replied sweetly, thinking the man had delayed far too long before asking for her help, but she would wait until they were alone to make that point. She left the house immediately, hoping Christina would not be too difficult to find. Fortunately, the timid girl never strayed far from the house and had gone only as far as the corral that enclosed their two mules.

As MaLou came up to Christina's side, she realized she had no idea what to say. Clearly the girl was terrified of Jesse now, although she could not imagine anyone being afraid of the charming man. Deciding it would be best to think of another topic of conversation, she chose something Chris had said. "What did your brother mean about everyone's being rich now?"

Christina eyed MaLou's pale blue gown with a longing glance as she wiped away the last of her tears. "Our claim is a very good one. My brother can explain far better than I can, but there's enough silver in the ore to provide both us and Mr. Garrett, too, with a fortune. We can build a nicer house, buy new clothes, make proper friends. Everyone likes people with money, don't they?"

MaLou laughed at her question. "I don't know if wealthy people are necessarily well liked, but their company is usually sought. It must be very lonely for you, living here all alone with your brother, but I hope that whatever new friends you'll make will like you for yourself rather than your sudden wealth."

Christina chewed her lower lip nervously as she considered the truth of MaLou's comments. "Yes, I understand what you mean. I won't trust anyone too quickly." That matter settled, she turned the conversation to more practical matters. "You have such pretty clothes. Do you think you might help me pick out some new things? I've always made my own, and I'd like to own a dress someone else has sewn now that I can afford it."

To be asked for advice on fashion was so unexpected that MaLou needed a moment to respond. "Why, yes, I'd love to go shopping with you. Tucson has shops with ready-made garments as well as seamstresses who can create a fashionable wardrobe for you. It would be wonderful fun to help you. I've really just begun worrying about my own wardrobe and still lack many things I should have."

Christina did not see how that could possibly be true, since on the two occasions she had seen MaLou MacDowell the young woman had been beautifully dressed. When she saw her brother and Lance approaching, she quickly made plans to meet MaLou in town the next day and did her best to smile at the two men.

Lance gave MaLou a questioning glance, but she shook her head slightly to warn him to be still. "It seems I'm to be well rewarded for my confidence in you and Chris, Christina, and I'll be happy to advise you so you two can invest what monies you earn from the mine wisely."

"Oh yes, we do want to make it last and last," the bashful young woman agreed. "But I will be able to buy a new dress or two, won't I?"

"Of course," Chris assured her. "Buy a dozen dresses if you like."

The two couples parted company after the women had decided where to meet the following day, and as soon as the buckboard had covered a sufficient distance from the house so they could not be overheard, Lance turned to MaLou. "Well, what did she say about Jesse? Did she give you her side of it?"

"She didn't mention the man, Lance. She seems to be more concerned about having new clothes than about him. Why didn't you tell me what had happened? You certainly had plenty of time while we were riding out here. Didn't you think I'd be interested?"

Lance shrugged slightly. "I should have told you. I know that. It's just that I'm used to keeping everything to myself, and I shouldn't have this time."

"No, you shouldn't have," MaLou readily agreed. She was sorely tempted to make her protest in far more emphatic terms, but he seemed so sincerely contrite she held her tongue. "I've been dreading going over to the Spencers'. Why don't we just stop by their place on the way home and I'll get the beastly scene we're sure to have over with as quickly as I can."

"Is that my punishment for not telling you about Jesse?" Lance asked playfully.

"Yes, you can consider it as such."

"Good. I'm really going to enjoy this," Lance stated confidently. "Remind me to thank him for mentioning the champagne. I might have forgotten to order it for our wedding if he hadn't asked me about it."

"Oh, Lance, you wouldn't say that!" Yet MaLou could see by the devilish sparkle in his eyes that he most certainly would.

Chapter XXV

MaLou thought later that "beastly" had proved to be far too mild a term to describe the wild scene Lance created at the Spencers' ranch. When they drove up to the house, Josh came running out to meet them. He deliberately ignored Lance, but he was so thrilled to see MaLou he reached up to grab her waist and swung her down from the buckboard. Rather than setting her upon her feet and stepping back, however, he wrapped her in a boisterous bearhug and proceeded to give her a deep and lingering kiss.

Appalled to find that Josh thought such a familiar greeting appropriate, Lance hesitated no more than an instant before leaping down from the buckboard. First he struck Josh's shoulder with a forceful shove to set MaLou free of his confining embrace, then Lance slammed his right fist into the amorous man's face. That crushing blow dropped the astonished young rancher in the dirt, but Alex had stepped out onto the porch, and seeing his son was getting the worst of a fight, he jumped right into the middle of it.

MaLou moved quickly to stay out of the way as Lance then began to tangle with Alex Spencer. Constance had followed her husband to the door, but seeing the dust kicked up by what looked like a brawl involving a dozen men rather than only three, she began to wail in a high-pitched scream. Ranch hands responding to that piercing shriek soon surrounded the combatants and began yelling encouragement to their boss and his son, neither of whom had been able to land a single blow despite the brutal punishment Lance was eagerly inflicting upon them.

While MaLou did not doubt that Lance could whip both Josh and Alex single-handedly, she did not want to see the odds get any worse, and fearing more men would soon join the fray, she climbed back up into the buckboard and reached for the loaded shotgun her father had always insisted she carry on trips into town. She quickly fired one blast into the air and prepared to fire a second, but it proved to be unnecessary. Startled by the noise of the shotgun, Alex and Josh staggered backward and stood clinging shakily to each other while Lance nonchalantly brushed the dust from his clothes.

Keeping a firm hold on the shotgun, MaLou adopted a proud stance and a murderous glance to return the curious stares of the Spencers and their hands. "Good afternoon, Constance, Alex, Josh, and the rest of you," she began with more than a touch of sarcasm. "I asked Lance to drive me over here today so I could tell you we're planning to be married soon. If you'd rather not attend our wedding though, we'll understand." She nodded to Lance then and he climbed back up into the buckboard. As soon as she was comfortably seated, he clucked to the team of horses and they started off for home before Josh or his parents had the presence of mind to object to her announcement.

When they reached the road MaLou turned back to make certain they were not being followed before giving vent to her anger. "What in Heaven's name got into you?" she asked Lance accusingly, her question in itself a scathing rebuke.

"What got into me?" Lance responded sarcastically. "Jesse got accused of attempted rape for far less than Josh was doin'!"

"Don't be ridiculous," MaLou argued with a disgusted frown. "Josh was just trying to show you up, just like when he asked you about the champagne."

"Oh, damn it all!" Lance swore angrily. "I forgot to

thank him for suggestin' it. I told you not to let me forget to do that," he chided with a sly chuckle that swiftly grew into a deep, raucous laugh.

Lance had apparently found the disgraceful incident at the Spencers' wonderfully amusing, while MaLou did not see a shred of humor in it. "Another couple of minutes and you'd have found yourself at the bottom of a deep pile of surly ranch hands. Have you no sense at all? If I'd known how badly you were aching to fight Josh, I'd have insisted we meet him on neutral ground."

"I can look out for myself," Lance assured her.

"Obviously," MaLou replied as she leaned down to lay the shotgun at their feet. "But I'd rather the whole town didn't think I'm marrying you rather than Josh just because you can throw a harder punch."

"Well, I can't say whether I do or not, since none of his punches hit me." Lance knew he should not continue teasing the feisty blonde, but he could not help himself. His spirits were too high to be squelched by her disapproval.

MaLou shook her head sadly, wondering how she would ever be able to face her lifelong friends again. "I would have made Josh understand I didn't want him to kiss me like that ever again. You needn't have interfered."

"Look, you know they wouldn't have wished us happiness no matter what you said, so just forget the Spencers. They aren't important to us."

"You're a fool if you think Alex Spencer isn't important, Lance. Maybe Josh is of slight consequence, but I don't want Alex for an enemy when he's my closest neighbor."

Lance had not thought of anything but peeling Josh off MaLou, and he was not sorry he had done it either, even if there were repercussions he had not considered. "Let's see now, if I'm not mistaken, my list of enemies is gettin' dangerously long. The Hatcher brothers must still want me dead. The Spencers probably hate me after what I did to them today. Your foreman, Nathan, has never been fond of me, so I've learned not to turn my back on him. From what Jesse says, most of the population of Tucson wants every Indian in the Territory hunted down and killed. I can't be popular with that group either, since it must be common knowledge I've driven your cattle to Camp Grant on three separate occasions. Then there are the men who've lost all their money trying to beat me at poker. There are too many of them to name, but one of them might decide to come after me someday soon."

When Lance paused for a moment, MaLou was afraid he was about to name several others who might wish him ill. "Must you be so terribly pessimistic? I've no wish to become a widow before I'm even twenty-one, or ever, for that matter."

"As long as you stay so quick with a shotgun I'm not goin' to worry." Lance put his arm around MaLou's shoulders and gave her a loving hug. "I ought to go back to El Gallo tonight, but I don't have to sleep there unless I'm not welcome at the ranch."

MaLou slipped her arm around his waist and rested her head upon his shoulder. "Is that a question you think you have to ask?"

"I hope not." They fell into the comfortable silence he found so enjoyable and his thoughts gradually strayed to the day he had first ridden into Tucson. He had been looking for a job and a few good friends, but he had certainly found more than he had bargained for at the MacDowell ranch, a great deal more. "What have you heard from your mother lately?"

"Not a thing since she took the money. I doubt I'll ever hear from her again, but at least the ranch is all mine now, just as it should have been in the first place. It will take me a while to pay back the loan Candelaria gave me, but I hope she'll be patient."

"From the assayer's report Chris showed me, I'd say paying back that loan won't be any problem at all," Lance remarked with a satisfied smile, delighted that for the second time he would be able to save the woman he loved from having to face a difficult financial problem alone.

"Is that true about the Buchanans' mine? Is it really

producing so much silver it will make all three of you rich?"

"Looks like it. I told you I didn't care if I ever made a dime out of that investment. I just didn't want to see those two end up not only broke but brokenhearted like so many other people who've come out West hoping to strike it rich. It's goin' to be real embarrassin' if I end up gettin' rich for tryin' to do a good deed."

"I know a lot of people who'd love that kind of embarrassment. You wanted to make a name for yourself before we were married. I think you've succeeded."

Lance frowned slightly. "Yes, ma'am, I have definitely made a name for myself, but are you certain it's one you'll be proud to share?"

"Yes," MaLou replied confidently. "I'm sure I will be."

When they reached the ranch, Lance helped to unload the buckboard, gave MaLou a kiss far more memorable than Josh's, then rode Amigo back into town. He had not forgotten just how many men would rather he did not arrive there safely though, and kept a close eye on the road.

It was nearly midnight when Lance returned to the ranch, and MaLou greeted him with such a desperately passionate kiss he swept her up into his arms and carried her straight back to her bedroom. She was already clad in her nightgown and he placed her upon the bed and sat down beside her to pull off his boots. "You give me that enthusiastic a welcome each time I come home and I won't ever want to leave."

"I've been thinking about what you said about enemies," the lovely blonde explained anxiously. "With you traipsing back and forth into town at such odd hours, it's only a matter of time before someone tries to ambush you."

"It's not all that easy to hit a man dressed in black riding a black horse at midnight, MaLou," Lance pointed out cheerfully. "I'm usually gone before dawn, so that's no problem either. I didn't mean to frighten you this afternoon."

MaLou hugged her knees and rested her chin atop them. "Maybe you didn't mean to, but you certainly did. I don't know what I'd do if I lost you, Lance. I think I'd just cease to exist."

Lance leaned over to give her a reassuring kiss. "Nothing is going to happen to me, MaLou." When he saw his words had failed to lift her downcast mood, he grew more thoughtful. "All right, maybe I should take your warning more seriously. When the word gets around that we'll be married soon, everyone will expect me to make frequent trips out here to see you. I have to be at El Gallo at night and unfortunately that makes my routine pretty easy to predict."

MaLou frowned slightly as she made an attempt to phrase her request tactfully. "I think it would be best if I came into town to see you. Not even the Hatchers are low enough to ambush a woman, so I'll be far safer on the road to Tucson than you are."

Lance reached out to catch one of her bright curls in his fingertips. "How often do you plan to come into town?"

"As often as I can," MaLou replied in a seductive purr. "Your room at El Gallo is very nice and I'm certain we can arrange to meet there discreetly."

Lance stood up as he began to unbutton his shirt. "This is a ridiculous conversation, MaLou. I think we ought to make plans to be married by the end of the week. Then we can divide our time between Tucson and here without havin' to make excuses to anyone."

"Well, I'm certainly not going to argue about when we have the wedding," MaLou assured him sweetly.

"You'll agree then? We'll be married as quickly as it can be arranged?"

"Is tomorrow too soon for you?" MaLou's glance swept over him hungrily as he peeled off his clothes. She knew his body as well as her own now. Each plane and curve was familiar, yet endlessly exciting. "I love everything about you: the way your hair curls over your collar, the width of your shoulders, the flatness of your stomach." Her eyes strayed lower, but she ceased to enumerate his remarkable array of physical assets as her eyes returned to his. "You must be as close to perfection as any man ever born."

As Lance joined her on the bed, he thought himself extremely fortunate to have found such an incredibly loving young woman. "Thank you," he murmured huskily as he pulled her into his arms. "But if either of us is perfection, it is you."

MaLou rubbed her cheek against his. He had shaved late in the afternoon and his skin still felt smooth. "When I'm with you, it's easy to forget the rest of the world exists."

Lance hugged her tightly as he made a heartfelt confession. "You are my world. Until we met, I had all I could do just to live from one day to the next. Now, because I care so deeply for you, I care about others as well: for Jesse, the Buchanans. Even the Chiricahuas at Camp Grant matter to me now. You've given me a world filled with good people I was too lost in my own pain to see, let alone want to know. In every way you have taught me far more than I will ever teach you."

MaLou was deeply touched to discover her effect upon him had been so profound. Best of all, she considered his revelation wonderfully honest. "Thank you, for that lavish compliment and for finally trusting me with the truth."

"Oh yes, ma'am, from now on I will tell you nothin' but the truth." He nuzzled her throat playfully, losing himself in the fragrant scent of her glorious curls as his fingertips pushed the hem of her nightgown above her thighs, where the warmth of her skin invited a far more intimate touch. In response to his wandering caress, she removed her gown with a careless tug and cuddled closer. His hand then slid over the silken flesh of her stomach to the soft swell of her breasts before his lips found hers. Her tongue met his with a saucy curl and he found the unrestrained joy of her loving, as always, the greatest of thrills. Love flowed between them with the ease of sweet music floating on a warm summer breeze. She was his perfect mate. She was his very soul, and he longed to spend not simply the whole night, but all of his life, pleasing her.

As she lay enfolded in the warmth of Lance's embrace, MaLou's slender fingers combed through his thick curls as she searched her mind for phrases pretty enough to describe the marvelous way he made her feel. A talented poet might have been able to adequately describe the exquisite sensations he created within her heart, but she could not find words that even approached that beauty, let alone fulfilled it. "I love you," she sighed softly as his mouth left hers to explore the alluring contours of her breasts.

The depth of her emotion was plain in that whispered vow, and, inspired by it, Lance treated her like the rare treasure he knew her to be. His loving kisses traced lacy patterns on the fair skin of her stomach and thighs, decorating her with affection as he sought to give her pleasure in a dozen different ways. He adored her, and when at last he brought their bodies together as one, his passion was tempered with tenderness. He moved with deliberate care to guide her through the exotic maze of love's most tantalizing mysteries until he could no longer think or plan, but only feel to the very depths of his soul the ecstasy they had again created together. He felt it throb within her and then echo through him with a furious rhythm that thundered in his ears and drowned out his own exuberant cry of joy.

"Surely you are already my husband," MaLou murmured softly as she drifted languidly on the last waves of their shared rapture.

"Yes, I am," Lance agreed, "but for our children's sakes we should make our union a legal one."

"What children?" the sleepy blonde asked in a lazy whisper. "Do you know something that I do not?"

"Perhaps," the Southerner replied. "At least I plan to use every opportunity I have to ensure we'll be parents soon."

"Is that your only concern, Mr. Garrett? You simply

want to give me a child?"

"No," Lance admitted readily. "I want to make love to you until you beg me to stop."

"What a delightful challenge." MaLou was suddenly wide awake, and since she loved a contest, she wanted it to begin immediately. Her fingers moved restlessly through the tangle of dark curls that covered his chest as she realized that any such contest between them would result in a tie. "I know what you like," she revealed in a throaty whisper as she slipped from his arms and moved between his legs.

Lance's laugh turned to a low moan of surrender as her deep kiss flooded his powerful body with pleasure and again carried his spirit aloft to paradise. Her long curls covered the flat planes of his belly like a silken cloud, and when he opened his eyes, he was surprised to find they had not left her room. They were still reclining upon her bed, not drifting among the stars, but he was positive for a few remarkable seconds they had actually touched the moon. "Tomorrow. We are getting married tomorrow," he promised in a voice still slurred by the bliss of her loving.

MaLou slid over him, bringing their bodies into perfect alignment as she kissed his lips with teasing nibbles. "Do you think we'll have the time?"

"We will make the time." He wasted no more of his breath in idle talk when the hours before dawn were so few and the ways to spend them so very splendid.

Despite their early-morning plans, MaLou had prevailed upon Lance to postpone their wedding until the end of the week so she might invite the people who had been her father's friends. She went first to the church, and then she called on Candelaria, who insisted upon hosting the reception since MaLou had no relatives. Because Lance and Jesse had grown so close, MaLou was hopeful that Lance would not object to her acceptance of the gracious woman's kind offer.

After a morning spent driving about town issuing

invitations, MaLou met Christina in front of Claire Duchamp's shop and hurriedly ushered her new friend inside. "You'll need lingerie as well as new gowns, so this is the perfect place for us to begin our shopping spree."

Claire showed the two slender blondes into her largest fitting room, but when MaLou removed her gown so her measurements could be taken, the woman recognized her pink silk corset immediately. "You must be Mrs. Garrett." Claire spoke her thoughts aloud, for MaLou looked like such a proper young woman she was certain her initial impression of Lance Garrett had been incorrect and he had indeed been shopping for his wife.

MaLou saw Christina's face fill with a bright blush, but she was not offended. "I will be Mrs. Garrett in a few days, but I don't mind answering to that name now."

"Oh, I am sorry," Claire apologized quickly, pained she had not been wise enough to ask her customers' names rather than assuming that she knew them.

"You needn't be. I know this is where Lance purchased my lingerie. That's why we've come here. As soon as I've picked out the things I need, Miss Buchanan would like to make some purchases too."

Once the helpful woman had taken MaLou's measurements and gone to check her stock, Christina found the courage to approach a subject that had worried her for a long while. "You and Mr. Garrett seem to be very much in love," she began nervously.

"Why yes, we are. He is a wonderful man and I am delighted he is as fond of me as I am of him."

Christina paced the small room with tiny steps as she continued their conversation. "Did you know him for a long while before you fell in love with him?"

MaLou frowned thoughtfully as she replied, "I can't remember when I didn't love him. The first time I saw him I found him so attractive I knew I wanted to get to know him. He wasn't all that cooperative at first, but as soon as he relaxed a bit we became friends and the feelings I'd always had for him became love." MaLou stopped before revealing how swiftly they had become lovers. "I suppose every courtship has a different set of problems, but we've resolved all of ours and I'm certain our marriage will be the happy one we both want it to be."

Christina nodded as she tried to imagine how love must feel. "I see. I suppose it is easier to fall in love with some men than with others. Mr. Garrett is very handsome."

MaLou shook her head emphatically. "No, Christina, it is not simply Lance's good looks that I love. He's very bright and wonderful fun. He's a joy to be with, since he knows so much about life that I do not. I've come to depend upon him for so many things, but he readily admits that I've added a great deal to his life too."

Christina could see by the undisguised joy of MaLou's expression that she loved Lance Garrett, but that did not help her understand what love truly was or how it felt. Before she could think of another question to ask about love, they were interrupted.

Mrs. Duchamp returned with a selection of fine lingerie as well as a white silk nightgown elaborately trimmed at the hem, neckline, and cuffs, with deep borders of lace. "Every bride must have a special nightgown and this is my finest."

"Yes, it is lovely," MaLou agreed, though she doubted she would spend much of her wedding night wearing it. She bought it, however, and when she had made several other choices she encouraged Christina to begin trying on things.

Christina was ashamed to let the shopkeeper take her measurements, since her muslin undergarments, while clean, were quite worn, but the charming woman seemed not to notice. She chatted happily about silks and lace, then left them alone again while she went to get the items Christina had requested.

Christina's questions had aroused MaLou's curiosity and she could no longer put off asking some questions of her own. "I'm sorry you had such a difficult time with Jesse. He is usually very charming, but perhaps he's still not feeling like himself just yet."

Christina sat down upon a padded stool and wiggled

anxiously as she waited for Claire Duchamp to return. Since there seemed to be no way to avoid responding to MaLou's comment, she tried to do so tactfully. "He's very unhappy to be so helpless, but he was real nice to be with until . . . well . . . until that last day."

When Christina seemed unwilling to continue, MaLou encouraged her to talk about herself instead. "Did you have many boyfriends before you came to the Arizona Territory, Christina?"

The shy blonde shook her head. "Oh, no. My mother was very strict, and what few men came home after the war got their pick of far prettier girls."

"Well, you're very pretty too," MaLou assured her, for when the bashful girl smiled, she really was quite pretty. "If you haven't had a boyfriend, are you certain you didn't mistake Jesse's affection for something other than what it was?"

Christina refused to accept that possibility. "Oh no, that wasn't affection. It wasn't. If only it had been," she added, sighing wistfully. "But what's the difference? I'll never see the man again, so there's no use worrying about him."

MaLou was intrigued by her revealing comment, for it showed Christina had some feelings for Jesse despite her confusion over his behavior. They were an unusual couple in many respects, but still she was so happy herself she longed to see her friends happy too. When Mrs. Duchamp returned with another armload of lace-trimmed silk, she was impressed by the way Christina examined each garment to see how it was sewn before she tried it on. She caught the older woman's eye in a silent plea for patience, though Claire was so delighted with the purchases MaLou had made she was happy to extend to her friend the same attentive service.

When they left Mrs. Duchamp's, they then began to look for a dress MaLou might wear to her wedding, and since Christina and her brother had been invited to attend, she needed a new dress too. It was late afternoon by the time they parted, but rather than returning directly to the ranch, MaLou went to El Gallo first. She had not come expecting a romantic tryst, but merely to say hello to her fiancé.

"Good afternoon," she greeted Lance warmly. "Do you think I could see Jesse for a moment? The man has to be bored to distraction and I think he'd welcome a visit from me."

Lance rose from his chair as MaLou entered the office. In her red and white dress she looked as fresh and pretty as the spring day and he pulled her into his arms and kissed her until the green of her eyes grew misty with desire. "I thought I was the one you'd come to see," he teased.

"Of course I wanted to see you, but didn't we decide to get married before our passion for each other causes more gossip than we can live down? Wasn't that our plan?"

"Yes," Lance admitted reluctantly. "But that's little help now."

"You will survive the few days until our wedding. I'm sure of it."

"Oh, I will undoubtedly survive, but I won't be happy," Lance confided as he pulled the lithe blonde back into his arms to sample another of her delectable kisses.

MaLou responded eagerly to his lavish display of affection but finally drew away. "Please don't make it impossible for me to leave. Now, may I see Jesse before I go, or is he 'sleeping'?"

Since he had heard Jesse yelling quite loudly at Carmen just before MaLou arrived, Lance was certain the man was not asleep. Nor would he be in a particularly good mood. "Don't stay long. Frankly, he's so miserable, I doubt you'll be able to tolerate more than a few minutes of his company anyway."

"Does he miss Christina as badly as that?" MaLou asked perceptively.

Lance nodded regretfully. "I'm afraid so. How is she?"

As they started up the stairs, MaLou found it difficult to describe the girl's mood. "She asked me about love, poor dear. I'm certain she feels something for Jesse, but she's not sure what it is."

Lance was relieved to find that Carmen had gone to

fetch Jesse's supper, but he was annoyed by the smile the man gave his fiancée, or at least made an effort to give her. "MaLou wanted to see how you are. Since you look so fine, I guess she can be on her way."

"Lance!" MaLou scolded playfully. "Maybe you should leave us alone if you can't be civil."

"I'm not leavin' you in any man's room," Lance replied calmly as he closed the door and leaned back against it.

Jesse shot his friend a menacing glance. "I have already ravished my quota of pretty blondes for the year, Lance. MaLou is quite safe with me."

MaLou had not expected Jesse to look so battered, and her heart went out to him. "Christina is very young. Give her a little time and I think she'll want to see you again."

Jesse's once even features took on a dark scowl as he shook his head. "That is a fantasy I will not pursue, MaLou. Please do not mention her name to me ever again."

Shocked by such a grim request, MaLou turned to glance over her shoulder at Lance, but he frowned slightly to warn her to be still. "You will be coming to the wedding on Friday, won't you, Jesse? I'd really like to have you be there."

"He'll be there," Lance called out. "Even if we have to get married here in his room he'll definitely be there."

"And you call yourself my friend?" Jesse scoffed loudly.

MaLou leaned down to kiss the injured man's cheek. "Yes, we are your friends, Jesse. Don't you ever forget that either."

Tears filled his eyes as Jesse reached out to catch MaLou's hand and bring it to his lips. "Thank you," he murmured softly before releasing her and turning away.

MaLou was near tears herself after his sweet gesture and she hurried to the door. When they reached the landing, she whispered to Lance, "He's given up, hasn't he? He's not even going to try to win Christina's love."

Lance opened his mouth to say it was none of their business what Jesse did about Christina, but before the words crossed his lips he knew better than to speak them.

"Weddin's are romantic occasions, aren't they? Why don't we wait until then and see what happens between them?"

"How can anything happen with her brother there?"

"That's a good point." Lance thought for a moment, then began to chuckle. "I will invite Carmen and make certain she distracts Chris so completely he doesn't know or care what is goin' on between Jesse and Christina."

"But isn't Carmen interested in Jesse herself?"

"What Carmen is interested in is money and I'll drop a little hint that Chris has plenty."

"That is either a brilliant ploy or impossibly foolish, Lance, but I'm not certain which," MaLou admitted frankly.

"Neither am I, but if I can't think of anythin' better I'll give it a try." He escorted her out to her buckboard and was surprised to find Pablo waiting for her. "I'm glad you didn't come into town alone, but—"

"But nothing. Pablo can manage the horses and I take care of the shotgun. We are the perfect team."

"No, you and I are the perfect team," Lance corrected with a teasing wink. He leaned down to brush her cheek with a light kiss, not caring who might be passing by on the busy street and observing them. "See you later," he whispered.

"But I thought—"

Lance shook his head. "No arguments." He gave her a sly grin and stepped back out of the way as Pablo turned the buckboard into the dusty street. Discretion be damned, he thought to himself. He loved her too dearly to give up a night in her arms for any reason.

Chapter XXVI

Friday morning, the twenty-eighth of April, 1871, dawned bright and clear. The wedding was to be at noon, and although it had begun as a simple ceremony, the guest list kept growing until MaLou feared their marriage would indeed be the year's most spectacular social event as Lance had at first suggested. All the hands from her ranch wished to attend, and since they were like family to her, she had always planned to include them. It was the endless stream of people she had not considered close friends who kept appearing at her door with gifts and good wishes who could not be excluded from the ceremony.

Alex Spencer had ridden over to ask who would be giving her away, and when MaLou admitted she had forgotten that detail, he insisted as her father's closest friend he should be the one to do it. He still had a few cuts and scrapes from his fight with Lance, but his offer seemed so genuinely motivated by affection she accepted it gratefully. As soon as he had left, however, she was overwhelmed with sorrow that her own dear father would not be with her. His death had never seemed more senseless and she longed as never before to see his murder avenged.

That Lance had shared her bed frequently before their wedding was not a secret MaLou would reveal as Candelaria and Christina helped her dress. She had found a gown of ivory satin that had needed only slight alterations to fit her slender figure perfectly, and Candelaria had provided a white veil of delicate Spanish lace, which not only covered her upswept hairstyle but trailed to the floor in a graceful train. Since her wedding night would bring none of the surprises recalled with regret by Candelaria and which Christina imagined in awestruck wonder, MaLou found herself attempting to calm her companions' nerves rather than needing to be soothed by their presence. She wanted only to get the ceremony over with quickly so she and Lance could at last publicly acknowledge their love and live their lives together openly as man and wife. She touched the locket he had given her for Christmas, pleased to have such a dear token to wear.

As noon approached, Lance's situation was in many respects identical to his future bride's. Since Jesse would dress in Mexican attire as he always did, Lance again decided to wear the elegant black suit his friend had given him before Christmas. His spirits were as high as MaLou's and he needed nothing in the way of encouragement to bolster his courage since he was delighted to at last be marrying the young woman he loved. He found the darkness of Jesse's mood nearly impossible to lift, however. They had worked all week to build his friend's endurance. Jesse was now able to stand alone and walk about for a few minutes at least. He would have a chair close at hand in case the ceremony proved too tiring for him. It was the changes in his appearance that worried Jesse far more than his lack of stamina, however.

Lance stood behind his best man and helped him to adjust what had once been a close-fitting jacket. "So you have lost a little weight. A man looks better when he is lean. It only makes you look younger, if that is a concern."

"I do not consider myself old!" Jesse snarled anxiously as he limped toward the mirror to get a closer look at himself. His face was no longer swollen and bruised from the beating Chris had given him. The jagged scar crossing his right cheek had healed more rapidly than he had dared hope, undoubtedly due to his aunt's potions, but he knew he would carry it with him for the rest of his life. Combined with the neatly trimmed beard he had decided to keep for awhile, his features were so changed he wondered if he would be recognized. "I look like the meanest son of a bitch who ever lived," he confided to Lance. "I've seen more handsome faces on wanted posters."

Lance studied his friend's sorrowful expression and made one last attempt to improve his outlook. "You are not only lucky to be alive, but damn lucky you've still got both your legs. I know you tire easily, but you'll have your strength back soon. As for your face, since it's so much like mine, I won't criticize your looks. Your smile will still melt a woman's heart. All you've got to do is use it."

Jesse felt not at all like smiling, but he had not meant to be so self-centered when Lance deserved better from him on his wedding day. "Forgive me. You'll not hear another word of complaint from me. Now how am I to get down the stairs? Or did you just plan to toss me out of the window?"

"That's not a bad idea, but I think we can make it down the stairs. Do you have the ring?"

"It's in my pocket." Jesse made his way slowly to the door and braced himself against the wall as they walked down the hall. He had practiced walking with a cane, but that had proved to be so depressing he had not considered using it that day. When they reached the top of the stairs, he waited for Lance to take his arm and they managed to arrive at the first floor without mishap, but then he had to sit down and rest before he could make it outside to the buggy. He took out his handkerchief and mopped his brow. His stomach was queasy and he felt faint, but he was determined not to let Lance down by giving in to the weakness caused by his pitiful physical condition.

Lance waited patiently for Jesse to rise to his feet again, then took his arm to help him out through the back door of El Gallo, where he had tied the buggy. It was nearly noon and he did not want to be late. He gave his friend a helpful boost to propel him into the buggy, then walked around to take his own place. He remembered that the first time he had washed the elegant little vehicle had been when he had taken MaLou to the dance at the Pioneer Brewery. Since that was a night he would never forget, he began to smile widely as they made their way across town.

"You cannot walk into the church grinning like that, Lance. Everyone will know exactly what you are thinking," Jesse cautioned him sternly.

"Surely my thoughts are no different than any other bridegroom's," Lance replied with a careless shrug. "MaLou is goin' to make the best of wives. Why shouldn't I be happy about it?"

"Happiness is appropriate, of course, but you would be wise to keep at least some of your joy more fully contained."

"I'll remind you of that on your weddin' day," Lance countered slyly.

"I will never marry," Jesse insisted bitterly.

"Would you like to put a little money on that? I've got fifty dollars that says you'll be married before the year is out."

"I would simply be stealing your money if I took that bet. Use it instead to buy MaLou a present."

Lance shot his morose friend a skeptical glance but did not argue. What the man needed was a tough-minded woman like MaLou who would give him a swift kick in the seat of the pants for acting like such a melancholy ass. Unfortunately, there was not another woman alive like MaLou. He doubted Christina had enough self-confidence to restore Jesse's belief in himself and convince him that he would soon be well and no less good-looking. At least Lance thought the man's appearance had suffered only a slight impairment until they arrived at the church and he noticed more than one woman turn away quickly as he helped his friend climb out of the buggy. Such a shocking lack of sensitivity disgusted him thoroughly, but he doubted he would have an opportunity to talk to each of the women attending the wedding and reception to encourage them to treat Jesse as they always had rather than as some pathetically scarred invalid for whom they felt only pity.

As Lance and Jesse entered the church, Christina followed their progress with an inquisitive glance. She had not expected Jesse to be well enough to attend the wedding and from the deliberate care he took with each step she could see the effort to be Lance's best man was costing him dearly. While she admired his courage, she had to swallow hard to force away the tears that had suddenly tightened her throat into a painful knot when she had first caught sight of him.

Chris was seated by her side. He was also dressed in fancy new clothes and she thought they made an attractive pair. She knew they did not look out of place at the gathering, but Christina did not feel at home either. Now that she knew Jesse was there, she wanted to leave the second the ceremony was over, but Chris had been looking forward to the party afterward and she doubted he would allow her to return home alone. As the church continued to fill, she realized the reception would be so large that Jesse would probably never notice she was there. She was not certain if that would please her or not, but for the time being she supposed it was silly to worry about what might happen later at the reception when the wedding would surely be enjoyable in itself. Forcing herself to think only happy thoughts, she sat back and waited patiently for the ceremony to begin.

MaLou could not help but wonder why so many people had turned out for her wedding. Perhaps the majority had come out of loyalty to her father, but she was certain there were a good many who were curious about what sort of couple she and Lance would make. Those people would be the ones who considered him a gunslinging gambler, she supposed, but she never thought of her beloved in such derogatory terms. He was a man of courage and conviction, in her view, and she was quite proud to be marrying him, but when Alex took her arm to escort her down the aisle to the altar, the walk suddenly appeared to be at least a mile long. There were no strangers in the church—every face turned their way was a familiar one—but somehow that made it no less difficult to take a deep breath. Candelaria had given her a bouquet of pink and white roses from her garden, and she clutched the ribbon-wrapped blossoms tightly, afraid she might drop them and trip. She had never heard of a bride who had fallen down on her way to the altar and did not wish to be the first, but she had never felt so terribly clumsy. Maybe that was why a bride always had her father as an escort, so he could keep her on her feet. She looked up at Alex then, and wished for the hundredth time her father could have been there with her instead.

Lance felt Jesse swaying slightly at his side and hoped the man would have sense enough to sit down before he fell down. MaLou's features were obscured by her veil, but he could tell by the way she was clinging to Alex Spencer's arm that something was desperately wrong. He was certain she had not changed her mind about marrying him, but he could not imagine why she would be so subdued when he had half expected her to skip down the aisle to meet him. When finally she reached him, he gave her a teasing wink and she tried to smile, but he saw the tears glistening upon the tips of her eyelashes and was tempted to stop the ceremony right there to ask her what was wrong.

MaLou knew it was permissible for a bride to cry at her wedding, but she had no clear idea of why other women might be moved to tears. Not wanting Lance to think she had suddenly developed misgivings, she straightened her shoulders proudly and listened attentively as the pastor began to read the service. She gave the right responses in a steady tone, and when she looked up at Lance she was smiling, but she was as eager as he to see the service end.

Jesse produced the gold wedding band at the proper time, then, certain everyone's attention was focused on the bride and groom, he stepped aside and collapsed into the chair that had been placed nearby for his convenience. He was pleased with himself for having been able to do his part, but at the same time he doubted he would be able to enjoy the gaiety of the reception. Since he had always been so fond of parties, that was a depressing thought. When Lance and MaLou were pronounced man and wife, had embraced happily, and then bounded up the aisle, he suddenly realized they would take the buggy to his aunt's home, but he would have no way to get there himself. How he could have forgotten something as basic as that he did not know, but as the crowd cleared the church he remained in his chair, horribly depressed at being stranded, until Candelaria appeared at his side.

"You're coming with me, my darling. My carriage is at the side door. Shall I call my driver to help you reach it?"

Jesse was momentarily perplexed, for when he had thought he would have no way to reach his aunt's home, he had done his best to convince himself he did not really want to go there. Now that she had suddenly provided transportation, however, he felt a surge of childlike delight. "No, I can walk that far," he assured her, though it was not an easy task.

"You must spend the night at my home. Just choose one of the guest rooms and go to sleep the minute you begin to feel tired."

Jesse was grateful for the comfort as well as the privacy afforded by the expensive carriage. He was already exhausted but would not admit that to his aunt. "I want to give Lance and MaLou my presents, so I will have to stay awake that long."

"Would you like to take a nap and then join the party?" Candelaria offered considerately.

"No, I can sit with grandfather and the babies and be all right." His attractive aunt had not winced when she saw him, but, he reminded himself, she had visited him often, so his appearance had not been a shock to her.

MaLou and Lance were surrounded by well-wishers as

they left the church, but as soon as he could manage it, Lance escorted MaLou to the buggy for the brief trip to Candelaria's house. He had been surprised the woman had offered her home for the reception, since he was the groom, but he had not wanted to insult her further by refusing. He had said nothing to MaLou about the hostility that existed between him and the Mexican beauty and hoped now that they were married Candelaria would no longer have any objection to him.

"You looked so unhappy when you started down the aisle I was afraid you might have changed your mind about marryin' me. Did Alex say somethin' to upset you?" Lance asked the minute they were alone.

MaLou slipped her arm through her husband's and gave him a warm squeeze. "No, he was a perfect gentleman and I hope Josh will be too. As for changing my mind, you must have known I wouldn't do that. It was just that I didn't expect so many people to be there and . . . well, I kept thinking about Dad and wishing he were there. I've thought of him so often these last few days. It just isn't right that his murderers have gone unpunished."

While he was certain this was an unusual conversation for a new bride and groom to be having, Lance understood her sorrow and did not try to change the subject. "I've done my best since I've been at El Gallo to learn all I can, but I haven't gotten a single lead I could follow up, MaLou. The rustlers either vanished into Mexico, or—"

"Or they never set foot in El Gallo," MaLou interrupted coldly. "It had to have been the Hatchers, Lance. Look what they did to Jesse." She shuddered then, remembering the night he had been shot and how frightened they all had been. "They are precisely the type of vermin who would rustle cattle and ambush a lone man."

Lance nodded. "I think you're right, but if I go gunnin' for what's left of the Hatcher clan with no proof they killed your daddy, then I'll be no better than they are. Tell me the truth about somethin' else, will you? Jesse is horribly depressed about the way he looks, but I don't think he looks all that different, do you?"

MaLou could see that her answer was important to him and she chose her words carefully. "It's not just his looks. He's like a completely different person, Lance. It's not simply that he's thinner or that he's grown a beard either. That scar is bad, but I wouldn't describe him as being disfigured. It's just that he used to be so damn superficial. He was always smiling and nothing he said ever struck me as sincere. Frankly, I think he's changed for the better, but I doubt he'll see it that way if all he cares about is his reflection in a mirror."

Lance considered her opinion a bit harsh, but he had to admit that he had not liked Jesse much until he had gotten to know him well. The man was his friend now though, and he was worried about him. "All Jesse needs is a woman like you who would love him in spite of his best efforts to force her away. I've never met another woman like you though, so I'm afraid he's out of luck."

"You're wrong there. A man like Jesse Cordova makes his own luck," MaLou assured him. "Speaking of luck, did you invite Carmen to the reception?"

Lance laughed as he shook his head. "Not when I found out Jesse always keeps his family and his 'ladies of the evenin'' separate. I remembered he has quite a few attractive cousins though, and I'm hopin' one will catch Chris Buchanan's eye."

"Let's hope they all do, so he'll be too busy to notice what Christina is doing."

As they reached the walled entrance to Candelaria's home, Lance pulled Duke to a halt and leaned back to rest a moment. "This is supposed to be our party, MaLou, not merely an occasion designed to get Christina and Jesse back together."

"You said yourself weddings are romantic occasions. I don't plan to take their hands and push them off into a dark corner together. Either they will take advantage of this opportunity to be together or they'll waste it, but we can't interfere in their lives."

"We can't?" Lance asked with clear disappointment.

"Well, perhaps just a little bit," she admitted as she

reached up to give him a kiss.

Candelaria's carriage arrived then, followed by more than enough guests to fill the patio. *Mariachis* provided an abundance of lively music, which, combined with plentiful food and drink, ensured the success of the party. The bride and groom had a marvelous time celebrating their marriage and when it came time to open their gifts they were touched by how thoughtful and generous everyone had been.

When Lance found an envelope addressed to him in Jesse's flamboyant scrawl, he was puzzled, for the man had already given them an ornate silver tray, which he was certain had been very expensive. He read his friend's brief note, then read it again before handing it to MaLou. He knew where to find Jesse, since he had been sitting in the shade at the far end of the patio all afternoon. It was unlike the Mexican to be on the fringe of a party rather than at the center, but Lance understood his reasons and went over to speak with him immediately.

"You can't give me half interest in El Gallo as a weddin' present, Jesse. That's just too much. I'll soon be able to buy in as I originally planned. It won't take me much longer to save up the money and I'll pay you back that seven thousand I borrowed too."

Jesse shook his head, then broke into an engaging grin. "No, *amigo*. Had I died, El Gallo would already be yours. Since I survived, I can give away half if I want to. My only condition is that you do not sell your interest to anyone else. If you will agree to that, then we will become full partners, fifty-fifty. As for the other money, pay me back when you can."

Lance thought the man's gesture far too generous to accept, but he had not seen his friend smile in a long while and knew he would succeed only in insulting him if he refused to become his partner until he could pay for that privilege. With a mock bow, he agreed. "Jesse, I am overwhelmed, but I will gladly accept your gift. Did I remember to ask for a few more days off so I can celebrate my marriage as I should?"

"We are partners. You need not request time off from me. Just take it," his friend insisted with another cocky grin, but when Lance returned to MaLou's side, Jesse found it impossible to continue to pretend he was having a good time. His relatives had all been attentive, but he had known they would be. The others present regarded him as something of a curiosity, but he was not certain if that was due to the unfortunate change in his appearance or the fact that Tucson's finer citizens did not usually socialize with him. Not that the men did not frequent El Gallo or The Silver Spur, but that that was how they knew him was not something they wished to admit with their wives present. Since he could not dance, he had tried to enjoy watching the others move in time to the spirited tunes, but that pastime had eventually lost its charm. Feeling very tired and alone, he decided to accept his aunt's offer and seek out a quiet room for a nap.

Christina had spent most of the afternoon watching Jesse watch the others at the festive party. She had danced several times with her brother, once with Lance, and then it seemed as though she had been asked to dance by every other man present, but she had been far too self-conscious to truly enjoy the lively dances everyone else seemed to find so entertaining. For the last few minutes she had been standing near the refreshment table, trying to catch her breath after the last set of dances. She hoped no one would notice that her main interest that afternoon had been in a man who had shown no interest in her. She had known Jesse could not ask her to dance, but she had hoped he would at least come sit with her and talk. That had been a very foolish dream, she realized, but when she saw him struggle to his feet, she held her breath, hoping he would make his way to her side. When she saw him enter the house instead, her heart fell. He was never going to speak with her again and she searched her mind frantically for an excuse to start a conversation with him. Finally recalling the forgotten pillow slip, she raised the skirt of her new gown above the toes of her slippers and followed him into the house.

Jesse was moving down the hall so slowly, Christina easily overtook him. He had frequently caught glimpses of her during the afternoon, but the sight of her had caused him so much pain he had deliberately focused his attention elsewhere. He opened a bedroom door, meaning to slip through it quickly, but she was far more agile than he and blocked his way. "Go away, Christina. It will be better for us both if we pretend we never met." She was dressed in a pretty sapphire blue gown, which made the pale azure of her eyes dance with a brightness he had never before seen. Her hair was styled attractively too, but he remembered how lovely it had been flowing about her shoulders and had to look away.

"But we did meet," Christina reminded him as she reached out to catch his sleeve.

"I will do my best to forget it and I suggest that you do the same."

"No, I can't do that," the blonde insisted. "I won't." Where she had gotten the courage to argue with him she did not know, but when she had seen him leaving the party she had known she could not let him slip away without making whatever effort it took to see him again.

Not relishing the prospect of another confrontation with Chris, Jesse took the precaution of glancing down the hall. The *mariachis* standing on the patio filled the whole house with the sound of their blaring trumpets and he doubted he would get any sleep as long as the party lasted, which he was certain would be half the night. For some reason, however, he no longer felt nearly as tired. "You know what will happen if your brother finds you with me again, don't you?"

Since he seemed to be weakening, Christina moved closer still. "He's been surrounded by pretty girls since we arrived, and he won't notice I'm gone. We can speak for a few minutes without arousin' anyone's curiosity."

There had been a time when he had wanted very much to speak with her, to beg for her forgiveness, but he had buried that longing under so many layers of self-pity he had nearly forgotten he owed her an apology. "Yes, we do need to talk." He pushed the door open, then limped over to the bed and sat down. Gesturing toward the nearby chair, he offered another suggestion. "Leave the door open. Then there cannot be any gossip."

He was behaving in such a cold, distant manner, Christina was not even remotely tempted to follow his instructions. She stepped into the room, and disregarding his directions, she not only closed the door but locked it. She then ignored the chair he had indicated and instead went to the bed and sat down beside him. "We were in your room alone together for nearly two weeks. We never worried about gossip then. Why should we now?"

She was so elegantly groomed and dressed, he was fascinated by her newfound sophistication, and it took him a moment to realize she had asked him a question. "You look so beautiful today, but you are still quite naïve, Christina. I am concerned about your reputation even if you are not."

"I'm tired of everyone telling me I'm naïve, when what they really mean is that they think I'm stupid," Christina confessed with an uncharacteristic show of temper.

Startled, Jesse was certain she had misunderstood him. "I did not say you were stupid. There is a great deal of difference between stupidity and innocence."

"No, not really," the blonde argued. She folded her hands in her lap and tried to concentrate upon her neatly manicured nails rather than on the warm brown of her handsome companion's eyes.

Her spirit, as always, seemed so fragile despite her surprisingly defiant attitude that Jesse put his arm around her shoulders and gave her a comforting hug. "I am the one who is stupid, Christina, not you. I liked having you with me very much, but I did such a poor job of showing my affection I frightened you badly. I am very sorry for that. Now I think you'd better go before I do something else we might both regret."

Christina lifted her chin proudly. "You needn't say that

just to be kind."

"I beg your pardon?" Jesse asked politely, now thoroughly confused.

"If you cared anything at all for me, you'd have found a way to send word to me that you were sorry. You would not simply have ignored me as you have. I've been in your aunt's home for several hours, and you did not even have the courtesy to wish me good day."

"Then I apologize for that too, but I thought I was the last person you'd ever wish to see."

The longer they talked, the worse Christina felt. She had not meant to back the man into a corner and make him apologize to her endlessly. What she had wanted from him she was not certain, but it was not this patronizing indifference. "My brother is overly protective of me, but now that I have money of my own I will insist he treat me like an adult and respect my friends." She brushed Jesse's hand off her shoulder and rose to her feet. "I left the pillow slip I was embroidering in your room. I'd like to have it back as I'd already completed the other one and I want to have the set."

"For your hope chest?"

"Yes. I will undoubtedly marry someday and I want to have plenty of linens."

Christina was staring at the floor rather than at him, but he could feel the power of her emotional turmoil, and unfortunately mistaking it for hatred, he reacted badly. "Well, you will have to do without that particular pillow slip because I have been using it and I'll not give it back."

"You've used it?" Christina asked accusingly, her furious glance now focused upon his.

"Yes, I wanted to use it, so I did. If you insist the pair must remain a set, then just send the mate over to me at El Gallo."

"But it took hours and hours to do all that embroidery and you had no right to use it!"

"I'll do as I damn well please!" Jesse shot right back at her.

"Oh yes, I already know that!" Christina rushed to the

door, then, blinded by tears, she had trouble turning the key to unlock it.

Jesse knew she was going to run from him again and while he could not blame her for hating him, he moved as quickly as he could to stop her. By the time he had hauled himself clumsily to his feet, she had finally unlocked the door, but as she pulled it open he managed to lunge across the distance separating them and slam it shut. That effort cost him so much energy he had to lean back against the door and try to catch his breath.

Christina raised her hands, meaning to shove him aside, but when she saw how pale he had become she grew alarmed. "Oh Jesse, what have you done to yourself?"

Jesse smiled weakly as he spoke in a breathless whisper. "I wish I had known you before I got shot. I could dance all night without getting tired and I was easily one of the best-looking men in town. Now I have to take naps like a baby and I'll never be considered handsome again."

Christina brushed away her tears as she studied his expression with a puzzled frown. "What are you talkin' about, Jesse? You're gettin' stronger every day, so you should be able to dance before too much longer, and if there's a man in Tucson who's better lookin' than you I haven't seen him."

"What about Lance?" Jesse asked with a trace of his old lively manner.

"Are you just fishin' for compliments? The man looks like your twin except for his eyes."

"You are a sweet girl, Christina, but I know how I look."

He looked as he always had to her, heartbreakingly handsome, and she reached up to kiss his scarred cheek lightly. When he wrapped his arms around her waist, she laid her head upon his shoulder and snuggled close.

Jesse held her in a light embrace, afraid she would bolt again if he dared to ask for more. "I wanted only to kiss you that day, Christina. That's all I meant to do."

Christina leaned back slightly so she could look up at him. "Is that the way you like to kiss?" she asked shyly.

Jesse nodded as he studied the pretty curve of her lower lip. "There are a lot of ways to kiss and all of them are nice."

He was leaning back against the sturdy wooden door and seemed fairly comfortable, so Christina ceased to worry about tiring him. "Perhaps you could kiss me a little more gently?"

"I suppose I could try." He kissed her forehead lightly, then her cheek, before brushing her lips tenderly with his own. "There, is that better?"

"Much," Christina assured him as she raised her arms to encircle his neck. "It might take me a while to learn though. Do you think you could show me again?"

"We'd better go back to the party," Jesse warned hoarsely.

"Not yet," the usually bashful blonde replied in an inviting whisper.

Jesse's reluctance to continue was short-lived as her lips met his. His response was a lingering kiss he deepened when Christina's lips opened willingly to lure him into giving more. Still he held back, caressing her tongue only lightly with his until she pressed so close he could no longer breathe and had to pull away. "That is the end of the lesson, Christina. It has to be."

While she doubted her brother would come looking for her any time soon, Christina understood the cause of Jesse's anxiety and stepped back. "I'm sorry. You are right, of course. I do have a reputation to protect. I can't spend the rest of the afternoon here with you, no matter how much I'd like to do it."

Jesse moved aside to open the door. "There will be other afternoons," he promised with a ready grin.

"Hmm, yes, perhaps," Christina murmured softly as they stepped out into the hallway.

"What do you mean perhaps?" Jesse responded too loudly. "I thought you'd forgiven me for being so reckless where you are concerned."

"Well, yes, if forgiveness is all you wanted, then you

have it."

Jesse shook his head. "It's not all I want, but I do not think I dare propose until I am strong enough to stand up to your brother should he object to our marriage."

"Are you bein' serious?" Christina asked in a voice filled with wonder.

"Yes," Jesse admitted readily. "You convinced me I should not waste another moment before taking a wife, and you seem the perfect choice."

"I do? Why?" the fair-haired young woman asked as they reached the sun-drenched patio.

Jesse stared at her for a long moment, wondering how he could explain that at first he had been attracted to her because she was blonde but had been so enchanted by her refreshingly sweet innocence he had swiftly fallen in love with her. That was when his uphill battle had begun. "How could I not love you? You're the only woman in town who still thinks I'm handsome."

Christina reached out to give him the same type of playful shove she frequently gave her brother, but she then had to grab for him to keep him from toppling over. "Oh, I am so sorry!" she exclaimed.

Jesse laughed as he pulled her into a loving hug. "We are both going to have to learn to be more gentle, it seems."

"I will try if you will," Christina promised happily.

"Oh, I will," Jesse vowed as he gave her cheek a light kiss. "Come with me. There's something I have to give to Lance."

Without explanation, Jesse handed Lance fifty dollars, then flashed a wicked grin before taking Christina's hand and going off to find an unopened bottle of champagne.

"Another present?" MaLou asked as Lance tucked the bills into his pocket.

"No, I just won a bet."

"Well, Jesse certainly did not look unhappy about losing it."

Lance took a moment to glance around at the guests to

make certain no one was looking their way before he replied in a conspiratorial whisper. "No, but I'll explain later. Now I want you to follow me inside. The buggy with our things will be at the back door, but we're just going down the street to Jesse's. His home is as nice as this one. His servants are expecting us and he promises they will treat us like royalty for as long as we wish to stay. I haven't forgotten about taking you on a trip, but since we've yet to decide where we want to go, Jesse's house seems like the perfect place for the time being."

"I think it's a charming idea. Let's slip away while everyone is having too much fun to notice we're gone."

"Of course," Lance explained with mock seriousness, "we could stay until midnight if you'd rather. I didn't mean to make the choice for you."

MaLou gave him a disapproving frown. "If you don't know what my choice is by now, then I am dreadfully afraid I have married the wrong man."

Lance gave her a sly wink as he reached for her hand and without further teasing he spirited her away to begin a marriage he hoped would be a lifelong honeymoon.

Chapter XXVII

While many of their friends and neighbors were attending MaLou and Lance's wedding, the leaders of Tucson's Committee of Public Safety were busy elsewhere. The group still had no conclusive proof the Indians encamped near Fort Grant were responsible for the recent raids in the Santa Cruz Valley, but nevertheless they considered the Chiricahua settlement an excellent target for reprisal.

Hiram Stevens was the chairman of the militant organization, but when it came time to take decisive action, William Sanders Oury assumed the leadership role. In addition to being an attorney, he was a former mayor of Tucson who took great pride in his reputation as an Indian killer. Another active member of the group was Juan Elias, a rancher, who was currently serving on the town council. He and his brother, Jesus, volunteered to recruit Mexicans for the raid.

One of the most important members of the committee, Samuel Hughes, Adjutant General of the Arizona Territory, was one of the many not present at the raid, but he not only furnished arms and ammunition but enlisted the aid of nearly one hundred Papago Indians led by their chief, Francisco Galerita. Often the victims of Apache raids themselves, the Papago were sympathetic to the Committee's goal of ridding the Arizona Territory of that hated tribe and had eagerly seized the opportunity to participate in an attack upon an enemy they thoroughly despised.

There were more than eighty citizens on the Committee of Public Safety, but when it actually came time to carry out the vicious details of the plot they had helped to create, most chose to hire others to take their places. Some of the men who accepted that type of work were known outlaws, while others were merely indigent Mexicans. Therefore, on the morning of April twenty-eighth, William Oury and the Elias brothers were joined by only a handful of their bravest coconspirators. Wealthy merchant Sidney De Long had once been in the Territorial Legislature. D. A. Bennett owned a hotel and saloon. Charles Etchells was a blacksmith and ironworker. James Lee operated the mill and was accompanied by one of his employees, David Foley. It was a poor showing as far as the committee members present were concerned, but it proved to be enough to carry out their diabolical plot.

The heavily armed band that set out that Friday morning was an unusual war party: six Americans, forty-eight Mexicans, and ninety-four Papago warriors. They were united in a single purpose, however: to kill as many Apache Indians as they possibly could. While William Oury believed the bulk of public sentiment was with them, he nevertheless was clever enough to send a message to Hiram Stevens to post sentries at Cañada del Oro to stop all traffic on the main road from Tucson to Fort Grant until after the morning of April thirtieth. Marching as a single column, the group traveled both day and night, following the winding course of the Rillito Creek. They passed the twenty-ninth hidden in the thick vegetation at the edge of the San Pedro River and before dawn on the thirtieth moved to avenge the crimes they insisted had been committed by Apaches they accused of enjoying the protection of the United States Army between their murderous raids.

The vigilante force split into two groups, with the Papago taking the right bank of the Arivaipa Creek and the Americans and Mexicans taking the left. Skirting

Camp Grant undetected by the Army, they found the Apache settlement five miles upstream. The first to die were a man and woman, sentries stationed on the bluff overlooking the encampment, who were passing the chilly hours before dawn playing cards. They were clubbed to death before they could sound a cry of alarm. The Papago then attacked the settlement below where Chiricahuas considered to be prisoners of war by the United States Army had been provided with rations in exchange for their promise to lay down their arms and live in peace.

Coordinating their efforts, the Americans and Mexicans shot the fleeing Apaches who had managed to escape being brutally murdered by the club-swinging Papagos. In half an hour the bloody raid was over and William Oury and his band of cutthroats enjoyed a hearty breakfast and congratulated themselves on a job well down. The Papagos, taking a more practical stance, made plans to take twenty-seven children they had captured alive to Sonora, where they would sell them as slaves.

Soon after the raid, a courier from Fort Lowell arrived at Camp Grant with the unsettling news that his commanding officer suspected from the large numbers of men missing from Tucson that an attack upon the Chiricahuas might be imminent. The man explained he had been detained at Cañada del Oro, but he hoped he had not arrived too late to avert such a tragedy. Greatly alarmed, Lieutenant Royal Whitman, who was again in charge of the fort in Captain Stanwood's absence, immediately sent two interpreters to the Chiricahua camp to warn the Indians and bring them back to the fort, where the Army could protect them from all possible harm. The interpreters soon returned with the horrible news that they had found the Indian camp in flames and the ground littered with the mutilated bodies of women and children. They could find no Indians left alive to bring into the safety of the Army post.

Blissfully unaware of the carnage that had taken place at

Camp Grant, MaLou and Lance spent the weekend in each other's arms. The large patio of Jesse's spacious home was such an inviting spot, they ate their breakfast outside each morning and basked in the sun's warmth until long past noon. Free of all distractions, save each other, they enjoyed every minute to the fullest, but on Monday the time seemed to have flown by so quickly they could think of no reason not to remain in the gracious home for another few days. Isolated from all care, they thought the beauty of their love would protect them from the troubles of the outside world forever.

Since news of all types swiftly reached Jesse Cordova's ears, however, he learned of the raid at Camp Grant within minutes of William Oury's return to Tucson. While he had known that the members of the Committee of Public Safety had a virulent hatred of Apaches, he had not expected them to carry it to such shocking extremes. The massacre swiftly became the town's sole topic of conversation, and fearing Lance and MaLou would learn of it from his servants, he knew he would have to pay them a call first. It would bring their brief honeymoon to an abrupt end, but he knew knowledge of such a catastrophe was not something that could be kept from them indefinitely.

On Wednesday morning, Jesse rehearsed several versions of the incident but found that none would cushion the horrid nature of the truth. Finally, he braced himself for the worst and took a carriage to his home. He found MaLou and Lance seated on the patio, peeling freshly picked oranges and eating the delicious *pan dulce* his cook had prepared so often for his own breakfast. Refusing to take a piece of the sweet bread himself, he began with an apology.

"Forgive me for intruding on you like this."

"Nonsense," Lance contradicted with a ready laugh. "This is your home, not ours. You needn't apologize for coming here. We were just talking about packing our things, for we've no wish to overstay our welcome."

"No, there is no reason for you to leave." Jesse knew he was merely stalling for time, putting off the inevitable, and forced himself to reveal the purpose of his visit. "I have some news, very bad news, I'm afraid, and I did not want you to hear it from someone else."

"Oh no!" MaLou gasped sharply, hoping Jesse was simply being melodramatic. "What's happened?"

Jesse tried to give a clear, concise account of the facts he had placed together about the massacre, but he soon found it impossible to remain detached. "Whitman reported one hundred twenty-five slain or missing. Only eight were men. The rest were women and children, even tiny babies. Some of the women were raped and then shot dead. More than two dozen children were taken captive by the Papagos. Most will never see their parents again, if their parents are still alive." MaLou and Lance were simply staring at him as if his story were too ghastly to be believed, but he understood their shocked silence for what it was and continued. "I do not condone what happened, although it seems everyone else does. To kill innocent women and children in retaliation for raids carried out by braves is obscene in my opinion, but as I say, I hold the minority view. The whole town is celebrating as though the massacre were the greatest of triumphs," he revealed with a shudder of disgust.

MaLou slumped back in her chair, the horror of Jesse's words almost impossible for her to comprehend. Finally she looked up at Lance. "They had very pretty children, didn't they? What kind of an animal would murder a child? A defenseless child?"

"They were all defenseless, MaLou," Lance reminded her. "The Indians had no weapons. They weren't supposed to need any." He laid his hand upon his bride's shoulder in a comforting clasp, for he had been as deeply shocked as she by Jesse's horrifying tale. The only difference was that he had been through four years of sheer hell during the war and had had his fill of grim images of death. Women and children had never been his prey, however, and he was totally outraged by what had happened at Camp Grant. "Is it known who was with Oury? Are their names known so they can be charged with this hideous crime?"

"They are all heroes, Lance. No one is worried that killing Indians might be considered a crime."

"Well, I sure as hell consider it a crime to murder women and children, regardless of their race, and I am certain President Grant does too."

Jesse nodded. "Let us hope that he does."

When the two men fell silent, MaLou looked up at her husband. "It was all for nothing, wasn't it? My father's efforts to help the Army bring peace to the Territory, everything he believed in—it was all for nothing. The Chiricahua will never listen to another proposal for peace, nor should they. Oury and his damn 'committee' have shown all white men to be lower than snakes. Was Eskiminzin killed? Was he one of those slain?"

"No, I don't think so," Jesse replied with a frown.

"You know what he'll do, don't you?" MaLou asked her companions, already knowing the answer without having to be told.

Lance bent down beside her. "This means war, of course, and it will be a long and bloody one Eskiminzin can't possibly win, but I know which side I'd prefer to be on."

Jesse agreed. "I am tempted to let my hair grow and ride with him, I am so disgusted with my own kind."

"Killing isn't the answer, Jesse. We can't just kill each other until there is no one left to fire another shot."

The Mexican looked over at Lance and saw by the set of his jaw that his friend agreed with him. Revenge could be surprisingly sweet at times, but perhaps it always appealed more to men than women. His sad message delivered, he rose slowly to his feet. "I wanted you to know what had happened, but there is no need for you to return home. I am very comfortable at El Gallo and it saves me the effort of having to travel back and forth."

"No, I want to go home to the ranch," MaLou announced suddenly. "Right now, this very morning."

"I am so sorry," Jesse repeated again. He leaned down to give MaLou a light kiss upon the cheek, then turned away.

Lance walked his partner to the gate. "MaLou has been thinkin' a lot about her daddy, so I know this is goin' to hit her real hard. I'm glad she heard about it from you, though."

"Do not let her think the man died for naught. He was right, and it is the fools who populate Tucson who are wrong. Dead wrong."

Lance nodded. "I have plenty of experience being a champion of unpopular causes, *amigo,* but I'll do what I can for my wife. I'm glad to see you are better able to travel about. That's good news at least."

Jesse climbed into the waiting carriage, then leaned out the window. "I have a good reason to want to get well," he revealed with a sly grin. "But you know who she is."

Lance waved as his friend drove off, his thoughts an uncomfortable mixture of sorrow and rage. He thought of Royal Whitman and knew the lieutenant must be overwhelmed with despair, for the massacre at Camp Grant would put an end to his dream of bringing peace to the Territory without bloodshed. It was a rotten way for such a noble dream to die, he reflected, and he returned to MaLou, not knowing how to ease her pain but certain he would share it in full measure.

Christina had left the reception Friday with her brother. On the way home he had scolded her for spending the last hours of the party talking with Jesse Cordova, but she had not revealed the nature of the lengthy conversation he had observed on the patio or the very private one they had held in the house. When Chris had seen them, Jesse had been telling her about his family, about life in the early days of Tucson, and, as always, she had found his comments both intelligent and entertaining. As her brother had criticized her choice of companions, she had simply smiled to herself and kept the fact that Jesse had mentioned marriage a very private secret.

She spent the following week daydreaming about the handsome Mexican and longing to see him again.

Thinking it unlikely he would come to her home when Chris would make him feel so unwelcome there, she realized if they were going to have any time together she would have to go into town to see him. Since Chris was busy all day at the mine, she hoped she could go into Tucson and return without him ever knowing she had been gone. She did have some shopping to do, and if Chris caught her, she would have a few packages to show as an excuse for the trip.

Hoping to spend the afternoon with Jesse, Christina took a long time getting dressed in one of her new dresses, then went into town late Friday morning. She made her purchases, then entered El Gallo del Oro through the back door. The hallway was dark, but she went first to the office to see if Jesse might be there before climbing the stairs to his room. When she heard voices coming from behind the closed door, she stood aside, hoping his visitor would not be long, but she soon realized he was involved in an argument of some sort with a woman. She could not understand their words, but Jesse's voice remained low while the woman's grew increasingly shrill.

Thinking perhaps she should come back later, Christina started toward the back door, but before she reached it the office door swung open and then slammed shut. She tried to step aside to avoid blocking the narrow hallway, but as Carmen reached her side the brunette stopped and regarded her with a cold, insolent stare.

"You are so skinny and pale, I cannot believe Jesse finds you pretty." She leaned closer then, speaking in an evil whisper as she made each of her insulting words count. "Be careful of him, little one. When he tires of you, he will put you to work at the Silver Spur. Most of the girls get two dollars, but as the only blonde, you could ask for five. With half a dozen men a night, you will be able to live very well, but do not say I did not warn you if you find our way of life too ugly to enjoy."

When Carmen suddenly turned away, Christina watched in stunned silence as the haughty young woman departed, too astonished by the vile nature of her remarks to realize they could not possibly apply to her. She remembered Chris had said Jesse owned other things beside a saloon. Was one of them a place called the Silver Spur? She had never heard of it, but she had a good idea what the women who worked there did. How could Jesse possibly own a place like that? she asked herself.

His work finished for the morning, Jesse opened his office door and stepped out into the hall. He saw a shadowy figure lurking near the back door and thinking it was Carmen plotting some mischief he called out to her. "I'll not give you another dime, Carmen. Now go on back where you belong." As the back door opened, sunlight streamed in and he saw that the fleeing woman had not been Carmen after all, but a slender blonde. *"Madre de Dios!"* he swore to himself, knowing that if Christina had been waiting outside his office to see him, Carmen would not have missed such an excellent opportunity to do him some real harm.

He started after Christina, but his progress was so slow she had already mounted the mule she had ridden into town and was headed away. He shouted her name, but she did no more than turn to look back at him with a glance so filled with sorrow his worst fears were confirmed. He would have to go after her, but rather than waste any more time hitching a team to a carriage, he borrowed the horse belonging to his bartender, Vance, which was saddled and tied to the hitching post near the back door. He had not ridden since he had been shot and had considerable difficulty just getting into the saddle, but the pain of riding was not so great he could not do it.

Not realizing Jesse would follow her, Christina slowed her mule's pace as soon as she had left Tucson's crowded streets. She felt like a complete fool and was so angry with herself she could not stand it. Chris had tried to warn her about Jesse, but she had paid no attention to him and now she was dreadfully sorry that she had not.

When Jesse saw Christina meandering along up ahead,

he slowed his mount to a brisk walk so he would not upset her further by overtaking her at a furious gallop. As he reached her side, he greeted her warmly, as though they had planned to go riding together. "I'd hoped you would come into town. There are so many things we need to discuss and—"

"What goes on at the Silver Spur?" Christina asked accusingly.

Jesse winced, then refused to explain. "Nothing that would interest you. Now won't you come back into town with me? I'd like to take you to lunch."

"I don't feel like eatin'," Christina replied as she drew her mule to an abrupt halt.

Jesse had talked himself out of many a tight spot, but he felt totally inept where Christina was concerned. That did not keep him from trying, however. "Carmen took your place as my nurse when you left me. Now she wants to argue about the amount I paid her. It is not an issue I will discuss, however, and I am sorry if she tried to get back at me by hurting your feelings. She is not a nice person." Although she had remarkable talents in areas he would not mention to Christina, he had had no interest in sampling her charms in a very long while. That was the real issue, he knew. Carmen was furious with him because she liked to think of herself as his mistress and knew that fantasy was at an end.

"Are you a nice person?" Christina inquired bluntly.

"I like to think so, yes." Jesse felt at a great disadvantage, not knowing precisely what Carmen had said. He was beginning to feel tired and knew he had overtaxed his small store of strength. There was a large acacia growing near the road and since it cast an inviting patch of shade he gestured toward it. "Please come and sit down with me for a minute. I need to rest or I'll not be able to ride back into town."

"I should go on home," the blonde argued.

Exasperated he had failed so completely to improve her sullen mood, Jesse shook his head sadly. "You should know what kind of man I am by now, Christina. If the words of a jealous woman can turn you against me, then I am afraid there is no hope for us."

Christina wanted to leave, but confused by his remarks she hesitated. When he rode over to the acacia and nearly fell trying to dismount, she realized he was not faking his clumsiness. She leapt down from her mule's back and led the animal over to where Jesse had sat down. "I think maybe I'd better ride back into town with you to make certain you get there."

"I thought you were in a hurry to get home," Jesse reminded her.

"Well, yes, I am," the distracted blonde admitted reluctantly.

Jesse knew he could not spend all his time chasing after a young woman who would just hate him when he caught up with her. He looked back toward town as he refused her offer. "You go on home if you have to, and I'll get back into town as best I can."

Christina fidgeted nervously with her mule's reins. "I can't leave you sittin' here all alone."

"Why not?" Jesse asked with a cunning grin, hoping he was beginning to make some progress.

Christina looked down at him, over at his horse, then up at the cloudless sky. She did not know how to answer such an obvious question and blurted out what was on her mind. "Every time I think I know you, Jesse, I find out I'm wrong. That hurts. It really does."

Touched by her plaintive lament, Jesse patted the grass at his side. When Christina sat down beside him, he reached for her hand. "I told you we have many things to discuss. I agree with you. It is not proper for a family man to own a place like the Silver Spur and I will sell it immediately. I have received offers in the past, and I will simply take the best one. My family has many business interests. I can make money to support us in a dozen different ways, but I would not do it in a manner that offends you."

Christina was amazed he would make such a decision so casually. "Wait a minute. A place like the Silver Spur earns a lot of money, doesn't it?"

"A great deal," Jesse admitted readily.

"And you would sell it just to please me?" She had come from a family where a shortage of money was a chronic problem and was astounded he would give up a lucrative enterprise simply to impress her.

Apparently Christina had had very little in the way of love and attention before she had met him, but that only made Jesse love her all the more. "If you will become my wife, I will always do my best to please you."

The bashful blonde was both flattered and thrilled by his proposal, but she was still a little bit frightened too. "Is there anything else I ought to know, Jesse?"

"Like what?" he asked with an amused smile, not about to confess he had lived the type of life he knew she would never condone.

Christina shrugged apprehensively. "I don't even know what to ask."

Hoping to impress her favorably, Jesse offered the most reassuring reply he possibly could. "I come from a fine family and have many nice friends. I have always been honest in all my dealings. I treat my employees well and am proud to say I have their respect."

The mention of employees brought a bright flush to the fair-skinned young woman's pale cheeks. "Just how do you find your employees for the Silver Spur, Jesse? Are they all women you no longer love?"

It took the clever man no time at all to guess where Christina had gotten such an absurd idea. "Is that what Carmen said to you? That I seduce pretty virgins and turn them into whores?"

Christina was so horribly embarrassed by his question that she turned away. If the man owned a whorehouse, surely he had slept with the women—if not all of them, then some. That idea was so revolting she could not face him, and she did not know if she would ever be able to again.

Jesse waited a polite interval and when she still had not replied, he realized she never would. "Carmen will be pleased to learn her filthy lies have turned you against me. It seems I was a fool to think if you loved me only the future mattered. Let us be on our way." He tried to rise then and was disgusted to find it was far too difficult for him to get up from the ground alone. "I am sorry to be such a burden, but I am going to need your help to stand."

Christina rose to her feet instantly, as though relieved to have an excuse to go. Having lived most of her life on a farm where the chores were endless, she was quite strong. She offered her hands and easily pulled Jesse to his feet. He did not release her immediately, however, and she was forced to meet his gaze. The sorrow of his expression mirrored that which filled her heart so exactly she felt the sharpness of his pain and her eyes overflowed with tears. She knew instantly that if anyone was wicked it was Carmen, who had selfishly tried to hurt her, not Jesse, who spoke only of love. "Oh Jesse, I'm bein' real stupid, aren't I?"

Her question was so unexpected Jesse could not help but laugh as he pulled her into his arms. "No, you are not in the least bit stupid, *querida*. You are simply very innocent and sweet. That's why Carmen's lies hurt you so deeply and you need not apologize for it."

Christina tried to wipe away her tears before they soaked his jacket. "But I am sorry, truly I am. It's just that I know so little about you and—"

Jesse silenced her complaint with a gentle kiss he waited for her to deepen. He found her shy affection not only delicious but wonderfully exciting as well. As they kissed again, he reached up to pull the pins from her hair to let it spill about them like a silken veil, and several minutes passed before he realized they were standing at the side of the road. It was fortunate no one had passed by, for surely any travelers would have stopped to laugh uproariously. He stepped back slightly then. "As much as I would like to, I know we cannot stand here all afternoon. Please come back into town with me and while we have lunch together you can ask me whatever questions you like."

Christina scooped up her hairpins from his hand and quickly wound her hair atop her head and secured it. She then smoothed out the skirt of her pink gingham dress and asked shyly, "Do I look all right? I'd hoped only to see you. I hadn't thought about havin' lunch somewhere."

"You look very pretty," Jesse assured her. "That dress is new, isn't it?"

"Yes," the blonde admitted, pleased that he had noticed. "MaLou helped me pick out some new clothes. Her things are all so pretty and I'd love to look as nice as she does."

"MaLou did not even wear dresses until quite recently." Jesse stood close by as Christina mounted her mule, then did his best not to fall and break his neck as he got into the saddle. When he was comfortably seated, he gave her a satisfied smile. "But perhaps she told you that herself."

"Why no, I'd thought she'd always dressed like a lady."

Jesse shook his head. "No, she did not. She has changed a great deal, so I am certain I can change too."

As they started back up the road to Tucson, Christina began to argue with him. "I don't want you to think you have to make lots of changes, Jesse. I like you the way you are right now."

"Well, thank you, but I know there is at least some room for improvement."

Christina considered that possibility for a moment, then dismissed it and asked, "When do you think you'll be strong enough to face Chris?"

"I did not realize you were in such a hurry to get married when only a few minutes ago you were protesting you did not know me well enough." It was all he could do not to laugh at such a contradiction, but he did not want to risk hurting her feelings.

Christina giggled at his remark, for she found it quite amusing. "I know how I feel about you. Isn't that enough?"

"Yes, but if you will have just a little more patience, I

promise you I will make a far better husband when I am again fully well."

The shy blonde knew precisely what he meant by that promise, and although she again could feel the heat of a bright blush flooding her cheeks, she had no trouble returning his smile.

Chapter XXVIII

Lance reclined lazily against the pillows as he read the *Citizen* article on the May seventeenth election. "It's a clean sweep, all right. De Long is the new mayor, Samuel Hughes and William Oury are on the council, Hiram Stevens is now city treasurer, and Juan Elias is the dogcatcher. I shudder to think what men like that will do to the city of Tucson," he stated with exaggerated sarcasm.

"Murderers or not, obviously they can do no wrong in the public's view," MaLou reminded him with a caustic cynicism far angrier than his.

Finding the sight of his pretty wife a great deal more fascinating than following the political careers of the men responsible for the Camp Grant massacre, Lance tossed the paper aside. He would never tire of watching MaLou, but like all her actions of late, her gestures were brittle, filled with tension. She was now drawing her brush through her long curls with such furious strokes he feared she would soon grow bald. "MaLou," he called invitingly, "come to bed."

Readily accepting his invitation, MaLou tossed her brush toward her dresser with such force it struck and nearly shattered the mirror. She did not even bother to turn back to make certain it had not been cracked before she climbed up upon the bed. She was clad in the lace-trimmed nightgown she had bought for her wedding night, since it had quickly become her favorite, although she had never actually slept in it.

Lance pulled the agitated young woman into his arms and buried his face in her gardenia-scented curls, knowing the wildness of her mood would again enhance their physical pleasure. That was selfish, he knew, but if passion helped her to unleash the rage she could not otherwise express, he was glad to provide that release. "There's just us, darlin'. No one else matters but you and me and what we are to each other."

While MaLou slid her fingers through the dark curls that covered his bare chest, she decided his words were impossibly romantic, and completely untrue. "How can you say that when we are surrounded on every side with the kind of unreasoning hatred that cost my father his life?"

Lance promised himself for the thousandth time that he was going to get those responsible for Thomas's death, even if it was the last thing he ever did. "I wasted too many years livin' in my own private hell, MaLou, to ever let anything that happens to us, no matter how bad, make me that cynical ever again. I won't let the evil that pervades the town touch us. I just won't."

MaLou's lips trembled slightly as she reached up to kiss him. She had not gone into town since their wedding, and would not return unless she absolutely had to, since she knew she would not be able to show anything but contempt for so many of the people she would meet there. The recent election was only the latest proof that murder was considered the best possible solution to the Territory's problems with the Apache. "I don't think we can make our own world, Lance. No matter how hard we try, someone will always intrude to ruin it."

"That's not goin' to stop me from tryin'," Lance vowed dramatically as he sought to end her melancholy mood with affection so lavish she would have no time to dwell upon sorrow and death. He liked her lacy nightgown too, since it gave her such an angelic appearance, but he worked quickly to remove it since he liked her bare skin all the more. With a mock growl he pulled the silk garment over her head, then ravished the curve of her throat with teasing nibbles that brought a breathless rush of giggles from her lips. He loved to make her laugh, and as she began to tickle his ribs playfully, he gave in to laughter himself. Making love with equal parts of passion and play was his favorite pastime and he cradled her tenderly in his arms as he let the magic of his deep kiss and soft, slow touch turn her blood to flame.

MaLou clung to her handsome husband, luring him down ecstasy's path with an endearing charm all her own. She loved the sight of his muscular body unclothed, the scent of his deeply bronzed skin, the power of his desire, which flooded her senses with erotic dreams she knew only he could fulfill. He never seemed to tire of her company, nor she of his, when the enjoyment they shared continually grew more rich.

As he turned her gently in his arms and spread a trail of light kisses across her shoulders, she curled back against him and ran her hand down the length of his thigh. They did create their own world together at perfect times like these, she mused dreamily. His hands moved over her breasts, teasing the tips to firm peaks. His fingertips then crossed the smooth flatness of her stomach before he pulled her back against him. With the fluid ease of the most adept lover he parted her thighs and with a soft upward thrust plunged deeply into the tantalizing heat of her lissome body's sweet, moist center. Captivated by her charms, he strove as he always did to make this new union even more pleasurable than the last.

Enfolded in the warmth of his loving embrace, MaLou welcomed each of his thrusts, letting the wave of rapture he created within her swell until she could no longer sense any separation between them and they were truly one. Their bodies were entwined in an ageless clasp while their spirits were borne aloft on a gracefully upswept spiral of love that continued to turn until at last it dissolved in the heady mists at the shores of paradise and left them awash in the warm glow of perfect contentment.

"MaLou?" Lance whispered sleepily, but her reply was

no more than a deeply satisfied purr and he snuggled against her, grateful he had again provided such a peaceful entrance to the world of dreams. He was ready to fall asleep himself, but he knew when they awoke they would again make love and the splendor of that thought kept a smile on his lips the whole night through.

Early the following afternoon, Lance began counting out the payroll at El Gallo. He had taken the precaution of locking the office door so he would not be disturbed, and when someone began to knock insistently, demanding entrance, he was annoyed to be interrupted. "Just a minute," he called out loudly, then scooping the cash he had laid out on the desktop into the drawer, he went to see who the untimely visitor might be.

Josh had his hat in his hand and pushed by Lance the moment he opened the door. "I need to talk with you," he said in an urgent whisper.

Lance checked the hall to make certain Josh was alone before he closed and again locked the door. "Yes, what is it?"

Making himself at home, Josh perched himself on the front of the desk as he began to explain the purpose of his visit in an excited rush. "I was down at the tannery just now and I saw something real peculiar."

"And for some reason you thought I'd be interested?" Lance leaned back against the door and crossed his arms over his chest. Since he had been the one to marry MaLou, he had no reason to continue his feud with Josh, but he was still surprised the man had come to see him, no matter what the reason.

"I know you will be interested. Just before I got there, Randy Hatcher had arrived with a wagon load of hides. When he left, the clerk asked me to take a look at one because he thought the brand looked strange."

"Well, did it?" Lance asked hurriedly, beginning to think he knew what was coming.

"It sure as hell did. The Hatchers had burned their *H*

over another brand. They'd made a real mess of the original, but we could still make out what it had been. It was an *M* joined with a *D*, the MacDowell brand."

A slow, satisfied grin spread across Lance's face, for he was elated to at last have the proof he needed that the Hatchers had been rustling Thomas's cattle. Since the man's death, not a single head had been found missing, but to sell a hide with an altered brand was such a stupid mistake he had difficulty believing even the Hatchers would make it. "Where is that hide now?"

"I left it at the tannery. I thought maybe you'd want the marshal to pick it up as evidence."

That was not an option Lance thought worthy of consideration, since from all he had seen, the concept of justice was unknown in Tucson. "No, I think I'll just pay the Hatchers a visit myself."

Astonished by such a suicidal prospect, Josh leapt off the desk and began to argue. "You can't go out there alone. Don't even try it. You've gotta let me go along with you."

Lance scoffed at his offer. "This doesn't concern you, Josh. Just go on about your business and I'll take care of the Hatchers on my own."

"It does so concern me!" the young man insisted heatedly. "I knew Thomas MacDowell my whole life and I want to see his murderers punished just as badly as you do. Maybe even more. Why, if it hadn't been for her father's death coming when it did, MaLou might be my wife now instead of yours. Let's just go on out to the Hatchers' ranch now and get this over with as quickly as we can."

Lance knew Thomas MacDowell's untimely death had had nothing to do with the reason MaLou had not married Josh. He would never have allowed her to marry another man, but that was not a point he cared to take the time to explain. "It would break MaLou's heart if I got shot in the back. You know that, don't you?"

Josh swore an incredibly filthy oath before he replied. "You were her choice, Garrett, and I'd never stoop to making her a widow in hopes she'd marry me to ease her grief."

Impressed as he had been in the past by Josh's obvious sincerity, Lance relented. "All right then, come with me, but I am goin' to be the one doin' all the talkin', you understand?"

"Talk as long as you like," Josh replied with a wicked grin. "I'll be ready to back you up when you need me."

Lance took the time to lock the desk drawer to safeguard the payroll, then walked out the back door with Josh. When they found Jesse standing just outside bidding Christina an extremely passionate farewell, they halted abruptly. While Lance kept quiet, Josh's snicker alerted the amorous couple to their arrival. Christina came by El Gallo frequently to see Jesse, but Lance knew his partner had kept their courtship an admirably chaste one, despite the love that was so obvious in their good-bye kiss.

Jesse stepped back slightly but kept his arm around Christina's waist to keep her close. "Yes, did you need to see me?" he asked Lance, looking more proud than embarrassed to have been caught kissing the bashful blonde, while she appeared absolutely mortified to have been observed at such an abandoned moment.

"Josh and I are goin' out to the Hatchers'. I wanted you to know where we'd gone." He quickly described what Josh had found at the tannery, and his friend's reaction did not surprise him.

"I will come too," Jesse volunteered. He then turned to Christina. "Go on home and I will see you in a few days." He gave her another light kiss to send her on her way, but with a surprising show of stubbornness she refused to depart.

"Wait a minute. It was men named Hatcher who shot you, wasn't it, Jesse?"

Jesse glanced first at Lance, clearly regretting that his friend had mentioned his errand in front of Christina. "Yes, but this is another matter entirely. Now please go on home as I asked you. You need not worry about us. We will come to no harm."

"Does MaLou know what you're doin'?" Christina asked Lance pointedly.

The Southerner gave her a reassuring smile as he replied, "No, but I'll tell her all about it this evenin' at supper. Jesse's right. You needn't worry about us."

Christina looked at the three men's smug grins and grew even more certain they were up to no good. Knowing she could not stop them, she hoped they were just half as smart as they thought they were. "You be careful now," she scolded softly, and mounting her mule, she rode away, though she was not bound for home.

"I'm sorry," Lance apologized immediately. "I'd forgotten she would recognize the Hatcher name."

Jesse dismissed the problem with a careless shrug. "I do not want her to worry when there is no need. Do you have some sort of plan?" he asked as they started for the nearby stable where Lance left Amigo during the day and Jesse boarded several of his horses.

"I'd like to take a look around and see what I can find before I confront them with what I know. My guess is that Randy was just careless and brought that hide in by mistake, so there might be others lying about. The more evidence I can find of their crimes, the easier it will be to turn them against each other and find the man I want."

"I say we just go in shooting," Josh proposed enthusiastically. "Ain't one of the Hatchers that's worth wasting the effort to put on trial."

"Go get your horse, Josh," Lance dismissed him curtly. "I'm not plannin' a killin' spree."

"You've got no reason to love the Hatchers either, Jesse," Josh called out as he turned away. "Talk some sense into him."

"You know I have no love for any of the Hatchers," Lance confided in his partner, "but I won't shoot them down in cold blood. The only one I want is the man who killed Thomas, and I think I can persuade one of them to tell me who he is."

Jesse frowned slightly as he gave his own opinion. "Josh has a point, Lance. It matters little which of the brothers killed MacDowell. They were undoubtedly all involved in the rustling and any one of them could have been the murderer. They have no concept of honor. That is precisely what they proved when they went gunning for you and ended up shooting me."

"Rex and Rad got themselves killed for that mistake too, and if one of them shot Thomas, then I'll just see the others are charged with rustling and tell MaLou her father's murderer did not escape punishment after all," Lance vowed calmly. He quickly saddled Amigo himself while Jesse told one of the stable boys to saddle his mount. While they were waiting for Josh to return, Lance began pumping his partner for information. "Are Mr. and Mrs. Hatcher still livin'?"

Jesse hesitated a moment, then shook his head. "No, I'm sure they've been dead for a number of years. There must be a few hands on their spread, but I doubt they would be loyal. Our problem will probably just be with the brothers. Randy you know well enough. He talks big but has no guts at all. It's no wonder he was not with Rex and Rad the night they came after me, or you—whichever way you wish to look at it. Darrel isn't much better, but from what I have seen of Donald and Hank, they go out of their way to be mean just for the fun of it."

"How can you tell them apart?" Lance asked in dismay.

"I have had years to study them, while you have had but a few brief opportunities. None of them came around The Silver Spur, but that is probably because they know they'd not be welcome there."

When Josh rejoined them then, Lance cautioned him to be careful. "The hide you've seen is evidence enough to convict the Hatchers of rustling, but what I want is proof of murder, or a confession."

"Oh hell," Josh argued. "They're all as guilty as sin."

"Perhaps, but I'm not goin' to be accused of takin' the law into my own hands and murderin' innocent people the way some of the citizens of Tucson feel so free to do."

"The Hatcher Ranch ain't no Camp Grant," Josh pointed out quickly.

"You're damn right it isn't," Lance assured him with a steely glance. With that barely veiled threat, he led the way out of town. The Hatcher Ranch lay to the east off the same road that eventually led to MaLou's home. Not about to come riding in the front gate, they skirted the property and approached the house and barn from the rear. Leaving their horses concealed in a gully, they studied the neglected buildings from a well-protected rise.

The house was built of adobe bricks, but there were only a few traces of flaking whitewash to prove it had once been white and no plants to provide a touch of color except for scattered clumps of cactus, which had been growing there long before the house had been built. The dilapidated barn was in even worse repair, so it appeared the Hatchers cared as little for their animals as they did for themselves.

"Except for a few scrawny chickens and the half-dozen horses in the corral, the place looks deserted," Josh whispered hoarsely.

"Good. That will make it a great deal easier to search the barn for the rest of the hides," Lance reminded him.

"Wait." Jesse reached out to grab his friend's arm. "There is a dog sleeping behind the rocking chair on the front porch and he looks like a very large, mean one."

Disgusted that he had not seen the pale gray animal himself, Lance decided to spend a few more minutes scanning the scene for signs of trouble. "There's a goose," he pointed out. "They can be as noisy as dogs." He removed his hat to wipe the sweat from his brow. He had left El Gallo in his shirt sleeves, but the day was a warm one. When they could discover no other perils, Lance turned to Josh. "I want you to give your rifle to Jesse for the time being, and Jesse, I want you to stay right here and keep us covered."

Since he knew he was too slow to run across the barnyard without being seen, Jesse did not argue about his assignment. When Josh handed him his rifle, he slapped Lance on the back and wished him luck. "If you find nothing, come right back."

Lance nodded, and leading Josh, he made first for the cover provided by a clump of cactus, then dashed on to the remains of a rotting wagon. When that brought only one restless honk from the goose, which failed to wake the dog or summon anyone from the house, they hurriedly crossed the last open space and rounded the corral to reach the rear of the barn. The sagging doors groaned as Lance pulled them open, but he and Josh darted inside without mishap.

Except for hay stored in the loft and a few bales scattered about the floor, the barn at first glance appeared to contain little of any value, but as their eyes grew accustomed to the dim light that streamed in through the holes in the roof, Lance saw what appeared to be a mound of hides piled in the far corner. "Come on. Let's see what we can find."

Josh lit a lantern he found hanging on a hook by one of the empty stalls, and, holding it above the hides, he watched with rapt interest as Lance began to sort through them. The first dozen were all marked with an *H*, but the next one bore a brand he recognized instantly. "Christ Almighty!" he wore. "Look at that! That's our Lazy *S!*"

Lance shook his head in disbelief. "I knew the Hatchers were not only stupid but careless too." He sorted through the rest of the stack but found none with more than the Hatchers' single *H*. "Well, I guess it is unlikely they rustled only our cattle, but that's not the evidence I'd hoped to find." As he stood up, he heard the distinctive rattle of an approaching buckboard and in the next instant the frantic barking of the dog.

"That must be Randy coming home," Josh warned apprehensively.

"Douse the light," Lance called over his shoulder, and with the blond man close on his heels, he moved to the shadows behind the last stall and knelt down to wait for Randy to drive the buckboard into the barn.

Randy stopped outside, however, and, leaving the team of horses standing in their harness, he went into the house. A few minutes later he came back out the front door with his brother, Hank, and the two quickly crossed the yard to the barn and threw open the doors. "Why are you so upset that I sold a few hides, Hank? Hell, I got a good price."

"Did you look at 'em real careful, or just grab some off

the heap?" Hank growled in response. He strode over to the pile of hides, and seeing the lantern sitting where Josh had left it, he picked it up and lit it. "Hey, this thing's still warm."

"Can't be. I didn't use it," Randy explained with a puzzled frown.

"Then you didn't check the hides, you damn fool!" Holding the lantern in his left hand, Hank used his right to give his younger brother a sharp jab to the mouth, but his blow barely staggered the overweight young man.

"Hey, cut it out!" Randy stepped back to avoid being hit again as he attempted to defend his actions. "Look, the hides were all ours. They had to be. Or the cattle had our brands on 'em when they were slaughtered. Shit, we haven't taken a head of anyone else's stock since the day you and Rex had the run-in with MacDowell."

"You shut up about that!" Hank replied in a menacing hiss. He was still holding the lantern and raised it as he turned slowly to gaze about the barn. "If you weren't using this lantern, then just who in the hell was?"

"Stay put," Lance whispered to Josh, and drawing his ivory-handled Colt from his holster, he stepped out into the closest ray of sunlight. Knowing Jesse was correct in his assessment of the Hatchers' sense of honor, he began to do his best to turn one man against the other. "I was. You're right about Randy, Hank. He made the careless mistake of selling a hide with the MacDowell brand still clearly marked on it. Now he's done me another favor by tellin' me which of you cowards killed Thomas MacDowell. With a brother that stupid you sure don't need enemies. Now I'm willin' to give you a choice. I'll take you into town where you'll surely be hanged for murder, or you can go for your gun and I'll put you out of your misery right here and now."

Hank was not only mean, but he possessed enough intelligence to see he had a third choice. With surprising speed for a man of his bulk, he hurled the lantern straight at Lance's head. Lance fired as he ducked out of the way, striking Hank in the chest, but when the lantern struck the hay-covered floor at the Southerner's feet, it broke open instantly, creating a leaping wall of bright orange flames. The fire then shot out over the trail of the splattered kerosene, quickly spreading the blaze in a dozen different directions and igniting everything in its path. Lance and Josh suddenly found themselves on one side of a rapidly expanding barrier of smoke and flame, while Hank and Randy were on the other.

Lance could no longer see well enough to get off another shot, and hearing Josh choking on the dense smoke that was rapidly filling the air, he ran back to the corner where he had left him. He grabbed the young man by the arm and made certain they both made it out the rear of the blazing barn before it became totally engulfed in flames. As they paused for a moment to gasp for air, they heard shots coming from around front and knew that Jesse had opened fire. In the next instant the horses drawing the buckboard, terrified by both the fire and gunshots, raced by with the wagon pitching wildly behind them as they headed for the safety of the open range.

Once that peril had rattled past them, Lance stopped to open the corral to free the horses inside, then again led the way. He stayed close to the side of the barn, where the smoke billowing out of every crack and hole provided good cover. They saw Randy sprawled face down in the dirt near the house, where Jesse's bullet had found him. Donald and Darrel, responding to the sounds of gunfire, had run out on the front porch, where they had taken up positions to return Jesse's fire. Their dog was barking furiously and leaping at their legs, but there was no sign of Hank.

"This is almost too easy," Josh whispered as he took aim for the men on the porch.

Lance shoved his arm down before he could fire. "Wait! Those two don't even know what's goin' on!" To remedy that situation, he called out to them. "We've got proof you've been rustling cattle. Throw down your guns. We're taking you in."

"You son of a bitch! You're a dead man, Garrett!"

Donald fired at him then but missed, while both Lance's and Josh's shots hit their mark, silencing him instantly.

"Don't shoot!" Darrel screamed as he threw down his gun and stepped over Donald's body. He raised his hands above his head and looked with a frantic glance toward the rise, praying Jesse would hold his fire too. Confused and frightened, the noisy dog scooted into the house through the open door and remained inside.

"You handle whichever man that is, Josh," Lance commanded sharply. "I want to find out what happened to Hank." Lance crept around the side of the barn, half expecting the man to leap out at him, but while the door was standing open to reveal a raging inferno fed by burning bales of hay, there was no sign of Hank Hatcher. Always a cautious man, Lance circled the barn, then waved to Jesse to come down to the house to join them. Stopping briefly to turn Randy over, he was surprised to find him still alive. He had a neat hole drilled through his shoulder, but Lance took a perverse pleasure in ripping up the young man's filthy shirt to bind the wound so he would live to stand trial for cattle rustling.

When Jesse reached them, he quickly gave a report of his part in the action. "I heard a shot and when Randy came running out the front of the barn I saw no reason to allow him to reach the safety of the house. I knew Hank was inside the barn because I saw him go in, but he did not come out." He turned then to look at the flaming remains of the barn's roof. "He will not be coming out now either."

"I thought I hit him," Lance replied matter-of-factly, feeling no sense of pride in the man's death. He looked over at Darrel, who was seated upon the porch steps crying pitifully. "He looks like he'll be in a mood to talk. Help me get Randy over to the house and I'll ask his brother some questions." The two men then dragged rather than carried the injured man over to the porch, where they laid him in the shade.

Josh had tied Darrel's hands behind his back, but Lance doubted the woebegone fellow had any fight left in him and sat down by his side. "Randy will recover to stand trial with you. You're not all alone. Now I want you to tell me everythin' you can. How long have you boys been rustling stock and what do you know about what happened to Thomas MacDowell?"

Darrel continued to cry so dejectedly, Lance looked up at Jesse for help. "What is this man's name?"

"Darrel, that's Darrel." Jesse sat down on the hapless man's right side and gave his pudgy thigh a comforting pat. "Why did you boys start rustling? You have good land here."

Darrel looked up then, his eyes filled with hatred as he screamed his reply. "It was all his fault—Garrett's, that's who!" He tried to spit at Lance then, but succeeded only in slobbering down his own chin, which brought on a fresh torrent of frustrated tears.

Lance gave Darrel only a few seconds to sob, then grabbed a handful of the man's greasy hair and jerked his head upright. "I want to know the whole story, Darrel, and now. Do you understand me? Donald's dead, Randy's out cold, and neither Josh nor Jesse will dispute my word if I want to say you died in that burning barn along with Hank."

"You wouldn't!" Darrel cried out in alarm.

"I am not a patient man," Lance threatened softly as he released his hold on Darrel's hair and wiped off his hand on his own pant leg. "Now tell your story or say your prayers. The choice is yours."

Darrel stared into the icy blue depths of Lance's determined gaze, and, as though he had come face-to-face with the Grim Reeper himself, he shuddered uncontrollably. "I'll tell you everything." He gasped for breath, then still stuttering between heart-wrenching sobs, he began. "It all started that day in the Congress Hall when you shot Randy. Hank and I weren't even there, but none of the others ever forgot it. They just kept talking about it, over and over, and every day they hated you more for making them look like fools. We started rustling MacDowell's stock when we couldn't get to you."

Lance glanced over at Jesse, who nodded in agreement.

The Hatchers were indeed fools, but apparently very dangerous ones. "Go on. You were the ones who tried to kill me from ambush the first time I came back from Camp Grant, weren't you? Wasn't that you boys who shot Manuel?"

Darrel hesitated a minute and then nodded. "Rex was in town and overheard one of the men from your spread saying where you'd gone. He camped out for two days waiting for a chance to shoot you, then missed." He shook his head then, obviously regretting that error as though it had been his own. "He decided to steal some more cattle then, but it was Hank who shot MacDowell when he spotted them helping themselves to his cattle."

Jesse spoke up then. "You must have been pleased to hear Lance had gone to work at El Gallo, since he'd make a much easier target for you in town. Why did only Rex and Rad come after him the night you shot me?"

"We was all there, all of us, just like the first time we went in there after him. Nobody saw the rest of us is all," Darrel admitted sorrowfully. "We got away clean."

Josh was leaning against a sagging porch rail following Darrel's confession as closely as his companions. "You took cattle from our spread too. Why? You got some sort of a grudge against us I don't know about?"

"Naw, we just took one or two of your strays you'd never miss."

Lance rose to his feet and took a few steps away before turning back to face their miserable prisoner. "That's a mighty convenient story, Darrel. You're giving Rex, Rad, and Hank all the blame for the shootings, while Randy, Donald, and you just did a little bit of rustling? That won't make a bit of difference to Donald now, since he's dead too, but it could save your neck and Randy's. Is that what you're trying to do?"

"No! I told you the truth!"

"I doubt you'd recognize the truth if you woke up in bed with it!" Lance exclaimed angrily. "Your argument was with me, not Manuel, MacDowell or Jesse! Wasn't there one man among you who had the guts to come after me instead of going after them?"

"We was always trying to get you! Always! They were just in the way!"

"How many years does a man get for rustling cattle? Five? Ten?" Lance asked Jesse, who shrugged noncommittally.

"Am I goin' to have trouble with you two as soon as you're released from prison?" Lance asked pointedly.

"No, never!" Darrel screamed as he saw Lance's hand slide toward his Colt. "We ain't never coming back here. I swear we ain't!"

Lance stepped closer then and lowered his voice to a menacing whisper. "Jesse talked me out of comin' after you boys when he got shot. That was a mistake. I won't make the same mistake ever again. I ever see you walkin' the streets of Tucson a free man, you'll be a dead one. You understand me?"

Darrel bobbed his head up and down quickly. "I understand."

Before Lance could make certain he did, Josh called out, "There's riders coming this way. Looks like quite a group from the dust they're kicking up. Do you suppose it's someone trying to be neighborly and help put out the fire?"

Lance did not take his eyes off Darrel as they waited for the riders to round the barn. When he heard MaLou calling his name, somehow he was not surprised and quickly went to meet her. Christina was with her, and Chris, along with about a dozen hands from the ranch. "I said I'd tell my wife all about this afternoon at supper tonight, Christina. Didn't you believe me? Or perhaps I wasn't the one you were worried about."

He had guessed the truth and Christina blushed deeply. "Of course I was worried about you—about all three of you." She looked over at Jesse then, and, leaving the rifle with Josh, the Mexican got up and came over to join them. He still walked with a limp, but it was only a slight one.

"Christina and her brother came to me for help," MaLou explained as she glanced at the smoldering ruins of the barn. "Doesn't look like you need any."

"No, we could use a hand or two," Lance admitted with a smile. "We'll need to catch up with the horses pulling the Hatchers' buckboard so we can use it to take what's left of their family into town." He dispatched a couple of men on that errand, then helped his wife dismount, and taking her hand, he led her some distance away from the others. "It's been the Hatchers who've caused our problems all along. They were tryin' to get even with me for shootin' Randy, but it was Manuel, your father, and Jesse who bore the brunt of their anger instead."

MaLou swallowed hard to force back her tears, and while she spoke softly, her voice was filled with rage. "I'd never yell at you in front of the men, but you were a damn fool to come out here today. All three of you could have been killed. Why would you take such a stupid risk?"

"I've always wanted to put your mind at rest, to find the man who killed your dad and make him pay for it," Lance explained calmly. "Once Josh provided the proof I needed, I succeeded too, so there's no reason for you to be angry with me."

"No reason? Have you lost your mind? Have I said so often I wanted to find my father's murderer that you thought that quest was more important to me than you?" MaLou inquired incredulously.

"No, not at all," Lance insisted. "But it was something I had to do, something I owed your dad as well as you. Now it's done. Hank was the one who shot him and there will be nothing left of him but ashes by the time that fire's finally burned itself out."

MaLou glanced back over her shoulder at the barn, then up at her husband. "I wish you hadn't taken such an awful risk, but thank you, Lance, for me and for Dad."

Lance pulled her into his arms and gave her a comforting hug. "You're very welcome, Mrs. Garrett. Now let's see if we can't finish up here and go on home."

MaLou recognized the teasing sparkle in his eyes for the promise of love that it was and quickly agreed. "Say something to Chris, will you? Christina wants to marry

Jesse so desperately it's pathetic, but she's afraid her brother will never allow it."

"Are you sure?" Lance nodded toward the three people she had mentioned. They were standing close together, apparently engrossed in a serious discussion. "Looks like Jesse is doin' all right to me." As they rejoined the group, he found his observation to be true.

Christina was smiling brightly as she stood clutching Jesse's hand. She gave her brother a nudge, and after a slight hesitation Chris stepped forward. "I guess I'm the last one to learn what's goin' on, but if my sister really wants to marry you, Jesse, then I won't stand in your way."

Jesse flashed the grin he had once used so often. "Thank you. You do not know how relieved I am to hear you say that. I had fully expected to have to convince you of that with my fists, and I did not want to be any more battered at our wedding than I already am."

"What?" Chris asked in dismay.

"He's just teasin' you, Chris," Christina insisted quickly, even though she knew Jesse had been telling the truth. "You'll come to our weddin', won't you?" she asked MaLou and Lance.

"We wouldn't miss it." MaLou gave both Christina and Jesse a kiss, then waved to Josh, who was still keeping an eye on Darrel and Randy. "We'll have to find a bride for you too, Chris. Josh knows lots of pretty girls and I'm sure he'd be happy to introduce you to some."

"I am doin' all right on my own, Mrs. Garrett," Chris admitted with a sheepish grin. "All your pretty cousins will come to the weddin', won't they, Jesse?"

"I will make certain they do," Jesse promised readily. He winked slyly at his future bride, knowing she would be pleased at how easily he and her brother would become friends.

Not wanting to remain at the Hatchers' ranch any longer than absolutely necessary, Lance took charge then, and while several hours passed before he was able to meet MaLou back at home, he found her mood as good as when they had parted. "I'm sorry to be late, but I wanted to make certain Darrel repeated to the marshal exactly the same story he told us."

"I'm sure he would with you standing there."

"Yes, ma'am, he sure did."

MaLou slipped her arms around her husband's waist and rested her head lightly upon his chest. "You're so thoughtful, but you needn't apologize for being late for dinner after a day like this. You're really a wonderful husband, Lance, and I'll bet you'll make a marvelous father."

"Is that just an idle compliment, or should I start buildin' a cradle?" Lance asked with a low chuckle.

MaLou began to giggle as she stepped back so she could look up at him. "I can't believe you're all that surprised to hear you're going to be a father."

"I'm not surprised at all, just delighted!" Lance scooped her up into his arms, and after giving her an enthusiastic hug and kiss, he carried her back to their bedroom. "Let's celebrate."

"Don't you want to have dinner first?" MaLou asked as she nibbled his earlobe playfully.

"Later, darlin'. Right now all I'm hungry for is you."

"Lucky for you that's an appetite I'm so willing to indulge, sir," MaLou replied in an seductive purr.

"Well, ma'am, I've always been lucky, and especially so where you're concerned."

As his lips met hers for a lingering kiss, the delicious excitement he had always been able to create with merely a teasing glance or a gentle caress again flooded her heart with love. She made a silent promise to herself then, vowing he would spend his whole life thinking himself a very lucky man indeed.

EXPERIENCE THE SENSUOUS MAGIC OF JANELLE TAYLOR!

FORTUNE'S FLAMES (2250, $3.95)
Lovely Maren James' angry impatience turned to raging desire when the notorious Captain Hawk boarded her ship and strode confidently into her cabin. And before she could consider the consequences, the ebon-haired beauty was succumbing to the bold pirate's masterful touch!

SWEET SAVAGE HEART (1900, $3.95)
Kidnapped when just a child, seventeen-year-old Rana Williams adored her carefree existence among the Sioux. But then the frighteningly handsome white man Travis Kincade appeared in her camp . . . and Rana's peace was shattered forever!

DESTINY'S TEMPTRESS (1761, $3.95)
Crossing enemy lines to help save her beloved South, Shannon Greenleaf found herself in the bedroom of Blane Stevens, the most handsome man she'd ever seen. Though burning for his touch, the defiant belle vowed never to reveal her mission—nor let the virile Yankee capture her heart!

SAVAGE CONQUEST (1533, $3.75)
Heeding the call of her passionate nature, Miranda stole away from her Virginia plantation to the rugged plains of South Dakota. But captured by a handsome Indian warrior, the headstrong beauty felt her defiance melting away with the hot-blooded savage's sensual caress!

STOLEN ECSTASY (1621, $3.95)
With his bronze stature and ebony black hair, the banished Sioux brave Bright Arrow was all Rebecca Kenny ever wanted. She would defy her family and face society's scorn to savor the forbidden rapture she found in her handsome warrior's embrace!

Available wherever paperbacks are sold, or order direct from the Publisher. Send cover price plus 50¢ per copy for mailing and handling to Zebra Books, Dept. 2325, 475 Park Avenue South, New York, N.Y. 10016. Residents of New York, New Jersey and Pennsylvania must include sales tax. DO NOT SEND CASH.